Rebecca J. Caffery is a queer romance author from Birmingham, UK, whose stories celebrate love, electric chemistry, fierce emotion and found families. She rediscovered her passion for writing in 2017 during a study abroad year in Canada, and she's been writing one too many enemies-to-lovers tropes since.

Rebecca is best known for her high-octane F1 romances, *Pole Position* (2024) and *First to Finish* (2026), where fast cars meet even faster hearts. With hopes to expand her writing repertoire into small-town romances, she continues to craft stories that celebrate queer love in all its intensity and joy.

When she's not writing, Rebecca can be found devouring queer romance novels, binge-watching romantic dramas and romcoms, or passionately (read: screaming at her TV) supporting the Arsenal Women's football team and the McLaren Formula 1 team.

📷 instagram.com/RJCafferyAuthor

Also by Rebecca J. Caffery

Pole Position

FIRST TO FINISH

REBECCA J. CAFFERY

One More Chapter
a division of HarperCollins*Publishers* Ltd
1 London Bridge Street
London SE1 9GF
www.harpercollins.co.uk
HarperCollins*Publishers*
Macken House, 39/40 Mayor Street Upper,
Dublin 1, D01 C9W8, Ireland

This paperback edition 2026
1
First published in Great Britain in ebook format
by HarperCollins*Publishers* 2026
Copyright © Rebecca J. Caffery 2026
Rebecca J. Caffery asserts the moral right to be identified
as the author of this work

A catalogue record of this book is available from the British Library

ISBN: 978-0-00-868488-4

This novel is entirely a work of fiction. The names, characters and incidents portrayed in it are the work of the author's imagination. Any resemblance to actual persons, living or dead, events or localities is entirely coincidental.

Printed and bound in the UK using 100% Renewable Electricity
by CPI Group (UK) Ltd

All rights reserved. No part of this publication may be reproduced, stored in a retrieval system, or transmitted, in any form or by any means, electronic, mechanical, photocopying, recording or otherwise, without the prior permission of the publishers.
Without limiting the exclusive rights of any author, contributor or the publisher of this publication, any unauthorised use of this publication to train generative artificial intelligence (AI) technologies is expressly prohibited. HarperCollins also exercise their rights under Article 4(3) of the Digital Single Market Directive 2019/790 and expressly reserve this publication from the text and data mining exception.

This book and every book that comes after is for you, Mom. Love and miss you forever.

Playlist

Dirty Little Secret - The All-American Rejects ♥
Felt Good About You - Gracie Abrams ♥
the grudge - Olivia Rodrigo ♥
Sports car - Tate McRae ♥
You Proof - Morgan Wallen ♥
I Love You, I'm sorry - Gracie Abrams ♥
Tennessee Orange - Megan Moroney ♥
If He Wanted To He Would - Kylie Morgan ♥
GO HOME W U - Keith Urban, Lainey Wilson ♥
The Painter - Cody Johnson ♥
decode - Sabrina Carpenter ♥
parallel universe - Lauren Spencer Smith ♥
Block me out - Gracie Abrams ♥
Too Well - Reneé Rapp ♥
i hope i never fall in love - Maren Morris ♥
Opalite - Taylor Swift ♥

Chapter One

Johannes

11:59 ticks over into midnight, and that's it. He's really forgotten my birthday.

Four years ago, I was basically the focal point of his whole world. Granted, it was on his racing blog and podcast, where he mostly tore apart my rookie year, but still. There's no way in hell he doesn't know what today is.

My phone is full of pleading messages from my friends, begging me to come out and celebrate my birthday; Instagram notifications from fans wishing me a happy birthday; even a message from my agent telling me to still enjoy my day, despite *fucking up* – his words – in the race today. I came sixth. Which, whilst not my best performance, is still in the fucking points. Still better than fourteen of the other best drivers in the world.

Yet, nothing from my stupid boyfriend.

I sigh and lean my head back against the plushest velvet

headboard I've ever seen. Like a fool, I unlock my phone again, just in case I've missed something. But I haven't. I'm living in a dreamland if I think he's stepping out of the office to do anything special for me today.

Daddy's got him on a tight leash as he grooms him to take over stupid Team Hendersohm. Hendersohm was already my biggest rival on the track and now they're competing for my boyfriend's time and love, too. It's a joke.

At a minute past midnight, there's a knock at the door. When I say knock, it's actually multiple fists pounding away.

Part of me wants to pretend to be asleep, noise-cancelling headphones in and dead to the world, so I don't have to get the door and put on a happy face for my friends. But the other part knows them too well to think that if I ignore them, they will go away.

In moments like this it would be so nice to tell my best friend that I'm having relationship troubles and need some time by myself. But my relationship is such a big secret right now that I may as well have signed a flipping NDA.

Falling in love with Jackson Calder wasn't part of my life plan. Not when his father is the team principal of my biggest competition. Not when the man I love can't bear to be seen in public with me. Or even in private, if tonight is anything to go by. It's not like how it used to be before his dad asked him to give up everything and become a fucking workaholic as team-principal-in-training.

Sometimes, when I swipe back through the pictures in the password-protected folder on my phone, I don't recognise the couple who went on all those skiing holidays and quiet lake retreats in the first year of our relationship. Those images don't marry up with how lonely I currently feel.

The banging on my door doesn't stop, so I pad over to the door in just my boxers, peer through the look-out hole just to be sure it's the assholes I believe it to be, and crack the door once I confirm it's them.

Harper glares at me, less than impressed. I'm not sure if it's because of how long it took me to open the door or the fact that I refused to join them tonight, but the disappointed stare almost makes me want to wilt. Harper's never made me feel like that before.

'Okay, so now that your birthday is officially over, would you please come and join us downstairs for steak and a drink?' he asks wearily.

Behind him, Elijah's leaning up against the wall looking bored and pissed off. 'Yeah, please come and fucking eat. We've been sitting downstairs in the bar all night waiting for you, and Harper wouldn't let me have anything but honey-roast peanuts. I'm fucking starving.'

Like that will make me want to celebrate. Like I was hiding away just to piss him off. It wasn't even a big birthday. Twenty-nine. I just wanted to spend it wallowing in misery. Alone. Because if I can't be with *him* on my birthday, then I don't want to be with anyone. God, the self-pity is really starting to take over. I swear, no one should be so bitter this side of thirty.

'You're both idiots. You should have eaten without me. I don't feel like getting dressed and going downstairs. Like I said a few hours ago, I want to get an early night before we fly to Europe tomorrow.' First stop, Harper and Elijah's home race of Silverstone. Harper's practically bouncing on his heels at the thought. He's just one race away from being reunited with his fiancé.

What a feeling that must be. To know he's heading home to

someone who loves the freaking pants off him. Someone willing to promise him forever.

'Okay, so what if we order room service? A bucket of beers and some steaks. Then you don't have to go out and we can all still eat dinner together.'

'I can feel my resolve slipping and before I know it, Harper's flashing me his puppy-dog eyes – that don't normally work on me – and I'm letting the pair into my room. Elijah pounces on the room-service phone as Harper flops down on my bed like it's his own.'

'Ash and Cole joined us for a while to see if you'd come, but they had to go to bed to be up early for a meeting. Nils also declined in favour of some hook-up. Said you'd told him multiple times you weren't celebrating.' I'm more than glad that it's only this pair stinking up my room right now and not our full group of friends.

I wave off Harper's comment as Elijah finishes placing our order then I grab a T-shirt and some tracksuit bottoms from my suitcase so I'm not having dinner in my underwear.

'Move over,' I say, slapping Harper's thigh so he's not star fishing on my bed. He relents and makes room for me and then for Elijah as he drops down onto the end of the bed.

'All ordered, and just so you know, I pretended to be you and I name-dropped a lot after they told me the kitchen was already closed for the night.' He's grinning like a stupid idiot, but I can't bring myself to care. I try not to throw my name around anymore, but when my stomach grumbles loudly I'm glad he's done it.

'Great,' I reply as Harper settles his head against my shoulder, like the affection-hogging guy he is.

'Has he always hated birthdays?' Elijah asks my best friend of fifteen years.

'Nope. Before he got boring, we'd spend them partying the night away.' Harper nods at me. 'Didn't you have a threesome for your twenty-third?'

I shrug. I think it was after winning my first race of the year in that category. It was probably well earned.

Today's performance wouldn't have got me so lucky.

'You two were wild so that doesn't surprise me.' Elijah came into this sport already in a relationship with his childhood sweetheart, whom he then married and had kids with, so he never got to experience the crazy nights of celebrating race wins like we did. I probably should feel sorry for him, but I wish, like him, I had someone to go home to with all my trophies.

I just 'hmm' in response. There were some good times, I can't deny that. The fact that I've now celebrated more birthdays with Harper in my life than without is one of the good things about turning twenty-nine.

Harper and Elijah slip into a conversation about birthday sex – which apparently isn't on the cards for me tonight – but I can't switch my brain off. My thoughts are racing with all the things I'm currently missing out on right now. The years when everything is meant to be good and easy are slipping away from me because the guy I love keeps me dangling. Because he keeps me as a secret. How much have I lost? How much time have I wasted?

For the last three years I could have been dating other guys, finding someone willing to show me off or maybe just, you know, hold hands with me in public or acknowledge my existence. Right now, I could be having shared experiences with my loved-up friends, trading happy stories of our trips away together and plans for the future. Instead, my life's become a vault I can't open to them. Instead, he's turned me into someone who lies to the people I love.

It's exhausting having to be so careful and secretive. It's draining the life out of me.

I blink and find I'm alone in the bed. It takes me a second to realise that Elijah's at the door accepting our food, Harper hovering behind him eagerly.

'Can you at least put down some towels?' I scold Harper before Elijah can start laying out the plates on my bed sheets. I'd prefer not to be sleeping on sauce and oil stains tonight.

'Ohhhhh, I haven't heard you say that in so long! For a second, I almost felt a thrill.' Harper runs to the bathroom to grab a couple of big fluffy towels, while I swallow uncomfortably. That's not a memory I want to think about anymore.

'Sometimes I forget you two have shagged,' Elijah contributes helpfully as he lays the dishes down on my newly protected bed. 'So strange how Harper's slept with both of my friends.'

'I wish I could forget, too,' I reply, but there's no forgetting. Ever. I don't regret it, though, not when it's part of why we're so close today.

'No one ever forgets this ass, don't you worry.' Harper gives his perky little butt a tap, before seating himself in front of the ridiculous amount of food we seem to have. I'm pretty sure Elijah's ordered every possible side dish on the menu to accompany three hulking pieces of steak.

As I swallow a piece of the tenderest, butteriest steak, it hits me how grateful I am for these two. I wanted to be alone, but now I'm glad I'm not.

'Thanks guys,' I say around a piece of tenderstem broccoli. 'I do appreciate you both coming tonight.'

Harper drops his fork onto his plate with a clatter and throws his arms around me, tugging me close as I try not to choke on my mouthful of steak. 'We love you, okay? All we want is to celebrate you.'

It's not the kind of love I was looking for tonight, but as my best friend clutches at the back of my T-shirt, I realise it's better. I'm lucky that I haven't pushed them both so far away that they don't want to be here for me.

'Love you, too,' I mutter into his curly hair, before pushing him away. 'Now let me eat my steak.'

We settle into conversations about the rest of the season and where we're flying to next and then fall into shared food comas once Elijah moves all the trays to the cart in the hallway. It's a good evening, once I embrace it. I look at the time and see it's just before 2 a.m. – and whilst I have a flight tomorrow and should probably be asleep, I don't want them to leave.

I contemplate suggesting we all bunk down here, in my room, like we aren't grown men who have their own beds in this hotel tonight, when there's a knock at the door.

'Did you order yourself a rent boy for the night?' Harper teases as the knocking doesn't stop.

'Or maybe it's the hotel staff coming to tell you to shut the fuck up,' I say. Harper is fond of singing along to whatever background music is playing.

'Unlikely. I have the voice of an angel.'

'Sure you do,' Elijah says sarcastically.

'The hotel's been taken over by racing drivers and team

staff – it's probably someone who's wasted and got the wrong room.'

'Well why don't you answer it and tell them to bugger off,' Elijah suggests irritably.

I shrug Harper off and pad to the door and the second I open it, I regret not looking through the peephole first, because there he is.

The only person I really wanted to see tonight.

His wavy brown hair is scraped back into a bun on the top of his head and his chocolate-brown eyes are hugged with dark shadows. His glasses rest on his nose in place of his usual contacts, so I know he must be tired, and I find myself softening towards him. But it takes him precisely three seconds to go from exhausted to panicked as he realises I'm not alone.

I can't speak. If I do, I'm going to give the game away because the only thing I want to ask is where the fuck he's been and why he's been ignoring my messages. I want to tell him how pissed off I am that he forgot my birthday. That with him, I never ever come first. Yet I can't say any of that in front of Harper and Elijah. I'm sure even a quick glance over my shoulder right now will make them both immediately suspicious. So, I just stand there like an idiot and don't say anything at all.

The panic slides away as he schools his face into a blank expression. He forces out a laugh and pretends to catch sight of the others. 'Shit, sorry, I must have the wrong room! I was looking for—' he's playing calm-and-collected very successfully. But then he struggles to find a name. Eventually he comes up with: 'Anna.'

'Wrong floor, man,' Harper offers from the bed. 'She's on four, I think, not eight.'

'Of course, sorry, only just finished for the night. Clearly my brain isn't working.' It's a believable lie, because why else would he be wandering the hotel at 2 a.m.? 'Sorry to interrupt your night.'

'You didn't, don't worry,' Elijah replies, holding out a hand to Harper to pull him up off the bed. 'We were about to call it a night anyway.'

I'm almost hopeful that that means Jackson might stick around, but I'm clearly delusional. 'No worries. I'll walk back with you. Maybe I'll actually end up on the right floor this time.'

All three of them laugh, but I can't move, let alone speak. Harper and Elijah have to contort their bodies to get around me to join Jackson in the hallway. I'm not sure I've even spoken since he arrived. Or breathed.

He refuses to meet my eye, instead smiling at his drivers as they tell him he needs to take a break more often or he'll end up like his dad.

Joke's on him, because little do they know that's exactly how this will end.

'We'll see you in the morning, okay?' Harper's looking at me curiously, perhaps confused by my awkward silence and complete lack of social skills right now.

'In the morning?' It's a stupid question, he's just trying to say goodnight, but my brain is completely lagging in this moment, trying to catch up on what the hell is happening.

'We're crashing your breakfast with Nils. We all want to hear about his new woman. Maybe she's the one.'

Three years ago, I couldn't imagine Harper James understanding what *the one* even meant, never mind making it his life's mission to help his friends find their own. Falling for Kian Walker really did a number on him.

It doesn't help that every time we go for dinner or a drink, he points out every guy he thinks could be a possible match for me. Like I don't have a long-term boyfriend. If only he knew. It's so fucking stupid. I can't believe I'm still keeping this ridiculous secret from him. It's past the point of making me feel like I'm fourteen again and sneaking around with my first boyfriend behind my parents' back. Now the secret is eating me up inside, making me feel ashamed of who and what I am. Making me hate myself. And I hate Jackson for that. Almost more than I miss him.

ARGH! This is some seriously toxic shit.

'Oh, okay, yeah, see you in the morning.' And then, just when I thought this couldn't get any more fucked up, I wave at him.

Harper's not an idiot. The media used to make him out to be a fool, but I've known him a long time and he's anything but.

'Night, Jo,' Elijah calls over his shoulder as he trails behind Harper towards the lifts.

It hurts to watch them all walk away, leaving me completely alone. But then I catch Jackson looking back. That's what completely guts me. I hope, desperately, to see remorse, regret, or an apology in those eyes that once upon a time made me feel warm and safe.

But they hold nothing but relief.

Relief that, yet again, we've got away with this. He's made it through another close shave without this stinking, festering, toxic secret getting out.

It's only when I shut the door that I realise he all but

pretended I wasn't even there. He talked directly to Elijah and Harper and didn't even acknowledge my presence.

What the fuck?

I don't even know whether he remembered my birthday.

As I reflect bitterly on how this night turned out, I begin to think that perhaps he came knocking on my door to get his own needs met and not because he wanted to meet mine. And yet all I feel is pitifully grateful that he remembered my existence at all.

That's fucking tragic.

Happy fucking birthday to me.

As I get back into bed, it's hard to see how twenty-nine is going to be any better than twenty-eight.

Chapter Two

Caleb

Becoming Johannes Müller's race engineer was meant to be one of the most exciting moments of my life. And, for maybe nine or ten races, it lived up to all my expectations. He was on that podium every week and I was being heaped with praise for basically not changing anything after his last guy retired and I was brought in.

Yes, he was performing, but he wasn't the fearless spitfire I'd watched from the garage in my previous role. His risks seemed unusually calculated and there was less freedom and ease as he sped around the track. He wasn't focused. He was too in his own head.

When he finished sixth in Canada, there were already whispers of – *What the hell's going on? What's changed?* – and so many of those questions were being thrown at me. There'd been no significant changes to the car, so that meant it had something to do with the driver. That meant it could be something to do with me. At first, I convinced myself it was one sub-par performance, only bad in relation to the incredibly high standards Johannes had started setting himself last season. Then he qualified eighth at Silverstone yesterday, and the headlines about him overtook those about Harper cruising home in pole position.

His last two years with Racing Borough Force (RBF) were pretty great, especially last year when he finished third overall and hardly ever left the podium. Although he's actually still sitting in third overall, the gap between him and the top two is gradually increasing. Yesterday's eighth place qualification isn't going to help that at all.

I'm sure Nathan, the RBF team principal, must be thinking that the only thing that's changed is his race engineer. I see it in the way he glares at me when Johannes doesn't make it anywhere near the front row, yet again, and in the way he stormed off before Harper even had a chance to sign his pole-position tire.

It is, of course, possible to turn it all around here at Silverstone. There's room for him to work his way up the points *if* he puts in the effort, *if* he finds his way back to the Johannes who isn't afraid to put it all on the line. But he has to be prepared to take risks. And right now, Johannes doesn't seem prepared to do anything.

He's sluggish as he gets into his suit; vacant as he stands with the others for the British national anthem. And it takes me two attempts to get him to do a radio check before the formation lap.

'Johannes, you okay?' I ask in a whisper, because if he's not, we really shouldn't be letting the other teams know, but I can't stop myself. He looks like he hasn't slept and that's really not good. I didn't sleep either because I stayed up half the night analysing his race from Silverstone last year, but that doesn't matter because he's the driver and I'm not.

He was magic out there last year. Finished top of the podium, pissing off his best friend and closest rival on the track by preventing him winning his home race. But this year, there's none of that fire. I don't get it. It's like he's just going through the motions. It's almost like he … doesn't care.

It's hard to watch.

He grunts out a 'yes' in reply and it tells me everything I need to know. He doesn't want to talk. Did my predecessor Gary ever have this problem with him? I'd have to ask Ian, Nils's race engineer, if Gary had ever talked to him about Johannes's quirks. I need more insight, more understanding – because despite being part of this team (albeit in the garage) for the last few years, I don't know him and he doesn't know me.

He needs to get in the zone so he can fight to climb back up that grid to where he actually belongs. He has it in him, I know he does, but I'm not sure *he* knows. Not right now, anyway. To be honest, I have no idea what's going on in his head.

That's the problem. In our first set of races together, he was on the radio a lot. Both he and his teammate are talkers. Nils doesn't stop running his mouth throughout his whole drive, filling the line with things he doesn't need to air on the radio. It annoys Ian to no end – he's someone who enjoys a bit of peace and quiet. But whilst Johannes is active on the radio, it's always with helpful insight and commentary about the car and how it's moving on the track. It made settling into my role easy, but just when I thought we might be starting to form a good partnership, he completely shut down on me in Montreal.

He didn't get the best result, which is definitely not what he wanted on his birthday, but he had mentally checked out before the race even started. He had nothing to say all weekend, just a few grunts punctuated by German swear words.

When I finally got back to my room, after multiple meetings and crisis talks about Johannes's starting position, my family group chat was full of concerned messages from my parents and three older brothers checking that I was okay after such an awful race.

Despite them being much older than me, we're still close. When I was offered the promotion to race engineer, I went to each of them for advice about whether I should take it. At thirty-two, I'm reasonably young for this position, and so much weighs on your shoulders when the driver is out on the track. I know there was some worry, especially from my oldest brother, Gregg, who has almost two decades on me, that I was taking on too much, especially alongside the PhD I'm also working on.

I was so proud to have proved myself to them when the first ten races went so well, watching Jackson win and take podiums at every track, only for it to crumble away last week. And now it's like the first ten races didn't matter, because Johannes has had a bad one. I know they're worrying about me, but I'm only thinking of Johannes.

It feels like an age that they sit on the grid, waiting for lights out. I can only imagine what it's like for him in that cockpit, in the downward spiralling headspace he seems to be in. It's like he's lost confidence in his ability, like he doesn't trust himself out there anymore. It's so hard to watch.

When the lights finally go out, I send up a silent prayer that Johannes makes a good move into turn one…

It's almost a miracle when straight away he pushes into sixth before everyone is even off their mark. I knew he could do it!

I cheer, only for Johannes's move to be rendered completely redundant seconds later when Kinsley goes straight into the back of Hunter before turn one. Hunter's car rolls across the gravel, leaving him upside down. Immediate red flag.

A whole heap of groans ring out up and down the paddock, because the red flag means a complete restart. Any gains made are therefore void. Damn it.

Of course, my focus goes straight back to making sure Hunter's okay and not injured, but his team and the safety crew will be all over that. My priority has to be letting Johannes know what's happening and preparing him for the restart. Hunter upside down in the gravel. Red flag. Restart looking lightly.

'*Scheiße! Scheiße!*' Johannes screams, before turning his radio off.

He needed that start – and the element of surprise is now lost as the two cars he jumped ahead of will be aware of his tactic. It's unlikely he will be able to pull off the same move again.

Everyone files slowly into the pit as we wait for the driver extraction. There's a buzz as we plan our restart strategies, but there's also a heightened awareness of how risky this sport is, and how the drivers put their bodies – and their lives – on the line. There is palpable relief when we hear that Hunter is breathing and alert and on his way to hospital.

When the drivers come in, they end up in a messy queue in the pit lane. There's still no word on when we're going to restart. Some get out of their cars and chat with mechanics and teammates in the paddock. Nils is at the pit wall, talking Ian's ear off about what he thinks he can do better in this restart, and Ian's nodding along and making suggestions. It's nice. They're an odd pairing, but while Ian sometimes seems to just be tolerating Nils's chattiness, he has huge respect for the young driver, too.

My driver remains in his car. Silent. The mechanics have put the tyre warmers on and his engine is off, but he makes no effort to move. I'm almost tempted to go over there and see if he'll speak to me, face-to-face, but I don't want to annoy or unsettle him when he's obviously already struggling. I don't want him to get an even worse result because of something I've done. If I can't even get him to talk to me on the radio, why would he want to do it face-to-face?

I watch him sit there, resolutely facing forwards, as still as a statue. His gaze seems locked on something – or perhaps on nothing – ahead of him.

What's he thinking? I wish I knew. I wish I could get through to him. I wish I could help him. I wish I knew what he needs to hear from me right now.

I feel like I'm watching his confidence drain away with every second that passes. I feel completely useless.

They finally announce a time to restart. Nils gets himself ready and gets back in his car, and I'm left with Ian's questioning stare.

'Johannes doing okay?' he asks.

'Your guess is as good as mine,' I mumble before letting Johannes know the track will soon be clear for another formation lap. He'll be headed back to his spot on the fourth row – exactly where he doesn't want to be right now.

'He can pull this back,' Ian says. 'He won from eighth last year.' Not here, though. Not on this track. Not at Harper's home race, where he'd probably run even his best friend off the track to win here. His fiancé will no doubt be watching on from the garage like the proudest man possible. Harper's not losing today.

Even if we could just climb to the top half of the points, that would be better than last weekend. I know he's capable of it.

Except, of course, we aren't that lucky. The lights go out for the second time, the track roars back to life, and Johannes can't get out of eighth position, no matter how hard he tries.

And he tries – he really tries – but his frustration gets the better of him and he gradually falls even further back, the gap between him and P7 increasing with every turn. He slips back closer to the driver in P9 and if he's not careful he's going to lose P8 to him.

If Johannes were on top form, we'd be enjoying the British battle at the front as Elijah tries to force his way into first, Harper defending his position like his life depends on it. Except we can't enjoy it, because I have my foul-mouthed driver on the radio cursing out his car, the other drivers, the officials, the course – and eventually the whole world – as he battles the demons inside his head.

I keep checking and rechecking the technical data and I can't see any issues with the car. On screen and on paper, everything looks good right now. Which means it's driver error. But I could have told you that without even looking at the stats. He's pushing hard, but it's like he's fighting himself instead of the other nineteen cars on track.

The crowd is going absolutely wild for a British 1-2-3 as Harper leads, Elijah trailing just behind him, and Jon trying his absolute best to keep up in a position he's completely unused to. The atmosphere is electric.

But my focus is locked on my own driver as he catches gravel at turn one, steering back onto the track in a cloud of dust. It's exactly what he doesn't need, and he quickly loses a place to Ogum. Johannes is now P9.

'Fuckkkk,' I grunt under my breath. This can't be happening.

Now he's left battling Nils who's closing in behind him like the up-and-coming driver he really is. While it's good for Nils personally, this is not in the best interests of the team. Of course they want Nils fighting for points, but they don't want it to be with the driver who's their best chance of being the championship winner this year.

I want to slam my head down on the desk and throw my headphones across the paddock. This sport, no matter how much I love it, is the most frustrating thing in the world. One millisecond can change the outcome of a race, and one race can change everyone's opinion of you. For better or worse.

Two bad results in a row means we have a serious problem.

'You're fucking kidding me,' Johannes groans into the radio, just when I think things surely can't get any worse in this race. 'Why is my steering so heavy?'

I look to our pressure notifications and half a second later it's flickering away as his front right tyre pressure drops completely. 'Box, box!' I call out almost immediately. 'There's a puncture.'

It's the worst news I could be giving him right now. Any chance of a one-stop strategy is now completely out the window as we have to pit on lap ten. Even if we go on hards right now, it's going to destroy his race to try and catch up. But if we go on to softs, we're fucked in fifteen laps' time and he'll have to come back in. The call needs to be made fast and it's up to me to make it.

'Let's go hards. He can do this. He'll ease the tyres back in and there's a chance he might not have to stop again.'

We should have started on hards like most of the rest of the grid, but no, we went a different way, hoping for a free pit stop at some point if a safety car came out. It turned out to be a bad call, but it's not just the tyres working against Johannes. I can feel the race slowly but surely slipping away.

Johannes is furious as we attempt a fast stop, but can only make it three seconds short before he rejoins the race. Luckily, when he does rejoin the race, he's in P10. He's at the back of the pack, struggling to keep any kind of pace behind the top of the grid.

Johannes doesn't climb any spots. The hard tyres take too long to wear in before he can find his true race pace behind Nils in ninth; and at that point, Nils is long gone and too quick to catch. Nathan's practically spitting venom before the chequered flag even drops for Harper to take it home.

It's the first time Nils has ever finished ahead of his teammate so the mood is going to be bittersweet in the RBF garage this afternoon. Of course, I'm happy for Nils, but I'm beyond gutted for Johannes.

Johannes almost finished outside of the points and I'm dreading what this means. For him, for the team, for me…

Surely the only way from here is up.

Chapter Three

Johannes

P fucking 10. My worst finish in longer than I care to remember. Everything from climbing out of the car to being weighed and then dragged in for some doping tests is a complete blur.

Until I walk smack bang into my supposed secret boyfriend who's clapping my best friend on the back.

Jackson's gaze on me is cold, the way a stranger looks at you. I don't know if he's in control of it anymore. It's like a role he automatically slips into every time we meet in a professional capacity. I'm not close enough to hear the words exchanged between him and Harper, but as I approach, Jackson makes a hasty exit.

Harper hauls me into his arms and I cling to the warmth I've known from him for so much of my life. It hits me in a zap of bitter ice down my spine how much I miss him right now, how much our gradual drifting apart has impacted me.

'Congratulations,' I murmur into his hair, ruffling the sweaty curls with my free hand.

'Thank you,' he whispers into my shoulder and I peer around, checking for documentary cameras. They don't need to capture this moment. It belongs to us, just us. Best friends who haven't been around each other enough recently. My fault. Not his.

Thankfully, there's not a camera in sight, but his fiancé is watching. He gives me a little wave and nods in approval as I hold the love of his life close to me. Maybe he knows how much I need this. Or maybe he knows I've not given Harper enough time recently.

'Are you okay?' Harper asks and I want nothing more than to break down and tell him how much I'm not, but I can't. The only way to keep a secret is to tell nobody at all. I promised Jackson I wouldn't tell anyone and I haven't. Even when he lets me down, over and over again, I've kept my mouth shut. I know how volatile Harper can be, especially when someone he loves has been hurt this much, and in a very short time Jackson will take over from his father and become Harper's boss. I won't put Harper's career at risk just because I got my feelings trampled on.

'Yeah, just a bad day.' It's not a lie. I have had a fucking awful day. But not for any reasons I can give Harper.

He pulls away from my grasp, eyes scanning mine for the truth. He sighs as he steps back, and I can sense the tidal wave of disappointment washing over him. 'I know this is really poor timing because I *know* you aren't okay right now, but I need you tomorrow. By my side. When I marry Kian.'

'You what?' He can't be serious right now.

'We're tired of waiting. All week Elise and Grant have been

helping us pull it together and tomorrow we're going to tie the knot. It'll be a small, intimate ceremony. Private. *Really* private. No press.'

I feel bad that he didn't even ask me for help, and that Kian's sister and brother-in-law have had to do all the work. I've been so focused on my own misery that I've been blind to what's going on in his life. If it's possible, I now feel even worse.

Even so, I can't help but admire how brave he is to think he can pull this off. The day after winning his home race, two of the biggest racing drivers ever getting married, in private, is a lot to ask. But I wouldn't want to be anywhere else other than at his side. No matter how much my own heart is currently hurting.

'You know I'll be there. You two are fucking crazy, but I'll be there.'

Which is why, just eighteen hours later, I'm in a small dressing room at one of the most beautiful hotels in England, helping Harper with his bow tie.

A moment of silence flickers between us as I tighten the knot. It contains all the years we've been friends, the handful of times we've been something more, and all the love that's brought us to this point. It's weighty, but in a comforting, meaningful way. I wish I could be honest with him. But today is not the day for that. Today is about Harper and Kian.

Elise comes in wearing a beautiful lilac dress to tell us it's time to head down to the marquee. I tell Harper I'm proud of him, we hug one last time, and then we go.

Kian's niece and nephew walk down the aisle first in matching outfits. I can feel the other guests melting at how adorable they are. Harper and I follow and when we get to the front I stand by his side as he watches Kian and Elise walk down. I watch Harper's expression as his soon-to-be husband approaches and I am ashamed of the big black hole that opens up inside my chest. I'm not jealous and I'm not afraid of losing Harper to Kian. I'm *envious*. I envy what they have together because I want that for myself. I want a man who loves me the way they love each other. I wish I could feel nothing but joy for them, but I feel so utterly and completely sorry for myself that I can barely breathe. I hope one day I can look back on this scene and treasure it for my best friend's sake, but it won't be today.

I refuse to ruin it for them by drawing attention, though. I bury my longing and my envy, my hurt and my shame. The years of modelling gigs pay off big time as I force my signature smile and let everything else wash over me.

Of course, Kian and Harper have written their own vows. They talk of the love they share and will share until the end of time, of the good and the bad times, of the pride they have in each other, of how they can't wait to make more memories, of how they want to grow old together.

The photographer catches every angle and I'm sure in the background he'll capture my tears. They'll be noted as happy tears for my best friend. Everything will look exactly like it's supposed to, and no one will ever know how empty the day makes me feel. How alone. So alone.

Alone, when supposedly I'm in a long-term relationship with someone who's meant to love me like this pair love each other, but it takes watching Harper and Kian vow to spend the rest of their lives together to make me realise what a big, fat lie that is. Love isn't supposed to make you feel like this. It's supposed to make you feel like *that*, I think as I watch Harper and Kian seal their marriage with a kiss then break away and smile as the guests clap and cheer.

Jackson won't even give me a date, never mind the promise of forever.

There's photo's on the lawn. Group ones, family ones, groom shots and then ones of me and Harper – and then me and the happy couple. God, it's miserable. I can't even look at the camera screen as the photographer shows them off to us. I'm afraid I will see all the pain reflected in my eyes.

I drift through the rest of the reception, going where I am told, smiling whenever someone holds up a camera. I eat steak and the creamiest of mashed potatoes and make conversation with any and everyone. I make jokes and laugh at other people's stories, because it's important to me that no one knows what's really going on inside me. How could I tell them that on the happiest day of my best friend's life, I feel like I'm dying inside?

I tune back in to the conversation around me.

'It was a beautiful day,' I comment, lights twinkling around us. Hard to go wrong with a simple comment like that, right?

'What, my win or this?' Harper gestures to the room of guests. It's not a huge, celebrity wedding, but there's more than a handful of famous faces. It's intimate, hand-picked, special. Every single person here matters to the happy couple. I swallow painfully.

'Both, I guess, for you.' The laugh I choke out is forced and he eyes me speculatively. It's a look with which I'm becoming all too familiar. Ever since I first hooked up with Jackson, something's been different between us.

He knows something is going on – he's known for some time – but even when he's pushed me about it, I haven't given him much. I want to, I always want to, but Jackson wouldn't like it and it's not fair to ask Harper to keep a secret from Kian. I'm competitive and I want to win the Championship, but not by messing with the dynamics of Team Hendersohm.

'It's really quite something to be on top of the world in both my personal and professional life,' Harper says. 'You wanna talk about what happened yesterday?'

I know he means my P10, but I can't tell him that it's because I'm so in my own head, so mentally fatigued, that my racing is suffering. And I can't tell him why. So, I shake my head. 'Not today, Harps. Today is about you and everything you've achieved. Congratulations, my friend. You deserve it. You both do.' I even manage to squeeze out a cheeky grin. 'I'll get the next one.'

He sighs but drops it. I know Harper so well I can read every inch of movement in his face, the way the crinkles around his eyes scrunch as he scrutinises my decision to push him away again. The disappointment that flickers in his eyes before he turns to his husband, seeking reassurance, which of course he gets in the form of a kiss to his forehead, and the shining beam of loving attention.

We hardly speak for the rest of the evening. I hate that I'm probably triggering the abandonment issues he's worked so hard to overcome when I don't let him be a part of my life anymore. It's the last thing I want him to feel today. I wish I could hide it better.

I mingle with Cole and Ash and we share memories of the

newlyweds over the last few years, before Harper and Kian join us again.

'Look at you two,' Ash says with a sigh, his arms wrapped around the woman I've come to learn is his childhood sweetheart. Neither of them is wearing a ring so I assume they aren't married or even engaged. 'Some days I still can't believe it.'

'Well, now there's no going back. He's stuck with me.' Harper's hanging on to Kian's arm, eyes a little hazy from one too many beers, but it's nothing compared to how he used to be.

'Like herpes, it seems,' Elijah jokes as he approaches us, his wife and kids long since having gone back to the hotel.

Everyone laughs and I allow myself to get caught up in it and laugh, too, because he's not wrong at all.

'I do have a question, though,' Elijah says. 'Was doing it like this, so quick and secretive, worth it now you have no wedding gifts?'

'I already have the best gift of all,' Kian replies, tugging Harper closer to him. They look ridiculously good together, like a proper power couple, and them being married will only make that stronger now.

Elijah, Cole and Ash all gag on cue and Kian flips them off but is quickly distracted by movement behind me.

'Oh, there he is,' Kian says with a smirk looking right over my shoulder. 'What time do you call this, mate?'

I don't even have to turn around to know who he's speaking to. I have the sound of his footsteps ingrained in my mind and the scent of his Burberry cologne infiltrates my nostrils and leaves the hairs on my arms upright.

'It was you who decided to get married the day after one of

the busiest races of the year for the team, especially after your husband decided to win the damn race,' he says.

And then he walks past me like I'm not even here.

Instead, he goes straight in for a proper hug with Kian and then a half hug with Harper who looks more than ready to drag his husband away from the reception.

It's like I don't exist. How is he able to make me feel like I don't exist at my best-friend's wedding?

Eventually, he turns away from the pair and shakes hands with Elijah, then Cole, then Ash before offering me a polite hello. This is insane. This is the man I share a bed with, the man I share my body with. The only person I've ever fallen in love with. The guy I thought was my future. And he's treating me like I'm nothing more than an addition to this little Hendersohm group.

There's a childlike tantrum waiting to erupt inside me. I want to stamp my feet and demand he acknowledges me. I want to demand he takes my hand, kisses my cheek and holds me like the other couples around us.

And then suddenly, it's all just too much. I've let this go on for far too long. We need to talk.

'Excuse me.' I pat Harper's shoulder as I step out of the little circle we've formed and head towards the front of the marquee. I need air. Or another drink. Or both. But mostly I just need to be away from all of … that.

Not even the sharp air of a chilly summer night can stun me out of the way I'm feeling. I'm all over the place. Maybe I should have been pushier. Maybe I should have made it clear I needed a public relationship, but I thought it would come eventually. I thought I just had to be patient and let him go public on his own terms, but I'm not sure he's even trying.

Now we're over two-and-a-half years in and we have nothing to show for it. We don't own anything together, no house or car or even a sofa. There's no engagement on the horizon, no marriage, no talks of a family in the future. I can't even remember the last time he told me he loved me. And as far as I know, not one single person even knows we are together.

How did I get this so wrong?

Footsteps on the gravel behind me almost have me ducking behind the marquee, but before I can hide Jackson is calling my name.

'Oh, so now you want to talk to me?' I'm aware I sound like a petulant child, but I am no longer capable of hiding how I feel.

'Jo, come on.'

'No, not come on, Jackson. I'm aware you don't want to be my boyfriend around our closest friends but you're so cold I was basically iced out of the circle.' My voice is rising and he shushes me, which only makes things worse. 'Don't fucking shush me, right? Who the fuck do you think you are right now?'

'I just want to talk, Jo, that's all.' For a conversation he doesn't want anyone to overhear, he's standing awfully far away from me. It's like he can't bear to be physically close to me.

There was a time when this was exciting. We were a secret moment in a crowded room, a lingering glance amongst a group of friends and no one knew but us. Sneaking around was exhilarating and it made getting each other alone even more thrilling.

Now the air between us hangs stale. He can't even look me

in the eye, and it makes the secret feel dirty. And not in a good way.

'So, talk,' I say. 'I've been trying to talk to you for months and all you've done is avoid me. But here we are. Talk away.' I wish I could soften my tone, but I think I'm past that now. I'm angry, and hurt, and really fucking tired of putting up with his bullshit.

'I'm so sorry, Jo.'

The way he says those four words makes my stomach drop. I know what's coming next, and although I'm pissed off at him right now, this is definitely not what I want to hear. He might be sorry, but he's doing this anyway.

'I can't do this anymore,' he says.

'And by this, you mean our two-and-a-half-year relationship, right?' I don't want to be this person, but I can't believe he thinks my best friend's wedding is the right time to do this. I can hardly go back in there upset because I would never intentionally ruin their big day, especially when no one even knows about Jackson in the first place. And then a sneaking, creeping suspicion enters my mind: maybe that's precisely why he's doing it now.

'I'm sorry. This isn't easy for me, Jo. I love you, but this is too much.'

I want to scream, to thump the ground and beg for it to swallow me up so I don't have to go through this break-up.

'You love me?' The words are so bitter as they leave my mouth. I snort. 'Don't kid yourself. You wouldn't know love if it hit you in the face. Those people in there,' I say, jabbing my finger towards the marquee, 'they know love. What they do is love. The way you treat me is not love.' Hot tears start to pour down my cheeks as everything I've wanted to say for months comes out. 'I put up with it for so long because I love you. I actually love you. But you? You don't love me, and I'm not sure you ever did.'

'That's not true, Jo. You know how hard this has been. You know the pressure I've been under.'

'Pressure? PRESSURE? You think I don't know pressure?' I exclaim.

'I didn't mean—'

'Yes, you did. That's exactly what you meant. Because the only person you think about is yourself. You have no idea how hard this has been for me. You won't talk about it with me and you won't let me talk about it with anyone else, so you've made sure I am completely and utterly alone in my misery and my pain,' I say, having to gasp for air to force out the words. 'You've made me lie to everyone in my life, but I did it because you asked me to.'

'I'm sorry, Jo. I never meant to hurt you. I'm sorry. I'm sorry. But my life is changing … and, you know, with taking over Hendersohm, I can't have a relationship with a rival driver anymore. It's just not possible. I'm sorry.' For a second, there's a look of anguish on his face, but it's gone as quickly as he is. He's walking away before I can do something stupid like take back my words or beg him to stay.

But it would all be a lie. As much as I love him and want him, it's been over for a long time. I have to let him go.

Luckily, there's a bench nearby and I sink into it, head in my hands letting his words sting every nerve ending in my body as I try to process that I'm single now.

'What was that?' Harper asks. I didn't even hear him coming but he's already standing in front of me.

'Nothing,' I mutter as I quickly wipe away all the evidence of tears from my face.

'Nothing?' He questions, glaring at me like my whole body is on fire with the lie. 'So you're sitting out here on your own, in tears, looking like the world just ended for nothing? What did Jackson say to you? Was he having a go at you? Will you please tell me what's going on?'

'Just leave it, Harps. It's honestly nothing. I'm not in a great place right now and I don't want to spoil your day.' It's a lie only of omission.

There's a beat of silence. He looks over at me, and I know he's not buying it.

'You're not spoiling my day. I wish you would talk to me, though. I feel like I have no idea what's going on with you anymore, Jo. The season was going so well. What's changed?'

'I don't know.' The lie instantly flies out of my mouth – I'm so used to telling them at this point. It makes me hate the person I've become. 'I'm sure it'll get better. I'll be back on top next race.'

He offers me his hand. His suit is slightly rumpled, his tie has gone and the top couple of buttons of his shirt are undone. It's the look of a happily married man.

'Come on. Let me cheer you up. I want a dance with my best man before we call it a night.'

I allow him to pull me up and into the tightest of hugs. My hands crumple the back of his jacket as I hold on for dear life, allowing myself to sink into him. We hug for longer than normal friends probably do – even normal best friends – but I need it right now and I am so grateful that he can tell.

When it's over, I let him sweep me back into the marquee and onto the dance floor. Jackson is, thankfully, long gone and most of the other guests have left, too, so it's a special moment shared only by the two of us. Every second reminds me of how much I've missed him. I need to try harder to be a better friend so I don't miss out on being a part of his life. It wouldn't surprise me if in a couple years' time, he and Kian think about children, and I want to be the fun uncle they would expect me to be.

The DJ announces it's the last song of the night and Kian taps my shoulder to take over. I happily let the pair share this final dance, congratulating them again as I step back. Elise hugs me as I gather up my discarded suit jacket and tells me not to be a stranger in Norfolk. It's nice, and not what I expected from Kian's sister when I'm not part of their little family, but I appreciate it, nonetheless.

She's also arranged for cars to take us back to wherever we need, which makes it easier for me to get back to the hotel where the rest of the team is staying, but the drive passes in such a blur. My face is slightly wet as I watch the countryside roads go by in the darkness of the night, silent tears slipping down my cheeks.

Back in my room, the tears dry up and a kind of numbness settles into my bones. I'm left to face the reality of this break-up alone in a dark, cold hotel room.

To be honest, it's been over so long already that the only difference I truly feel from the last few months is a weird sense of relief that I never expected. For the first time in what feels like forever, I fall asleep quickly and sleep through the night without tossing and turning.

Chapter Four

Caleb

A triple header is the busiest period of the racing calendar, so when I board the plane for Hungary just a couple of days after the race at Silverstone, I can feel the exhaustion in my core.

Ian takes a solo seat and cracks on with a race report he says is overdue. The rest of the plane is full of chatter, until I reach the back and find Nils sitting quietly, not chatting his teammate's ear off like normal. I wonder what's wrong with him until I turn and see Johannes with his knees tucked up on the other side of the aisle, headphones on, hood pulled up, eyes closed. We've been flying together all season, and I've never seen him like this. I look at Nils but he just shrugs and puts his own headphones on.

I hate to disturb Johannes, but the seat opposite him is pretty much the only one remaining and the flight's only a few hours. I take the seat and he doesn't even flinch. If I hadn't seen him board the plane a few minutes ago, I might have believed he was asleep.

The flight takes off without drama and I'm quick to open my laptop to get some work for my PhD done. At some point during the flight, whatever Johannes is listening to must end and his eyes shoot open, clearly shocked to see me.

'Sorry. I hope I didn't disturb you.' I apologise quickly, half closing the lid of my laptop.

'No, you didn't. Don't worry. Just forgot I was on the plane for a moment.' He tucks his headphones in to the side of the seat and plucks a neck pillow from the top of a backpack.

'Late night?' I say. It's my way of asking what's going on without actually asking him what's going on.

At first he doesn't say anything, but I catch an expression crossing his face that I can't quite read. It's fleeting but also … desperately sad.

'Long weekend, you know.'

I get the impression he wants to say more but he doesn't.

'Oh? You and Nils went out last night? I saw some photos from what looked like a party. Guess he's enjoying scoring points.' We both turn at the sound of heavy snoring from across the aisle. I can't help but laugh, but Johannes doesn't even crack a smile.

'Nah, just an event for a friend. Didn't expect it to be such a late one, that's all.' He doesn't have to tell me if he doesn't want to, but I still wish he would. He's obviously not okay, and something tells me it's more than his P10 finish at Silverstone. 'They have you working on the flight?' He asks, gesturing to my laptop.

'This? No. I'm working on my PhD. I have to cram it into every bit of free time at the moment, which has been difficult with the triple header.' It's been hard all season, to be honest. My thesis has had to take a back seat really and I'm probably going to end up having to ask for an extension because I can't see how I'll get it done in time as well as do my job. But that's the cost of living my dream.

'Oh, so you're super smart? Is that what you're telling me?' It's the first drop of real emotion I've heard from him today. 'What's it about?' His next words are tight, like it's an effort to find them and speak them aloud.

If he'd prefer silence, I wish he'd just say so. I could do with the extra time to finish the chapter I'm writing.

'It's Automotive Engineering. My thesis is on aerodynamics.' I'm not shy about my achievements – it doesn't pay to be in this industry. It's cutthroat and they only employ people who will help their team win.

I've earned my promotion to race engineer, working my way up from the bottom. With my undergraduate degree and a master's under my belt already – and almost a decade of experience, the PhD will be the icing on the cake.

'Get you. Very fancy. But good for you. Honestly. I only just about finished school, so I can't imagine doing all that studying.'

'I think you're doing pretty good for yourself, superstar.' He makes more in a year than I will earn in a lifetime, so he's doing perfectly fine without an education. I've managed to save a little bit, though, because I'm mostly on the road and my living expenses get covered. One day I'll put down roots somewhere. Maybe. If I meet someone who would want to do that with me.

'Caleb? You got a minute?' I hear the team manager calling me over. It looks like he's having a meeting with some of the other higher-ups, so I unbuckle my seatbelt and slot the laptop into the side of the seat.

'You want anything from the bar while I'm up?' I say to Johannes.

'Nah, all good, man.' He waves me off and tucks his long legs back up under his body. It's a sad sight to watch him sink back into himself. I've never seen someone look so lost.

It can't just be the bad performances. He's missed the podium a few times in the last couple of years – he's even had a couple of DNFs after crashes and car failures – but normally he rallies so well and comes back fighting even harder.

I join the bosses and make some contributions to their discussion. When they move on to a new topic, I excuse myself and take a piss in the fanciest plane bathroom I've ever seen. It still gets me, even after all this time, that I get to do my business in luxury. It's bigger than the one bathroom my entire family shared growing up.

It even has a shower. What plane has a damn shower? And why? I guess it makes more sense for long-haul flights, but, like, still. It seems really over the top.

When I get back to my seat, I'm quickly stopped in my tracks by the saddest sight I've ever seen.

Thick, fast tears are sliding down Johannes's cheeks. Headphones on, hood up, eyes closed, he probably doesn't realise I've returned. I don't know what to do. I don't know how I'm meant to handle this. Why doesn't the team therapist fly with us? I look around, but no one else seems to have noticed.

It definitely can't be the race result – no way in the world.

We might not be close friends, but the Johannes I'm beginning to get to know doesn't cry over a bad result or two. They happen, he knows that. He spent a whole season at another team in a poorly performing car, barely scraping points every week, and he never gave up. He worked harder and got better and he started winning.

No, I know those tears. They are heartbreak tears. Break-up tears. I haven't shed them since I was twenty-two years old and I refuse to ever let them ruin me again. No man is worth that much heartbreak.

The tears don't stop as he stuffs his face into his pillow. I will say he's mastered the art of crying quietly.

What should I do? I want to give him the biggest of hugs, but I can't imagine that would be well received and I'm sure he wouldn't want me to draw attention to him after all his efforts to keep his pain private.

I scan the plane, hoping that there's a spare seat so I can give him some space, but without forcing my way into the senior-management meeting – I would rather die – there is only my original place opposite him.

Well, here goes…

'Hey, sorry, um, sorry… I don't want to interrupt your … invade your privacy but there's just nowhere else to sit.' That wasn't too bad, I think, so I carry on. 'Are you okay? Is there anything I can do?' I reach into the mini fridge by our seats and hand him a bottle of water. Crying on a plane has to make you dehydrated.

He wipes furiously at his face with his sleeve, but even without the tears his bloodshot eyes paint a pretty clear picture. He takes the bottle and chugs down several swallows.

'Ignore me. I'm just … having a bad time.' A fresh tear

starts to fall and the second he feels it, he swipes it away. 'Things are shit right now and it's hard because I can't talk about it. It's just a lot.'

'Look, even if you can't talk about whatever's going on, I'm here if that changes, or if you just need someone to sit with you. Also, never apologise for crying. It's the healthiest way to process things, trust me. You haven't seen tears until you've seen me crying at 4 a.m. over a paper that's threatening to beat me.'

A laugh gurgles in his throat and a snot bubble forms out of one nostril. It's not a pretty sight, but it might be the most human I've ever seen him. This is weirdly the most connected I've ever felt to Johannes since becoming his race engineer – and I keep him alive on the track for a living!

I hand him one of the fancy private-jet napkins from on top of the mini fridge so he can blow his nose. He takes it and once he's cleared himself up, it hits me that I just watched Johannes Müller cry.

I don't know why I feel shaken at having seen him look so broken. He's usually so happy, posing up a storm, flashing his good looks, his dazzling smile. When he wins, he celebrates like no driver I've ever seen before. It could not be more different from the crumpled shell of a man in front of me.

He takes a big breath and starts to sit up straighter.

'I'm sorry,' he says quietly, eyes flicking around the rest of the jet. I hope for the sake of his pride that no one's noticed.

'You never have to apologise to me, Johannes. We're all human, we all go through bad times, and if you needed a big cry then that's what you needed. End of. If you ever want to talk about what's going on, I promise I'm a great listener.'

I offer him a smile and he smiles back tightly, before pressing the button on the side of the chair to raise the leg rest.

'I'm going to try and nap for a bit,' he says. 'I have an interview right after we land and I'd prefer not to look a mess on camera.'

I almost go to tell him that I don't think he could ever look a mess. Even in his current state, he still looks like absolute perfection. He'll always be one of the most stunning men I've ever seen.

Except I don't, because that would be inappropriate for our professional relationship.

'Good idea. I'll type quietly,' I reply, gesturing back to the laptop I discarded earlier.

He nods appreciatively, before stretching out and wrapping himself in a blanket. I don't know that he'd be happy to hear how adorable he looks, his six-foot frame encased in a snuggly blanket, his face tucked into a plush pillow.

I have to look away before I do or say something stupid. I force myself to focus on my screen, but an hour, and nowhere near enough words written, later, turbulence shakes the plane a little and he startles from his nap.

Groggily, he pushes himself up into a more seated position, blanket still wrapped around him as he rubs at his eyes. 'We landing?' he asks, his voice a little husky.

'Still about three-quarters of an hour to go. We were just flying through some turbulence.'

'Feel like I was asleep for hours. It was definitely needed. You get much done?' He gestures to where my laptop is half closed on the table.

'Nowhere near enough.' I don't add that I was distracted by

the beautiful, sad man opposite me because that would be creepy.

'That sucks – but you should also try and relax. These triple headers are exhausting.'

'What is this relaxing thing? Not sure I know what that is.'

'What do you do outside of work for fun?'

I gesture to my laptop.

'What about time with friends or a … partner?'

I almost laugh at him trying not to assume I'm gay, when I'm pretty sure he must know I am.

'No, no boyfriend. I don't have time for anything beyond this team and the words that live in this computer.' I'm not even remotely kidding. There hasn't been a man for a decade now, except the occasional hook-up and I don't plan to change that any time soon.

'I'm surprised. You give off … relationship, settling-down vibes.'

He's not wrong. I do want that. But now is not the time – for a lot of reasons, none of which I want to discuss right now.

I decide to deflect instead. 'You're starting to sound like my mom. She tried to set me up with her dentist this weekend,' I groan, thinking about last night's conversation.

'But you're not into him?'

'I've never met him. But I spend nine months of the year travelling and then half the winter break supporting at the factory with analysis and data. I'm hardly in one place long enough.'

'Yeah, I get that.' He clicks his neck from side to side before stretching his arms above his head.

'I'm sure you could have someone if you wanted to,' I say. 'Probably anyone you wanted.'

He stills, but it's too late. I wish someone would gag me sometimes.

The silence hangs as he stands up to stretch out his long limbs.

'Excuse me,' he says quickly, before taking off towards the jet's fancy bathroom.

Fuck. Why did I not think before I spoke? I hope I haven't damaged our working relationship by making him uncomfortable.

He's gone for ten minutes, so unless he's got a bad stomach, he's definitely avoiding coming back to this awkward conversation.

Great. Well done, Caleb.

When he finally returns, there's a forced smile on his face. I'm so used to seeing those pearly whites on show but this one hardly even pulls at his cheeks.

'Wanna play some cards?' I suggest quickly to cover my embarrassment.

He nods and I flip out the table between us, then pull a pack of cards from my backpack.

I let him win the first game of poker as a way to help repair things between us. After all, I'm trying to cheer him up. But I'm too competitive to keep losing, so I even things up in the next game.

'Fucking hell! You're a hustler, Caleb! Good thing we aren't playing for money,' he says, chucking his cards down on the table as I win for the third time in a row.

The plane has begun its descent, and when I peek out the window, the trees and houses are completely visible.

'I played a lot at university. It's how I paid for my master's.'

Perhaps not the most ethical income, but I didn't have time for a part-time job.

'Remind me never to invite you to a poker night.'

'No, please do! I'd love to crush you and all your friends,' I say with a smirk.

'You're cocky!' he says, raising one eyebrow.

'I know what I'm good at, and I'm really, really good at this.'

A heavy silence follows that's very different from the awkward silence we shared before. This one is electric.

'No way are you hustling the guys at poker night – unless you train me first.'

'Train you?' I lift a brow.

'So I don't walk away a complete loser.'

'I'm sure I could teach you a thing or two.' Our eyes lock and his are ablaze with surprise and … heat? It can't be. I must be imagining it. Fucking hell.

Shut up, Caleb. Don't ruin it now.

The sudden jolt of the plane landing breaks the tension between us. My stomach is still churning with adrenaline.

As everyone's phones pick up signal, there's a series of buzzes and beeps across the cabin. I look down at the notifications on my phone, and I'm immediately met with news headlines of Kian and Harper's wedding last night.

'You were 'just out with friends' last night, were you?' I ask, flashing the phone screen at Johannes.

He shrugs. 'Well, you know, it was a secret wedding for a reason.'

'You're clearly good at keeping secrets.'

His face falls and I wish I could stuff the words back into my mouth.

'For Harper, always.'

This man knows loyalty, even when it's with his biggest competitor. It's admirable – one of his best qualities. The more I get to know him, the more good qualities I see.

As soon as we hit the tarmac, Nils and Johannes are whisked away in a car to their photoshoot.

As I watch him go, I kick myself for spoiling things with my stupid comment.

Chapter Five

Johannes

When I wake up and open my eyes, for a second my mind is free of everything that went down in the UK and I can breathe. Then I sit up, and it hits me.

Tenth place.

The wedding.

The break-up.

Three monumental things in the space of twenty-four hours come at me full throttle. I feel winded.

I can find neither the energy nor the will to get out of bed. It's Wednesday. I have two days till I'm due back at the track. These should be rest days, but I'm so booked up with appearances and events that rest is impossible. I can't remember the last time I wasted my days off in bed, but right now I can't imagine doing anything else.

I never cancel. I never bow out of commitments. But a moment later, I'm sending a text to my agent to get me out of anything I have today. When he asks why, I say I'm sick. Heartbreak is a form of sickness, right?

He obliges without protest – presumably because I'm normally so conscientious – and my calendar is wiped clean for the day. I want nothing more than to turn my phone off, lock my bedroom door, and be left in peace for a little while, but I know that going dark on my friends will only bring them to my door, and I don't want that right now.

So, I reply to some texts, let people know I'm sick, then turn on the shower in my en suite. The water is scalding hot on my shaved head, but I let the water splash over me until the steam is thick and my skin feels seared. I head out into the lounge, sweating from the hot shower and clutching my water bottle like it's a lifeline, and I force out a bit of a cough.

'You look like shit. Don't come near me,' Nils warns from the couch, pulling a cushion up over his mouth and nose like a mask.

'You're all good,' I croak out, pushing my bottle up against the water filter on the fridge. 'Just filling my water bottle up and then I'm going back to bed.'

I cough a final time at the fridge for good measure, then scurry back to my room and lock the door. Mission accomplished.

Once I crash back down on my bed, reality truly hits. I hear the front door go and assume it's Nils leaving for the gym. I am alone again. But like, really alone. Solo. Single. Alone. For the first time in almost three years. It hurts more than I thought it would, considering how strained my relationship with Jackson has actually been.

What do I do now? How do people start again after so long?

After being so in love? Except I don't feel in love right now. I don't feel desperate to go and beg for him back. The relief I felt when I fell asleep after it was all over is still there, but now it stings.

Stings like an absolute bitch that he had the power to do this. That he strung me along for so long.

My blood bubbles angrily that I allowed that. I could have broken up with him. I could have listened every time he told me that him taking over Hendersohm was inevitable and he could not be in a relationship with the driver of a rival team. When he started dropping breadcrumbs, I shouldn't have acted like that was all I deserved. I should have been stronger and walked away first.

When was the last time we were actually properly in that relationship?

Our last full day together was a year ago. A YEAR. A whole fucking year. I only remember because I insisted he take me back to his hometown. It was all very hush-hush, but I just wanted to see where my boyfriend of two years grew up – we were already in the UK for Silverstone, so it wasn't that far to go.

At the time, I convinced myself that we had a great day, that it was an important milestone in our relationship, but I don't actually have any good memories from that day. I remember the sunglasses and caps and the driver partition screens. I remember not being able to go to the village pub together because people would recognise him. I remember holding my breath as he snuck me up the stairs at his dad and step-mum's house – and then having to hold it again the next morning as we tiptoed out, because of course, no one could know that I had stayed the night. I remember telling myself that the sick feeling in my stomach was adrenaline, anticipation, adoration…

Have we even spent a full night together since then? When was the last time we even had sex? Proper sex, not a quick hand job or blow job in a stolen moment.

Looking back at your relationship, even when it's over, should not be this gut-wrenchingly depressing. I actually feel less alone right now than I did for the last year because I'm not longing anymore. I'm not waiting for him. Pining. Yearning. It's over.

And all I'm left to feel is embarrassed that I put up with it for so long.

I sleep until grit forms in the corners of both my eyes. I wake to a light tap on my bedroom door, and a bowl of soup accompanied by a plate of toasted bread on a tray left just outside. Nils shoots me a thumbs-up from the other end of the villa. He's dressed in dark, baggy jeans and a stupid vest that's a little too cropped, indicating he's heading out. I realise it's already dark and I've slept all day.

Now, I know Nils didn't make this soup – thankfully we have a nutritionist and chef who takes care of us in our European villas – but it's the thought that counts. He went to the trouble of asking for this dish to be made for me, because I'm *sick*. I wave pathetically at him as he leaves the villa for whatever he has planned this evening.

I open the sliding doors that lead from my room out onto our patio and while it's not exactly warm out there right now, I could do with the fresh air. So I set the tray down on the bistro-style table for two and collapse into one of the chairs, pulling the strings of my RBF hoodie in close around my head.

The place we're staying is fairly removed from Budapest,

where I imagine Nils is heading tonight. There's green land as far as the eye can see. It's peaceful and so needed.

All I want is for my brain to switch off in the dark silence and be quiet. I want a goddamn break from all the anger and fury I'm currently feeling both towards Jackson and his stupid team and well ... myself. For letting this happen and having no one to blame but me.

I haven't won a race since Bahrain, eight races ago. I haven't been on the podium in three. I was almost out of the points last weekend. And for what?

For what? I almost want to scream it into the darkness. I've gained nothing except the deepest pit of sadness and anger in my stomach and a side dish of low self-esteem.

If I can't keep my head, I don't deserve to win. But did I deserve this? Did I really deserve this? So what if I was on my knees sniffing for scraps being tossed at me like I was a dog in the street. Did I deserve it then? No, and yet...

In the end, he chose his team, his job, his new life. And the fucked-up thing is that he told me right from the start that's what he would do.

That's what hurts the most. *I'm* the one who convinced myself that he would love me enough to choose me anyway. I took his casual crumbs when I should have got up off my knees – literally – and walked away at anything less than a three-course meal on fucking gold-plated dishes. And that's on me.

Thankfully, the soup scalds my tongue, momentarily refocusing all of the pain in my body. At least it's better than the heartbreak.

I sit for an hour, maybe two – I'm not sure without my

phone out here – polish off the whole bowl of soup and the bread and then collapse back into bed.

I grab my phone from the nightstand and switch it on.

There's a whole barrage of texts. From Harper, checking in multiple times. From Elijah, too. From my agent confirming he's cancelled all of today, but that I have no choice about my commitments tomorrow as it's media day.

There's even one from Caleb.

> Hey, heard from Nils that you aren't well. I told him about my mom's soup recipe. She used to make it when we were sick as kids. Said he'd give it to your guys' chef! Feel better.

That's unexpected, I think.

But then, he wasn't what I expected either. After winter break, Gary announced that due to health problems he was retiring to be with his family. I was shocked to then be paired with someone almost half his age. Someone that looked like a ginger Clark Kent. Somone seemingly so smart and so in tune with my car.

And now this. I cringe when I think about him seeing me cry on the plane. He clearly has a big heart.

I reply to Harper and Elijah that I'm okay but not coming out tonight, and they respond with a picture of them in a bar, Nils nestled between them like their child. I'm grateful they're looking after him when it should be my job.

I think about what to reply to Caleb. A simple thank-you would probably suffice. I could let him know how good the soup was, but somehow that doesn't feel like enough.

I decide to take another shower while I think about it some more. I shuck my sweat shorts and hoodie and try to let the hot water carry my heartache away as it curls around the drain. I put on a fresh T-shirt and shorts and climb back into bed.

The sheets are cold after leaving the patio door open for too long and I sink back into them, letting the duvet envelop me as I settle down.

> Thank you. The soup was really good, very needed.

I quickly hit send before following up with—

> And, about yesterday, I'm sorry.

I'm just about to drop my phone back on the charger on my nightstand when it buzzes. I expect it to be Harper with further night-out updates but it's Caleb, with the fastest response known to mankind.

> Absolutely nothing to be sorry for. Bad days happen and it's okay to cry. Better out than in. Look after yourself and I'll see you tomorrow.

Tomorrow. I find I'm looking forward to it, which is unexpected after my truly shitty last few days.

I fall back to sleep and am woken by my alarm. It feels far too early and I'm annoyed that a day is all I get to grieve my relationship before I'm expected to be back on top form.

If yesterday was about allowing myself to feel absolutely everything, today I have to numb myself completely in order to get through a long day in front of the cameras. It's a day of stupid challenges, soundbites, and having to laugh constantly to produce great content with Nils for the social-media team and various other media outlets and interviewers.

It's exhausting. I'm mentally, physically and emotionally drained as we get to what they tell me for the *third* time is going to be the last clip of the day.

Except I'm done. I'm so done.

Normally I love these days. They're so much fun and when Nils and I first became teammates it really helped us develop a much closer relationship, but today it's just too much. I've been running on fumes for too long and now there's nothing left in the tank.

'I need a break!' I practically shout, as Krissie, one of the RBF social-media team, explains what she needs from us in this video. My chair skids across the vinyl flooring and I accidentally nudge the table as I get up, spilling both glasses of water. My feet carry me across the room without being directed – at least that's the way it seems – as I desperately search for a dark corner to hide in while I try to get my shit together.

But I don't get a moment of peace because Nils follows me.

'Look, I don't want to be all up in your business, but what the fuck's going on, man? First Austria and now this.' He gestures from the table, where several people are cleaning up the mess I made, to where I'm sitting on the cold, hard floor trying to compose myself. 'Talk to me.'

'I can't,' I say through gritted teeth. There's nothing, because what can I say? My secret boyfriend that you didn't know about for the last almost three years broke up with me and now my brain is so scrambled I can't get my head in the game?

That won't lead to more questions.

'Is it ... that guy?' he asks and I forget how closely we live on top of each other and how annoyingly observant he is.

'There is no guy,' I grunt, and now it actually is true. Jackson isn't anything to me anymore.

'Wow, you're such a bad liar.'

He crouches down in front of me, almost as if he's trying to get a better look at my sadness and I can't even bring myself to tell him to fuck off. This isn't Nils's fault.

'I'm still sick. I need to go back to bed,' I say.

'If you say so,' he says, but we both know he doesn't believe me.

'Let's get this last one done and then you're free to go back to the villa and be boring there. Can you do one more?'

I want to scream and cry and tell him no, but I'm supposed to be setting a good example for him.

'Yeah, I can do that. Give me a minute?' I say hopefully, and he leaves me to it.

If I'd been able to tell anyone about Jackson in the first place, I wouldn't have to grieve the loss of my relationship alone. I'd have support and people would understand and give me space when I ask for it.

I count to sixty, and then I go and apologise to everyone for my outburst. I put a smile on my face and we get the final video.

On the drive back to the villa, Nils tries to convince me to go out to dinner with some of the team, but I can't face it – the only thing I want is my head in a pillow. So when we get back, I head straight to bed and fall asleep to the sound of him getting ready for the evening.

I wake before my alarm, and even though I could sleep for an hour or two more, I can't ignore the fact that I haven't worked out since Silverstone. Time to get off my arse and go for a run.

Before it turns six, I'm forcing my body into a vest and a pair of sweat shorts and lacing my feet into my favourite pair of running trainers whilst I try to convince myself that I'm going to enjoy this run and I will feel better afterwards. I want to rot in bed until Jackson is nothing but a distant memory, but the experts are right about the power of exercise to develop a healthy mindset.

I set a timer for an hour then I run and run and run until my legs ache and the timer goes off. It's freeing to get lost on unfamiliar trails and streets, and for the first time in days, my brain doesn't feel like someone's trying to squeeze the life out of it. While my heart rate comes down and my breathing returns to normal, I stretch out my hamstrings and calves against a wall. I notice there's a coffee shop and decide it's a reward from the universe for getting my lazy, pathetic arse out of bed.

I straighten up and crash directly into someone. I grab his arm and shoulder to stop him crashing into the gravel, exclaiming 'Shit! Sorry!'

Once he's stable, I let go of him, and when he turns around those green eyes are instantly on me.

'Caleb! Fuck! Sorry! I wasn't looking where I was going.'

'All good, man! You okay?' he asks as he catches his breath.

'Yeah. Just got a run in and I was about to get a coffee.' I point stupidly to the coffee shop. What's wrong with me?

But his face lights up and I'm drawn immediately back to those eyes. Have they always been that green? Are eyes supposed to change colour with excitement? Because I swear there's a shimmer of tropical sea when he gestures to the door, as though to suggest we head in together.

I follow him in, still slightly dazed by the collision outside.

First to Finish

I don't remember the last time I got coffee with someone or did anything with anyone who wasn't Nils, Elijah or Harper. I barely know Caleb – not the way I knew Gary – and now is as good a time as any to start.

'I have to warn you, I'm a bit particular about my coffee. I like things a certain way, but also, I'm a sucker for getting something sweet and stupid at the same time. Don't judge me.'

He holds his hands up. 'Judgement-free zone,' he replies as we step up to the counter.

'Do you have a menu in English?' I ask the barista, because it's vast and I can't take it all in. 'And do you roast your beans instore?'

'Yes. Every day,' she says. I'm glad she has good English as I don't have word of Hungarian.

'Which would you recommend? I prefer a darker, richer roast,' I say, and she reels off a couple of suggestions. 'And what milk alternatives do you have?'

'Oat, soy, almond, coconut.'

I order what I want and then, with a quick glance at Caleb, I say, 'With a shot of salted caramel, too.' My eyes wander over the cake stand, I could easily crush several of the dark-chocolate brownies they have, but I can't cheat on my dietician's pre-race meal plan in front of my race engineer, so I quickly avert my eyes. 'And whatever my friend wants.'

'You don't have to do that,' Caleb tries to protest.

'I almost knocked you over. It's the least I can do,' I reply, waving him off.

'Okay, thanks.' He orders a tea to go and a pain au chocolat, and I'm instantly envious when he takes a bite of the pastry.

'Which way are you going?' I ask, when we step out onto the street with our beverages.

'That way.' He gestures right. 'I have a meeting to get to, so I'm going to walk to that. You heading back to the villa?'

I nod. I'm disappointed we aren't going to walk back together. I mean, he's a good distraction from my negative thoughts. That's all I mean.

'Well, maybe I'll see you around?' I say.

'You'll see me at work later.' He laughs. 'Sorry, I need to get a move on. Don't wanna be late or Nathan will have my head.'

I consider asking if he wants to get lunch or go for coffee later – just so we can plan my comeback – but it's too late. He's already walking away before I can even say a proper goodbye.

Chapter Six

Caleb

Johannes arrives to the first free practice of the Hungarian weekend looking so vacant I'm worried he's not actually there. It's like his body arrived at the track, but his soul's still back wherever he left it.

He smiles – tightly – at the mechanics who stop him to chat, but he's gunning for his little room in the garage, I can see it. A place just for him where no one will disturb him until it's completely necessary. I can't hear him, but I can tell by his hand gestures alone that he's making his excuses to end the conversation, and ten seconds later he's closing the door to his room behind him.

I can't say it gives me any kind of hope for the weekend. I know he's been sick and if he fucks it this weekend, the team will use that as an excuse, but he was crying his heart out just three days ago. That wasn't because he was ill. That was a personal kind of pain. I might not know what's going on with him, but even I could see that. I found myself in the same position ten years ago, except it was on my mom's tatty couch that I curled up crying snotty tears, not the comfy seat of a private jet.

I've scoured the internet since to see if it was maybe a break-up, but he's never been reported to have been in a serious relationship. A whole bunch of hook-ups and a casual fuck-buddy relationship with his best friend many years ago, but nothing more. Maybe it's a relationship he never disclosed? A secret relationship? *Secret* is probably the wrong word; he's entitled to a *private* life after all. But it's my job to do whatever it takes to get him back on top of the podium.

And I have a feeling that this weekend, it may take a lot.

I've been analysing all of his film from this track, calculating every statistic from every practice, qualifier and race he's done in Hungary, and I've come across something I'm desperate to show him to remind him of the real Johannes.

So, the first time he emerges from his room, I pounce on him. 'Hey.'

He jumps a little, eyes wide but not bloodshot like they were on the plane.

'Sorry, didn't mean to startle you. I just, uh, have something I want to show you. Do you have a minute?'

For a second he doesn't move. I can tell he doesn't want to listen to me, but more of the same isn't what he needs right now. I open my eyes wide and smile, adding, 'Please?' in my gentlest tone. As I said, I'll do anything.

'Okay,' he says, gesturing. 'Lead the way.'

It's only a short walk to where my laptop is set up, a number on a PowerPoint page on my screen waiting for him.

'Do you know what this is?' I ask, my mouse highlighting the numbers – **1:16.623**.

He shrugs with what feels like apathy.

'The record for the fastest lap on this track.' I pause for dramatic effect. 'You know who set it?' The right corner of Johannes's lip tilts upwards a fraction. 'Of course you do. It was you. Last year when you beat Harper by seven seconds. Seven!'

I've watched that race so many times in the last twenty-four hours. I know exactly which lap won it for him. The image of him celebrating on top of the car is burned into my brain. And then there's the podium. He had a completely blissed-out look on his face as he took it all in. It wasn't even his first win, but it was the first time his name went into the racing history books. It clearly meant a lot to him.

He stares at the numbers for a long few minutes. I keep waiting for him to ask why I'm showing him this, but he doesn't. Watching his face is like seeing a whole movie scroll across his features. Emotions pull at his features as he contemplates the numbers. He glares at them like they might come to life and kick him in the balls. Then he smiles and closes his eyes and sniffs suspiciously. I hope I haven't done the wrong thing and upset him. I hope it's pride, not sadness, that's currently choking him up.

'Johannes,' I whisper softly, the paddock starting to fill up around us. 'You did that. *You*.' I know he needs to go and warm up, stretch, get into his suit and prepare himself to head out onto the track for the practice hour.

'Thank you,' he replies, sucking in a breath and releasing it slowly. 'Thank you,' he repeats, and then disappears back into the garage.

Well, that went…

Well?

I don't think he spoke more than ten words to me, but I thought I was going to have to fight him more. I thought he might shrug it off. I'm not so naïve that I believe I've 'fixed' him. Nothing that causes a person the pain and anguish he's obviously experiencing can be fixed so quickly or so easily. But maybe it's a start? A baby step?

I don't know.

Then we let him loose for the first free practice. Unfortunately, Ogum goes into the side of Johannes in minute three of track time and Johannes spends the rest of the session in the garage trying to school his frustrated face.

Thankfully, the issue is fixed quickly and he's back on the track for the second practice. I watch for the full hour, unable to stand still, waiting, hoping…

He's courteous and gives feedback on the mic when prompted, but he's not his usual chatty, perky self. He performs better than he has in the last few weekends, but it's nowhere near his usual standard, and he takes off so quickly to his room after the second practice that it's like he's a puff of smoke.

Even in the evening debrief with the rest of the team, he contributes nothing to the discussion. It's like he doesn't trust himself to speak and it makes me sad, because normally he has really useful feedback.

They cater dinner for us in the garage, but Johannes is long gone. Nils sticks around to eat with everyone and talks excitedly about the weekend. The buzz of consistent point weekends has filled him with so much more confidence.

It's great to see, but I'm still watching the door, hoping Jo might return.

'Is Johannes okay?' I ask Nils, catching him slightly off-guard.

'Why?' he asks, like I'm a head teacher about to get his friend in trouble.

'I just ... I'm worried about him. Don't you think he's a bit...' I try to search for an appropriate, professional word, but Nils beats me to it.

'All over the place? Fucked up? Man, I wish I knew. You should try living with him. It's not a fun time in the villa right now. Lots of moping, no partying, no hook-ups, just him locked in his room.'

'Has something happened?' I ask, but Nils only shrugs and shakes his head, and unfortunately, that's not enough for me to work with. 'Look, I'm not asking you to break a confidence. I'm trying to prevent another Spielberg and Silverstone. He's not himself. He's not performing. He's not ... happy. I just want to help him. Please?'

'I don't actually know anything, man. We're friends but he doesn't tell me anything. And I don't think Harper knows either.'

It has to be bad if even Harper doesn't know.

'I'm close to shaking him, too,' Nils continues. 'He earned us both a talking-to from Nathan yesterday after he was rude to one of the social-media girls.'

'That doesn't sound like Johannes at all.'

I hope it's not worse than I've been imagining.

'If you find out what's going on, will you please let all of us know? Because he refuses to talk about it and it's beginning to piss off his friends.'

'Yeah, of course. Have a good rest of your evening. See you tomorrow.'

Thinking about Johannes keeps me awake. I toss and turn, trying not to ruminate on his issues. They aren't mine and I should not be this worried about him, but I am. I can't help it. I don't want whatever it is to eat him up inside and leave nothing but bones. I couldn't bear that.

But what more can I do without invading his privacy or crossing a line he's clearly drawn around his personal life?

The next day, I watch him complete his third practice. He finishes sixth in the standings, but he's 1.2 seconds off Harper at the top, which is a big gap for Hungary. He can't perform like that in qualifying if he wants to be anywhere near the front row.

He's whisked away to do some media before I can even check in with him.

'I need a coffee. These triple headers aren't for the weak.' Ian groans as he stretches himself out next to his pit wall.

A big cup of coffee sounds very much needed right now.

Coffee.

Coffee.

His face in that café... The way his eyes lit up as the barista described the different kinds of beans they used... The pure relief on his face as he cradled the cup at his lips...

If a coffee was all it took to put a driver on top of the podium, they'd all be doing it. But it's not about the coffee itself. It's about what the coffee represents – how it might make him feel to have someone notice him, care about him, do something nice for him.

I'm hotfooting it out of the garage before I can stop myself.

First to Finish

I don't have any free time, but my job is to make him perform better, and if this could help, then I have to try.

I summon a car and while I wait for it to arrive, I google independent coffee shops and check the reviews. I choose one that's a little further away because it has the best customer feedback. When we get there, I ask the car to wait. I have no idea what it'll cost, but it'll be worth it to get back to the track quickly.

Inside, I scan the menu, struggling to decipher what's what. Thankfully, the barista speaks English and I tell her about my friend and his coffee preferences and what I saw him order last time. She recommends something and I agree, because I know absolutely bugger all about roasts and blends and syrups and foams and whatever.

I just want this to cheer him up. At the last minute, I spot a fudgy-looking cake on a display stand and ask for a piece of that, too. He won't be able to consume it before the qualifying race today, but it can be something to look forward to afterwards. I saw how he was eying up the brownies and my pain au chocolat in the coffee shop and I may have heard him say in an interview how much of a sweet tooth he has. Hopefully this will satisfy that.

I'm in and out in less than five minutes, to the taxi driver's delight, and I make it back to the garage within forty. When I get back, Johannes and Nils are nowhere to be seen, but the garage is filling up with engineers, strategists and analysts. Nathan's also roaming about, so I need to be swift like a ninja to get in and out of Johannes's room without them asking what I'm doing. I don't know what I'd tell them if I was caught, because a sweet coffee right before qualifying is not in his race plan or dietician's schedule, but I don't care.

Keeping my head down, I weave through the garage to his room. I knock lightly in case he happens to be in and count a couple of seconds before I open the door and slip inside.

I put the takeaway cup and sweet treat on the table beside his bag.

I contemplate leaving a note, but I'm not doing this for recognition. I tell myself it's for the team, for his performance, for my job, but I know it's also because I can't bear to see Johannes hurting like this. I'm in and out of his room in the blink of an eye, but as I close the door behind me and walk away trying not to look suspicious, mentally I'm back in his room, waiting to see his face when he takes a sip.

I can't help how aware I am of where Johannes is and whether he's been back to his room yet. I linger, trying to get a glimpse of him, but I'm due in the pit and have to leave before I see him. I feel wired – like I'm the one that's had too much coffee – bouncing from foot to foot, unable to sit still. Ian gives me a look and I force myself to calm down.

Then, just as I'm beginning to lose my mind, the teams start their grid walks and I see Johannes with his arm around Nils taking a selfie on the track. They're both smiling but I'm focused only on Johannes. I see crinkles in the corners of his eyes, his mouth stretched wide, and his shoulders relaxed. In one hand is the takeaway coffee cup.

He takes his last sip and bins the empty cup as he comes off the track, and I feel myself holding my breath.

'Looks like we're in for a good time this weekend,' Ian comments from beside me. Nils has only been getting better and better this season, which is only giving Ian more confidence. 'Nils should score points, maybe even decent points if the practice today is anything to go by.'

But all I can think about is Johannes.

While we're probably too far down the rankings now for the constructor's championship this year, Nils has another year on his contract and with Nils showing so much promise, we could be real contenders next year.

'Johannes looks slightly more alive this afternoon.'

'For sure. He's just got to put the last two weekends behind him and focus on what's in front of him. He can do it. He'll show us all what he's made of, just you wait.'

I sound more confident than I feel, but I know he has it in him to pull it back. I'm just waiting for him to know it, too.

Less than an hour later, it's like magic on the track again. The garage is alive with excitement as Johannes and Nils both make it into Q3 to compete for pole position on the grid tomorrow. Nils is performing above his expected standard, upping his game again here in Hungary, but Johannes is on fire.

Not literally, thank God.

He's focused and driven, making fearless choices and finding the smallest opportunities to exploit. He's working the car to its limits and feeding back to us any issues he's picking up on along the way, which makes our life easier to get the car ready for tomorrow. He's back in tune with the vehicle, and it's so beautiful to watch him come back to life out there.

'Fastest lap out there right now,' I tell him, with seven minutes to go of this final round of qualifying. Of course, so much can change in that time and I'm watching on the second screen the way Harper completes a purple first sector, but the boost is good for Johannes after his last two races. He needs to hear he's doing well.

Two minutes later, Harper's back in P1, pushing Johannes down to P2, but it's better to be P2 than to be out in Q1 or Q2. Elijah's fighting to challenge Harper and Johannes's times, but he's not even putting in personal bests right now, his sectors turning yellow, so I'm more than confident that Johannes will take up the second slot of the front row of the grid.

Nils is still in P6 when the timer runs out and everyone finishes the lap they are currently doing. I watch intently for any change, but thankfully, there is none.

'You'll start front row tomorrow, Johannes. P-Two, man!'

He whoops down the mic and the whole garage cheers, clearly happy to see their main man back in action.

I can finally take a deep breath, and it feels so, so good.

Chapter Seven

Johannes

I'm actually excited when Nils and I enter the paddock on race day. My body feels looser than it has in weeks and my mood is much better, too. The atmosphere is frenetic as teams gear up for the race this afternoon, and for the first time in almost a month, I feel like it could be my day.

There's no lying about how rough this week has been, but this sport waits for no one. Not even a heartbroken idiot like me. And yeah, maybe I've had to give myself one hell of a pep talk, but I'm ready.

I'm not even tempted to hide myself away until I'm actually needed. I might stick around, sign some fan stuff, actually interact with my fellow drivers. The pain that was drowning me, I'm determined not to let it win. Instead, I'm going to use the anger I'm beginning to feel instead to push myself to be a better driver. Prove to him that it's his loss, not mine.

'You're happier this morning.' Nils throws it out there like it's the most casual thing ever, especially with cameras flashing around us capturing our race-day-outfit pictures. 'Did you have a good run this morning?'

Nils was still fast asleep when I crept out of the villa at 6 a.m. It wasn't even hard to wake up this morning, especially with the chance that if I got lucky, I might bump into Caleb again. Despite circling the area a couple of times, I didn't see him, but there's always tomorrow.

'Wasn't bad,' I say. 'Good to be up and about to get my head in the game.' I offer my signature smile to every cameraman and woman on the grid and in the stands.

'You're crazy. I slept for ten hours, and I still feel tired.' Just to prove his point, he punctuates the admission with a big yawn.

'You've just got no stamina, kiddo,' I tease, nudging his shoulder.

'I have plenty, I'll have you know.' He shoots me a sly grin and I fake a gag.

'I'd rather not know, to be honest.'

'Fuck you! You're just jealous, old man, because I'm getting lots and you're being mopey. I'm going to find Ian. Catch ya later.' He takes off in a jog.

'I'm sure he's really looking forward to having his ear talked off all day,' I yell after him and he just shoots me the middle finger.

Whilst he goes to annoy the man who looks after him on the track, I'm scouting the paddock for my best friend. I need the pre-race chat we've been having since we were gangly teens in go-karts.

I spot him, but then my stomach lurches. I'm frozen in place.

Harper claps his hand on Jackson's shoulder as they both laugh about something I'm too far away to hear. Why can't this man just disappear back to his damn computer screen, his stupid podcast, and his even stupider blog?

I feel my breakfast loosen in my stomach.

As long as I continue to race, I will never get away from him.

Bile rises in my throat, a bitter taste stinging the back of my mouth and I clasp a hand over my mouth so I don't spill it all over the floor outside the Hendersohm garage.

Fucking nepo babies and their fucking privileges. And on the first day I'm finally starting to feel like I don't want the duvet to consume me forever, too.

I tear my eyes away from my best friend and ex getting on like an absolute house on fire. I hate it. I hate that everyone likes him so much. But most of all, I hate that he's fine while I'm a mess.

I abandon my pre-race ritual with Harper and hurry back to my own garage to take some deep breaths. Or maybe scream into a cushion in the privacy of room.

I cannot allow him to get to me like this. I made a promise to myself after the caffeine gods shone on me yesterday that I'd stop letting him put me in such a foul mood. I definitely don't need it on a race morning.

I keep my head down as I pass through the garage, grateful that for once no one seems to want a piece of me. Or maybe it's just the scowl on my face scaring them off. Either way, I'll take it right now.

Ten minutes. That's what I'll give myself. Ten minutes to

wipe his existence from my mind and then I'll be back to focused Johannes, ready to go out there and win. Ready to move on from this disaster. Just ten minutes.

I push open the door to my room, slowly forcing out a controlled breath. But as I release and breathe in again, the smell of coffee infiltrates my nostrils.

Sitting on the table is another steaming takeaway cup of coffee, and it smells absolutely incredible.

I peel the lid off and take a sip. The flavour is rich, the roast of the bean very fresh, but in the background there's a sweet, creamy flavour like a mocha. It's perfection in a cup and God I need this right now.

I realise way too slowly that I'm grinning like a total idiot at a polystyrene cup. At least I'm alone in my room, even if the door is still open and anyone could see in if they walked past right now. I look back at the table and just like yesterday there's a paper bag there, too. I peer inside and it's the gooiest chocolate brownie I've ever seen. I can't eat it right now, obviously, but it gives me something to look forward to post-race.

The caffeine fills my veins giving me a much-needed boost, but it's the taste that lingers in my mouth and has me forgetting all about the rage that bought me in here. I think about the track, the car, the twists and turns, where the opportunities might lie, the weather report, the feeling of qualifying in P2. I think about the fact that I set the record for this track and I still hold it. I sip and think, sip and think.

When I'm finished, I stride confidently out to the pit wall where set-up is taking place. Thankfully, Nathan isn't around and Ian and Nils are focused on their own strategy, but it wouldn't matter because I'm focused. I'm ready.

I see Caleb, headset already on and eyes fixated on his screen, scribbling down notes. He cares so much about my drive, and about this team. I don't know why I never noticed it before, but now it feels like I won't be alone out there. It's not just the coffee that feels like warmth inside my body.

I allow myself to be guided away by the team to warm up, suit up, and stand for the national anthem.

Rolling my shoulders back as I finally climb into the car, I let out a big breath and the tunnel vision kicks in. I have to crush this today. I need to make the Hungarian track my bitch and prove to everyone that I'm neither down nor out. That I'm still here and I'm still the best that's ever been seen here.

Everyone is fighting today, especially the Hendersohm guys, but I'm relentless as the three of us battle on the narrow roads. I'm grateful for the start I got from P2, because I was able to put myself out front from the very beginning. And that's how it stays for almost seventy laps. An utter domination of the Hungaroring.

I'm so hungry for this win that even Harper almost causing contact doesn't distract me, and I take the opportunity to floor it between turns eleven and twelve as I try to put as much distance between us as possible. It's beautiful going into clean air after lapping the stragglers at the very back, not a car in sight as I let it sink in that I'm going to win, that this could be a turning point if I just let myself fucking embrace that my life is going to be better from now on because I'm free of the dead weight arsehole who's been dragging me down.

That sometimes shitty things do happen so that better things will come.

One door closing and another opening, and all that shit.

In this case, I'm hoping the door that's cracked open leads to potentially being world champion for the very first time.

'Final lap,' Caleb confirms as I cross the line for the penultimate time, heading into the straight for one last beautiful lap.

'Time between me and Harper, please?' I ask, but I can hear him behind me – it can't be as much as I initially thought.

'Point two. Keep pushing. You've got this.' I believe him, but less than a second later Harper's right behind me, practically fucking rear-ending me in a last-ditch attempt to win. He pulls around me and flies out of my defensive reach.

'Fuck!' I say. Of course he couldn't just let me have this. He never would. And I respect him for that, because I would do the same. But still…

I hate having to trail him to the chequered flag because I led for an hour and a half, but P2 is P2 and a hell of a lot better than P10.

When I pull up behind the second-place stop sign, I know I'm back. It's joy but it's also relief. I'm back. I'm fucking back. Thank God.

I finally get released from media and time in the cool-down room and on the podium, desperate to be out of my sweaty race suit and to celebrate a good result on the track. Checking my phone, Harper's already messaged in the group chat that we're going out this evening and to bring *everyone*. I'm not sure who he means by everyone, but I can guarantee he means at least Nils, so I fire off a text asking if he fancies it tonight.

He replies immediately with a big, screaming YES as I walk towards our pit wall.

Caleb's still at the screens, chatting away with Ian and gesturing animatedly to something on the screen, whilst Ian takes notes. It's kind of cute how excited Caleb seems about whatever it is, and I find myself lingering a few metres away to observe. He's still working and I don't want to interrupt him, but I owe him a proper thank-you for getting me through the last month or so.

'Hey, superstar!' Caleb calls over Ian's shoulder, and I realise I must have zoned out while watching him, because I didn't even notice they were packing up.

'Hey, Caleb, Ian.' I offer Nils's race engineer a nod, which he returns with a tight smile before tucking his notebook and laptop under his arm and heading back into the garage. 'Did I say something to offend him?'

'Ian? Nah, think he's got a bit of a headache. Nils was chattier than normal on the radio today. Boy, he's got a comment for literally everything, good or bad.' He shakes his head, but he's grinning at the same time. I can imagine watching Nils and Ian work together is a real treat.

Not that he needs to tell me about how much Nils can talk, I have to live with him when we're in Europe. 'He's absolutely buzzing about coming sixth today, so I can't blame him. He's doing so well the second half of this season,' I say.

'Trust me, Ian is happy with his performance, too. In his own way.' We both laugh, but I'm completely distracted by the way the corners of his eyes scrunch up as he laughs, even if it is a godawful sound that he produces – like a cross between a wheeze and a cackle. How have I never noticed that before? 'You okay? I thought you'd be off celebrating already,' he asks.

'I had a press line a mile long to deal with first. Apparently, I made a comeback today.' I can't help but smirk as I say it.

'You did, indeed. Focus was back on point, and you made well-timed decisions like the Johannes we all know and love.

It could have been either of you for the win. Harper was sneaky today, but next time it'll be you.' I've heard it from almost every journalist out there, but it's much sweeter hearing it from him because I know it's genuine.

'Thanks, man, and, fuck, I'm sorry for being such an arsehole recently. I'm not going to give you a sob story, but I shouldn't have been rude or disrespectful to you. I hope you know that's not the kind of guy I am.' My parents, my mom especially, would have been so disappointed in the way I'd spoken to him. 'And thanks for keeping me going. I mean it. It's been a shitshow, but you've listened and helped and kept me motivated when I didn't want to be motivated. I appreciate that more than you know.'

I'm word-vomiting, but I want to make sure he understands. So much of the time I don't think we value the guys outside of the car who make every single race weekend possible.

'You're welcome. I'm just glad you've been able to pull it back—'

'We. *We've* been able to pull it back. We're a team, Caleb.'

'Sure, yeah, but my point still stands. You work hard, Johannes. You deserve this, and we'll prove it at the end of the season when you win the championship.'

My phone pings, and I see that it's Harper asking for an update about whether I'm coming tonight and I realise I made sure Nils was in, but didn't actually give Harper an answer.

'Sorry, I have one very demanding best friend. He gets needy if I don't respond within ten minutes,' I tell Caleb, and quickly fire a text back letting Harper know I'm in. His response is rapid, asking how many people I'm bringing as they're booking a table for dinner first.

'Yeah, I can't imagine patience is one of Harper's finest skills, either on or off the track,' Caleb says.

He's tucking his things into a satchel as I contemplate what I want my next move to be. No, not *move*. I'm not making any kind of move on him.

'Do you want to get dinner?'

'Dinner? With you?'

Yep, I see exactly how that might sound, because his face registers a confusing array of emotions. This was not the way to go about it.

'Um, Harper's asked me to go for dinner with him and Elijah and I'm guessing some of the other guys from the Hendersohm team – they're pretty tight. Nils is coming, and I wondered if maybe you'd like to join us. Celebrate the weekend. Might be some drinks after if you fancy seeing the reformed and happily married version of messy Harper.' He'll still want to drink everyone under the table, but he'll be sober enough to have FaceTime sex with Kian. His words, not mine.

Caleb's eyebrows tug as he rearranges something in his bag. Shit. Maybe I should have organised dinner with just me, Nils, and Ian instead of throwing him in at the deep end. We don't have to be besties, but it would be nice to properly get to know the guy I trust with my life. Plus, from everything I've seen over the last couple of weeks, I think he'd fit in well with our weird little mish-mash group of racing people we're collecting. The group includes both of Hendersohm's race engineers, Cole and Ash, so he could at least talk shop all night with them if he truly desires.

The silence lingers for a second too long, and now I'm trying not to regret asking him.

'I mean, obviously you definitely don't have to. I just

thought it would be nice. I dunno, we live in this crazy bubble for nine months and it's hard to be friends sometimes with the competition, but we make it work and I feel like you might enjoy getting away from the garage to celebrate our win, you know?'

Stop talking, Johannes, you fucking prick.

'Yeah, um, I would, you're right. I'm in. Text me where you guys are heading. I need to finish a few things up here and head back to my room to get changed, but I can probably be ready for seven?'

'Perfect. I need to round up Nils. I think he's taking selfies with every single fan in the stands! See you later.'

I throw him a wave, glad the awkward moment is over. I'm pleased he's coming out tonight, but I wish I could read him better. I guess that's the point of getting to know him.

Two hours later, I'm throwing yet another outfit on the floor, unable to decide what to wear. Nils walks in, fully dressed and ready to leave.

'You can't go out like that! Or, well, I guess you can if you want to spend the whole evening being ogled.' Nils is the straightest person I've ever met, but even he's eying my mostly naked body.

'Oh, really. Thanks, man, I'll just get dressed, then.' I kick the suitcase I've emptied all over the floor hoping for some inspiration.

'That would be good considering we needed to leave five minutes ago.'

'Shit!'

'I could hear you having some kind of crisis in here, so I thought I'd see if I could help?'

I've had every pair of jeans and trousers on my body, but nothing looks right. My shirts are too sheer, too tight, too bright, too … not quite right. I've walked runways in some of the most uncomfortable outfits in the world, yet I can't bring myself to wear my normal clothes for this dinner with friends.

'Nothing looks right,' I grumble, knowing exactly how pathetic it sounds.

'I saw you wear those black jeans just the other night and they looked fine.'

'Yeah, I was hoping for something a bit better than *fine*, young one.' Since when is looking *fine* considered Johannes-worthy?

'What about the navy trousers with the pleat in the front? They look good on you. With a white T-shirt? This dinner isn't fancy, right?' He peers down at his baggy, mid-wash blue jeans and basic tee, and the black bomber jacket tossed over his shoulder. It's very Nils; it suits him. I wouldn't wear it, but the late-teen skater style works on him with his baby face and white-blond hair.

'I don't think so.'

'So why does it matter? Unless … are you looking to get laid tonight?'

'No,' I fire back almost immediately, which doesn't help my case at all. 'No, I'm not, but you know the cameras will be crawling tonight with all of the top three hanging out, and I finally feel like I'm in a much better headspace, so I don't need someone tearing apart my outfit.' The words feel gross on my tongue. I never normally give a fuck about what the press think of my clothes. I've always been known to dress quite androgynously and never felt pressure to change that.

Yet I am, surrounded by mountains of the clothes I would never normally let touch the floor. 'Fuck! This is such a mess. I haven't even moisturised yet.' I flop down dramatically on the bed.

'Ok, well, tidying up will have to wait. You go and moisturise and I'll pick out an outfit for you.' I glare at him, but he just shoos me into my en suite. I can't believe I'm letting Nils pick my outfit, but my brain is so overwhelmed right now, and I desperately want to hold on to my good mood.

I take a minute at the sink, forehead pressed against the cool glass. Even my skin looks ashy because I haven't taken very good care of myself recently. I don't know why I'm freaking out. I got P2 today, and this is a night out with my closest friends. Why am I so stressed?

'Get your shit together, Johannes,' I say to my reflection before opening my skincare fridge and grabbing my moisturiser and eye cream. I cleanse first, the icy cold water making me feel a little more alert, before I slather my face in luxury.

Finally, my skin has that signature glossy, brown Johannes glow that not even an outfit picked by Nils can dull.

'Thirty seconds to get dressed!' Nils calls from the doorway, tapping his Rolex.

'Who put you in charge?' I reply, before grabbing the black silky trousers he's left out for me with one of my favourite Gucci belts to accessorise. 'Not bad, young one.' His smile grows and he finally leaves me to it.

I pair it with the soft-pink crisp cotton shirt Nils has selected. I'm surprised and impressed. Leaving several buttons open, I pull on the white trainers I got from a sponsored ad I did a couple of months ago. One final glance in the mirror and damn, I look hot.

'Let's go!' I call out, grabbing my wallet and phone from the dresser. 'Come on, why aren't your shoes on? Get moving.'

'I hate you!' He reaches down to pull on his trainers, before eying me. 'I did good, huh? You look great. All the men will be dying to take you back to *theirs* tonight.' Is that a hint, I think.

'You did okay, now move your ass. I'm surprised Harper's not blowing up my phone right now.' Right on queue it buzzes in my hand and we both laugh. 'You've sorted us an Uber right?' He blanches and I take that as a no. 'So you rushed me to get ready and we can't even leave? Do I have to do everything around here?'

'Jeez, give me a break.' He's lucky I'm fond of him, but I've got a fair bit of making up to do after the way I've been acting recently so I let it go.

'Right, it's two minutes away. You got your wallet? I'm not covering you again tonight when you conveniently forget.' He flashes it from the small bag slung across his chest. 'Good, now move it!'

It's a quick car ride over and before I know it, we're pulling up at the restaurant-bar Harper's chosen for the occasion.

'Oh, is that Caleb? Did you invite him?' Nils asks as we linger by the bar, my eyes scanning for our table. They quickly fall on his ginger curls that for once don't look crushed and sweaty after being stuck under an RBF hat. Whatever product he's using is really working for him right now.

His lean body looks great in the denim jacket he's rocking, sunglasses that he definitely doesn't need tucked into the breast pocket. *Okay, Caleb. I see you.*

'Yeah, yeah, I didn't think you'd want an evening with Ian, so I didn't extend the invite. But Caleb's cool, right?' I look to him before we make our way to the table, and he glances back and forth between Caleb and me.

'Mmmhmm. *Coooool.*'

Wrapping an arm around his shoulders, I clip his ear before guiding him to our table.

'Don't worry, the party has arrived! Call off the search, the evening can begin,' I announce dramatically, then slide in next to Caleb. Nils sits opposite me, next to Elijah. Harper sits next to him, with Cole next to him and Ash opposite, beside Caleb.

At first it was just me and Harper against the world, but now it feels so good to have the table full. It's nicer than I could have imagined to have a little gang of friends. I catch Caleb's eye and smile.

Nice, indeed.

Chapter Eight

Caleb

I'm on edge, sitting at the table alone with our competition and the driver who beat Johannes to P1 in today's race. Don't get me wrong, Harper and Elijah and their two race engineers have been nothing but welcoming towards me, but I really wish Johannes wasn't late right now.

'I did tell him seven, but he's not answering his phone and Nils's seems to be switched off or on DND, so fuck knows.' Harper shrugs, before taking a swig of his beer.

'I'm sure they're fine, just stuck in traffic or something,' Elijah suggests with the same nonchalance.

The set of villas and apartments we are staying at are completely locked off to paparazzi, but the second you're out of there, they are an assault on the senses, and who knows what hassle Johannes and Nils are facing trying to get here.

But if Johannes doesn't show for some reason, and I'm left here awkwardly on my own...

I breathe a sigh of relief when the bar cheers and my eyes shoot straight to Johannes's six-foot frame, his hand on Nils's shoulder guiding him through the crowds.

The contrast between the two men is striking. Nils is baby-faced with that white-blond hair, and despite no longer being the youngest driver on the circuit he still looks like such a kid compared to Johannes. He's dressed casually, while Johannes, with his shaved head and strong features, is dressed to impress in silk trousers that hug him in all the right places, accentuating his long legs. He's left several of the buttons on his pink shirt undone, leaving what feels like miles of gleaming chocolate skin on show. This man is a sin. An absolute sin.

I'm very much afraid that my mouth is hanging open. I close it with a snap, but I'm not the only one who's noticed that Johannes is radiant tonight.

The friends all greet each other enthusiastically.

'Hey,' I finally say after Harper stops ribbing him about being late because he was doing his hair. Being in such close quarters, it's impossible to ignore how good he smells. It's sweet like vanilla, with a nutty hint – maybe pistachio? – and with top notes of femininity that make him intoxicating.

'Hey, yourself. Sorry I left you alone with these knuckleheads. Apparently, I'm incapable of getting ready in half an hour.' He chuckles before spreading his arms out across the back of the booth, relaxing into the plush seat.

'Oh, no problem,' I rush to reassure him. 'They were getting a bit restless, though. I think Harper's already put in a food order for everyone. It took him like five minutes to reel off, so I hope you're hungry.'

'Oh, don't you worry, I can eat. That's why I run so much,' he says, patting his flat stomach. I'm all too aware that under the pink shirt is a set of washboard abs. I lift my eyes back up to his face and realise he's caught me looking. I hope my pale skin isn't revealing the heat I feel flood into my cheeks.

The most obnoxiously sized plates of wings and ribs, alongside a bunch of potato sides are delivered to our table, and the way the six other people dive in reminds me of animals in the wild. Part of me almost feels like a bit of a spectator at the table. It's not that I don't fit in – I'm as much a part of the racing world as all of these guys – but I don't really know them.

Even Nils seems quite relaxed with them, and I know he wasn't really part of this group last year. I didn't know Cole or Ash were either, to be honest.

It feels like I'm back in senior school, which is kind of pathetic when I'm almost thirty-three years old. So, I grab a wing and bite into the juicy flesh. It's spicy but the ranch dressing they've provided helps take the edge off. I've definitely had better in America, but it isn't the worst attempt at it.

'Good, huh?' Nils comments from across the table, hands already sticky and hot sauce coating his lips.

'Did the kids' meal not come with wet napkins?' Johannes asks Harper. Nils sticks his tongue out at him in reply. 'Seriously, wipe your mouth, you animal. Can't take you anywhere.'

Nils doesn't. Instead he sucks the meat off a rib in protest, blue-cheese dipping sauce trickling down his chin. It's the messiest meal I've eaten in a long time, but as the bones stack up and the trays of fries go down, we all end up resembling Nils. Except Johannes.

Torturously, he sucks the sauce off his fingers between every piece of meat, dabbing a napkin at his lips to catch any sauce. I almost drop a forkful of fries the first time I see him do it. I have to force my eyes to look away from each mesmerisingly delicate suck. It must be the multiple beers I've sunk, because my mind is going places it really shouldn't. Not at a table surrounded by colleagues. Not at all. It's not a place I often let it wander. My life is full enough between work and education. I don't have room for anything else. I wish my brain would tell my body that before I embarrass myself.

I focus back on the food, joining in on conversation about a soccer game that's being shown on one of the screens. I think there's a big European competition going on right now, but it's not exactly a sport I follow. The US Men's soccer team isn't anything to write home about.

The Brits and Johannes have a whole bunch of opinions, but when I squint at the screen I don't think it's either of their teams even playing. I'm just happy to be here, to be included, even though I have no idea what's going on on the pitch. I have no idea what time it is, and I feel relaxed and loose.

When the match is over, they turn the music up and Chayce Beckham's song '23' starts playing.

'I love this song.'

I'm not sure if I said the words out loud, too, but they echo my thoughts exactly. I turn to Johannes beside me and we both laugh at the same time, shifting so our knees clack together.

'Oh, no. Now there's two of them,' Harper mutters, shaking his head at us across the booth.

'I didn't know you liked country music,' Johannes says,

and I can't stop the grin that's splitting my face. I've only had three beers, but there's a thrum of excitement racing through my veins.

'There's probably a lot you don't know about me.' I don't mean for it to sound as flirty as it comes out, but the words fizz in the very small space between us.

'I'm sure.' The energy between us is suddenly charged like I've never felt before with anyone. What I thought was going to be awkward drinks with colleagues and the enemy, now has sweat collecting at the nape of my neck. 'What got you into country music?' he asks.

'Well, I was born and raised in Tennessee. I used to spend weekends getting the train to Nashville with my dad to see live music in bars and it was always country music. What about you?'

'I actually have no idea. Neither of my parents are fans but I remember hearing Carrie Underwood for the first time and I was hooked.' He's smiling, his whole body turned into the conversation, shoulders hanging loosely once more. It's so good to see him like this after witnessing him being so broken on the plane to Hungary. 'God, Nashville though. I can't believe how many times I've been to the US and never visited.'

'I'll have to show you the sights one day, all the local hangouts.'

'I might just hold you to that.' And I want him to. I hope he does. I hadn't realised how much I wanted to see him smiling again and enjoying life.

He holds my gaze for a beat – two, three – then bites his lip and turns away.

I can't believe the way the energy suddenly seems to crackle between us. There's a churning feeling in my stomach and it's not down to the ridiculous amount of ribs and wings we just consumed. I don't remember the last time I felt like this. I've practically made myself immune to chemistry.

Johannes's knee settles casually against mine and he doesn't move it away. He's speaking to Nils and Harper across the table, not even looking at me, but I feel every inch of that touch. I know I'm not reading too much into it. I know he feels it, too.

This is not a good idea, but I don't move my leg away.

I shouldn't have come tonight – and still I don't pull my leg away.

My attention is thankfully pulled by Ash on the other side of me. I take a big gulp of beer and focus on what he's saying. I'm intrigued by how these guys are all such good friends, despite being fierce competitors on the track.

'How long have you two been at Hendersohm?' I ask as Cole leans in across the table to be involved.

'Like, six years now I think,' Ash answers. 'I was Elijah's race engineer and now I'm Harper's.'

'Dare I ask who you prefer?' The three of us chuckle before he mocks zipping his lips.

'That would be like choosing a favourite child, which is weird considering I'm only a couple of years older than Elijah. They both have their qualities – Elijah's easier to talk to in high-tension moments, but Harper offers a ton of insight. It surprises people when I tell them how smart he is about the car and race.'

He's gone from being a rookie to being on top of the racing world in such a short amount of time, and that's simply not possible unless you truly understand the drive.

'I've been with Hendersohm for longer than I care to admit,

but I can't imagine not working there. I started the year the team was formed – Kian's rookie year,' Cole replies.

I can't even imagine what it would be like to be a part of Kian's story. He's going to forever be one of the biggest legends in this sport.

'I bet you were sad when he decided to retire?' Even I remember the little clench in my chest as I watched his final press conference.

'Yeah, but it was his time. I wouldn't have wanted him to race if his heart wasn't in it anymore. Plus, who doesn't want to go out on a high?'

'Yeah, his last season was incredible. I'd say the sport isn't the same without him, but the potential of the kids coming into this level of racing right now is astounding.'

I'm thinking of drivers like Nils, who's having a career-changing season so far. It's like he's finally comfortable in the car and is just shining.

'No kidding,' Ash chimes in. 'I look at our academy team and I can't believe how well they perform. It's insane. There's so much promise. Not that I think we'll ever get Elijah out of a car. When his leg was broken and he couldn't race, it only ramped up his love for the sport.'

I can see that. The way he's been performing since that season out, it's like he's even hungrier. He's yet to win a championship, but he warms the other podium spots like no other driver.

We start discussing our reserve drivers, then the new regulations that are being whispered about, and then the fact that both Cole and Ash have lived in the US at some point in their life. We share amusing stories from being on the radios with drivers, and someone keeps bringing rounds of drinks.

I haven't even got a single round in yet – I have no idea who's paid for everything we've had so far. When I look down at my smart watch, I see it's just past midnight and I can't stifle the yawn that comes out.

'Past my bedtime,' I say to the pair. I turn to Johannes to ask him to let me out but he's not there and my path is clear. 'Going to the bar. Be back in a second.' They both nod at me but are quickly distracted by Harper and Nils.

Johannes is leaning against the bar, and I'm just about to let him know I'll get the next round when he jumps in before I can speak.

'They're talking about going clubbing,' Johannes says as I approach him. He's already got the next round – shots and six bottles of beer and a glass of water. 'I'm not gonna go as I'm getting a headache, but you should. Seems like you're getting on well with Cole and Ash.'

'Yeah, they seem like good guys, but I'm not someone who enjoys a club, if I'm honest. I'm not even sure I want that shot. I could do with getting up early tomorrow.'

If I can get a sunrise run in, I might be able to carve out three or four hours working on my PhD thesis before we have to pack up and meet with the team to fly to Belgium.

'I'm exhausted, too,' he says. 'I know my brain will be up and ready to go at like 6 a.m. I want to try and get a run in, so I'll probably be up and out before Nils is even home.'

I turn back to our table where Nils and Harper are dancing by the edge of the table.

'You, uh, fancy a run together in the morning? I normally run around that time and I don't think we're staying too far apart.' The words sound so casual coming out of my mouth, but my brain has been thrust into a vat of boiling anxiety as I overthink how he might take it.

Harper and Elijah are close enough with their race engineers to go out clubbing with them, surely we can be friendly enough to go for a run together? It's nothing crazy. Nothing serious.

'Yeah, sounds good. You wanna walk back tonight? It's not too far and then I can see which apartment you're in and knock for you in the morning.'

I'm nodding way too fast so I grab my beer bottle off the tray to give myself something to do other than nod. 'Sounds good.'

'Cool, let me know when you're ready and we can head off. I'm just going to make sure Nils has got his key.'

He takes off with the tray of drinks, leaving me leaning against the bar with my beer. I'm ready to leave now, if I'm honest. Both the bar and restaurant side of the establishment have started to empty out as they wipe down tables and mop floors, but the music seems to have got louder. I bet the staff would like to go home, too, if they weren't aware they have four drivers in here posting about what a great night they've had – which probably means a generous tip.

I down half of my beer and go back to the table to say my goodbyes.

'Come dance with us,' Nils says with stretched-out arms, but I'm quick to shake my head.

'I'm good. You enjoy yourself, though. I'm heading out.'

'With Johannes?'

'Erm…' I splutter a little and Nils winks at me, still dancing with Harper. 'We're going to walk back together, yeah. Have a good night.' I tap Harper's shoulder to get his attention. 'Thanks for a great evening, man. Let me know who I owe for dinner. Enjoy the club. Keep him out of trouble.' I gesture at Nils.

Nils flips me off as Harper tells me not to worry about it. He says dinner was his treat.

Elijah, Cole and Ash are deep in a debate about a soccer result as I reach into the booth to grab my jacket. 'I'm heading off. Thanks for a great night.' Ash claps me on the back as Elijah and Cole lean over the table to shake my hand.

'Don't be a stranger!' Cole calls out. 'You've got our numbers. Give us a shout if you want to hang out. We both get how demanding this job can be when it comes to your social life, plus it's nice to have extra support to keep these guys in line when we're out.'

I laugh, but I'm not sure even Harper needs keeping in line anymore. At some point he disappeared for half an hour to FaceTime his husband. He's a changed man.

'Thanks, guys. I appreciate that.' I gesture to Johannes and Nils. 'Is it weird that they sometimes feel like our children?'

'Ha! We keep them alive. Isn't that what parents do?' I nod in agreement.

'See you around. Enjoy the club.' When I slide out of the booth, Johannes is waiting for me. 'Ready?'

'Yep, see you all later!' he shouts over the music before we head towards the door.

After being in the warm bar for hours, it's a shock when the chilly air hits my face, and I have to stop for a second to put my jacket on. It might be summer, but the evenings are colder than I expected.

'You have a good night?' he asks as we start the trek back to our accommodation.

'I really did. Thank you for inviting me. For including me. You've got a great group of friends in there.' And I really mean it. It's hard to be friendly in this sport when even their own teammates are competition.

'I was thinking exactly that earlier. Not to get too deep at midnight, but for so long I only had Harper. We were what therapists would probably call co-dependent.'

Yeah. For a long time, all I ever saw were headlines about the pair of them being thick as thieves, so that makes a lot of sense.

'But now, now the group is bigger and we both welcome it. Plus, obviously Harper has Kian, which has changed our dynamic. Not in a bad way – like, Harper's found something that I couldn't and didn't want to give him.'

I've no idea how true the stories claiming the two of them were an item are, but I have no desire to pry further.

'Yeah, him and Kian were a shock, huh? When that news broke, I had to read the article twice.' I remember the news blast, the way everyone in the garage stopped working and had to pinch ourselves because it didn't feel like a possibility that there could be a couple in this sport, never mind in the same team.

Not that there's anything wrong with Harper, it's just that they seemed like two wildly different people.

'I know, right! Harper was a mess when he told me. I couldn't understand the words coming out of his mouth. I was convinced he was off his head, but now when I see them together, I can't imagine them being apart. I've never seen two people more in love.'

I've seen the wedding pictures and that checks out.

The more I scrolled, the more a tiny bit of loneliness gnawed at my heart.

I didn't feel lonely tonight. Not surrounded by a great group of guys, all very different but with a shared common interest. I decide to make an effort to get to know Ash and Cole, because I'm great at agreeing to things when I'm in a social situation and poor at following through.

'Good for him. Honestly, don't we all deserve a bit of love like that?' says the guy whose whole life was turned upside down by a bad relationship and hasn't been on a date ever since.

Johannes goes quiet. The strains of music from bars on the strip are now far behind us as we turn into a more residential area.

Did I say something wrong? I go over everything I've just said in my head and hope I haven't offended him. After all, I hardly know him. One evening out and a couple of coffees doesn't give me the right to pass judgement on his friend's relationship.

The silence hangs because I'm afraid to break it. I notice Johannes shiver and I realise the man's made no attempt to button up his shirt.

'You want my jacket? I at least have a shirt with more buttons done up under this.'

A smile pulls at his plush lips. 'It's the look, you know?'

'My chest is way too hairy for that. It would be like an auburn bush peeking through.'

'Oh, really?'

Why did I say that? I can feel my face flushing. I'm grateful that it's pitch-black out here and the streetlamps are doing a poor job of illuminating our way, never mind shedding light on my strawberry cheeks.

'I rescind my offer. You shall freeze.'

'I'm good, thanks. It's not too far now.'

And he's right, because as we reach the end of the path it joins the road to the complex where we're staying and before I know it, I'm pointing out which block I'm in and he's leading me up the path to the door of the part where most of the RBF engineers have been allocated accommodation.

We stand on a doorstep that isn't really big enough for both of us, and I'm grateful that the security light doesn't seem to have come on because if anyone were to look out the window right now this could seem … compromising.

Even though we aren't actually doing anything.

Just standing really close. To the point I can hear him breathing and see the glimmer in his chocolate-brown eyes.

It would be oh-so-easy to lean in a fraction and test the waters. I'm not even sure what I'd be testing for, because this is Johannes Müller. Supermodel. Millionaire. One of the best racing drivers in the world right now. And I'm just me. A decent guy, but still an average person.

Yet there's definitely curiosity in the way he's looking at me, and in the way he runs his tongue across his generous bottom lip.

'You were right earlier. We do all deserve a bit of love like that,' he whispers into the small space between us, the night air absorbing the words before I can process what he's referring to.

I almost throw caution to the wind. I almost kiss him, even though I have by no means forgotten what it's like to have a man ruin your life, but before I can make the move he's stepping backwards.

'See you in the morning,' he calls over his shoulder as he jogs away, small white clouds puffing from his lips as he goes.

I have to take a second to catch my breath in the cold air, hoping it'll knock some sense into me. Because there is absolutely no reason for me to be watching Johannes until he disappears into the night. And absolutely, definitely, no reason to think about kissing him.

Chapter Nine

Johannes

'Why did we decide to drink so much the night before a flight?' I ask as I drop into the seat next to Caleb. His hair's all mussed, like he's not had time to do anything with it, and his head is resting up against the closed window shield.

'Don't. I haven't drunk like that in a while, and my head feels like there's men with tiny little hammers bashing at my skull.' He doesn't even open his eyes to reply to me, which tells me everything I need to know.

Now that the triple header is over, we're flying back to the UK for a few days of strategy and media at the factory. But I could do without two hours of alcohol sweats in front of my colleagues. We tried to go for a run this morning, but we were both a bit of a mess so it wasn't a spectacle of athletic prowess. I hurled into a bush and Caleb panted wretchedly as he fought hard not to do the same. It's fair to say we didn't get very far or at any kind of pace.

I used to be something of a big drinker, but these days my tolerance is non-existent and despite all the wings and ribs I ate last night, I'm yet to feel anything other than that I must surely be dying.

Having said that, I'm in significantly better shape than the Norwegian who's locked in the bathroom right now. The plane falls quiet as we prepare for take-off and poor Nils chooses that moment to hurl loudly. My fellow passengers cough uncomfortably.

'Jesus, he didn't get back till after four. I'm not sure he even knew his own name,' I say, settling into my seat. If I'm lucky, I'll sleep through the whole flight.

'And that's exactly why I knew going to the club was not a good idea,' Caleb says as Nils saunters out of the bathroom, wiping his mouth on his sleeve, and sits down opposite me like nothing's happened.

'You good?' I ask. Several sets of important eyes fall on him, but if he notices he doesn't seem to care. He's paler than I've ever seen him – which is saying something – and his blue eyes are bloodshot to within an inch of their lives.

'Yeah, but I'd give the bathroom a minute. I'm not sure what I was downing last night but my puke is blue.'

I feel my stomach lurch and Caleb lets out a quiet, 'Urgh.'

'What?' Nils questions. 'Just because you middle-aged bores were tucked up in bed at the stroke of midnight, it doesn't mean I can't celebrate.'

Five years ago, when Harper and I were having the best season ever in F2, we were celebrating like this after every race. 'You know I'm not judging you, just your gross sick. It was probably curaçao. Harper used to love that shit.'

At least he made sure Nils got home safe. I heard him

yelling from the taxi at half four this morning, shortly before Nils noisily stumbled into the suite.

Whilst Nils is way more awestruck by Harper's husband, Kian, than by Harper himself. I know there's still a part of him that can't quite believe he's partying with drivers he's looked up to for years. But he's worked hard and deserves his success. Who am I to deny him the fun that comes with it.

We're barely off the ground when Nils passes out, head smushed into a pillow, corner of his mouth open and drooling.

'Nikolas Beck, everybody. Future world champion. Apparently.' I sneak a quick photo – to tease him with later.

'Oh, to be young again,' Caleb jokes as he kicks up the footrest of his seat so he can get comfortable.

'You're not old. You're, what? Early thirties?' I'm only guessing based on his expertise, his many degrees, and over a decade of experience working in motor sports. He doesn't look a day over thirty. His features are strong, but his skin is clear and smooth, giving him a youthful look.

'Just turned thirty-three and feeling every ounce of it this morning.' He's dramatic in the way he curls his body into the seat. Luckily, there's plenty of room for his lean frame in the large seats of the team's private jet. When he shifts his body to find a comfortable position, his T-shirt rides up and I catch a glimpse of lean muscles and pale abs.

Holy fuck. Caleb is hot. Why on earth has he been hiding that underneath team polos and sponsored RBF apparel?

'You okay?' he asks, cracking one eye open to observe whatever freaked-out look I must have on my face right now.

'Yeah, sorry, just in the market for a nap and a big cup of coffee.' It's not a lie – I could use way more sleep than I got last night and then a big hit of caffeine. I'm not scheduled to be at the factory till tomorrow, but of course my agent loves to pack out what should just be a travel day with a tonne of other commitments.

'I feel you on the nap front. I should be working on my PhD, but I don't think I've got it in me today, you know?' He offers me a *what can you do about it?* kind of smile, which is all sorts of sleepy and adorable, before pulling a blanket halfway across his body and closing his eyes.

He doesn't drift off nearly as quickly as the snoring horse sitting across from me, but he looks so peaceful doing it. Ginger curls fall across his face and soft little sighs leave his plush lips every now and then.

I'm staring. I know I'm staring and I shouldn't be, but I can't look away. Luckily, we're tucked in the back corner of the plane, so no one is witness to me freaking out at the realisation that I've been blind to this man for years.

Obviously, I've seen other attractive men during my relationship with Jackson, but I was committed to him and never allowed myself to really look. Not that it got me anywhere, considering I'm now sitting on my single ass checking out yet another man who should have a big 'off limits' sign flashing in neon letters above his head.

What's wrong with me? I have to shake this off. Turning over in my seat, I get comfy facing away from him, legs fully stretched out in the recliner as I allow the exhaustion of the triple header to wash over me and lull me to sleep.

I'm woken by a jolt of turbulence just over an hour later. It also seems to awaken Caleb, because the second I open my eyes, I'm met with his face, all soft and sleepy as he yawns and pushes his hair out of his face.

'Morning,' he says, voice thick with sleep and a huskiness that perks a certain part of me right up.

'Hmm,' I hum as I wrestle the blanket from where it's become tucked underneath me, my whole body suddenly too warm. I peer over at Nils and see that he's still fast asleep. I think the plane could be free-falling right now and he wouldn't wake up.

I need to pee and find coffee, that's my prerogative right now – not sit here and mull over the warmth that blossomed in my stomach when waking up next to my race engineer. That thought needs to be banished to the skies and left there for good.

'Just going to…' I gesture with my thumbs towards the toilet and then quickly disappear into it.

Luckily, it no longer reeks of alcohol – or worse – and I am grateful to whoever it was who's been in to clean it. I take a piss and then slump against the sink. I look tired. The mirror is a sad reflection of what three weeks of non-stop racing – and a lack of self-care – can do to you. My brown skin looks ashy and dry.

It's not that I don't love the pressure of the circuit – because I really do – but when those three weeks also included a traumatic break-up and a big racing slump it really knocks it out of you. I need a face mask and a good hot-yoga session to sweat out some of the toxins and get my skin back to its optimum glowing state. I could also probably use a good buzzcut because my head is feeling quite stubbly right now. A week back in the UK won't do me any harm before we jet back to Europe for Spa in Belgium.

It's one of my favourite tracks, and the perk of being back in mainland Europe is that I can whizz home to see the parents for a day or two without missing anything. Yeah, this will be good for me. A chance to unwind a little, get my head back in the right place for the second half of the season. I'm not about to let Jackson Calder ruin what should, and could still be, *my year*.

Pep-talk over, I wash my hands, splash my face and find a kind air hostess to make me a mug of coffee. The smell of caffeine gets Caleb's attention and his wide green eyes tell me I should have got him a cup, too, but I was desperately trying not to think of him when I was in the bathroom.

'Sorry, that was rude of me. I'll flag down Josie the second I see her again.'

He says not to bother, but I catch him eying the aisle every couple of minutes as we settle into the last hour of the flight. Luckily, Josie comes round and services his caffeine needs with a tea and we slip back into a comfortable silence. He taps away on his laptop while I flick through a bunch of notes for a podcast I'm a guest on this evening.

It's an easy rhythm of his keys clicking away and Nils's light snores, but I find it weirdly relaxing. We all spend so much time together – on this plane, in the garage, the endless meetings – you get used to these everyday sounds of each other. Now I'm apparently getting used to Caleb being part of that mix, even after only six months of working together.

I can see where and how he fits into this team – his intelligence and the knowledge he has about the car and the way it runs on track. He must be exceptional to have earned this spot at such a young age – he's the youngest race engineer in the paddock right now. I listen to him type furiously, working away on his PhD, and I know that I – we, RBF – are lucky to have him.

I finish reviewing the approved questions and talking points for the pod this evening, trying not to be distracted by the little groans leaving his lips in response to a series of text alerts on his phone. I don't want to pry. It's none of my business, but I can't help sneaking a look. His face pulls and his brows knit together as he scrolls through whatever he's reading.

He sighs deeply, fingers swiping over the screen, and I can't stop myself getting a better look at what's got him so agitated.

'Who's that?' I know I shouldn't be peering over his shoulder, but there's a very good-looking man on his phone and my eyes can't exactly avoid the sight.

'Urgh. This is prospect number six-hundred-and-ten at this point.' He groans, before swiping over to the next photo – a shirtless version of the previous man. He's got a toned six-pack, tanned skin and dark, neatly trimmed body hair. He's the full package body-wise, at least.

'Sorry, prospect what? Why are you pouting over a hot man?'

'I'm not pouting. It's just this is like a weekly occurrence at this point – my mom sending me a Facebook profile of a guy she'd like to set me up with.' His mum has great taste because this guy is gorgeous. As Caleb minimises the picture, I spot that the guy's occupation is listed as 'Doctor'.

'Hot and smart. What's the issue again?'

Caleb zooms in on the guy's location, showing it to be Caleb's home state, then shows it to me.

'And?' I say.

'Sorry, do we not spend nine months together on the road?'

Oh. Makes sense. Wow, I'd never thought about it like that, which is ridiculous because in this sport, unless you work together – which I obviously would not recommend – you aren't going to see your partner a lot of the year.

'Okay, you have a point. How do you, uh, deal with that?'

I'm not sure what I'm asking, but it's out before my brain registers that it's an inappropriate question to ask a colleague.

'I don't. I've completely sworn off relationships.'

'Forever?'

I'm astounded.

He shrugs, so clearly there's a story there. But I definitely can't ask about it, especially when I haven't been forthcoming with *anyone* about my relationship troubles.

'My first and last boyfriend, Brad, was my college sweetheart. We were together for four years – I graduated from college, in three years, by the way – and he wanted us to move in together that final year. So we did. His parents bought, yes, *bought* a twenty-one-year-old couple a house and life was brilliant. We lived there for six months and I was crazy enough to start looking at rings. Then, the day I found out I got into my master's programme, I came home to find him shagging another guy in our bed.'

When he's finished speaking, he physically heaves out a breath, like he knew that if he stopped at any point during the story he wouldn't have continued.

I wish I could throw my arms around him, because that must fucking suck. It does fucking suck. To think you're about to spend forever with someone and then poof! Gone. Betrayal.

'I'm so sorry, man. He must have been a fucking idiot. You're a great guy. Fuck him, because look at you now. In a fantastic job, with one of the best teams in the world. And, well, you get to work with me every day.'

I nudge him with my elbow, drawing a smile out of him.

'Well, when you put it like that.' He's smiling, though, so that's something. 'I'm just over it. I don't feel like going through that hurt again. But my parents, they love love. All three of my older brothers are married with kids. My parents have been married just over fifty years. They think I need the same thing to be happy.'

'But you don't?'

I would have agreed with him until I watched Harper fall madly in love and how it's only made his life better. I gave it a try and got fucked over, so either I was doing it wrong or I'm not one of the lucky ones. Or maybe I just don't deserve it. I flinch inwardly.

'I love my job, I love this sport, I love the travel, and I love working on my PhD. It's enough.'

'It's a lot, for sure,' I say dumbly. But is it enough?

I'm too hungover to be getting this deep thirty-thousand feet in the air.

He shrugs again, offering me a half-smile, which tells me that maybe he's only half happy. Half happy is more than I am right now, but maybe once I get another win under my belt I'll feel more like the old Johannes.

'Try telling that to my mom. She would love for me to come home and live on their street with my husband and our kids. Don't get me wrong, she supports me following my dreams, but I know she'd love to have all four of her boys close by.'

'The same street? That's ... close.'

He shoots me a glare. 'Two of my brothers live on the street and my other brother lives two blocks over. The only house close enough for her would be next door.'

'Wow, that is ... a lot.'

'I love them, though. They've always been such good parents, so I can't complain.'

The captain announces that we're beginning our descent and asks everyone to prepare for landing, so I return my seat to its normal position.

'What's your plan for whilst you're in the UK? Do you have somewhere to stay?'

'I don't have a permanent place. Even though we're in the UK more than anywhere, it's too much hassle to manage it while we're away, so I normally get like a short-term lease or an Airbnb, but I haven't this time, so it's the hotel for me with some of the other guys.'

It's on the tip of my tongue to invite him to stay in my London apartment. It's where, once upon a time, Harper and I lived together. But would that be weird? I've had Nils stay with me before when he first joined the team, but most people do their own thing. We're on top of each other for most of the year, so people appreciate having their own space whenever possible.

Except, it does get kind of crappy spending so many nights a year in a hotel room, doesn't it?

Before I can stop myself, the words are flying out of my mouth. 'You can stay with me.'

The plane touches down with a solid thunk and we are pushed backwards in our seats as the brakes engage. Caleb stares wordlessly at me like I've just dropped from outer space.

'If you want...' I add, trailing off uncertainly.

Chapter Ten

Caleb

You can stay with me. The words hang between us.

Neither of us says anything while the plane comes to a halt and everyone around us comes back to life, including a very disorientated Nils.

'We on the ground?' he asks, and all I can do is nod as Johannes gets up and swings his bag onto his back. 'Cool.' Nils doesn't make any effort to move, just stares bleary-eyed at the goings-on around him, waiting for everyone else to deplane before he does.

The bulk of people start to file out, but both Johannes and I seem to be lingering. Him, probably because he's waiting for an answer, and me, because I don't know what to say. It's a nice offer and all, but I'm not an idiot; we both felt that slight crackle between us last night. It hit me like a big red warning sign as I stood on the doorstep of the apartment I was sharing with Ian and a bunch of the other mechanics.

That was after just one night of being out with him – in a group. A few hours in normal civilisation. He's talking about seven days. Six whole nights. That's a long time to have to sit with this charged energy between us and do nothing about it. Maybe he didn't feel it. Or maybe, because he's Johannes Müller and can have any man in the world, he gets this all the time so barely clocked it.

Maybe.

I tell myself it would be nice not to be confined to the four walls of a hotel room. It would be nice not to wake up alone. Not that I'd be waking up to him, of course. I don't mean that. I just mean, it would be nice to wake up to someone drinking coffee in the kitchen. I bet he has so many fancy machines. I wouldn't have to eat room service for a week. We could even travel into the factory together. It would make the days and evenings here a little less lonely.

Although, he might have plans and is actually just offering me a place to sleep – a bed and nothing more. Not company in the kitchen, homecooked meals, or time spent hanging out before or after work. My brain feels like it's in overdrive. I should just let him know I'm grateful for his offer, but the hotel is fine. I should really have sorted a place in the UK already, especially with summer break coming up, but I've been so busy writing up my thesis in every spare minute that it's not been my top priority.

I'm stalling. The plane is mostly empty and I just stand here, unable to take a single step towards the exit.

'Um, were you serious?' I ask Johannes.

'Yeah, of course, man. Don't we spend enough time in hotels? You shouldn't have to do it whilst we're at base, too.'

He's smiling like he means it and I really would be a fool to turn him down.

Or maybe a fool to agree, but here we are.

'Okay, well that would be nice. Thank you.'

'Of course. We'll head there now. I ordered a big food shop to be delivered yesterday so I'm well stocked, but let me know if there's anything you want and I'll get that sorted today. I have a podcast to record this evening and a couple of sponsorship videos to make, but then I can cook us dinner, if you like?'

'You don't have to do that.' I wave him off. We've got a busy few days. The last thing he needs to be doing is running around after me as well as all his work commitments.

'No, I want to. I like to cook, so let me. Any allergies I should know about?' I shake my head. 'Good, let's go.'

Nils is finally up on his feet, walking down the aisle in front of us when Johannes's hand finds the small of my back, guiding me off the plane. I feel like my whole body's been engulfed in flames. How can such a light touch burn me to my core? And yet the last thing I want is for him to move his hand.

'You good?' he asks Nils as the Norwegian stretches his whole body in front of us on the tarmac. Most of the team staff have disappeared into various cars and taxis, but there are still two waiting next to the plane.

'Yeah, I'll see you tomorrow.' They share a bro hug and Nils eyes me, still looking a little sleepy. 'You going with him?' he asks. There's a deceptive tone to his voice. Almost as if he thinks he has everything between Johannes and me figured out, when there's nothing to figure out. Nothing at all.

'He's staying with me whilst we're getting work done at the

factory. See you tomorrow,' Johannes says, and Nils waves as he heads for his car.

Johannes asks one of the ground crew to load our luggage into the back of his car and before I know it, we're off and heading to London.

'Does Nils have a place in the city?' I ask.

'No. Don't ask me who he stays with when he's here, but it's someone. An ex-hook-up or something, I think. But every time we're here, he goes there. For someone who usually loves to share the details of his sex life, he's quite private about this person.' I hear exactly what Johannes is laying out: this person is different.

I struggle to imagine Nils being serious about anyone, but then four years ago I would have said the same about Harper James and look at him now.

'As long as he's all right, I guess?'

'Exactly. He's twenty-three and living his best life. None of our business who he stays with as long as he's not out of control or being stupid or hurting himself, so who are we to stop him?'

We settle into a conversation about what we were like at that age as we drive through the outer boroughs towards the centre of the city.

I can't stop a breathless '*Wow*' from leaving my lips as we step out of the elevator into Johannes's penthouse apartment. Because it's truly stunning. So modern, so sleek, but not soulless or boringly white like a lot of these places.

There are nice hues of blue and purple on some of the walls. His kitchen is decked out with a sleek black counter-top and the cupboards an eye-popping shade of electric blue. This is not what I was expecting at all, but it's so very Johannes at the same time. Edgy, yet refined. You're never quite sure what you're going to get with him, but the package as a whole makes total sense. It's nicely decked out, with appliances on the island, a fancy coffee set-up (of course) and a six-burner high-end range cooker.

He leads me into a big living area furnished with a massive TV and one of the biggest L-shaped couches I've ever seen. But what steals my attention – and my breath – is the giant naked photograph of him on the wall above the mantel. It's tastefully shot, but everything is on display except for his dick, which is covered by one of his racing helmets. It captures a lot of his side profile, so I get a complete view of the delicious curve of his ass and ... wow, I need to stop staring but I can't take my eyes off it. I will not be able to spend a single second in here without my eyes drifting up to it.

'It's got four bedrooms, but when Harper and I lived here we turned one into a gym and the other is a mini home cinema, so there's only one guest bed but I think it'll be fine for you.' I follow him down the corridor, as yet unable to stop thinking about the glorious image of his naked body.

'En suite through there, and then there's a walk-in wardrobe, which is empty if you need to hang anything.'

'You know I'm only staying here for the week, right?' My jaw's practically hanging open at the ridiculous size of the bed in the middle of the room. It's already made up, which I'm sure is courtesy of whoever looks after this place for him, but it looks so luxurious.

'Yeah?'

I can't help but laugh. 'This is amazing. Wow. What an apartment. Thank you for letting me stay.'

'Of course. I get tired of all the hotels. I much prefer when we're in the villas in Europe, but it's nice to come back here, too.

'Is this not your permanent residence?' I can't imagine ever wanting to not live here.

'No, not really. I have a place in Germany – smaller than this – and I often stay with my parents when I'm over there. I don't really think of any of them as home.'

Now *that* I could relate to. I don't even have my own place in the States. I always stay with my parents when I'm back in Tennessee, which makes me feel like a child.

'Well, if you ever need a house-sitter, just let me know!' I'm only half kidding, because I would happily stay here forever.

'You're welcome here anytime, man. I'm probably not here enough. I have someone who comes and cleans it every week when I'm away, and who keeps an eye on the place.' He fiddles with the edge of the comforter on the bed as I pop my case down on the rug and unzip it.

'I have to go and film a couple of brand videos and then record this podcast, but I'll be done like five-ish, so dinner for six?'

'Sounds good. Thanks again.'

'Make yourself at home. Gym's to the left and the home cinema the other side.' He pulls the door halfway shut behind him and heads down the corridor to what I'm assuming is his bedroom.

I take a second to flop down on the massive bed, the amethyst-coloured comforter like a cloud beneath my back. I desperately need some sleep after last night's craziness, this morning's hangover and then the abortive early morning run, but in the back of my mind I know I should be working on my PhD thesis. The deadline is slowly creeping up on me and as work gets more and more busy, I can't afford to drop the ball.

Ten minutes. I'll just lie here for ten minutes and then I'll get up and maybe make use of the gym and settle in for some writing.

I wake up an hour later, legs draped half off the bed and my mouth dry, but at least I feel more human.

I run for thirty minutes on the treadmill and even try out some of his fancy weights machines, before showering in the biggest bathroom I've ever seen classed as an *en suite*. I change into a comfy pair of sweatpants and an RBF quarter zip. Grabbing my laptop, I head out into the lounge in search of a comfy place to sit and type, but the second I settle down in a chunky armchair I'm distracted.

My eyes should be trained on my laptop screen, focusing on the aerodynamics study I've been doing, but how am I meant to think about anything when there is such a masterpiece on the wall? His naked form is practically taunting me from above the mantel, every curve of muscle begging for me to drool over it. I keep forcing my attention back onto writing my paragraph, but my traitorous eyes slide up to the paragon of perfection on the wall. I admire the way the light kisses his brown skin, the dips and hollows where the shadows form, the way he exudes strength and vitality. But I'm most caught up in the beauty of his features and the teasing look in his eyes. It's like he knows he's being watched and he likes it, because he's the one in control of how I'm responding.

Indeed, my own body cannot help responding. My cock twitches and thickens in my sweatpants. I feel sparks racing up and down my spine and heat pools in my belly. I have to adjust myself to get comfortable again because my cock is springing up, hard now and aching for him to let the helmet fall so I can see the full length of him in all his glory. My hand creeps towards my groin because I'm starting to feel the need for release and—

Christ, I can't do this.

Slamming my laptop shut, I tuck it back into its sleeve and gather up my papers. I don't like to work in bed, but anything is better than this. I pass the home cinema on the way down the corridor and slip in there instead. The plush velvet sofa hugs my body as I throw myself down and stretch out my legs across the thick cushions. This will do.

It's been a while since I've had enough free time to actually lose myself in the research, but I soon get lost in the words, my hands flying across my keyboard as I flesh out the argument of my thesis, every point supported by data and references. It reminds me of everything I love so much about academia and how much my brain still burns with a need to learn.

I'm not sure how many hours pass; I don't even really notice the way my ass goes numb from sitting for too long without a break. It's worth it to see my screen full of my own words and ideas.

'There you are.' I almost jump out of my skin at the sound of Johannes's voice coming from the doorway. Then I make the mistake of peering over my shoulder to see what he wants, only to find him shirtless and in a pair of shorts slung so low on his hips that it should be illegal.

To add to the crime, his skin is coated in a sheen of glistening sweat.

I should not have agreed to stay here.

'Sorry, I didn't mean to startle you. I just finished up a workout and thought I'd get started on dinner but couldn't find you.' He's using a towel to dry his smooth, slick head but doesn't seem bothered about the damp stretches across the full compass of his abs and I have to mentally tell myself to look away and meet his eyes, to not make this awkward.

'It's fine, sorry, I made myself at home in here. This sofa is insanely comfy. I got so many words written.' Softly, I close my laptop and tuck it up under my arm as I push up off the sofa.

'Don't be silly, I told you to make yourself at home. I'm glad you got a lot done. I'm going to make beef and black bean tacos for dinner. That okay?'

Is that okay? A man who can cook, too? Yes please.

No. This is not a *yes please* kind of moment. We are colleagues. We work together. I'm not interested. And he can't be. There's no way. I mean, look at him!

'Caleb?' A smirk pulls at the corner of his mouth as my eyes track back up to his face again. *Busted.*

'Yep, sounds good. Do I have time for a shower?' A very cold shower.

'Sure. Food'll be ready in twenty.'

Plenty of time for me to get myself together – maybe get myself off so I don't spend dinner ogling him.

'Plenty of time.'

Chapter Eleven

Johannes

Every day Caleb becomes that little bit more interesting to me. He surprises me in the most unexpected ways. Like the way he couldn't keep his eyes off of me. Made me want to cook dinner half-naked, too, but the risk of hot oil splattering on my bare skin drove me to pull on a T-shirt.

I got to work frying off some beef mince and beans, flavouring it with paprika, salt, chilli flakes and a crack of black pepper. I whip up a chunky pineapple and tomato salsa, then mash up an avocado with some red onion, and shred some lettuce and cheese.

I'm just warming up the tortilla wraps when Caleb steps back into the kitchen. He's barefoot, wearing a different pair of sweatpants and his hair is a curly, wet mess.

Oh, boy.

In what world did I think asking him to stay was a good idea?

This is temptation city, and there is absolutely no way I can act on anything. Not when we have to work so closely together. Not when I'm fresh out of a heart-wrenching workplace relationship that's so severely affected my performance.

'Something smells incredible,' he comments from where he lingers on the other side of the island, a safe distance away from me. I'm glad such a big obstacle lies between us, and the electric the crackle of energy I keep feeling when I'm around him.

'Well, I hope you're hungry because I'm used to cooking just for myself and apparently don't know how to double a recipe. I've made enough to feed a family of four.' The pan is full to the brim with the beef and bean mixture, which I packed out with grilled onions and peppers.

'Absolutely starving. Who knew typing all day could be such hungry work?' he says, sliding onto one of the bar stools.

He looks so … natural, so at home. It shouldn't startle me, but something zings around my bloodstream like it's electrifying me. Luckily, the oven timer dings which gives me an excuse to turn away and take out the wraps while I get myself under control.

In the time it took him to shower I seem to have made us a build-your-own taco station. Normally I'd just cram everything into wraps from the bowls and pans I used to make the components, but I'm spooning things into serving bowls and everything. Don't know who in the Nigella Lawson I think I am right now, but Caleb's eyes light up as I call him over to help himself.

'This reminds me so much of being back home with my

family,' he says as he fills three wraps, not skimping on the cheese or sour cream like I am.

We settle down next to each other at the breakfast bar as he continues. 'Having four hungry boys to feed, plus my dad, Mom always used to just let us go for it and serve ourselves rather than spending ages plating up and letting it go cold. I'm the youngest, so I always just copied everything my brothers did – though they were grown men when I was just figuring out how to hold a knife and fork.'

'How old are your brothers?' I ask, mouth filled with taco.

'Gregg's fifty-one, Damon's fifty-two and Joshua's fifty-four so there's around a twenty-year age difference between us.'

I whistle. Being an only child, I can't even imagine that.

'How'd you find it?'

He ponders for a second, eyes on his plate like he might find the answers there. 'I love them all, so much, and their now-wives and all of the nieces and nephews they've given me. But, it was lonely at times. They were all away at college already when I was born and then when they graduated they all moved back in for various periods of time and then they were gone again with their partners to start their own lives. We all get on great now I'm older, but I'm closer in age to my nieces and nephews than I am to my brothers.'

'Yeah, I can imagine. Though I have no siblings, so I guess I actually can't! I don't even think I would have liked having one. I wasn't very good at sharing.' I don't tell him that I'm still not. That I hated sharing Jackson with Hendersohm. I definitely don't tell him how bitter it's made me.

'Luckily, I didn't have to share anything. They were off at bars and football games while I was still playing with toy cars in my bedroom. Then I told them I was gay, and I remember

Damon saying well at least they never had to worry about me stealing their wives.' That extracts a chuckle from me. It reverberates around my body, catching me off-guard, because I'm not sure when I last properly laughed like this.

Which turns into me laughing like an idiot for a solid minute whilst Caleb watches on in confusion. Eventually he starts laughing, too – it might be catching, or perhaps he's just laughing at me – but this feels so freeing. Like it's loosening all the tightness in my muscles, releasing the bones in my spine from where they've become locked. My jaw relaxes, my shoulders drop, and the lingering headache that's been gnawing at the base of my skull evaporates.

It takes me a good few minutes to collect myself before I can take another bite of my taco, but even then, a hearty smile lingers on my face.

'You good?' Caleb asks, polishing off his third taco, a blob of sour cream clinging to the corner of his lips.

I can't stop myself from reaching over to wipe it away. I brush my thumb over his lip and he just stares back at me, frozen in place, frozen but also hot. So fucking hot. His eyes are so clear and so green as they lock onto mine with an intensity that makes my toes curl. Everything slows down. I watch a flush creep up over his skin, staining his pale cheeks a rosy red. I see his eyes widen as I bring my thumb to my own mouth and close my lips around the digit. I suck the remnants of the sour cream off then slowly pull it out of my mouth with a wet pop.

'I am now,' I say.

His mouth drops open.

I can't believe what I've done. But mostly I can't believe how cute he looks when he blushes. I can see the pulse at the base of his throat bumping like it's about to erupt out from beneath his skin. He blinks slowly and I watch his auburn lashes graze the tops of his heated cheeks. I want to feel that heat with the palm of my hand, to push my fingertips into his hair, and trace the delicate skin under his eyes with my thumb. But that really would be madness.

I swallow audibly.

What the fuck am I doing?

Seriously, what the actual fuck?

'Um…' he says, still not breaking eye contact.

I cannot pursue this. I shouldn't even want to. A week ago I was crying my eyes out over Jackson and now I'm lusting over my race engineer? What the hell's wrong with me?

He shifts in his seat as though he needs to adjust himself. My eyes flick down to his sweatpants. They're pretty loose, but I'm sure I see the telltale signs of a growing erection.

Fuck.

I know I have to put a stop to this before we're both too hard and horny to do anything but make a massive mistake. Because it would be a mistake. Sure, it was a problem to be fucking the future principal of a rival team, but at least I don't have to see him every single day or hear his voice in my ear while I make split-second decisions that could deliver me everlasting glory, or a painful death in a blistering fireball.

I tear my gaze away – with considerable effort – and leap up from the barstool. I start clearing away plates and dishes, clattering crockery and clinking cutlery so there's no need to make conversation. I load the dishwasher and put the leftovers into plastic, food-storage containers and stack them in the fridge – all without looking at Caleb once.

I'm a coward, but it's for the best.

By the time I'm wiping down the counter, I feel ready to look up, but Caleb has gone.

We settle into an uneasy routine after that. We put in long days at the factory, attending different meetings and studiously ignoring each other. I spend a lot of time with Nils, recording different soundbites and clips, working in the stimulators, and doing strength training. I try not to notice what Caleb does.

But every evening we meet in the foyer and drive home together, then I cook dinner whilst he works on his thesis.

The second night, I feed him pork schnitzel using my mum's best recipe and the way he devours it has me hard for the rest of the evening. He clears up and sorts the dishes, like it's the least he can do to show his appreciation. Little does he know that the visual of him wolfing down the meal I cooked him – and licking his lips afterwards – is worth more to me than any effort to pull his weight with the chores. Or that I masturbate to the memory of it when I am alone in my room later that night.

On night three, I whip up the freshest of pasta salads using my favourite cold-cut meats and homemade pesto. I send a silent thank-you to my housekeeper for keeping my basil plant alive. And as I crush the garlic and herbs in a pestle and mortar, I try not to think of what I want to do to Caleb, or how I want to see that blush creep down his back, his thighs or his cock. I'm breathless when I finish grinding the pesto and my eyeballs are burning in their sockets from trying not to imagine Caleb's ears turning pink if I were to suck him off right here in the kitchen. While we eat, we talk about our families, life on the road, our goals and ambitions. Sometimes we laugh and joke, and sometimes it's more serious, but always, always, there is an unspoken undercurrent of desire that no amount of self-discipline can erase.

By nights four and five – homemade pizza and then enchiladas – I'm a churning mess of desperate craving and the need to prevent myself making another mistake that could cost me even more. I don't seem to be able to appreciate him without also wanting him the way I used to when he first started working with me. I tell myself that three years of being kept dangling by Jackson has twisted my sense of how fucking hot it is to do something dangerous and stupid, but I was doing dangerous and stupid things long before I met him. Caleb isn't dangerous or stupid. He fits in my home like it's always been his, too, and I enjoy seeing him working away in the cinema room, or closing his eyes when he gets a particularly good bite of food that I made him.

It feels natural to have him here. I like having him here. His presence fills me up in a way Jackson's never did because I was always chasing more with him and he was always holding back. Caleb doesn't hold back.

Tonight is our last night before we fly out to Belgium and our cosy flat-share is no more. I'm really going to miss it. I'm going to miss *him*.

He is brilliant. Watching him work hurts my brain, but he's so smart. One night I asked him to tell me about his thesis and wow. *Wow.* The way he understands the aerodynamics of the car is insane. He's wasted being stuck at the pit wall. But I also see, day-to-day in the factory, how much he has to offer to this team. I thought at first that he was shy and quiet, but he's quick to offer his opinion when needed and he confronts problems head-on. I see how much respect he's earned from the experienced guys on the team, how they listen when he speaks because he doesn't fill the air with unnecessary chatter. It's impressive.

It only makes him more attractive to me when it really, really shouldn't. I shouldn't be daydreaming in a strategy meeting about the braised-rib tagliatelle I'm going to make him tonight. How I'm going to spend precious time rolling out my own pasta like I'm applying to be on *MasterChef*, even though I have the ready-made stuff in my pantry. Maybe I'm hoping he'll let me teach him. I could wrap my arms around him and show him how to knead the dough, then together we could gently feed it into the machine and hang it to dry on the special stand.

The fantasy turns dirty in my mind as I imagine pressing myself against his back and kissing his neck. I conjure up an image of his little, pink-tipped ears as he feels the hard length of my cock nudging his ass cheeks. Perhaps he turns around and we—

'Johannes?'

I'm brought suddenly back down to earth as the meeting we're in seems to have wrapped up and everyone is standing to go.

Shit. This has got to stop.

I hope I didn't miss anything crucial.

'Yeah, thanks, see you tomorrow,' I say, standing up and acknowledging the voice that broke through my sexy little daydream. I carry my file of papers in front of me to hide the evidence of my arousal as we all file out of the room. It's been a long week and the team has been working harder than ever to make the second half of the season even better. We're getting an impressive package of upgrades to set us apart from the Hendersohm team. We won't win the constructor's championship this year, but I need every millimetre and millisecond to keep myself in contention for the driver's championship.

When we get back to my apartment, Caleb puts down his things and cracks his neck side to side, before rolling out his shoulders.

'What a week. I'm exhausted.'

'Me, too,' I say, watching his shoulders flex and roll.

'But I do love a week in the factory, and this has been a good one. I know I've already said this but thank you for letting me stay. It's been so nice to come home in the evenings and properly switch off from day-to-day work.'

'I've loved having you here. You're welcome any time.'

I mean it. I mean it so much I can't even begin to think about it deeply. I've never cooked for someone like this, put effort and care into making each evening the perfect relaxing occasion – pairing wine, adjusting mood lighting, making everything from scratch. I certainly didn't do it for Harper when he lived here, and Jackson never stepped foot in the place.

'Thanks. I'm going to take a shower. Do you need help with anything?' Caleb asks.

'Take your time. I can put you to work when you're ready.'

I pull out all the ingredients I'm going to need for dinner. Luckily, the meat has been roasting in the slow-cooker all day, so when I take it out, it falls off the bone. My mouth waters at the smell as I set up a station to make pasta, before slipping into the pantry to analyse the wine rack for the perfect bottle of red to cook with and another to consume with dinner.

I take my time, reading the labels and thinking about what will work. I'm definitely not waiting to hear the water go off and then for his feet to pad down the hallway to the kitchen.

It's pure coincidence that I'm weighing out the flour when he joins me on the opposite side of the island, his damp hair curling around his neck and brow in a way that makes my balls tighten.

'You fancy helping?'

I'm in so much trouble.

'Of course, put me to work.'

Don't tempt me.

He washes his hands, before stepping up by my side.

'Okay, so we're going to need to make a little well in the middle of the flour for the eggs and then we'll crack them in and meld it all together.'

'That easy?' he asks.

'That easy,' I confirm. I don't tell him this is just the start of what can feel like an endless process to get it right, not when his eyes light up with the excitement to learn. 'Make sure you keep the flour walls intact. It makes it easier for it all to come together.'

I crack three eggs into the nest he's built. He's quick to get stuck into the messy mixture because he's careful and takes instruction well. He kneads the dough, and I try not to watch the muscles in his strong forearms flex and twitch. I try not to think of the fantasy I had of pressing up against him. I force myself to stand back and let him do it on his own, because I know that if I put my hands on top of his hands, then I'm definitely fucking him tonight. Probably before we've even finished making dinner.

I blink to clear my head and before I know it he has a golden mound of dough ready to start to shape.

'Okay, break it into four and then we'll roll it out manually into ovals, before we pass it through the machine.' He gets on with that whilst I set up the pasta attachment on my KitchenAid.

I turn my back for two seconds and the ovals he's rolled out are pizza length and thickness. I chuckle to myself, before reaching round to stop him rolling the dough out to almost a see-through density.

'Too thin?' he asks.

'A little.' I gesture an inch between my thumb and first finger and a grin stretches across his face as he laughs.

'Where did you learn how to do this?' he asks.

'I did a course,' I say.

'You're kidding.'

'Just a one-day thing at a fancy restaurant in the city. I won it in a silent auction at a charity event.'

'And then you practised,' he says. It's a statement, and I bask in the warmth of his admiration.

'You haven't tasted it yet,' I say.

'You do everything well,' he says and then blushes.

I move closer to show him the right thickness for the pasta dough and realise I have rested my hand on his hip as he feeds it through the machine.

'I've never even thought to make my own pasta,' he says shakily as my thumb caresses the bare skin of his hip where his T-shirt's ridden up. 'Mom always just had like big ten-kilo bags in the cupboard. Feeding three football players always took a lot and I loved to eat.'

He's watching intently as the small blades separate the dough into tagliatelle-width strands, but I'm more mesmerised by him. How grass-green his eyes are from right here. How his auburn lashes flutter over his cheeks. How soft his hair looks and how much I want to run my fingers through it. How much I really want to.

I take note of every single freckle that makes up the constellation across his nose and cheeks and even some down the side of his neck. I long to pull his T-shirt over his head to see how far they stretch.

The final piece of dough runs through the machine and we spend a peaceful few minutes hanging them strand by strand to dry out. I stir the sauce that's coming together in a pan, and he opens the wine and pours us both a glass. We lean against the countertop, thighs and hips brushing as we sip, the homely aroma of a pasta dish coming together wrapping us up in a warm, cosy bubble.

I don't want to speak. I don't want to burst that bubble and let the outside world in. I want this evening to go on forever.

'You're thinking hard over there,' he says in barely a whisper, almost like he wants to stay trapped in the bubble, too.

'Just thinking about how much I've loved this week.' I gulp down a mouthful of a delicious red and rest the glass down on the counter. That same hand now snakes around to the small of his back and creeps under his T-shirt. We're in a bubble where the outside world can't touch us…

He shivers and leans into my touch. With a hum, he replies. 'Me, too.'

There's nothing more to say. There's no point pretending

we're talking about anything else but this domestic bliss we seem to have found.

The pan simmers away, the timer counting down on my phone until I can add the pasta to the salty water. I stroke soft circles on his back and his head gradually comes to rest against my shoulder. I don't want to compare this to anything Jackson and I shared, because I don't want his existence to intrude upon such a perfect moment, but it was never like this with him. Stolen moments are exciting – for a while – but they're not this. Never this.

Because this, right here and now … I could stay here like this for the rest of my life.

The timer dings and we jump apart. I have to catch my wine glass as it tips and nearly falls to the floor. It's for the best. I can't be thinking about forevers. Not now and not with Caleb. It would be monumentally stupid to get involved with him. I nearly blew this season over one heartbreak – I cannot throw away the rest of it on another.

I add the pasta to the water and shred the meat into the sauce. He lingers a little distance from me, cheeks flushed and eyes careful. I tell myself it's from the heat of the range cooker, but I hope it's from what my touch did to his insides.

'The pasta only needs four minutes as it's so fresh, so we're almost good to go. Would you grab the parmesan from the fridge?'

Something gnaws at my insides as I stir the strands of tagliatelle, but I won't let it consume me. Instead, I focus in on making this last meal together perfect, tasting the sauce to make sure it's seasoned enough and passing Caleb my favourite pasta bowls from the cupboard.

We share the meal at the little bistro table that takes

advantage of the big window, with its incredible view of the vast London skyline. The sky is a blend of purples, pinks and oranges fading into the horizon as the sun sets. It's beautiful, but nowhere near as beautiful as the man sitting opposite me.

We eat quietly, lost in the flickering of the candles I lit for ambience, which only makes this feel more and more like a date.

'This is delicious,' he says. 'You're such a good cook.'

'Thank you,' I say. 'But you made the pasta.'

He laughs and blushes, which I enjoy enormously.

When we've both finished, he clears the table. I wash and he dries, putting each item away in its rightful place. It occurs to me that he now knows where everything belongs. His movements are precise and intentional, and I find it so fucking hot. Since when did this become more of a turn-on than sneaking around having sexy rendezvous with a forbidden lover? Hell if I know, but it has.

Back when I was running around town with Harper, I wouldn't have cooked for Caleb or invited him to stay. I'd have got him drunk and fucked him. It would have been amazing and I'd have walked away without considering the collateral damage. There would have been no *moments*, just a seriously great night together. Maybe not even the whole night. Then came Jackson, just when I started to want these kinds of things, and I realise now that he didn't want them. Or perhaps he just didn't want them with me.

So now I don't trust myself to be silently feeling things for Caleb, never mind actually putting them out there for him to see and hear. I don't want to want things. I don't want him to want so much less with me than I want.

'I should get to bed,' he says in a low voice as he hangs up the tea towel. 'We have an early start tomorrow.'

'Yeah.' I can't think of anything else to say.

'The car's picking us up at five, so…' He hovers in the middle of the lounge while I blow out the candles. The night is over.

'Yeah,' I repeat like an absolute idiot.

Say something.

My brain pleads with me, but my mouth still doesn't move.

'Well, goodnight, then.' His face drops a little, the soft smile that's been there all night leaving his face.

He turns and walks down the hall, bare feet soft on the carpet.

'Wait!' I call out as his hand settles on the door handle to enter his room.

Finally, *finally,* my body kicks into action and I take off like a rocket after him.

'Is everything oka—?'

I don't even let him finish his question. I put my palm on his cheek, exactly like I've been imagining and haul our faces together. My mouth crashes against his as I take everything I've been fantasising about since I suggested he stay with me.

He goes completely still and I ready myself to step back, but then his hands find my shirt and fist around the fabric, pulling me closer. Our whole bodies clash together, and it's a battle for dominance.

'Holy fuck,' I mumble against him, but he uses it as an opportunity to penetrate my mouth, his tongue lashing over mine in a hot, wet fight.

His hand must find the door handle again at some point

because we stumble into his room. Clothes go flying – his, mine – as we fumble and curse and scramble to get naked, then we fall onto his bed in a jumble of limbs.

This is for sure going to be the stupidest thing I've ever done. And I don't even care.

Chapter Twelve

Caleb

It's like I blink and suddenly I'm under Johannes's naked body, our dicks lined up way too perfectly as we kiss, feverishly. I don't even get a moment to appreciate how gorgeous he is naked. I can feel the hard edges of his six pack as my fingers trail them like a map.

This might just be the best kiss of my life, and when his hand strays from where he was clutching the back of my neck down to my stomach, edging ever closer to our cocks, I can't stop the groan that echoes in his mouth.

Just when I'm not sure it can get any better than this, his big hand begins to wrap around both of our dicks, creating the perfect friction as he moves slowly against me. I can't stop the way my back arches off the bed, feeding his hungry fist, his thumb catching the first treacle of pre-cum to lube up his hand.

It's heaven on earth with every thrust, especially when his lips latch on to the side of my neck. They are gentle at first, delivering soft kisses, but then, as our pace picks up and each slide of our cocks becomes more slick and desperate, he begins to nip at a sensitive spot just behind my ear, his tongue quickly soothing over it after every scrape of his teeth.

When he pulls back, his eyes are molten brown and his gaze is so hot I can feel it on every inch of my skin.

'You're so fucking gorgeous,' he whispers, before dipping back into my neck and working down to my collarbone.

What. The. Fuck.

I still can't believe this is happening. I can't believe I've somehow managed to fall into bed with someone as hot as Johannes Müller. A world-class F1 racing driver. Who knows how to cook. Who knows about wine. Whose taste in music is immaculate. What kind of luck is this?

One hand is still tangled in my hair, tugging softly every time he needs better access to my neck or for grip, to maintain the friction between our bodies.

It's everything and hardly anything at the same time. I imagine this is nothing to Johannes. It's not like I haven't heard all the stories about his and Harper's sex escapades.

But I'm way too close to the edge for a little bit of frotting. There's warmth coiling in my stomach faster than ever before. It's *never* felt like this before. So perfectly aligned, so desperate. Like, I want to come so badly – but I also want this to last forever.

His hand slides down the side of my body, fingers making my skin tingle – especially as he scrapes down the curve of my ass before landing on my thigh. He pulls back to get a better look at us, pausing for a mere second before he takes us both in his hands, his knee settling between mine to line us up better again. His calloused hand is delicious as we both thrust upwards and I can't stop the way I cry out, 'Holy fuck.'

Johannes's grin widens to that perfect pearly-white smirk and I feel myself surrendering to him. I'm completely at his mercy, which is the total opposite from our day jobs.

Oh fuck. My job. Our jobs. Fuck, we should not be doing this. I mean, I'm pretty sure he'd be fine, but I'm replaceable. They could fire my ass for this, I'm sure.

'Stop, stop. Sorry. Stop.' He practically springs back from where he's been grinding against me, freeing both of our dicks from his grip, elbows catching him at the end of the bed.

'Everything okay? Was that too much?' He props himself up, and it's not fair that this man is such a work of art and I'm about to give up a chance of one night with him.

'Sorry, we can't do this. Fuck, we work together Johannes!' I swear I hear the moment his teeth clench together, the excitement fading from his face so quickly it's like I imagined it. What was I even thinking? This job, this job is all I have.

'You weren't saying that five minutes ago when you were sucking my face.'

And now he's being pouty, which I hate to admit looks really fucking good on him.

'I know, but I was in a horny haze and then my brain actually kicked in and remembered that the team would probably fire me for fucking their star driver.' Then what would I do? I'd have to crawl home to Tennessee with my tail between my legs to live in my childhood bedroom amongst the boxes of Christmas decorations and my mom's craft projects. I can't let that happen. Not even for what I'm sure would be the best night of my life.

He opens his mouth to speak, and then he must realise that

I'm right because he quickly pushes himself up off the bed, grabbing his boxers from where he discarded them not ten minutes ago. Shit! I don't want this to be awkward between us. Not when we've just started to find magic again on track.

Wordlessly he grabs the remainder of his clothes – he doesn't even bother to put them back on, just exits the room without looking back. The door clicks behind him and I start to drown in the heaviest silence imaginable.

I huddle under the duvet for comfort, but I'm wrapped in the sweet and spicy scent of Johannes Müller. It fills my senses and teases me with all that could have been.

I don't sleep a wink.

The silence continues at quarter to five the next morning as we move awkwardly around the kitchen, avoiding physical contact at all costs. I've become used to there being a slow country song serenading the cooking show Johannes usually puts on for breakfast, so the bitter quiet is deafening.

I can't think of the right words to say, and I hate how weird it already feels between us. What will it be like once we get back on the track? When I'm talking in his ear? When I need the feedback he gives in order to help him and the car perform at their best? Will he retreat into stony silence again?

My stupid big mouth went and ruined what could have been an incredible night with a god-like man who seemed to want me too. How many times in my life will that happen? Once is already more than I deserve.

And now we're stuck together.

My chest aches as I glide my suitcase towards the front

door. Seven days ago, I was anxious about accepting his invitation to stay here and now I wish I could go back and relive it – again and again and again.

Johannes nurses a travel cup of coffee, leaning against the very same counter he leant against last night while we made pasta, while his finger rubbed lazy circles on my skin and I felt my whole body come alive. I wish I could go back and—

What? Choose differently? Have one night together and then get fired from my dream job and blacklisted in the industry? No, of course not. But this is torture.

I avert my eyes from his masterpiece on the wall as I gather a notebook I left in there earlier in the week, poking it into my backpack before sweeping the penthouse one more time to make sure I have everything. I don't need to be leaving excuses to come back.

'Car's here,' I say as the notification pings on my phone. I allow myself one last glance around the kitchen. I want to catalogue all the memories we've created in here so I can relive them in my mind when I need something to get me through what lies ahead. I reach for the handle of the front door, still unwilling to leave behind what we had here.

'Hey, wait a second,' Johannes finally says, breaking his silence.

My heart leaps. He feels it, too, this sadness. I know he does. I turn, ready for him to say whatever it is he wants to get off his chest – an apology maybe? Not that he owes me one. Maybe he wants to forget anything ever happened. He probably already has. I have no doubt I'm making way more of this than he is.

My fears are confirmed when he abandons his suitcase next to the door and disappears towards his bedroom, returning a few seconds later with his charging cable, dangling it in the air between us to indicate his relief that he hadn't forgotten it.

Well, I guess that's what passes for closure around here.

We sit as far apart as is possible in the back of the car to the airport and then he plops himself down next to Nils at one end of the plane and I force myself into the seat next to Ian at the front, who eyes me, like he's not sure what I'm doing sitting here when the last few flights I've sat with Johannes. But he doesn't question it, for which I'm thankful.

Ian's not feeling chatty at all. He puts earbuds in then opens out a newspaper across his lap. I'm glad. I don't think I have it in me to pretend I'm fine, anyway. I put my noise-cancelling headphones on and press the play button. I don't care what I listen to, as long as I can blot out the way my heart leapt when I thought Johannes was going to say something this morning – and then dropped when I realised he's probably given me no more thought than the cable he nearly forgot.

A song starts playing and I feel my stomach drop all over again when the country-mix playlist Johannes and I made together the other night starts shuffling. It has a good blend of the classics he likes as well as the newer, indie country I enjoy. This is not going to help me forget his angry words last night. Does he think I'm just a cock-tease? That's what he seemed to imply. That I was just playing games, when that's not it at all. He must know that if there's a problem between us, then *I'm* the one who'll get fired, not him.

Lainey Wilson's melancholy voice suits my dark mood all too well as I pull out my laptop to get some work done. Spa is one of my favourite racetracks and I know it like the back of my hand, but now there's an added complication and it wouldn't hurt to be extra prepared. Since there will be no getting away from Johannes no matter what I do, I decide to dive in headfirst and watch the footage of his last couple of races here. Last year he won and the year before he finished third. Both, podium finishes, but I want to see the difference in the two drives again.

With the ghost-car footage system we now use, it's easy to see where mistakes are made, and the second I get started I spot an issue. The first corner of Spa is one of the tightest hairpins and immediately I can see how much better Johannes was at taking it last year versus the year before.

But there's another factor: weather. Last year it was slightly overcast and a little humid; the year before, torrential rain. There's a poor decision, in my opinion, about tyre strategy, which works against Johannes when the rain clears up about two thirds of the way through the race. He started on pole that day, but the tyre mistake is part of the reason he ends up in third, overall.

We all make mistakes and human error is, well, human, but not to learn from those mistakes is when that becomes a problem. Our weather experts obsessively track the forecasts, but I'll raise this point in our meeting tomorrow. It's my job to think about all these things so he can focus on the drive. It's my job to give him the best possible chance at winning.

I spend most of the flight studying the footage, making note of things we need to look out for and ignoring messages from my mom about coming home during summer break.

I should go home. I really should. But Mom's still harping on about that doctor she wants to set me up with. I swear she'll suddenly discover an urgent medical condition the day I land in Tennessee and make me accompany her to an appointment she's been able to make at short notice. I'm not exaggerating – she's done this before. I love my family so much, but I wish they would let me be sometimes. I live a very different life to any of them – a good life, an exciting life, the life I've chosen – but in their eyes none of this matters unless I'm married with a pack of kids and a house with a yard where I barbecue on Sundays and watch football with my brothers.

There's nothing wrong with that, and none of them mean to make me feel like I'm a loser for not having it, but they don't care about F1 the way I do. They don't understand that it's more than just a job to me. It's everything. And I won't put *everything* at risk just so another fucking Brad, or Chad, or Jason can rip out my heart and leave me with *nothing*.

I close my laptop and rest my notebook on top of it as a particularly sad song comes on the mix. This is not helping, but I don't skip it. I don't want to forget our week together, even if it didn't have a happy ending. Brad can go fuck himself. I'm only going to feel sad about Johannes now. The cabin crew announces we're about to descend and I pack away my laptop and notebook, ready to disembark.

Nils's laugh echoes up the plane, and I risk a glance along the aisle to see what's going on back there, but all I see is a stony-faced Johannes staring back at me. His eyes have lost their sparkle – though how I can tell that from this far away is anyone's guess – and I hope he's not going to fall back into the dark pit of sadness that robbed him of what he deserved in first Spielberg and then Silverstone. It can't be because of what happened last night. I'm the one making it out to be more than it was, not him. I'm the one holding on to how special it felt. He probably cooks for guys all the time, fucks them, and moves on. Not guys he works with, but still.

Johannes turns into his conversation with Nils, leaving me feeling hollow.

Hollow, like when he left the room without even saying a word last night. Hollow like this morning when he refused to even look at me.

He'll be fine, I tell myself. I can't let this ruin the season we're building together. Keeping Johannes performing is what's important here, and if that means I have to grin and bear it then I will. Whatever it takes.

A small voice whispers inside my head – *Whatever it takes? Maybe you should have fucked him, then.*

No, I have to move on and forget it ever happened. I have to focus on the driver's championship and giving Johannes everything he's ever wanted. *Professionally*, I mean.

Obviously.

Chapter Thirteen

Johannes

So, apparently, I'm now the king of making mistakes with people I work with. What is wrong with me?

The wannabe principal of our rival team? My race engineer? What am I even thinking? Am I thinking? Clearly not.

Waking up in Belgium from a dream about a ginger-haired, green-eyed man with freckles across the bridge of his nose and skin that flushes pink and red when he gets turned on is like a bucket of ice-cold water down the back of my neck.

I really don't want to go on this run. But if I lie here, I'll end up doing something that future me won't appreciate when I'm desperately trying to forget that night. Thinking about him while I touch myself will only cement the memory more firmly in my brain, and that's the last thing I want.

No, a run will clear my head, get me set up for the day –

and I can get a coffee before Nils and I go to record some promo clips for this week's race in Belgium.

The villa is silent and still, the rising sun casting a golden glow on my bedroom as I pull back the curtains and dress for my run. My shorts are snug after a week of wine and carbs that aren't on my dietary plan, but I don't feel sluggish as I grab my phone and keys, tucking them into the back pocket.

I'm just pulling on my trainers when my phone vibrates. I ignore it because it's so early in the morning that whatever it is, it will either be from someone in a different time zone or the kind of news I could do without. But when it vibrates again a second later, I abandon my laces to retrieve it.

Unfortunately, it's from someone who's definitely in the same time zone as me, and therefore it's not good news.

My heart sinks into my stomach.

> Hey. I know we haven't spoken since the wedding, but I miss you so fucking much, Jo. I know you probably don't ever want to speak to me again, but things are so much more settled than I thought. I'm going to be announced as interim team principal over the summer break, and I can see I've fucked up losing you. I think I can have both and I just didn't see it before. If you have time while we're in Belgium, I'd love to spend some time together. Please.

I hurl my phone onto the bed. I would have flung it at the wall, but I need it. Who the fuck does he think he is? To text me that, *weeks* after what he did. Like a few meaningless words can make up for all the heartbreak he's caused? After every date he bailed on, every call he never returned, every text left unread? He dropped me like it was nothing, and he thinks *this* will somehow make up for it?

No chance.

I pocket my phone so I don't get lost on my run, not even justifying his pathetic message with a reply, and tighten the laces on my trainers. Now I really do need this run. I need it. Now.

Jackson Calder can get fucked.

I set my watch to an *outdoor run* and stretch out my quads. As I look up to decide whether to go left or right, I spot a lone ginger-haired figure waiting for me at the end of the path leading up to our villa, running tights hugging his long, lean legs and stupidly perfect ass. An ass that I've seen naked, that I've had my hands all over.

Fuck this.

Really, universe. Why are you testing me so much this morning?

I pause my watch so it doesn't track something inaccurate and make my way up the path to where he's waiting.

'Hey,' I say casually. I notice his hands tucked in the pockets of the windbreaker he's sporting. I think he's clenching and unclenching his fists. I don't know what he's got himself so worked up about. He's the one that said no.

'Hey,' he begins. 'Um, I hope I'm not intruding, but I thought you might be heading out on a run this morning. Is it okay if I join you?'

I really regret us talking so much about our love for early-morning runs – and specifically how 6 a.m. is the perfect time for them. I regret a lot of things.

He's trying his best not to look at me too much, but not to look away too much, either. I know, because I'm doing the same. I don't want this to be awkward. It can't be awkward. I need him out there with me, fully focused and ready to guide me to the top of the podium.

'Yeah, of course you can join me.' The words are said through gritted teeth because I'm not sure it's a good idea at all, but we need to get over this quickly or my track times will suffer. That's the brutal reality of the mindset that's required to be an elite athlete – and another excellent reason why you shouldn't fuck your coworkers.

But I'd be lying if I said I don't already miss speaking to him, and it's only been two days. In such a short period of time, he's become an integral part of my life. I spent years watching Kian build a deep bond with his race engineer, then Harper and now Elijah. I never had that with my last guy. He did a good job, but I don't think he ever actually liked me. This connection Caleb and I have developed is good for my racing – the result in Hungary proves that. And now that we know each other even better? That must be a good thing. I just need to keep it out of the bedroom. I can do that, surely?

I hear Caleb take a deep breath, but he doesn't say anything. He takes another one and rushes out with, 'Look, I really want us to carry on being friends and working well together. So can we just forget the other night happened and move on?'

It hurts that he makes it sound so straightforward, but I need to turn my brain off and stop thinking about how it never felt like that with Jackson. And how I've never felt so at peace with someone in my space. I have to. I have to if I want to achieve anything this year.

Professional, friendly relationship. Yeah, let's go, I think without enthusiasm.

'Yeah, absolutely. We can do that. I could do with a big win this weekend.' I nudge his shoulder with mine and the spark that jolts my body has me pulling away almost immediately. Okay, that was a mistake. I'm adding *touching* to the list of things I can no longer do with Caleb.

'Did you, uh, have a route in mind?' he asks, hands now tugging nervously at the strings on his windbreaker.

'No, not really. I was just gonna go for half an hour and turn back. You?'

'Sounds good. There's, um, this coffee shop like thirty-five minutes away I thought we could head to and then come back if you've got the time?'

'Sure,' I agree. It sounds very like a date to me, but at the same time it's just a coffee. I can gulp it down quickly and then once we're running again we won't have to talk.

'Shall we go?'

I nod in reply, not trusting my words. At first, I'm slightly behind him, but once I realise it gives me a great view of his ass jiggling – which almost sends me tripping up a kerb as we cross a road – I speed up so I'm slightly ahead. Much better.

Professional thoughts.

Come on. I can do this.

I focus my eyes straight ahead and think about my calendar for this week. I run through all the meetings we have scheduled, the race weekend, the fact that it's a sprint weekend and there's an extra eight points available that I desperately need to keep me in contention for the championship race.

I'm doing well, until we come to a stop in front of a cute coffee shop with a little outdoor patio area. It's got perfect vibes.

'Oh, this looks nice,' I comment as we step inside, the smell of freshly ground coffee beans hitting me.

'Yeah, it has great reviews.' We're the only ones in the queue this early in the morning so he orders his tea and I order my coffee and we quickly take up one of the patio tables.

He's researching good coffee shops? As a non-coffee drinker. This isn't fair. We just agreed to forget everything that happened and keep this friendly and professional. The way I feel about him doing this for me is neither just friendly nor professional.

'You okay?' he asks.

'Yeah,' I lie, desperate to push my thoughts back into the professional zone. I shake my head to clear it. 'Just starting to think about the week ahead. How much I could do with those extra points.'

'You've got this. I'm going to make sure of it.' He sounds like he truly believes that, too.

'I could do without all the media commitments and that documentary filming.' I don't usually mind the documentary people being around, but I know they want us to film some reactions to the last bunch of races and I'm not sure I'm ready to answer all the questions that will undoubtedly be posed about my performance recently.

'Did they tell you they're doing a whole episode on the support teams this year? Apparently, it's like a 'behind the pit wall' kind of episode. They want to get footage of the race engineers, strategists and principals.'

'Makes sense. Unsung heroes and all that,' I say. I can already picture it, especially with the members of certain teams who already have a solid public profile, like Cole and Ash.

Oh. And Jackson. Fuck's sake. They'll lap that shit up, I

think. The handover of power from father and son. That's one episode I'll definitely be skipping.

'I've signed the form to be interviewed,' he says with an artless enthusiasm that's incredibly charming. 'Fingers crossed I don't come across like too much of an idiot.' He swirls his tea but doesn't meet my eye.

'You won't. You're way too smart for that. I'm sure you'll dazzle them with all your –' I wave at his face before realising what I'm doing '– expertise.'

He's downright gorgeous. The girls and the gays will absolutely lap him up – expertise or not.

'I've never done anything like it before. I hope I don't look too nervous.'

'You'll do great,' I say with an encouraging smile.

He smiles back, unconsciously reaching over to me – I assume to touch my hand – but at the last second, a flicker of remembrance flashes over his face. His face flushes – adorably – and he yanks his hand back.

'We should probably head back,' he says suddenly, standing up so fast his chair makes an ugly screech against the patio.

The run back to the villa is fast, as though we're both trying to outrun what's happened. The second I step through the door, I'm met by Nils, arms folded and already dressed to go for the day. 'Where have you been?' he demands.

'For a run?'

'It's quarter to nine. We have to go in five minutes. I've sent you like a hundred texts, you asshole. What gives?'

It's really something when I'm being lectured about being punctual by Nikolas Beck, king of making us late.

'My phone's on silent.' I don't tell him why it's going to stay that way for the foreseeable.

'Take a shower. You stink.'

Once I'm clean, I dress in an appropriate outfit for media, making sure I add my brand-partnership watch and join Nils at the front door.

'Hey, Jo, are you okay, man?' he asks, as I pull on some smart black trainers. 'You've been quiet since we got to Belgium. It seemed like you were doing better but now…'

Little by little, Nils has become one of my closest friends. When we first became teammates more than three years ago and he was this bratty teenager trying to follow me around to all the cool clubs with Harper, I had no interest in being pals. Now, I can't imagine life without him. We spend so much time together and he's really grown into an awesome person. I know he's asking because he genuinely cares.

'I appreciate you asking,' I say, 'but…' I don't want to tell him too much, but I think it's probably time to tell him something. 'There was a guy – *is* a guy, I guess. I don't know. It felt really good and I thought maybe it might go somewhere but, you know, things don't always work out the way you hope.'

He contemplates that for a minute, pausing with his hand on the doorknob. I hope I haven't said too much but he just shakes his head.

'Honestly, Jo, you deserve a guy that's going to treat you right. For a while recently, you've seemed happier than I've ever seen you, and I hate to see you become sad again. If he makes you happy, if there's a chance it could work, isn't that worth taking?'

When the hell did Nils get so wise? I feel like a proud big

brother, because three years ago he'd have given me some cocky answer about getting under someone else being the best way to move on. I think about making pasta with Caleb, about the moment our lips met for the first time, how enthusiastically he kissed me back. I know I didn't imagine that.

'Plus, the sex must be sensational to put a smile like that on your face.'

Oh, there he is.

I ruffle his wild blond hair and shove him out the front door, because now we really are going to be late.

Chapter Fourteen

Caleb

I love the thrill of a sprint weekend, but only having one practice session is not fun at all. Especially not on a track like Spa and in my first year as Johannes's race engineer.

He was absolutely superb last night in sprint qualifying. In rounds one and two he was the best driver on track, but in the final round – the one that counts – Elijah pipped him to pole by one thousandth of a second. It was a stunning lap, and I'm sure Johannes and I will sit down and watch it at some point and pick apart what makes Elijah so good in these sprint races, but there's no point dwelling on it now.

In the actual sprint race, things didn't go quite so well. He finished third and I know he's pissed. I wish I could have done more for him today.

He's frustrated, not because things didn't go well out there for him, but because they did go well and it still wasn't enough. He, Harper and Elijah all finished within half a second of each other – but at this level, a fraction of a second is the difference between first and third. Elijah comes alive over shorter distances and Harper is, well, Harper.

'Hey,' I say, grabbing Johannes's arm as he storms towards the garage. 'You were brilliant out there. The time sheet tells everyone exactly how good you were.'

'It wasn't enough though, was it? I needed all eight of those points.' He stops and sighs, leaning into my touch on his arm and I hate how good it feels. I hate that I want to pull him towards me and hold him close.

'It's still points, and that's better than no points, Jo. Go and clear your head then put this behind you. Don't let sulking over eight points cost you the twenty-five up for grabs in the main event tomorrow. The sprint is over. Focus on qualifying this afternoon.'

It's perhaps a little more than I meant to say, and a bit tougher than I've been on him in the past. I decide to get him a special coffee and a piece of cake for after to make up for it.

I don't see him again until qualifying as he's busy with media and warm-ups and then suiting up again, but I left his treats on the table in his room, the usual spot – he can't miss them.

The next day, the focused and fearless Johannes I remember from his pole position races appears in the cockpit. He actually cracks jokes over the radio. It's deeply refreshing.

He even *listens* when I suggest we move to strategy B, a one-stop technique that means he has to really nurture the tyres after a poor first stop costs him a whole bunch of time, giving Harper the lead of the grand prix for almost fifteen laps.

He approaches the Eau Rouge – the Spa circuit's most thrilling blind summit – with all the confidence of a man who laughs in the face of danger. When you come over the crest of the hill, you have no idea where you'll come out, so it takes balls – serious balls – to attack it the way Johannes does. It's even more satisfying when he crosses the line five whole seconds ahead of Harper. He's on a real high when he climbs on top of the car and pumps both fists in the air.

I'm too far back in the throng of team members crowding him as they celebrate the win. The closest people get hugs, but we lock eyes for the briefest of seconds and I feel that look right down to my very core. He deserves it, I deserve it – our risks paid off today. It's the first time I believe our new friendship might not be a disaster after all, and it feels amazing.

Mostly, I just love seeing him back on top, nothing but pure glee on his face as they hand him his trophy. My stomach flips. I can't help but match his smile, mine filled with such pride that I get to be a small part of both this win and his life. We've found a good push and pull, that rhythm so important between a race engineer and his driver.

I'm not quite sure how, but he manages to soak me with champagne, even though he's on the podium balcony and I'm down on the ground, but is it even a good race if you aren't a little sticky afterwards?

Packing up the pit wall in wet clothes, damp curls sticking to my forehead, is less fun, but the glow of the win makes up for it.

I want to make light work of getting everything done because I still have two meetings before I can leave for the day, but before I can get properly started, Johannes joins me at the pit wall.

'I know it's you,' he teases as he holds up the

congratulatory triple-chocolate cookie and coffee I left out for him.

'Know what's me?' I reply coyly.

'Who's trying to fatten me up.'

'I have no idea what you're talking about.' I turn away from him, back to where the race footage is still playing on one of the screens as the software we use churns out stats for me to review later on with the team.

'So, you're telling me there's just some kind of fairy going round who knows exactly how I like my coffee and when I need something chocolatey, and it all started right after we bumped into each other at that coffee shop? That's not suspicious at all.'

Well, he's got me there. Not that I'm going to give in and admit it.

'If that's what you think.' I shrug my satchel onto my shoulder so I can fill it with all the last bits, but before my hands can get to work, Johannes is all up in my space, the smell of his shower gel filling my senses. His hand softly pushes the sticky curls off my forehead, then he places a light kiss to my cheek.

'Thank you,' he whispers, his gaze locked with mine. He probably should be checking that no one's watching, but I don't care. Maybe this is how he thanks all his friends.

For a couple of moments no one exists but us. It's a beautifully perfect world.

Then he takes a step back and without another word turns on his heel and heads back to the garage. My fingertips immediately find the spot he just kissed and press against the tingling sensation.

Shit. I pull my hand away because I'm not some teenage

boy who's going to fantasise about this. I remind myself he's already kissed me – on the lips. He's already had my dick in his hand, already pressed it and rubbed it against his own. This is not something to get worked up over.

Yet my cheek burns from the slightest graze of his lips, and it's enough to have me questioning my sanity.

What is he doing to me?

It's a good thing we have a summer break coming up next. I think we could both use a bit of distance, and it's come at the perfect time. Because to go out on a high like this sets us up for the second half of the season.

Four weeks apart will be good for us. Sure, there'll be some days at the factory, but I'll stay in a hotel and there won't be any candlelit dinners or 6 a.m. runs.

I had agreed to go to Monaco with Johannes and Cole and Ash and the rest of their gang before – a trip we organised back before things got fucked up between us – but maybe I can cancel? My mom's still bugging me about going home, so I could potentially use that as an excuse. I can catch up with my brothers and get some family time in. They'll be too excited about the football season starting up again to ask about racing, so there'll be no need to think or speak about Johannes. That sounds perfect right now.

I'm about finished packing up the pit wall when Harper approaches me from the garage beside ours.

'Congrats,' he says ruefully. 'I thought you'd be with Johannes already?' My hands freeze on my laptop where I'm about to tuck it into its case. Does he know? Did Johannes tell him? I know they're best friends, but for fuck's sake, he should have told me!

I eye Harper for a second, trying to work out how much he

knows. 'Because of his win,' he adds, miming that he's been stabbed in the heart. Of course that's what he means.

'Oh, yeah, I'll be there shortly. I just like everything to be sorted first. Congrats to you too – and Elijah. You raced well today.'

He acknowledges my words but he's obviously already thinking about what's next.

'Oh, before I leave you to it. I stepped out to FaceTime with Kian before I spotted you. He reminded me the new farm shop he's opening with his brother-in-law is launching in just over a week and he could do with a few high-profile guests to make a splash. I've asked Jo and Nils, obviously, but thought you might like to come? Cole and Ash will be there, too.'

I should say no. I don't need to be seeing Johannes any more during the summer break, but this is what I wanted, right? At the start of the season, when I felt alone and envious of the friendships other people seemed to have developed. I was dying for friends who got what this world was like. That's what this group is. It's perfect, and I actually really like being a part of it. But neither me nor Johannes can afford a repeat of the other night. Not when things have finally started to go right.

'I'm heading back to the States for a couple of weeks,' I say, 'before we all go to Monaco. Otherwise, I won't see my family again till Christmas.'

Harper is so easy-going he doesn't even seem to notice the rejection.

'No worries, man. I get that. Family's important.' I nod along with him to show understanding, but I'm already wishing I could take it back and accept the invitation. 'Enjoy the break.' He offers me his hand and then pulls me into a full-blown bro hug, before disappearing back to the Hendersohm garage.

I'm proud of myself for staying strong, but just in case I'm less strong later, I pull out my phone and buy a ticket home for the Friday evening after we finish the week at the factory. Then there will be no excuse to spend any time with Johannes. And by the time we meet again in Monaco, that night will be long forgotten.

I have to laugh as I make my way back to the villa because at this point, I'm not even convincing myself.

Chapter Fifteen

Johannes

It's the first time I've been back to the penthouse in London since that awkward morning with Caleb. It's so quiet, but my ears ring with the echoes of Caleb laughing at my jokes, singing out of tune to country music, and explaining the statistical method of his PhD research.

It's disorientating and probably why I can't take it for more than a few days. I invite myself to stay with Harper and Kian for the rest of the time. I'm sure Harper was surprised by my request but he doesn't pry. He puts me up in the guest room, which is still as beautiful as ever. I can't believe that Kian gutted and redecorated this place mostly on his own. It's now the perfect home for them and I know they already have plans to extend the cottage to prepare for when they have kids.

I take lots of long walks to give Kian and Harper the privacy they probably thought they were going to have over the summer break. Not that it's a hardship – the land they live on is gorgeous. I even select my favourite sheep – Elise tells me her name is Bonnie – and I always look out for her in the field.

I cook for Harper and Kian every night as a way of saying thank you. Some nights I cook up at Elise's for the whole of the Walker crew. It's literally the least I can do.

'I forgot you can cook like that,' Harper says on a night when it's just the three of us in the cottage. Kian fully leans back in his chair, hands rubbing his stomach like he's an old man with a beer gut.

'Yeah, I guess it's been a while.' I too am completely stuffed and know I'm going to need a big old run tomorrow morning. For some reason they just don't hit the same anymore, now that I'm doing them on my own again.

'I'm so glad you two are leaving tomorrow. I need to get back to eating salmon and salad,' Kian says with a groan. 'Jo, you're gonna make a great house husband one day.'

'I can't believe you didn't cook for me like that all the time when we lived together,' Harper says, mock-petulant.

I roll my eyes.

'It was a different time,' I say, and it makes me feel a hundred years old.

'Sure was,' says Harper, eyeing his handsome husband. Kian puts his hand on Harper's thigh and squeezes.

I see the look they exchange and say quickly, 'I'm gonna head out for a walk and ring my folks. Harper did you sort the car for six?' We're annoyingly on a 10 a.m. flight to Monaco from Stansted, which is a bit of a drive.

'Kian booked it.' Of course he did. I shouldn't be surprised.

Harper doesn't even wait for me to get my trainers on

before he pulls Kian towards the bedroom. I hear them shriek and laugh as they tear each other's clothes off, and while I'm happy for him, I'm also insanely jealous of everything he has here.

I want what he has, but I want it with—

I don't let myself finish the sentence.

I'm kind of glad when we land in Monaco and it's just the guys. I don't want to be reminded of everything I want but don't have. And then in walks Caleb and he is everything I want but can't have.

Fuck.

For the first couple of days, we're very good about keeping our distance. He's just ... one of the guys. We go running together every morning, we play games in the pool with the other guys, we eat good food and drink expensive wine. We joke and talk and laugh like nothing ever happened between us, but the truth bubbles beneath the surface. Every day, the pressure builds, but we pretend not to notice. Fans snap pictures of us when we're all out together, and I'm reminded of why I don't have a place here like some of the other drivers.

Every day, Caleb's pale skin gets a little more sunkissed. Every day, another freckle pops out on his face. When we're all relaxing in the evenings, I like to make a mental note of each new one that appears. It's harmless, I tell myself. Completely harmless.

One evening, over dinner at a local restaurant, I watch him suck up a piece of linguine and I'm grateful for the napkin in my lap that just about disguises how hard I get. I feel like a teenage boy. By the time we get to dessert, my ankle happens to rest against his, and the merest slither of skin-to-skin contact has me on the edge of my seat, all my nerve endings sizzling away. It's torture, but the delicious kind, and I don't pull away. Neither does he. He must know it's my ankle. He must know. He can't not know. I feel like I've been branded and the creeping lush on his cheeks tells me I'm not alone. It makes me feel reckless.

Everyone's buzzed when we get back to the apartment, but one by one the others call it a night or slink off to call wives, girlfriends and husbands.

When Harper plants a kiss on my cheek and tells me he's going to call Kian, I am the only one left. Of course I am.

I carry the glasses and empty bottles into the kitchen and start loading the dishwasher. It's like living with teenagers. I crash about resentfully, making no attempt to hide my frustration. I'm not really mad at them. I just wish I had someone of my own to call.

Once it's all done, I slope off to bed, but find myself pausing outside Caleb's bedroom. I contemplate knocking. No one would know. The guys are all busy on the phone or already passed out.

It doesn't have to mean anything. Just like the ankle graze at dinner didn't mean anything. Or the way Caleb clenched his thighs around my ears the other day when we partnered up in a game of shoulder wars in the pool. And of course I had to hold on to him, tightly, otherwise he'd have fallen off as soon as Ash made contact. It's not like I threw my head back to feel his dick against the back of my neck – at least, I did, but it doesn't have to mean anything, right?

Sun plus booze plus Caleb is a dangerous combination. I'm already hard and all I'm doing is standing like a creep outside his door.

I don't want to ruin the friendship we've built. The team's success is important to us both, but I'm desperate to get my hands on him again.

I raise my fist about to knock. Drop it down, then raise it again, and pause.

Make good choices, Johannes.

'I can hear you breathing,' says Caleb.

Well, shit.

'And I can see your toes.'

'Oh,' is all I manage to say.

I shift my toes back from the crack under his door.

'Sorry, I was ... contemplating whether this was a good idea,' I whisper into the space between us.

'It's not,' he says, but it comes out strangled, which at least strokes my ego a little.

'I can't stop thinking about you.' I sound ridiculous, desperate even, but I am a weak man.

'I...' He barely makes a sound, but I catch it all the same.

'I'm glad you're here, Caleb. I'm glad you came.'

'Me, too,' he says in a soft voice.

'The guys love you and I know they appreciate that you've got me cooking again.'

I didn't even realise how much I'd missed cooking, until I had someone to do it for.

'Thanks Jo. That means a lot.' He's started calling me Jo on this trip, and I love hearing it. 'I've not been very good at connecting with people in this world, but I'm grateful you introduced me to your friends.'

'You're welcome,' I say. They've all raved about him to me at one point during this trip. Cole and Ash have set up a padel game with him and Elijah tomorrow, and Harper's been picking his brain about a trip he and Kian are taking to America this winter.

'It's been nice to be included. And even nicer to have a break from work.' He did seem to be fully switching off. He even left his laptop behind so he couldn't work on his PhD.

'It looks good on you,' I say.

I hear a noise, but I can't make out whether it's a word, a movement or a choked swallow.

Eventually he says, 'So, I should probably get some sleep. Cole's booked the court for nine.'

He's right. Of course he's right. And he's right not to have opened the door. But there's something about talking softly to each other from either side of a closed door that makes this conversation intensely intimate.

'So, goodnight?' I whisper.

'Goodnight,' he whispers back.

I wait to hear if he moves away from the door but there's nothing but the chirp and buzz of cicadas from outside the villa.

I know he's still there. I might not be able to see him, but I can practically feel his presence behind the wood keeping us apart. I can hear his breathing in rhythm with mine. I press my hand against the door and wonder if he's doing the same.

'Just so you know,' I whisper, 'I really want to kiss you right now. I know all the reasons why we shouldn't and you're right about all of them. But I still want to.'

I hold my breath.

Do I imagine it or does he say, 'Me too?

I wait, but he doesn't say anything else. I drop my shoulders in resignation, which makes my head thud dully against the door.

'What was that?' comes his whisper, sharper now.

'Just my head,' I reply.

I hear him stifle a laugh.

'It's not funny,' I murmur.

'If you say so,' comes his response, as well as a little snort. There's nothing like the need to be quiet to make everything even funnier.

'I'm going now,' I say.

'Okay.' A pause. 'Goodnight, Jo.'

I go to move when I feel a sudden pulse of cool air as he yanks open his door and I turn to meet him. He presses his mouth against mine and lets out the tiniest grumbling sigh, which is the biggest fucking turn-on. He's shirtless, his nipples a dusty shade of pink and very erect. He's so beautiful. It should be illegal.

I run my hands up and down his back while we devour each other hungrily. His fists ball up my T-shirt as he pulls me close and possesses my mouth with his. It's fierce and fiery and everything I've dreamed of. I grab his ass and press him against me so he can feel just how hard I am. I'm not thinking – there are no thoughts, only actions and reactions. Only mouths and tongues and hands and bodies.

Anyone could come out and catch us, which only makes it more thrilling. I groan into his mouth. It's louder than I intended and the sound bounces down the tiled hallway.

We break apart, panting. I'm so fucking hard. I ache for

him. I want to feel his mouth around my cock, sucking and licking and swallowing. Did I think that, or say it out loud? My pulse is pounding so hard in my ears that I'm not sure.

But then, just as suddenly as he appeared, Caleb is gone and the door is closed in my face.

Fuck.

Chapter Sixteen

Caleb

For the first time in more than five years, we are in France for a Grand Prix.

I wish I could say that the lead-up has been productive, except that's not the case. It's been heavily overrun with filming for the documentary series.

The handful of race engineers who are being featured in this episode sit around in the documentary crew's motor home, waiting to be told what to do. This isn't a good use of my time. We need to be studying the track – which my driver has never driven – and practising on the simulator to get data to feed into the model, but here we are.

At least I have the company of both Cole and Ash. Cole is doing a whole piece about being the race engineer for the legend that is Kian Walker. I feel like there are going to be a lot of tears while watching that bit.

Ash kicks back in his chair. 'How am I already this tired on a Wednesday of race week?' He says between yawns.

Naturally, we yawn, too, which leads to the three of us laughing at each other.

'Honestly, I feel exhausted. A cameraman followed me and Johannes on a run yesterday morning.' It was the most frustrating and pointless run we've ever completed, considering we had to keep stopping so they could set up each shot. We even re-took a section because Johannes stumbled on a loose rock. I'd have kept it in for comedic relief.

'Don't,' Ash starts. 'Harper's enjoying it all way too much. He keeps pranking me every time the cameras are rolling.'

Now that doesn't surprise me at all.

One by one, we're called into the filming room. I am left till last.

When I enter a room with a green screen and I'm asked to sit on a small black stool in front of many cameras, lights and panels, I suddenly feel very nervous, indeed. They tell me not to be – helpful advice, thanks – and I'm asked to introduce myself.

'I'm Caleb Hughes, race engineer for Johannes Müller, RBF, for the 2027 season.' I click the action board shut and when they call cut, I'm already laughing at how unreal this feels. 'Was that okay?' I ask.

'Yep, first guy to do it in one take today. We're happy with that,' one of the women co-ordinating the shoot says. 'Ash told us his name was Ash Harper and then laughed for a solid three minutes before we could go again.'

I hope they put together a blooper reel, even if it's just for social media.

'We're going to throw a few questions at you, nothing

tough, just the basics about your job. You good to go?' another of the co-ordinators asks.

I nod, shuffling around on the uncomfortable stool and trying not to let the big light aimed at my face put me off.

'Tell us about your journey to becoming a race engineer.'

Okay, easy. I launch into a lengthy discussion about my love for the sport – about my brothers only liking football so I was the odd one out. About my degree, my masters, the PhD I'm working on, and my time as an engineer within the broader RBF team – and how I worked my way up. I know it'll be cut down to be more of a soundbite, but it's still kinda fun to really lay out how far I've come since watching my first race as a kid.

I'm a little breathless and I can feel my cheeks blushing as I finish my spiel. I wish I could control it. I hate how it gives away how nervous I feel.

They ask some more questions about the team, the season, the competition, the car – nothing I can't handle.

'Last one, I promise,' says the interviewer, whose name, I've learned, is Cassie. 'What's it like working with Johannes?'

That's the most obvious – but also the most loaded – question they could ask. So many answers filter through my brain. So many that I'm not allowed to say. I want to tell them that he's the best man I've ever met. That he makes the job easy in the best ways, and so fucking hard in the worst ways that I can't let myself think about. That he cares very deeply for the people he holds closest. That I can tell when he's being too hard on himself just by the way his eyebrows pull inwards. That he's a sensational cook. That I dream every night of his mouth on my cock, and it makes me so hard it hurts. That I would do anything – literally anything – to make sure he never again cries like his heart is being torn from his chest.

'Caleb?'

Shit.

My face floods with heat. I must be beat-red.

Shit, shit, shit.

I haven't said anything in like a whole minute.

Cassie repeats the question, and I pretend to consider it, as though I simply misheard it the first time.

'Johannes is one of the most incredible drivers I've been lucky enough to witness on track, and working with him is a dream.'

Does that sound like I'm gushing? It definitely sounds like I'm gushing. Shit.

'He gives great feedback, he's always willing to listen and he's not afraid to try new things. We trust each other – the whole team, I mean – so he can take those big risks that see him set records and top the podium. I've only been working with him for the last six months, but I hope we have many more years together.'

My throat feels a little raw and I reach for my water bottle to wash down the emotion that seems to have been drawn out of me.

The big light flicks off, which takes some of the heat out of the room, but my face still feels like it's burning. Did I say too much? Fuck. I'm so in my head that I miss what Cassie says as they start to fold up equipment.

'Sorry?' I ask, this time genuinely needing her to repeat herself.

'I said we're all good.'

I hop off the hard stool, stifling a groan because one ass cheek has fallen asleep.

'The team will show you where to go for the next part – the technical panel with the other race engineers,' Cassie says.

The technical panel passes in a blur, and I hardly remember any of it.

'You wanna grab some lunch with us?' Cole asks as we are finally released from the motorhome for the day.

'There's this deli place we passed on the main road out of Marseille,' says Ash.

'Fuck, yeah!' I reply, as we push through the double doors into a very warm French afternoon.

'Or not…' Cole comments, his eyes sliding to the lamppost holding up the guy who haunts my dreams every night.

'We'll catch you later.' Ash claps his hands on my shoulders and gives me a small shove in Johannes's direction.

Do they know? I feel a sudden wash of panic, but I tell myself even a blind man could see there was chemistry between us in Monaco. It doesn't mean they know about the … other stuff.

But, then, I don't care, because *he's* here. Even if we can't be anything other than friends, he's waiting for me. I can't even comprehend why that means so much to me.

'Thought you might be hungry,' he says. 'Filming can be more exhausting than an actual race. So much waiting around.' He's not wrong – I've hardly had to use my brain at all today and yet I feel like I could fall asleep standing up.

'Did you come all this way just to take me out for lunch?' I tease.

'I had a meeting with some of the higher-ups and my agent – contract negotiations, ya know.' He shrugs, but there's a small smile tugging at his lips, so it must have gone well.

Apart from Spielberg and Silverstone, he's having a good season and I don't see any reason why RBF would not want to keep him on. Nils already has two more years on his contract here and him and Jo work together as perfect teammates. Why sacrifice that?

Unless he gets caught acting unprofessionally with another member of the team. Especially his race engineer, I quickly remind myself. Although, I'm pretty sure that I would fare worse if we ever did do anything stupid and management found out.

They aren't going to get rid of their star driver. Especially if he manages to bring home the championship this year.

'So, lunch?' He suggests again pulling me out of the panic I could easily spiral into if I think too much about it. I really can't afford to risk this job. That's a thought that needs to stay front of my mind.

'Uh.' I should say no. I really should say no, I should go back to my room and do some more tape prep for this weekend, but then my stomach grumbles and the pull towards Johannes is too strong for me to resist. 'Yeah, lunch sounds good.'

He tells me about a spot where they make fresh focaccia, complaining that he's never been able to make it as well himself.

'Maybe when the season's over, I'll get back into bread making. Kian cooks these amazing, land to table meals, and when I was there last month I was inspired to get back into fresh eating. I mean, Kian literally went out and retrieved the eggs we had for breakfast one morning.'

'You want a farm?' I can't quite picture Johannes, all manicured and stylish, working with animals.

He shakes his head, laughing around a bite of a very meaty-looking sandwich. 'No, not at all. I don't wanna have to get mucky every day. I mean, like, making things from scratch sounds good to me.'

I can't help picturing his strong hands as he guided me in the use of the pasta machine and how ridiculously sexy he looked doing it. I swear, I remember every popping vein in his hands and forearms.

We finish the sandwiches and reluctantly start to head back.

'Thanks for lunch,' I say as we linger on the path outside the café. 'You need a lift back?'

'Nah.' He shakes his head. 'I'm meeting Nils to help him pick out some clothes. Maybe he'll actually wear something that doesn't look two sizes too big if I choose it for him. I'll see you at the track.' He goes in for a full hug at the same time I do – a sideways bro hug – and the confusion and clash of body parts means there's some fumbling before his head falls to my shoulder and he holds me tight.

It's the least 'just friends' hug I've ever received from someone. His fingers dance along the dip in my spine and it makes me clench my hands around the back of his shirt. If someone, anyone, who recognised him sees us like this, it would not be a big leap to assume something's going on between us.

Which is why I have to break free from the hug before I do something stupid like wind my arms around his neck and kiss him.

'See you tomorrow,' I call out, abruptly abandoning him as I power-walk back to my car.

I try to limit our alone interactions for the rest of the weekend, but it does nothing to stop my feelings growing. This is bad. Really bad.

And it's even worse watching him fly off the blocks in pole position, several car lengths already between himself and Harper as they go into turn one. It's chaos a little further back as Nils overtakes Elijah to take that shock eighth place qualifying position. Elijah's gone from that big-sprint win and those huge, eight extra points, to struggling to hold on to any points at all in this race. It shows just how fast things can change in racing and why it makes such an exciting spectator sport.

Just to make things worse for Elijah, he drops it into turn eleven on lap eight and very quickly ends up in the barriers. It annihilates the six-second lead Johannes has built up over Harper as the safety car is deployed whilst Elijah's car is rescued and we all bunch up again on the track.

Johannes grumbles frustratedly, even as he checks in to make sure Elijah's okay. We decide not to pit, just eight laps into the grand prix, despite the fact it would be a cheap pit stop, and the pack of five trailing behind us follows suit.

I listen in to Elijah's radio from just after the crash, and the scream of '*Noooooo*' when he realises he can't reverse out of this with the damage he's sustained is bloodcurdling. He will be all too aware of how much this hurts his championship title challenge, especially with how vigorously both Johannes and Harper are battling now.

Luckily, that's the only chaotic part of the race and Johannes maintains the lead for pretty much every lap, except when he pits before Harper. Just two laps later when Harper pits, Jo steals it straight back.

Harper goes for a late lunge on turn one of the very last lap, but runs out of straight to make the move, and I breathe a sigh of relief. Johannes's defensive game is nothing short of flawless as he blocks all Harper's last-ditch attempts to overtake.

Watching Jo on top of that podium, the biggest grin on his face as he kisses the trophy, is almost painful. I have to look away or I'm going to end up falling into big, stupid love with him.

Chapter Seventeen

Johannes

After my win in France, I spend a week with my parents in Dortmund. My dad has a lifelong fear of flying, so they don't make it to many races, and even the closer ones are too much for them as they get older, but they are still the most supportive parents I could ask for and leaving them again was hard.

It's a short trip across the border to Zandvoort in the Netherlands. Harper flew in last night, so we're getting dinner together in an hour, just the two of us, which will be nice. I love our extended group of friends but it's rare we get to spend time like this anymore. That makes it feel extra special.

I'm about to head out to meet him when my phone rings.

'Hey, so I know it's meant to be just us two going for dinner tonight, but...' I wait for him to say that Kian's flown in early, rather than meeting us in Italy for Monza next week, or that Elijah's gatecrashing the evening. I sigh, though I've already accepted the inevitable. 'But, I just had a meeting with Jackson and, man, he's bummed out right now. I think he's really starting to panic about being announced as team principal.'

Wait … what? Is he cancelling on me to spend the evening with my ex? This is what happens when you keep secrets.

'We can go out another time, no big deal,' I say.

I'll stay in and game with Nils. No big deal.

'No, don't be silly. He's just going to come with us for dinner.'

That'll be a *fuck no* from me.

What the fuck is he playing at?

'Does he, uh, know that he's crashing a dinner out with me?'

'Yeah, of course. He needs this right now, Jo. I know you don't really know him very well, but he's a good guy. He and Kian have become good friends over the years. Ki's worried about him.'

I almost snort out a laugh at that. Don't know him very well? Like I haven't seen every inch of that man's body! Like I don't see through the charm to the asshole beneath.

'Sounds like you should take him out and you and I can catch up another time,' I say.

'Come on, Jo. Please?' Harper says.

Fuck my life.

This might actually kill me.

'Right, sure, fine.'

'Thanks, Jo! He needs this.' I need it like a hole in my head, but what else can I say?

'See you there,' I say tightly before ending the call.

I look at my reflection in the mirror. I'm wearing one of my tightest pairs of black jeans with a midnight-blue vest and sheer black shirt over it. I was going for an easy, casual vibe and I don't want to change to appease Jackson, but I feel very exposed and vulnerable right now. I want to pull on my comfiest hoodie and sweats to protect myself from him.

But fuck him, right? Fuck him.

'Are you okay?' Nils asks when I go out into the lounge where he's setting up his game console. 'You look a little grey.' I feel a lot grey, like I could be sick if I think too deeply about how tonight is going to go.

'Just tired, and I'm not very hungry, which isn't great as I'm meeting Harper and Jackson for dinner.'

'Jackson Calder?' Nils's crystal-blue eyes almost bulge out of his head as he springs forward, half a bowl of popcorn spilling over the sides and onto the armchair and floor.

'Yeah. Harper invited him because he's sad or something.' I'm impressed by how nonchalant I sound.

'And you're, um, all right with that?' The way he eyes me makes me feel even more sick. He knows. He knows. Fuck, he knows.

But wouldn't he have said something before now if he knew? If he'd put the pieces together before today, I'd never have heard the end of it from him.

I shrug, not at all convinced I'd be able to squeak out any more words.

'Do you … need an out?' He offers me a small smile before his eyes flit back to the screen.

Holy shit. Nils definitely knows about me and Jackson. He's never offered me an out before, because why would he? I'm not the kind of person who does things they don't want to do. Even my agent knows to pick his battles.

How long has he known? How did he figure it out?

Why hasn't he said anything till now? But the way he's handled it gives both of us plausible deniability and I respect him a thousand times more right now.

'All good, man, but thanks.' I slip on my trainers and make a hasty exit.

The restaurant is a thirty-minute walk. I'd planned to get a taxi, but I need the walk. I need some time to clear my head and mentally prepare myself for the evening ahead. Just a casual dinner with my best friend and his new boss, the man Harper has no idea is my ex.

Your standard Wednesday evening.

The walk does nothing to help me. As I get closer to the restaurant, I feel sicker and sicker. I stand frozen in the doorway. Harper and Jackson sit at a small round table, three beers already waiting, both laughing at something I can't hear.

It's hard to fucking watch. I hate Jackson so much. I despise the way he treated me, the way he strung me along. I despise how he made me feel about myself. He knew how I felt about him and he used it to take, take, take and give back crumbs in return. He was my first love, and he acted like that love was worth nothing. He made me doubt that I have anything to offer besides my body. He made me afraid to love again for fear it would be thrown back in my face.

Resentment coils in my stomach and I feel bitter acid rising up my throat. I have to swallow hard to control it. I haven't even made it to the table and I feel like I could throw up. How will I endure this?

I can't stop thinking about how many times he stood me up. Or pretended to barely know me at a party. I know exactly how many times he made excuses not to meet my parents because I counted. Twelve times. We were together almost three years, and he treated me like a dirty little secret.

And now he expects me to sit down for dinner with him and my best friend and act like he didn't break my heart? I swallow hard. I'll never be able to drink that beer if I can't settle my stomach.

As I watch him through the window, the only thought running through my head is that Caleb would never, *never*, treat me that way. Instead of engaging in a secret relationship conducted behind everyone's backs, Caleb explained honestly and openly why he can't take the risk. I understand and I agree – his position *is* more vulnerable than mine – and I see him struggle to stick to his principles every time our eyes meet or our ankles touch. And it only makes me admire him more.

There's really no comparison between Jackson and Caleb, and it makes my blood boil that I'm being manipulated into attending this dinner. What would happen if I went in there and told Harper everything? I allow myself to enjoy that thought for a second, but it's not fair for me to put my friend in that position with the new principal of his team.

Nothing else for it, I think, and square my shoulders then reach for the door of the restaurant when my phone buzzes in my pocket.

It's a message from Caleb.

> What you up to tonight? My head is hurting from reviewing tape and working on the conclusion to my thesis. Fancy an evening run?

I'm in no mood – nor outfit – for a run right now, but I do fancy getting the fuck out of here. I text back.

> Do you have a company car right now?

> Yeah why?

Thankful that he's fast on the reply, I quickly shoot back to him.

> Could you come grab me from this address?

I send a pin to him a few doors down, and with one final look through the window at the two of them sipping beer at the table, I get the fuck out of there.

I pace the pavement as I consider what I'm going to tell Harper as to why I'm not going to show, never mind how I'm going to explain to Caleb why I've asked him to come and get me.

I've already received three messages from Harper asking where I am and how long I'm going to be, and then eight messages that consist solely of a series of question marks.

I start typing but then delete the message and start again. I delete that too, and before I can start a third attempt, Caleb pulls up beside me and rolls down the window.

'Get in,' he says.

I do, and he pulls away immediately.

'You don't look like you're dressed for a run, so what's the plan?'

I don't have one. I can't even begin to think of one. 'I don't know. Can we just drive?'

I let out a long, slow breath. I run through every nightmare scenario that could have happened if Caleb's text had arrived just a few seconds later.

It's not fair that Harper's caught in the middle. It's not fair that I can't talk about this with anyone. It's not fair that Jackson gets to move on, seemingly untouched by our break-up. It's the stress of the job that's been getting him down, not dumping me. He was in there laughing and joking – completely unbothered by the prospect of spending an evening with me, while I was frozen to the spot, desperately swallowing down acidic bile at just the sight of him.

The motion of the car moving through stop-start traffic isn't helping my stomach.

I can't be sick in the car in front of Caleb. That would be truly awful for both of us.

I bend forwards and drop my head between my legs to stop the anxious waves of nausea that keep hitting me. It's not an easy position to maintain for a man over six-foot tall, but it's worth it when the churning in my stomach starts to ease. When I can finally sit upright again, Caleb's pulling into a parking spot next to the beach.

I'm out of the car before Caleb has even fully put it into park. I rip off my socks and shoes and jog along the beach a little way, enjoying the cool breeze of an early September sunset.

I face the sea and scream out my pain and frustration, scaring a flock of birds. When I feel hollow and empty, I drop to the sand, roll onto my back and close my eyes.

Caleb collapses beside me. I open my eyes to see him placing my socks and shoes by his side, then carefully removing his own.

Eventually, I am able to catch my breath and sit up.

'What's going on, Jo?' he asks gently.

Where do I even start?

'I just ... it's been an evening. I was about to walk in there and have dinner with my ex but I couldn't. I couldn't go in.'

There. That doesn't give too much away.

'Oh. Wow. Yeah. That's a lot.'

My hands are still shaking a little as I brush sand off my shirt.

'Then you texted and I panicked and ran away. I'm over him, but like, fuck, he seriously messed me up.'

Caleb brushes sand off my back, and the motion is soothing.

'It's why I overreacted when you ... you know ... the other night. In my apartment. In London.' As if there could be any other night.

His sand-brushing turns into gentle circles on my back, and I feel my body letting go of the hurt. I relax into his touch and then his arms are around me and he's holding me and for the first time since I answered the phone to Harper, my breathing feels steady, my heart stops racing, and my brain stills.

It doesn't fix any of my problems, but it does make me feel less strung out. Caleb doesn't push any harder for information and I'm grateful, because there aren't any words for this fucked-up situation. He's the most calming person in the world, I think, as I feel his peaceful energy sink into my bones. We sit there like that, watching the moon rise and the sky turn a deep shade of purple, until the air bites at my skin through my sheer shirt. I shiver and Caleb unzips his jacket and drapes it over my shoulders.

This is what it's supposed to feel like, I realise. Love. Not the stomach-churning uncertainty and self-doubt that Jackson convinced me was the thrill of a forbidden affair. It's perfect contentment in the arms of another while the world and its problems rage around you.

Chapter Eighteen

Caleb

We're at the point in the European slog when I wake up and for a moment, I'm not sure what country we're in. When I was an engineer and then a strategic advisor it was never this bad, never this intense. Now we're six races from the end of the season, after this one at Monza, and my brain is exhausted, but we're so close. Jo is back in second place overall and gradually creeping up towards Harper's points total.

Finishing second in Zandvoort was an absolute miracle considering the state I found Johannes in that night. He still looked a little fragile the next day, but by the time he was called up to do the first press panel, he'd bounced back like a champ.

I'm not sure exactly what happened, considering the complete lack of detail he gave me, but whoever this ex from the Netherlands is, he really messed him up. Seeing him so broken in that moment, though – fuck, it almost broke me as well. It took all my resolve not to swear on everything I hold sacred that I would never hurt him like that if we could just give whatever it is between us a chance. Except we can't. We shouldn't. That might solve his problems, but it doesn't address mine.

I wish I could have stayed wrapped up on the beach with him all night, but his skin was cold to the touch even after I gave him my jacket – a jacket he's still yet to return. It was just the two of us on the sand, waves crashing, sky darkening. I'd have liked it to be under better circumstances – but we can't have everything in this lifetime, it seems.

The perfect guy is being dangled right in front of my face, but RBF stands like a billion-foot tower between us. It's so tempting to try to slip through the tiny cracks that are showing, but I have to think of my career, my ambitions, my dreams. I won't throw it all away for a guy again, even if that guy is Johannes Müller.

So I'm back to trying to push Johannes into certain categories in my head. He's my driver, my running partner, a good friend. Those are the only acceptable boxes for him.

So why can't I keep the lids on?

It's Tuesday morning of race week in Monza, and I'm actually trying to make the most of the free time we have this week before the four days of chaos. Johannes and I ran yesterday and he told me he wouldn't be running this morning as he had a late media event last night, so I decide to have a lie-in. I eat a light breakfast and then set off with my satchel into the centre of Monza. The streets are beautiful, lined with small, independent shops that I dip in and out of.

I spend hours getting lost in the lanes, before settling in a café with a pastry and an iced tea. I open my laptop to edit my conclusion chapter for the fifth time. It's so close to being done. Then that'll be it. I won't be a student anymore. Every time I think about it, I feel sad. I don't want to be done with education; there's still so much to learn.

I'm about to let that sad thought take me back to my hotel room when my phone rings. The caller ID flashes up as Cole, so I quickly pick up.

'Hey, what are you up to today? I'm assuming you're already out here?' Cole asks and there's another hushed voice in the background, which I assume is Ash.

'Yeah, I'm here. I'm in town. Just grabbed some lunch. What about you?'

'Me and Ash are trying to round people up for padel. Harper and Johannes are out, but Elijah's up for it if you want to be our fourth.' I almost laugh at how many lonely days I've spent in foreign cities over the years I've been with RBF and now I have people who just randomly want to play padel with me on a Tuesday in Italy. How times have changed.

'Yeah sure, I'm in. Send me the location and I'll see you there.' I'll need to head back to my room to change first, but I've not strayed too far from where I'm staying.

'Cool. Can you be there in half an hour? I'll send you the place.'

When I check it out the location, it's walkable in fifteen minutes from my room, easy-peasy. I head back and change, and am still the first one there when the three of them arrive together a few moments later.

'What're you looking at?' I ask as they walk in, all gathered around Elijah's phone.

'Harper and Kian's official wedding photos. Kian just

shared the album with the guests,' Elijah replies and I see they're focused on a photo of the whole gang.

Kian and Harper are looking lovingly into each other's eyes, Elijah and his wife are the other side of Kian, then Cole and his husband, and Ash holding hands with his girlfriend next to them.

Standing on Harper's left, all alone, is Johannes, and he looks wretched. He's slapped on the fakest smile I've ever seen, and it can't hide that his eyes are a dull shade of grey and his fists are clenched. He looks angry, hollow. It's hard to look at. Then I remember how he cried on the plane after Silverstone. The morning after the wedding. What happened that night?

Elijah swipes over to a picture of Harper and Johannes, the groom and his best man. Again, Johannes's smile fails to reach even the midpoints of his cheeks. I hope he's not on his own when he looks at these. No one comments on how terrible Johannes looks as they flip through the album.

'Shall we play?' Ash asks, and I realise Elijah's put his phone away already and I'm just standing there, gormlessly staring into space.

We drop our bags in the locker room and head out onto the court where the match turns into a vicious competition, which I shouldn't be surprised about. I'm paired with Elijah, and it turns out he's a big old sulker when he loses. But it's fun to feel free for an hour or so – no racing, no PhD thesis, just my body feeling loose and excited to be here, with this group.

I'm sad when our time on the court comes to an end and we traipse back into the locker room and hit the showers.

I'm first out into the foyer, but I don't want to be rude and run off without even saying goodbye so I study the pictures on the walls and a noticeboard full of fliers. My attention is caught by a poster advertising a country-music festival in Milan tomorrow evening.

Now look, I don't believe in fate. But this has to be a sign, surely? Jo would love it, and so would I. I want to take him out and make him feel special. I tell myself it can only help his state of mind for the racing. Like that's why I'm doing it.

I google the festival and punch the air when I find there are still tickets available for it. I swiftly add two to my basket, but before I check out, I realise I should ask if Johannes is free first.

I craft a text that's casual but enthusiastic and explains why I think it would be good for him to go, but everything I compose sounds ridiculous – too formal, too jokey, too lame, too desperate. By the time I'm climbing in the car with the other guys for a lift back to my place, I still haven't sent the text. I'm probably running out of time to even ask, never mind buy tickets. He's probably busy anyway.

'You okay?' Cole asks while Ash and Elijah are distracted, squabbling over something in the back of the car.

'Yeah, just, I don't know, I'm very in my own head. This year, this job, it's not been what I expected.'

'In a bad way?'

I shake my head. 'No, not a bad way, just a lot. I feel like I have a lot to think about right now. Stuff I shouldn't be thinking about until after the season's over, but it'll be fine. Plenty fine for us to beat your ass this weekend.'

Cole laughs and rolls his eyes. It's big smack talk when his team are still looking likely to bring home both championships this year, but I'm nowhere near giving up on Johannes's chances.

'You're going to be fine. You're a smart guy, Caleb. You know what to do.'

I get out of the car and wave the others off, declining their invitation to join a big dinner tonight with everyone. I have a virtual meeting with my PhD adviser this evening that I can't put off any longer.

After the meeting, I tap out a casual text to Jo and hit send before I can rethink it.

Because fuck it.

Chapter Nineteen

Johannes

Italy in September is beautiful, cool breezes in the evening cutting through the heat from the day's rays.

It's nice to be out on a patio with the guys, eating and drinking all the stuff we really shouldn't before a race weekend. But we're all here and it's too nice of an evening to pass up. Nils has hung out with us so much recently that he feels like a regular part of the group, but tonight is the first night he gets to hang out with Kian in a causal, relaxed setting away from the track.

To say I'm a little scared of how excited he is right now would be an understatement. His face practically lit up when I invited him to dinner and he found out that Kian was going to be there.

'No hero-worshipping,' I remind him on the walk up to the restaurant. He makes me no promises, and the second we find the happy couple, the Hendersohm race engineers and Elijah out on the patio, he's gawking like he didn't share the track with Kian for a year. Yes, he spent most of that year right at the back, but it still counts.

But the second we get to the table, he edges himself into the seat next to Ki and is quick to start talking his ear off about his career and everything he achieved. It's adorable really.

We order pizzas and bruschetta to share and it's the perfect vibe for our first night in Italy.

'Okay, so, I have some news,' Elijah says, clinking a spoon against his beer bottle.

'You're a twat – we already know that,' Harper quickly pipes up, only to be pinched into silence by his husband.

'When you're quite finished?'

Harper mocks zipping his lips as Kian slips an arm around the back of his chair.

I ignore the little flip of jealousy in my stomach. I close my eyes for a second to re-centre and an image of Caleb holding me on the beach in Zandvoort pops up, causing me to shiver.

'So, I'm going to be a father. Again. Angie is fourteen weeks pregnant with baby number three.'

'Oh, man.' Kian practically hops up out of his seat to give his best friend the biggest hug. 'Congratulations. Hoping for a boy this time?'

'Nah, we're not bothered as long as they're happy and healthy. Angie's mostly just glad that her third trimester will coincide with winter break – so I'll hopefully be home for the birth.' The grin on Elijah's face is just pure ecstasy. Kids have never really been on my agenda, but I've seen how this man dotes on his and can completely understand why he's so happy.

'So happy for you, man! That's fantastic news.' I congratulate him, as the rest of the table offers up similar sentiments.

The conversation moves on to baby names. Nils is offering up a fun selection of Norwegian names for both genders, when my phone pings in my pocket.

Two new messages from Caleb. I feel like a giddy teenager.

The first message is nothing more than a picture, which is taking its time to download, but underneath:

> I know it's last minute and I'm not sure how busy your schedule is tomorrow night, but this seems like fate if you ask me.

I bite my lip in frustration as I wait, but then...

He's right. It's fate. A country-music festival not too far away, and I don't have anything on that evening that can't be moved.

I just wish it could be a date. I want us to go like any normal couple would.

I click back to the picture and can't help the grin that spreads across my face as I glance over some of the artists that are playing. There are a few I don't know, but a lot of them can be found on our shared playlist.

My phone chimes again and when I exit out of the picture, there's another message confirming he's got two tickets in his basket ready to check out and, God, I want to. I really fucking want to.

'And what is this?' Harper asks, waving his hand around in the vicinity of my face. 'Look at the way my Jojo is smiling.' Everyone snickers and I shoot him the middle finger, but he just uses it as an opportunity to try and snatch my phone.

Luckily, my reflexes are quick and I slip it back into my trouser pocket. 'What do we think, lads? Who is it making him grin like that?'

Kian's shaking his head at his husband, whilst the group laughs again.

'Right,' Elijah says, 'are we actually pretending we don't know who it is? Oh okay.'

That only sets everyone off laughing even harder. Fuck them.

'Oh, no, we all know,' Kian adds. 'You're not to pester him, Harper. He'll talk about it when he's ready.' He talks as if I'm not sitting right here. I hate that they all think they have any kind of idea what is going on right now.

'Remind me why you're even here again, Ki? Aren't you retired?'

He just laughs and I busy my mouth with my bottle of beer to prevent myself from saying anything stupid or incriminating.

'That sounded to me like someone's avoiding the question,' Nils quickly chimes in, and I shoot him my best death glare, the traitor. He's meant to be on my side.

'Why did I bring you again?'

'Because I'm awesome and you know it. Now, who's texting you?' He tilts his head and flashes what he thinks are adorably pleading puppy dog eyes, but that won't work on me.

'Just a friend,' I reply. It's not a lie. We are friends. Just friends. That was the agreement.

'Just a friend, my arse,' Harper snorts. 'We've all seen how much happier you've been since you became pally with a certain someone and how growly you got in Monaco when he was about to pull.' I'd banished the memory of some guy trying to make a move on Caleb when we went out for drinks one night. It's not like I actually growled at the guy, just stepped in the middle of them, cutting him off from touching Caleb at all.

Wow, okay, so they do actually all know. And have been letting me do my own thing at my own pace, which is kind of nice, But it's not like Caleb and I have been taking things slowly while we work towards a committed relationship. The only scenario in which we can be more than friends is if one of us loses their job – and that's obviously not an option. I'm sure the two other race engineers sitting here with us probably also think it's a stupid idea to be involved with a driver.

'Look, we just want you to be happy, Jo, and I don't think I've seen you this happy or excited in years.' Harper's eyes are earnest from where he's across the table.

Was it this exciting at the start with Jackson? I can't remember. It was … something. I'm not even sure how to classify it anymore.

'Your silence is speaking volumes over there. It's sharing time. Spill.' I shake my head at Harper. I know he's not about to let up about this, but I don't even know where to begin or how much I can say.

'If he's not ready, babe, you can't force him. How long did you keep us a secret for?'

Kian's not wrong there. I still remember the shock of hearing the pair had been sleeping together. Then I took one look at Harper, even though he was fairly drunk at the time, and I knew it was love. I knew that Kian was the one for Harper no matter how guarded Harper still was at that point. My best friend was radiating this warm glow, despite his tear-streaked face and tequila breath. He was in deep. And look at them now. Happily married.

Could that be me?

My silence is loud at the table, and I find myself looking at Nils in a silent plea to distract the table. He may be young and sometimes immature, but he gets the message and starts yapping on about some woman he matched with the second he got to Italy and how she's promised to show him the sights. The guys lap it up, speculating about the sights he'll actually be seeing this week, all while Harper glares at me across the table.

Guilt drips down my spine making me feel cold even in the Italian air. I've been doing this to him for the last three years. Shutting him out. Probably making him feel like an awful best friend because I won't let him in. But if I share even one thing, it'll all come spilling out, and it's not fair to put him in that position.

I shouldn't have to feel like this. Not now, not ever. I never should have.

'Say there was someone,' I blurt, interrupting Nils educating us on how to pull a woman – a topic half of us have no need of. 'Sorry,' I quickly add in his direction. 'I just, I have no clue what I'm doing.'

I let out a deep breath as I try to figure out where to start.

'Hey,' Harper says from across the table. 'It's okay. You don't have to tell us anything. I was just teasing. It's nice to see you happy, that's all.'

'I just … I really like him and we probably shouldn't even be thinking about being something other than friends, but we kind of fit. It's strange. Like, when we're together, it's like nothing else matters other than me and him. We share a lot of interests and hobbies, but also have differences that seem to complement each other. He lights me up inside. But he's also a really good person. He's so caring and he does all these little things for me because he knows they'll make my day better. I just want to be with him all the time and I think he feels the same way but there's too much at stake. For both of us. We can't be together. Cole, Ash, you get it, right?' There's sympathy on everyone's faces as I wait for someone, anyone, to say anything helpful.

'Okay, well, that's a lot,' Elijah comments unhelpfully and then winces as, I'm assuming, Kian kicks him under the table.

'You're telling me,' I mutter.

'Do you want to be with him?' Harper asks, like it's just that simple and maybe it is – or at least it should be.

And it's the easier answer I'll probably ever give in life. 'Yeah, I do.'

'Then isn't that all that matters?'

'Not really. What if it doesn't work out? What if it gets awkward? He's ... my race engineer, you know?'

'What?' Harper exclaims with mock surprise. Someone else around the table adding, 'No way!'

I shoot them all a look. 'It's the most important dynamic in the team, and winning is important to me.' I see nods from around the group. 'I know you all understand that because you feel the same way.'

'It's a fair point,' admits Ash.

'And that's only the part that affects me. If things get fucked up, it won't be *me* losing my job, it'll be *him*. Risking my success – even the team's success – is one thing, but risking everything *he's* worked for? *His* dreams? What would you do?'

There's silence from the group. 'No, seriously, please tell me, because this has been killing me.'

I look around at the faces of my friends and I see the uncomfortable truth reflected in them.

'I agree that none of that should matter. If you both want to try then that should be enough,' says Kian.

'But?' I say. 'Because there's definitely a *but* hiding there beneath all those *should*s.'

'But you have a point,' he admits grudgingly. I see a few of the others nodding, too.

'Kian!' exclaims Harper.

'Think about it, Harp,' I say. 'You know what it takes to top a podium. Nils, Elijah, back me up. It's fractions of a second. It's millimetres. It's a gram here or there. These tyres or those. It's the smallest disruption and you get shuffled to the bottom of the pack and then what has it all been for? It's the difference between P1 in Spa and P10 in Silverstone. We've all worked so fucking hard to get where we are. It's not fair to the team. And it's not fair to him.'

'That's fucking bullshit, man,' Harper replies.

'But he's not wrong,' says Cole carefully.

'To win takes sacrifice,' says Elijah. 'Everyone at this table knows that. I missed the birth of one of my children…' He looks down at his hands.

'I still say it's bullshit,' repeats Harper. 'You talk about sacrifice and fairness, but every single time we get in a car and race around a track, we ask ourselves, "What am I prepared to risk in order to win?" We look for slivers of opportunity and weigh up the odds, don't we? Ash? Cole? Isn't that what we do? We look for the merest fucking *slivers* of opportunity and we risk our very lives on those slivers because *that's* what it takes to win. All I'm saying is that Caleb is more than a sliver of an opportunity. You've had a couple of bad races this season and maybe that's made you afraid to—'

'Are you calling me a fucking coward?' I shoot back, standing up and stepping towards him.

'He's not calling you a coward. Are you, Harp?' says Kian, ever the peacemaker.

'Well, I'm not *not* calling him a coward,' Harp snarks.

There are a few sharp intakes of breath from the group.

'You risk *your* life, Harper,' I say coldly, 'but would you risk *his*?' I indicate Kian with my thumb. Harper jumps to his feet.

'YES! Of course I fucking would. Because I trust myself. Because I back myself. Because taking a risk is what got me this hot idiot in the first place.'

The tension is thick between us and you could hear a pin drop.

'Because maybe that's the difference between being at the top, like I am, and not being at the top, like you are.'

'Harper!' says Elijah, getting up in anticipation of having to referee a real fight between us.

I swear to God, I've never wanted to punch my best friend more than I do right now. I feel rage rising inside me. It's a blistering fury and it burns white hot, but mainly because there's a part of me that knows he's right. I stopped trusting myself. I lost confidence in myself. I clench my fists at my sides and feel the cold trickle of truth drip down my spine. I stopped believing in myself somewhere along the line because Jackson made me believe I wasn't worthy.

It's only since I've got to know Caleb, since we've become a proper team, that I've begun to find my way back to myself.

That I've begun to take risks again that have put me back on top where I belong.

'I don't know what the fuck's been going on with you this season because you refuse to talk to me,' says Harper accusingly. 'But that ginger hottie is the best fucking thing that's ever happened to you and if you don't take a risk on him, you'll regret it for the rest of your life.' He holds his hands up, palms out, as though he's said his piece and now he's done. He emphasises his point by sitting down and folding his arms.

I see the other guys looking back and forth between us, uncertain now about where they stand in this debate.

Nils puts up his hand, like he's a kid in school.

'What?' I say a little too aggressively, but my blood is still boiling.

'Just so we're crystal clear,' he says tentatively, 'I want you to know that I won't tell anyone in the team, okay? Or anyone who's not currently present.'

How did I keep Jackson a secret for years when I haven't been able to keep the way I feel about Caleb from the guys for a couple of months? I hope Caleb's okay about me telling them. I should have asked him first, but I didn't exactly plan to have this conversation.

'Jesus, man, you look like you've seen a ghost!! It's okay, you know? You and Caleb are fucking cute. He proper likes you. You should see the way you look at each other – it's something else.'

I melt a little inside, but then I frown at Harper who makes a dramatic gesture with his arms as if to say, *see, I told you so.*

I extend my middle finger at him and he huffs out a laugh.

I guess I'm going to that music festival after all.

Chapter Twenty

Caleb

J o's text comes quite late.

> Can't wait.

And now I can't wait.

At a certain point, I realised that despite our best intentions, we've already taken the leap, and all our careful self-denial means is that we're shouldering the risk without any of the reward. If things go sideways between us now because of the relationship we've already developed, he won't top the podium and I'll still lose my job, and then what will the point of any of it have been?

We've been trying to pretend we're still *just friends,* but the only people we're fooling is us. I'm so tired of wanting him and not being able to touch him. I'm so tired of the ache inside me when he skewers me with one of his heavy-lidded intense stares. I'm so tired of saying no when I want to say yes.

He's no Brad, of that I'm certain. And there are never any guarantees in life, are there? What would be the point of driving laps around a track if we already knew the outcome? I don't work in F1 racing because it's predictable; I do this job because it's exciting. It curls my toes and sets off fireworks in my belly – just like Johannes.

Ian would know, he's been here forever, but is there a subtle way to ask him? It's not like we're a small organisation, so I could be talking about anyone. He doesn't need to know it's Johannes.

'Hey.' I drop into the seat next to Ian as he sips his morning coffee, looking way more awake than I feel.

'Morning,' he replies simply.

It's just the two of us in our little cubby in the garage, both early for the pre-race engineer briefing, but I still keep my voice low. 'Uh, could I ask you something?'

He lowers his tablet and looks at me. 'Yeah, sure. How can I help?'

He's seen this team through almost three-hundred races so he really knows his shit, but the more I think about it, the more I'm worried he's going to dob me in straight away. But I need his advice or at least his factual opinion. 'I was just wondering if you knew about any rules in our contracts or within the team's code of behaviour that would prevent us, um, fraternising?'

Fraternising? Who do I think I am? The way he's looking at me makes me think I've definitely screwed this up. His brows knit together in an almost disgusted way.

And then I replay my words again. 'Oh shit, not us as in me and you, just like, say, two people within the RBF team?'

'Well,' he draws it out like he's really thinking about how to phrase his response. He's probably relieved that I'm not trying to seduce his married ass. 'I don't think there's anything in our contracts or behaviour code that strictly prevents it, so it's not going to get you fired, but I wouldn't recommend it.'

As fast as he raises my hopes, he dashes them. 'Why?'

'Because it would impact the dynamic, and if you two broke up, that would be bad for the team.' Why does it sound like he knows who I'm talking about when asking this question?

'It's just a hypothetical, of course.'

'Of course, but Caleb, my advice is don't do it. I know it's exciting right now because you're caught up in the rush of it, but it'll be a different story when it's over and a dark cloud hangs over you at RBF. They may not be able to fire you for it, but they can hold it against you.'

This is exactly what I said to Johannes back at his apartment. I've just been conveniently ignoring my own good sense because I don't want it to be true. They won't sack Johannes. Race engineers are replaceable, but superstar drivers are not.

I get all of my prep work done in record time, before declining dinner with a gang of the engineers. Ian sighs disapprovingly when I apologise for already having plans, like he knows I'm going against his advice. But I don't care. The only thing I regret is asking him for it in the first place.

My mom calls me on the drive back to the engineers' base after work and I'm practically giddy as I'm pulling into the car park to start getting ready for this date.

'Hey, baby, how's your day been? Up to anything fun tonight or just work?' she asks.

I'm almost tempted to tell her I'm going to a music festival with a super-hot guy who I'm head over heels about, but it's too soon. God knows, if I mention a man, she'll have the wedding planner booked before we hang up the phone.

'Not much, Ma. Got a dinner with some work people and that's pretty much it.' It's not a total lie.

'I'm jealous. I bet you're eating so well out there. Make sure to send me and your dad some pictures.'

'Of course. How was your day?'

She launches into a story about having the youngest grandkids over today, what Dad's been up to in the garden, and their plans for the evening.

'We've got Gregg and Kelsea and the kids coming for dinner, too. Dad's doing ribs and I'm making Mikey his favourite mac and cheese.' She explains that fourteen-year-old Mikey has decided to become vegetarian and my meat-loving family are still struggling to adapt to it. It's been a big affair in the Hughes household.

I listen to her on speaker as I pick out an outfit for the evening. It's still warm out there, but I also know that it could get chillier later so I go for knee-length, beige chino-style shorts with a white T-shirt and drape a hunter-green cardigan around my shoulder like a shawl. I'm just sad that I don't have a pair of cowboy boots on me. Lord knows, I have enough pairs back home in the US.

'What time's your dinner?' Mom asks as I rummage through my wash bag for my favourite cologne. It's tough to even get a couple of spritzes out as there's hardly anything left, but after a vigorous shake I manage to coat myself in it.

'Six. I'm just getting dressed now. When you have a chance, Mom, could you check the washroom cabinet in my bathroom to see if I have any Tom Ford Ombre Leather. I'm running out so need to know if I should grab another at duty-free or wait for winter break.'

'Of course, baby. Any more thoughts about getting your own place?' It's her second favourite question after when I'm going to find a husband.

I get it. I'm approaching my mid-thirties but it's not like I live in their basement eating chips and playing video games. There's just no point getting a place I'll spend all of a couple of months in each year.

'At some point, Ma. Just a bit pointless right now.' We've had this conversation so many times that my reply is automatic.

'The Davidsons are moving into a retirement home after Christmas. I'll send you the listing when it goes up for sale.' I roll my eyes, thankful she can't see.

What would I do with a four-bedroom house? I'm not even sure I could afford it on my salary alone, since I'm still technically in grad school. She's living in dreamland. 'You do that, Ma.' I'll take it just to have a little snoop at what the insides look like, but not much else. 'I'm going to have to head off, though, as I don't want to be late.'

'Have a great night, baby. Don't forget the pictures. Love you.'

'I won't. Love you, too, Ma.' We hang up and with a last once-over of myself in the mirror I'm out the door.

It's not that far to drive when I've got Luke Combs getting me in the mood for the night, and even when I have to park a bit further away from the restaurant I find it hard to be annoyed, because my whole body is thrumming with excitement for the evening ahead.

I'm almost giddy on the walk up to where we've agreed to get dinner, close to where the festival is taking place. I'm about to cross the road to the restaurant, when I spot a little stall selling glowsticks, feather boas and cowboy hats and I can't resist. They're plastic and flimsy and way overpriced at ten euros each, but I buy two hats before I can stop myself.

There's an idiotic grin pulling at my cheeks when I enter the restaurant and spot him already at our table. The second he sees me his eyes light up, and it makes my heart turn over. He spots the hats tucked under my arm and he laughs.

'I, uh, can see my … friend,' I tell the hostess, who lets me make my own way over there.

'Is that what I think it is?' Johannes asks, gesturing to the purple plastic.

'I thought they were exactly what we needed for tonight.' I pop them down next to him in the mini booth and blush at the fact that he can't seem to take his eyes off me. It's been so long since I've been aesthetically appreciated.

'You look really good, Caleb. I'm so used to seeing you in an RBF jumper or polo; the green looks good on you.'

I was told once, by my mom, that green complements pale skin and ginger hair, so I silently thank her for that.

'So do you, but then you could wear a trash bag and pull it off.'

'I once did for Halloween. I'm sure Harper has pictures somewhere.'

'Like you need your ego feeding with your millions of followers and international modelling campaigns. You have to know how gorgeous you are.' You only have to scroll for five seconds through Johannes's Insta comments to see thousands of people willing to tell him so.

'It sounds better coming from you.' His grin slips into something genuine and the way my stomach knots is ridiculous. It's so good to see him smiling again after how pained he looked just a few months ago. I can't help responding and I feel my cheeks flush with happiness.

'Now, what do you fancy?'

'I'm assuming *you* isn't the right answer?' His tone is so smooth, like butter wouldn't melt, as he looks me up and down. It's like we both know that tonight contains an implicit acceptance that we're no longer pretending to be just friends. It certainly feels like a date.

'I meant from the menu.' But it's too late. My face is on fire and I have to fan my cheeks with the menu.

'Mmm, of course you did.' He grins. 'I'm thinking of having the biggest bowl of pasta you can imagine. Coming to Italy every year is absolutely awful for my diet and my nutritionist hates me, but I can't stop myself.' I don't think he has anything to worry about regarding his diet. I've seen him naked, plus I know all his physical stats for the car. His body is magnificent.

In the end, though, he opts for steak frites whilst I go for a pizza with a burrata in the middle, because that just sounds stupidly delicious right now and nobody has my physical stats recorded on some computer program in the office.

'Busy day?' he asks as I settle back into my chair, our ankles brushing under the small table for two. My instinct is to pull away, but he locks my foot in place between his and even this small touch has goosebumps running up my leg.

'You know how it is, race-week fun. The days before the

race are very data driven, but I love Monza. One of my favourite tracks to watch you drive.'

'Is that so?' He strokes a foot up the side of my leg. He's not playing fair. We have a whole festival to get through this evening and now all I want is to drag him back to my car and finish what we started that night at his penthouse.

'You're really fishing for compliments tonight, aren't you? You're very needy.'

'I don't need to when you're so quick to give them to me.'

I shake my head at his cocky tone, but I don't miss the way his face lights up when he hears all the praise from me.

'How was your photoshoot?' I ask, I've already seen the helmet he's wearing this weekend and it's nuts. He loves a crazy helmet, but this is the brightest one I've seen so far. The fans are going to go wild for it.

'Not bad at all. The interviews this morning were harder than the shoot. It was for the documentary, and they love to ask me about Kian and Harper and I'm bored of it. Like, I want to talk about my racing not their love lives.'

I bet the documentary crew are gutted those two got married in secret and without the camera crew there. I bet they'd pay good money for footage of the event. I hope they don't get it, because I would hate for Johannes's sad, grey face that day to be broadcast all over the world.

'Their love story brought in a whole new audience to F1 and they want to capitalise on that. I'm not saying it's right, but it's good for the diversity and growth of the sport.'

'Harper's their man to talk to, then. Honestly, I didn't even know the wedding was happening until like just before.'

'That sounds chaotic and crazy stressful.'

'I can't imagine trying to plan a wedding in like a week

while my home country race is taking place and also trying to keep it secret from the millions of people who adore them.'

'From the pictures I've seen in the magazine spread, it looks like it was a gorgeous day.' I don't mention the album that Elijah showed us or how sad I thought Johannes looked. I want tonight to be perfect.

Something flickers across Johannes's face. There's a pinch between his brows and his eyes drop from where he was holding my gaze in conversation. 'It was,' he finally agrees, but doesn't expand on it.

The food arrives and we settle into a steady stream of conversation about how it all tastes, his highlights of being in Italy over the years and who we're most looking forward to seeing tonight.

Johannes gets the bill after I told him the tickets were on me and that I wouldn't accept any payment for them. On the way out, I slip on my cardigan, glad I brought it as the air has turned a little chilly.

'Hey, before we set off, I think we have to put these on.' He grabs the hats from where I've tucked them under my arm, and positions his securely on his head, before popping mine on, too.

His fingers stroke down my jawline making a beeline for the string to tighten it under my chin. My breath hitches. He really is the most beautiful man I've ever laid eyes on.

Chapter Twenty-One

Johannes

The festival grounds are alive with the sounds of guitars and people screaming in delight as we dip between different tents to see a couple of our favourite artists before securing a spot at the main stage to see Lainey Wilson, one of the headliners.

She's easily one of our favourite artists right now. I could listen to her all night. There's a thick smell of whisky in the air from one of the booths lining the paths between the stages and everyone is bopping and singing along as she plays 'Country's Cool Again'. The hats were a funny addition to our outfits, but almost everyone around us has one on. They also work to hide our faces.

I always feel part of something special when I'm out on the racetrack, but this is like coming home to my people as men around us tap their feet, swinging their partners round in smooth steps. It's maybe not what everyone expects from male model and race driver, Johannes Müller, but this is all I need.

She plays some more upbeat songs, before stripping it back to a slow one in 'Heart Like a Truck.' The atmosphere softens and people begin to sway together, husbands and wives wrapped up in each other as the lights dim to an evening glow.

This song in particular played too much during my break-up with Jackson. It's sad in the sense of her talking about how much of a beating her heart's taken, but hearing it now with Caleb standing next to me mouthing the words, it feels hopeful, too. It talks about dusting yourself off and opening yourself up to new love, more love, the love your heart actually deserves.

I think about what Harper said yesterday. I know he was baiting me by calling me a coward, but it takes bravery to keep your heart open after you've been hurt. I see that now. Caleb makes me feel invincible again. He makes me want to take risks again – on the track and off it, too.

Everyone around us is too caught up to care who I am or who I'm with, so I stretch my fingers out to graze his, giving him the chance to pull away. But when he flips his hand over and grasps mine, twining our fingers together, I squeeze back with all I have. I hope he understands how much this means to me. I wish I could hold him against me, but for now I'll settle for this.

'Hey,' he mutters into my ear as Lainey switches into another slow song.

'Mmm,' I reply over the strumming of the guitar. When I look at him he's got his phone out, ready to take a selfie.

'I want to capture this moment so I can remember it forever.' He swoops his arm up to get a good angle and we lean into each other, the rims of our hats touching as we laugh at the how they clash and get in the way. He takes so many I'm almost giddy, leaning into where he's clutching the edge of my T-shirt, wishing I could pull off this stupid hat and kiss him for all to see. For the thrill of it. For finally being able to take what I want.

'I'll send them to you later,' he promises, pocketing his phone again before slotting his hand back in mine. It fits perfectly.

For a while, I enjoy being anonymous in a crowd of strangers, just me and him and the music, and then the crowd goes wild and when I look up there's a man coming on to the stage and Lainey's introducing Keith Urban so they can play 'Go Home With U' to finish off the set. It's the perfect ending to a beautiful night.

We move in perfect time with each other and at some point, I shift behind him, my hands lightly resting on his hips as we sway together. I wish I could take him home with me. I wish we were going back to my London apartment tonight, where we were so happy.

'Take me homeeeeee,' I sing into his ear, lips brushing a spot along his jaw, and as he grinds against me, there's no doubt in the world that he can feel the way my cock perks up at his perfect little ass rubbing against it. I wish there was another act we could go see, someone playing some fast and dirty country music for us to get all sweaty and hide the fact that we're rubbing against each other, but now it is actually time to go.

We walk back to the car, recollecting our favourite songs and top moments of the night. I wish I had something for my hands to do rather than thinking about having them all over Caleb.

We play Lainey the whole drive home and I'll be making a playlist of all her songs before I sleep so that we can run to them tomorrow.

It's after midnight when he switches off the engine outside my villa. It's on the tip of my tongue to invite him in – after all, Nils has already promised not to tell anyone, so what harm would it do? But I want to do this right. I've already seen him naked, but I don't want our first time to be some quick fuck with our busy schedules for tomorrow playing in the backs of our minds. It's not what he deserves.

I want to see if my heart can fall in love again – this time without all the pain and hurt. I want to be brave enough to risk the sliver of opportunity we have, and I think he wants the same. But it's important that we're both on the same page about the potential consequences before we take any steps that can't be rolled back.

He unbuckles his seat belt and before I can even think about mine, he's at my door, opening it for me to step out. I swoon. *Swoon*. Find me a man that still does this? I've never experienced it, that's for sure.

We walk up the path together to the front door. 'I wish you could come in,' I mumble and he shakes his head.

'Not tonight.' It's not the same rejection that hurt me last time, at the end of our week in London. It's not actually a rejection at all. In those two words I hear the promise of a future opportunity, and that's all I need right now. I know what to do with *opportunity*, thanks to Harper's reminder.

'I had the best time,' I whisper into the silent night around us. 'Thank you for planning this.'

'Me, too. Nobody else I'd rather do this with.' Under cover of darkness, he leans in and I lean in, and every ounce of nerves vanishes. There's nothing but us on this planet right now.

The moment his lips touch mine, all thoughts disappear.

My hands cup the side of his face, cradling his cheek as I press my tongue into his mouth, deepening the kiss. I want to get lost in his mouth and never leave. His fingers burn the skin they've found under my shirt, and I feel an urge to press him against the wall of the porch and do something really stupid.

Instead, I tangle my fingers in his curls, pulling him as close as physically possible till we're bound together. I need to feel him, I want to taste all of him, but I settle for exploring his mouth. I swallow down every moan and happy hum as his hands slip into the back pockets of my jeans and squeeze my ass.

Fuck!

I want those fingers inside of me. I want *him* inside of me. It's been so long.

'Fucking hell,' I gasp against his lips as we break apart, both of us gulping down air.

'Yeah,' he confirms, and I'm glad that it's not just me who could feel exactly how perfect that was. How perfect we are together. I can't wait to strip him naked again and press my mouth on every inch of his skin to see how he lights up for me. 'I should go,' he says reluctantly. 'See you in the morning?'

'Can we do eight? I might still be dead to the world at six.'

'Of course. Sleep well, Jo.' He backs up until he reaches his car and slides into the driver's seat.

I throw him a wave. 'You, too.' I won't be able to sleep until

I sort out the raging erection I'm currently sporting and change my boxers, which are slick with pre-cum.

Only once I see him drive off into the night do I unlock the door and step into the villa.

'Oh, I was so right.' Fucking Nils. The twenty-three-year-old giggles delightedly.

'Shut it,' I say, but that only makes him laugh harder, which has me rolling my eyes as I kick off my shoes and tuck them under the cabinet by the door.

'You wanna tell me about your night or am I going to have to put the pieces together?' He gestures to the hat and then to the porch window where he just saw us kissing. 'You could have brought him in, you know? I'd have closed my eyes as you walked past and then put my noise-cancelling headphones on.'

'Shut it,' I say again, giving him a warning glare.

He backs off, grinning.

I retreat into my room so I can swoon in private. I got to hold hands with a man, in public, whilst singing at the top of my lungs to one of my favourite artists. We took pictures together. And yeah, we wore our cowboy hats most of the night, concealing our identities, but we weren't hiding.

I think I have maybe ten photos of me and Jackson from almost three years together. That's ridiculous. Caleb and I took more than that tonight alone.

I strip off my boxers and drop into my bed, the duvet tucked up under my chin as I change the background on my phone to one of the pictures we took tonight, thanking my lucky stars that Caleb has been quick to send them over. He truly is a stunning man. It's the eyes, the way they stare into the camera. It feels like they are piercing my soul, reading every single secret I have tucked away there.

I probably shouldn't keep this as my lock screen, but for right now I want to enjoy this moment. Every second of tonight plays on repeat in my mind – the dinner, the music, the dancing, the way he kissed me. I already have my hand on my dick and it's begging for a release.

It's not exactly hard to get off when I can still feel the ghost of his hands on my ass, the way he was grinding up against me earlier, the taste of his kiss. Those fucking green eyes. And then I'm shooting into my fist like a teenager with a dirty magazine.

I'd better do this a few more times before we do this for real, otherwise I'm going to embarrass myself.

What a hardship, I think and smirk to myself.

It goes like that most of the week leading up to the race. I am completely blissed out, and always hungry for more. We fit in a run most mornings, we time another lunch date perfectly and I sneak him into my little room in the garage for a short but sweet make-out session.

He always makes sure there's a coffee waiting for me before the race, but he delivers it to me directly, with a little peck on my lips before running back to get set up for the race.

Racing hasn't felt like this in a good while. Like it's just me and the car in harmony with each other, moving as one. Monza's never been my favourite track, but today I own it. When I'm on my last lap and Caleb tells me I'm fourteen seconds clear of my best friend, there's a fireworks level explosion of happiness inside of me.

First to Finish

I'm back.

I'm really back, and there's still time for me to be in contention for the driver's championship.

And it's all because of Caleb.

I see the chequered flag ahead of me and then I'm back on top of that podium again.

'That was for you, Caleb,' I say over the radio. 'Thank you for everything you've done over the last couple of months. I mean it, man. Couldn't have done it without you.'

I'm elated, almost saying too much on a radio that can be listened to by millions and millions of people around the world. I'm grinning inside my helmet, fist pumping outside of my car.

I embrace every second of the last bit of the drive up to the parking spot for first place, soaking up the noise of the crowd. Caleb's right there at the front, waiting for me, the biggest smile on his face. I want to leap over the barrier and into his arms. This man believes in me, even when I'm an asshole, even when I'm crashing the car into the barriers, even when I'm grumbling about my tyres and can't tell him why.

He's stupidly handsome with his green eyes and auburn curls. I need to stop looking before someone clocks the intensity of our exchange, but I can't look away. After giving the photographers that signature, climb up on top of the car winner's pose, I hurl myself towards those barriers and his arms are the first to find me.

The rest of the mechanics, analysts and our team principal roar in support, but all I can hear is Caleb telling me how proud of me he is.

I clutch the front of his shirt, hoping that none of these assholes drop me when we're just five races away from the end of the season and I'm making a great attempt at a comeback to be world champion.

But in the back of my mind, I just know that Caleb's got me; both up here and on the racetrack. I also know that if we're going to do this for the next two and a half months of the season, I'm probably going to need to stop looking at him like something I worship. Just in case management catches on and tears us a new one.

There will be plenty of time for us to celebrate together, just us. Plenty more wins. Plenty of time ahead for us.

Chapter Twenty-Two

Caleb

'Can you close your eyes and put in your noise-cancelling earphones please,' Johannes announces as we step through the door of his villa after his win at Monza. He skipped out on the team drinks to have dinner with *me*. I'm not even sure I want to know what this exchange is about. I kind of get it, but it seems like an inside joke.

Nils peers around Jo and scrambles to his feet. 'Absolutely I can. Have fun, guys!' he says, disappearing into his room faster than I've ever seen him on the racetrack. Johannes just laughs.

'You don't want to know,' he tells me. 'You want a drink?'

He walks towards the kitchen, but I shake my head and tug his hand towards what I'm hoping is the other bedroom.

All of my nerves about doing this, about sleeping with someone as experienced and gorgeous as Johannes slip away. I don't care about who came before, or the billboards he graces.

I only care about the here and now of this moment. How proud I am of him. How he looks at me like the sun shines out of my flipping ass. It's crazy, but it all seems so perfect.

'Caleb Hughes, are you taking me to bed?'

'Oh, Johannes Müller, you have no idea the night you're about to have. I'm so fucking proud of you.'

'Is me winning a turn-on for you?'

'What do you think?' The way he dedicated the win to me… Fuck, it turned me inside out.

He pushes the bedroom door open, everywhere beautifully neat just as I expected, and my lips are on his before he can even get the door shut. He shoves it with his foot, because this isn't a moment we want Nils witnessing, and then I'm walking him back towards his bed without detaching my lips from his.

His fingers slip under the hem of my polo and lift it up. I have to lean away for a second for him to get it off. I chase his lips the second it's discarded on the floor, but he holds a hand against my chest before pulling us both down onto the bed. But not even then does he let me continue. He lets his eyes appreciatively scan my bare chest, almost as if he's taking in everything he didn't get to enjoy the first time we did this. I was so torn up that night, but now I feel safe with him. And horny as hell.

'Fuck, you're so hot,' he grunts before tugging my head back down and into the most intense kiss of my life.

It's searing hot and our hands roam each other like we can't get enough. And I can't. There's no such thing when it comes to Johannes Müller. We break apart for a second so he can pull his team T-shirt off and my hands finally get the chance to map out all that bare skin. In person, it's just as incredible – and it's mine for tonight. For as long as he'll let me.

'You're so fucking hot. It's insane how hot you are.' He's sculpted in all the right areas, but before I can even take it all in, he's pushing down the pants he has on and his boxers all in one swoop. We tangle stupidly as he kicks them off and I'm laughing into his collarbone and, fuck, I've never felt so free. I don't think I've ever laughed so joyously while half naked with a sexual partner, but it comes so easily with him.

I unbuckle my belt and, in what I hope is a graceful move, shimmy my jeans and boxers down to my ankles and kick them off. It takes a millisecond for my brain to catch up that I'm completely naked with him, but I don't get any more time to think because he's pulling me down on top of him, skin on skin, back into another kiss.

Our dicks brush and I hiss at the friction, before searching it out again almost immediately. I could probably come just like this, but I don't want to. I want to take him apart. I want to enjoy this moment, and I want to start to learn what makes him tick under the covers, what he likes and what pushes him over the edge. Unlike in today's races, there's no rush to the finish line.

I break the kiss, but only so my lips can find the corner of his jaw, then the slope of his neck down to his collarbone and there's what feels like miles of dark brown skin ahead of me. I could do this for hours. I flick my tongue over his nipple and he moans, hips bucking up off the bed.

'Patience,' I whisper, looking up at him. 'We're getting there.'

I drag it out, mapping my way down his abs and his hip bone, nipping a little in the hope it will mark. He's panting and whining by the time I get to the inside of his thighs, even more so when my nose pokes into the incredibly tidy patch of pubic hair around his dick. Even right here, he smells incredible. It's a mix of whatever sweet scent he washes with and sweat and something uniquely Johannes, and I can't get enough as I breathe him in.

'I'm going to suck your dick, but you're going to tell me when you're close, okay? You're not coming like this.' His head tilts back to the ceiling like he's composing himself before he nods and I love that he's surrendering control to me.

He spreads his thighs out for me and I slide in between his legs, then engulf his entire cock in one fell swoop. I don't do random hook-ups much – and only when I'm desperate for a release my hand won't give me – but I always get told I'm really fucking good at blow jobs. It pays to have no gag reflex.

Johannes bucks up before I can stop him as his dick hits the back of my throat, I don't even choke. Spit pours out of the corners of my lips, but I'm quite happy to keep him here as his salty pre-cum slides down my throat.

'Oh, fuck, Caleb. What the fuck! Your fucking mouth.' All the curses only seem to keep coming as I roll his balls in my hand, pulling my mouth back slightly only to let him sink straight to the back of my throat again. It's incredible hearing him come undone like this, to see him clawing at the comforter to keep himself under control every time I bob back up to the tip of his dick and lick the slit, treating myself to how good he tastes.

Tugging at his balls with every stroke of my tongue leaves him panting and my jaw is finally slack enough that it doesn't ache too much to keep up the pace I've set. His hands settle in my hair, spiralling my curls around his fingers until they're tight and there's a pain in my scalp, but I'm not complaining. It only motivates me further.

'Stop, stop, fuck, fuck fuck!' he curses out and I come to a halt before pulling off completely. 'Sorry, I was about to cum, and you did say to let you know.'

I'm only a little sad because I was enjoying myself, but it was never meant to be the main event. I let myself catch my breath and look to him for a bit of a clue as to how he wants to play this. I don't mind being either top or bottom, but we've never actually discussed what we're down for.

'How do you want to do this?' he asks and my answer flies out of my mouth way too quickly.

'You inside of me?'

'I'm vers, so that's good for me. Plus, I'm dying to play with this ass. Fuck, you need to size down your work trousers. They are doing absolutely nothing to highlight this perfect globe.' He smacks my ass lightly, and I'd be lying if I said I didn't give it a little wiggle just to show it off.

He leans over me, reaching inside his bedside table, and grabs a condom and a bottle of the most expensive lube I've ever seen. 'So glad I put these here this morning. I had a feeling we would be celebrating tonight.'

'Oh, you thought it would take only one win to get me into bed?' I ask as he chucks them down on the bed next to me.

He raises a perfectly defined eyebrow at me and, okay, he's got me, because yeah, here I am. 'Fuck you.'

'I believe, it'll be the other way around, baby, but good try.' He gives my ass another firm slap and, fuck, when did I develop a pain kink, because I want to ask him to slap it again and pull my hair whilst he's at it.

'When we have more time to enjoy it, I'm going to eat this ass like you're my last meal because that's how much I want it.' My own cock is rigid as hell, and I feel my balls tighten painfully at that. Looking over my shoulder at him is a mistake because, fuck, his eyes are so bright as he eyes me like I'm heaven on earth, fingers padding across the plains of my ass.

No one has ever looked at me like this. No one has ever made me feel like every single nerve ending in my body is on fire. Like they're ready to worship me. But here's Johannes fucking Müller ready to do just that.

'Don't tease me. What are you waiting for?' I ask as both his hands cup my ass before letting it go to watch each cheek jiggle.

'I could honestly get off just watching this, I can't lie,' he comments, but he's finally reaching for the lube and I'm so fucking ready for this.

He presses a kiss to my left cheek before parting them to get a better look at my hole. I'm glad I did a little personal grooming last night in anticipation of whatever might come today.

'Jesus, Caleb. Fucking hell.' I'm pretty sure he's talking to my asshole at this point, but then a cold, slippery finger begins to massage the ring, getting it nice and soft and ready for him to enter. 'This is going to be embarrassing if I cum without being touched.'

'Don't you fucking dare. I need your dick.'

'Then I best make this quick, because there's no way I'm going to last if I watch your ass take my fingers.' Part of me can't believe that it's our first time and I'm on my hands and knees, ass literally hanging in the air for him to do what he pleases, but it's making him so damn happy.

He warms the lube between his fingers like the angel he is, before his first finger penetrates me right up until he's a knuckle deep. He takes great care in opening me up before sliding in a second and when I'm writhing back against the two, he adds a third for good measure. There's a slight burn with it, but it feels so good and if I'm going to take the thickness of his cock, I'm going to need it.

'Fucking hell.' It's my turn to start swearing up a storm, but how can I not when his free hand is digging into my thigh, holding me in place and no doubt leaving fingerprint-sized bruises, which I'll get to treasure as a memory of tonight.

'You ready for me?' he asks, leaning against my shoulder, his fingers grazing over my prostate.

All I can do is nod and squeeze the base of my own dick to keep this from being over too soon as I hear him rip open a condom and sheath himself.

The thick head of his cock breaches my hole and I puff out a breath, fingers gripping his comforter as I brace myself for a little bit of pain. It's been a while, and while Johannes doesn't have the longest cock in the world, it's easiest the thickest I've ever seen and he's currently splitting me in two with just the tip.

'You okay?' He's cautiously holding himself back, assessing if I'm ready for him to keep going.

'Yeah, just … fuck! Why is your cock so big?'

'Born this way,' he says, and I never thought I'd be laughing during sex with Johannes.

It causes me to edge back a little and it kinda hurts, but at the same time I feel so alive. 'Just give it to me. I don't mind if you're a little rough.'

'I'm seeing a whole new side of you tonight.'

I know I'm blushing, but it's something else to feel him all over me, to trust him to break my whole body in half.

He's good at listening to me off the track, too, it seems,

because he ploughs my ass like a tractor in a field during autumn harvest. The skin-on-skin noise echoes through the room and I hope Nils took Jo's advice about the noise-cancelling headphones. Between his balls hitting off my ass and the pair of us moaning and swearing, it's loud in here.

Every time he nails my prostrate my dick leaks a little more. I don't think I've ever been this wet during sex before. There's sweat dripping down my forehead and I'm so close, so fucking close.

'Fuck, shit, Caleb, I can't...' He nails me one more time and then I feel him still and then pulse inside me, which sets me off, too – long ropes of cum coating my stomach and his sheets.

I collapse face first into his pillows as I feel him pull out. The bed dips and I hear him go to the bathroom to get rid of the condom. I wince as a wet cloth swipes over my sensitive crack.

'Sorry, just clearing up the mess. Turn over and I'll do your stomach, too.' I roll onto my back and he swipes up all of my cum, before tossing the cloth back into the bathroom and sliding back into bed with me.

I couldn't move if I tried right now, but especially when he wraps an arm around me and pulls me close so my head's resting on his chest.

'Can you stay?' he asks.

I nod against his chest, words failing me as I catch my breath.

'Aren't you worried that the engineers you share your apartment with will know you've been gone all night?'

'And?

'Well, we aren't exactly public, are we?'

'How would they know who I'm spending the night with?

And anyway, when we're still going strong at the end of the season, or the beginning of next, I won't care.' We'll have to do it the right way and talk to management before we do anything else, but that's fine.

A zap of shock zings across his face and I realise he thought I was going to hide him away forever. Once we've been together a serious amount of time, and we're stable and confident in our commitment, there'll be no risk – or much less risk – in going public. I'm so proud to be dating him and I only wish I hadn't let fear stand in the way of us having had this a couple months ago.

He leans in to kiss me. Tugging the comforter up over the both of us, he pulls away and opens an arm for me to snuggle in next to him and I have absolutely no objections to being the little spoon right now. Not when his thigh slips protectively over mine and holds me in place.

'You're so good, you know that, right?' It might be dark, but I can see the conviction in his chocolate brown eyes.

'Wow, one night with me and he turns into a sap. What have I done to Johannes Müller?'

'Hey.' He swats my ass. I'm sure it's meant to be a punishment, but I really do think I might have found my kink. 'I'm trying to have a serious moment here. You make me feel like I'm worth it.'

I can't imagine a world or any single reason why Johannes should or would have had to feel any other way, and if someone did make him feel this way, I'd like to kill them. There's no one like him, not a single person I've ever met who cares the way he does. Who is so ready to look after you and make you feel like you can accomplish anything. I've watched him take Nils under his wing and show him the ropes – teach him how to be a winner.

'That's because you're beyond worth it, Johannes. I hope I get to show you that every day that you'll let me.'

'You already do,' he whispers into the darkness, before pressing a soft, final kiss to my lips. His head drops next to mine on the pillow we seem to be sharing tonight and with every single one of our limbs tangled together, I fall asleep happier than I can ever remember.

Chapter Twenty-Three

Johannes

'What's this?' I ask, as a photo pings into my WhatsApp messages from Nils. We're sitting together in the bar of our hotel in Singapore, scrolling on social media and making plans for our time here.

'Open it and look,' Nils replies before grabbing his beer bottle to take a swig.

The two weeks Caleb and I had off before flying to Singapore weren't enough. Caleb was really busy with the team, and then Nils and I skied for five days, and then the second Caleb was free, my agent bulked out my schedule with sponsorship meetings and photoshoots and a bunch of charity work. None of it I was unhappy to do, but it meant Caleb and I couldn't get away together like we planned. In the end, we managed a single night in my penthouse in London and that was it. One measly night that was never going to satisfy my desperate need to spend time with him. The next morning, we met Nils at an airstrip and the three of us boarded a private plane to Singapore.

It's not something I do very often. Normally I'm more than happy to fly commercial, but I wanted to be able to relax with Caleb and not worry about fans on the plane or having to be less handsy with the cabin crew around. Nils was in London for the same shoot I was, so it was easier to just bring him with us.

I open the picture and there's me and Caleb, fast asleep on the plane, trying our best to be wrapped up in each other. I want to be slightly perturbed that Nils was taking pictures of us while we were asleep, but it's too cute to be annoyed at him for. We both look so content, our faces smushed into a shared pillow, blanket only half covering us because it was definitely only made for one person.

'You're welcome.' Nils laughs, and I realise that I've been staring at the photo for way too long without saying anything.

'I appreciate it, but I thought you were asleep for the whole flight?'

'Eh, I got up to piss at some point and couldn't help myself.'

Well, that's a relief. We had checked he was sound asleep beforehand, but neither of us could resist getting a bit handsy on the plane. Not something I wanted Nils to hear or see, but I couldn't stop myself.

'Don't worry, if you pair joined the mile high club I didn't hear or see a thing.'

'Joined,' I scoff. 'Kiddo, you don't know me if you think that was the first time.'

'Ewwww! You did get off while I was asleep right in front

of you! I hate you.' He fake-gags, but then he's smiling and I know he's happy that we're happy.

I ruffle his hair, before returning to look at the photo, the beer I'm meant to be drinking with him forgotten about. Caleb and I look so right together, it's actually ridiculous. I have no idea how we're going to keep this hidden until the off season when we've decided we'll speak to management about our relationship.

'Guess who.' A pair of hands covers my eyes but I don't have to spend more than half a second thinking about it. I know that voice like I know my own name.

'Nils, is there an annoying fucker from Hendersohm behind me?'

'Afraid so,' he confirms and Harper smacks the side of my cheek as he pulls his hands away.

'Can I steal my best friend?' Harper asks Nils, moving round to stand in front of our booth. He's dressed in grey sweats and a white T-shirt, so I can't imagine where he's stealing me away to.

'Absolutely, I just found out he had sex on the plane right in front of me while I was asleep. So please, take his disgusting ass away.'

Harper raises an eyebrow, like he's trying to work out what the issue is, but I just shake my head.

'Perfect, come on Jojo.' He holds out a hand and I use it to hop down from the booth, but he doesn't let go as we walk towards the hotel lift. 'Which floor?'

'You know you're a married man, right?'

'Oh yeah, because this is me seducing you. In sweats and at the hotel both our teams are staying in.'

'You're leading me to my hotel room, man.'

'To have some quality time with my best friend, dickhead. I don't need your actual dick anymore, although I am glad to hear you're finally getting some. Even if you are traumatising Nils.' I can't help but laugh at that. I should probably feel sorrier than I do for the guy.

'Movie and room service,' he suggests as we enter my room, slipping off his shoes before throwing himself down on to my bed, quickly getting comfy.

'Sounds good to me, let me go slip into something comfy and I'll be with you. Order what you want.'

I grab a pair of sweat shorts and a vest and slip into the bathroom, washing my face quickly before throwing on my comfy clothes. Harper's just hanging up when I leave the bathroom and I dread to think about how much he's just charged to my card, but it's worth it to get this quality time together.

'They said food won't be for forty-five minutes as they're really busy tonight, but they have Disney Plus on this tv so I thought we'd watch Iron Man.' Because why would we watch anything new when we could just binge the Avengers series again like we used to do at sleepovers when we were fifteen? He fires up the first film and I get comfy on the bed next to him.

'I'm glad you took my advice,' he says, referring to Caleb.

'Thank you,' I say. 'For what you said in Monza. I needed to hear it, and I wouldn't have listened to it from anyone but you.'

'I love you, JoJo. You know that. I'm glad you're back to yourself again, even though you keep pushing me off the top spot.' He punches me lightly and I punch him back. Not everyone is so lucky to have a friend like Harper in their life.

'I just wish you'd tell me what was going on and why you wouldn't talk to me about it.'

'Harp, I…'

'What? What's so fucking awful that you can't tell me? *Me*. Your best friend.'

'It's complicated.'

'Oh, fuck off. There's no such thing when it comes to you and me.'

'I…'

'You really hurt me,' he says quietly. I still and turn to face him.

'I'm sorry, Harp. I just … couldn't. I can't.'

I feel him pull away from me a little. I'm not sure if it's a physical action or if it's a kind of invisible barrier he puts up between us, but either way it breaks my heart. And I've had enough of heartbreak.

I take a deep breath. 'Harp?'

'Yeah…?'

'If I tell you something, will you promise to listen and to trust me and not ask any questions?'

'Jo, what's going on?'

'Promise me, Harp.'

'Okay, okay, I promise.'

'It's not in your best interests to know what was going on with me.' If I tell him that the knowledge would put him in an impossible position then it won't take him long to work it out and that would defeat the purpose. 'Believe me when I tell you that I would have shared every part of it with you if I could have. I wanted to, a hundred times. A thousand. It's not because I don't trust you and it's not because I'm ashamed of anything and it's nothing you've done or not done. Just know that I've put it behind me now and I'm happy with Caleb, thanks to you.'

'Does it have anything to do with why you bailed on dinner in Zandvoort?' he asks suspiciously.

'I said no questions.'

'I just don't want us to drift apart again, and after Zandvoort I was worried we were heading back there.'

'Absolutely not. No drifting. But please don't ask me anything else, Harp. I promise I'll tell you one day.'

He eyes me sceptically. I can tell he's not satisfied but I hope he'll let it go for now.

'If you want, we can talk about how hot my new boyfriend is?' I offer.

I nudge him but eventually he plays along.

'Is it someone I know?' he jokes.

'He's so fucking hot.'

'He actually is. Okay,' he says with a sigh. 'Tell me everything.'

I get out my phone so I can scroll though the endless reel of pictures me and Caleb have taken together.

When the food arrives, we chow down, talking about everything except racing, from the date ideas I have for Caleb this week to the horses that Kian and his brother-in-law, Grant, are going to look at this weekend.

I polish off a steak with asparagus and broccoli and we split a bottle of wine. It's the tamest night we've ever experienced together, but I'm here for it. I hate to say it, but we're growing up.

'I'm not kidding, I'm worried that the next time I go home there'll be some kind of animal in our bed. Kian needs reining in, but it's hard to do from the other side of the world.' Never did I imagine it would be my best friend having to do the reining in, not the other way around.

'I love that this is your man's life now, though! I never saw it coming, but it fits Kian perfectly.'

The film ends and Harper's yawning his head off. 'Also, you can't stay the night,' I say, and he pouts before his eyes light up.

'Ohhh, your man's coming over to dick you down. I get it, hoes before bros. Sure, sure, when I can only get cyber dick right now.'

'Oh boo-hoo, your married ass isn't getting any right now. Let me enjoy this. You'll be home before you know it, and you can bug the life out of Kian for all the dick in the world.'

'I can't wait.' And he means it. His whole face softens at the mention of Kian and it's literally adorable – but also makes my heart flip because now I'm thinking about what Caleb and I can get up to over winter break. 'You'll come and stay won't you?' Harper adds. 'See all the improvements Kian's made since summer break. We'd love to host you both. Can I tell Kian? Please say I can. He'll be so excited.'

'Yeah, of course. I wouldn't expect you to ever keep anything from your husband,' I say pointedly. 'I'll talk to Caleb, but I can't see why we wouldn't be there.' God, I hope we're still doing this at winter break. I hope we're still doing this for a really long time.

The movie credits are hardly even rolling when I push Harper out of bed.

'You used to be fun and now you have a boyfriend you don't love me anymore,' he whines.

'Go FaceTime your husband,' I say. He pouts again, but I

lob one of his trainers at him, which he ducks and it smacks straight into the hotel room wall.

Luckily, he gets the message and slips into his trainers and with a kiss to my forehead disappears towards the hotel lift.

No longer than five minutes later there's a knock at the door, and there's my Caleb.

'Perfect timing. I finally turfed Harps out. He was gutted I wasn't letting him sleep over, but we had a really good night.'

'Did you talk about me?' he asks with an eyeroll.

'Obviously,' I say.

'Should I be expecting you down on one knee soon, then?'

'Not with that attitude. It would be an honour if you got to marry me.' I can't even believe that just a month into our relationship we're joking about marriage. Shit, I'm already in so deep with this man, and while it's daunting, I'm not scared of falling for Caleb. He's not Jackson. He isn't.

He slips off his shoes and jacket, folding it over the desk chair and then quickly strips down to just his boxers before climbing into bed. I follow suit until I'm left in just my underwear and slide in next to him. I open an arm for him to snuggle in next to me and he does so after flipping off the light next to the bed.

It hits me suddenly that he's here for the night. To sleep. Not for sex. This isn't a booty call, though maybe I'll wake him with a blow job. But this is purely so we can hold each other tonight and wake up to each other in the morning. It shouldn't be such a wild concept, but it is, and at the same time I feel perfectly content.

We fall asleep together, his head still on my chest, our bodies snuggled up tight together.

Chapter Twenty-Four

Caleb

Everything feels like a high right now. Between Johannes racking up another top of the podium finish in Italy and a second place in Singapore, the dates we've managed to fit in and of course, the sex, everything is stupidly good. Johannes is slowly gaining back the lost points, and with Harper finishing third in Singapore, it's a good bump for us.

The first two practices in Brazil yesterday were nothing but perfection for us. Jo's found his groove with the car and he's performing over and above even our highest expectations. He's a true winner.

Then comes the third practice on Saturday morning and it all falls apart in front of my eyes.

It's a ridiculously hot day and other teams' tyres aren't performing like ours. Which is how six cars end up being taken out in one slip-up from a Team Distraus driver. Johannes goes straight into the wall on one of the turns and it has me out of my seat at the pit wall desperate to run to him.

When he climbs out of the car, I probably should be looking at the record of damage as they lift his car off the track but I'm too focused on him telling me he's okay. That's all that matters.

'I'm so sorry to do this in FP3. Is there going to be enough time for them to fix the car?' He's breathless as he runs over to where I've been talking with a couple of the other engineers.

Both his and Nils's cars are an absolute mess. We're lucky to have four hours between now and qualifying and the best team of mechanics in the world. I'm not quite sure why he's apologising, though. It's not his fault that the newbie doing a test drive for Distraus wiped out a quarter of the grid towards the end of the session.

'Not your fault, Jo. Half the teams are panicking right now; we're just amongst the fun.'

He coughs as he goes to reply, which turns quickly into a wheeze, leaving him doubled over. 'Are you okaay?' I ask as he regains his balance, arms still wrapped around his chest.

'Absolutely fine. I'm going to go nap before the debrief and then pray that catering has that brown-rice salad thing I like.' He's clutching at his chest, moving slowly as he tries to step around me to head to his room.

'Woah, woah, woah, absolutely not. Medical needs to see you. Nils is already being checked over and then it's your turn. You hit both a car and a wall, mister.' Plus, there is pain etched in every tightly formed line on his face.

'I'll nap first and then get checked. Don't worry about me. I'm just a bit tired. Had a late night.' He waggles his eyebrows, before starting to cough again.

'Nope, medical then nap. Race engineer's orders.'

'But—'

'No buts.'

'But you have such a nice butt.' He grins like this is all a joke, but his health isn't a joke. Not in one of the most dangerous sports in the world.

'Jo.' The bossy tone he only gets to hear when he's being a dick on the track comes out and it stops him in his tracks. 'I'll walk you there myself, if I have to.'

He finally stops protesting and we head to the medical room where Nils is just leaving. 'All good. Just some bruising from some asshole hitting me.'

I don't think I'll ever be able to watch the footage of Harper's car flying into Johannes's car sending it spinning into Nils's car before both of them go straight into the wall. It was bad enough the first time. I've seen worse accidents in my career; I've seen cars catch fire, I've seen cars with their whole front missing. But this, this was the most stressful, to the point my smartwatch was like do we need to call an ambulance your heart rate is so high?

'You're welcome, dickhead. Not my fault. I was literally just the meat in a car sandwich.' Johannes ruffles Nils's hair, but I can tell he's just trying to delay getting checked over.

'I think I know someone who'd like you as the meat in a sandwich.' Nils drops me a not-so-subtle wink and I shake my head at this pair – stubborn and sarcastic, the both of them.

'As nice as this has been, Nils, he needs to see the doctor, so move along.' I shoo him with my hands, but he doesn't budge.

'Shit, are you okay?' Nils turns to Johannes. 'I think you took the brunt of everyone's force, to be honest.'

He's not kidding. I feel like I felt it, too, and I was only in Johannes's ear.

'Yeah, he's just being Mr Overly Cautious. Practically marched me over here.'

I can't see Johannes, but I'm sure he's rolling his eyes.

'Like you weren't doubled over coughing just a few minutes ago.' I shake my head. 'Now get in there.' If we weren't at work, I'd have probably smacked his ass, but there are too many people around and the workplace is a professional environment, whether people know about us or not.

'Shit, man, I'll leave you to it. See you in the debrief in an hour.' Nils takes off in the direction of the small room he has in the garage, probably for a nap like Johannes was planning.

'I'm waiting outside the door, by the way. I know you. You're too stubborn for your own good and you'll just ignore my orders otherwise.'

Johannes salutes me and slips into the doctor's office.

Twenty minutes later, and I'm still standing here, which considering qualifying is just over two hours away, is very unproductive, but I said I'd be waiting, and I just want to be sure he's all good. But then another five minutes pass with no movement.

'What's going on?' Nathan asks as he rounds the corner to the medical office.

'Johannes is in there with the doctor. He was wheezing and holding his chest after the crash in FP3.'

'Okay, well we need to speed this up a little, because we need to go through the data from FP3 and make a decision on tyres, and he needs to get his head in the game. A win today and we'll be within touching distance of Harper.'

'And he will, once he's been checked over by the doctor.'

I know we all have different priorities, but I refuse to let Johannes go back out there without being assessed.

'Could you try to hurry it up? We'll see you in the meeting room.'

I don't really want to barge into Johannes's appointment, but there's a lot riding on the Saturday of a race weekend. So I knock a couple times and wait a handful of seconds, just in case, and let myself in.

'So sorry to disturb you,' I say before the screen the doctor's showing Johannes catches my eye. 'What's going on?' I ask, stepping further into the room and letting the door close behind.

'Are you okay with him being in here?' the doctor asks and Johannes nods from where he's still laid out on the bed. 'I was just explaining to Mr Müller that he has two fractured ribs, and he's lucky they haven't punctured his lung.'

'Oh, Jesus, Johannes.' I get a closer look at the screen and can see where the breaks are. Fuck, that must be so painful.

'So, what do I need? Some strong pain meds? Do you still wrap broken ribs? I just need something to get through today and tomorrow, and then I have almost three weeks until we go to Qatar.'

He can't actually be thinking about getting in the car right now? There's no way, surely? I look to the doctor, hoping for some guidance. While he works for the team, if he advises Johannes to drive and Johannes ends up puncturing a lung or something mid-drive, I'm sure he'd lose his license.

'I would strongly advise against you getting back in the car today. Any kind of impact could cause serious further damage to your ribs – or even your internal organs, if you aren't careful. I'd recommend icing your ribs, rest, mixed in with periods of light exercise for a few weeks, then we'll reassess to make sure you're healing okay.'

I almost breathe out in relief. It's not that I don't want him to race. I don't want him to end up doing more serious damage.

'So, what? I can't race today? In what world is that going to happen?' Johannes scowls. I could have predicted this reaction a mile off. He's not the only stubborn driver on the grid. They could have limbs hanging off and they'd still be insistent about getting in their cars and going out there.

'I can't ban you from driving, but I have to make you aware of the consequences of such a choice. If you have another crash or even a bump, you could end up out for longer.'

Johannes looks up at me from where he's struggling to get comfortable in a sitting position. He's waiting for me to air my opinion. My professional opinion would be that he shouldn't race, but I don't know how to be impartial here.

'I'm not a doctor, so I'm going to have to agree with his thoughts on this, Jo. He is the professional after all.'

'Nathan will never go for it. He'd let me race with a broken foot if he thought I could still get points,' Johannes huffs. He tries to sit up way too quickly, which results in him wincing loudly.

'How are you planning on folding yourself into the cockpit in that kind of pain?' I'm struggling to watch him right now, never mind sit there for seventy-one laps letting him become more and more uncomfortable.

'Painkillers would sort it, I'm sure.' The doctor just shakes his head, and I see Johannes has had enough.

He tries to hop up off the bed, but only ends up almost

doubling over in pain, his breath coming out in wheezes as he clutches his abdomen.

'Yeah, you're definitely in a fit state to race,' I comment as we leave the room.

'Fuck, this is so fucking dumb! Stupid fucking rookie! Who let him do this? It shouldn't be allowed so close to the end of the championship. Can you get the guys to look at the chair? A small crash shouldn't have broken my ribs.'

'I'm not sure a double-impact crash could be classed as small, but I will obviously get the guys to look at the seat design if you think it had a bearing on the pain you've ended up in.

'Nathan's going to throw a fit. Having to put in a reserve driver with no practice is going to tank us today.' He's not wrong about Nathan, and I don't want to be the one to have to tell him this.

'Have some faith in Anton.' I try to sound confident, but the test practices he's done this year have not been great, and to be honest, I'm surprised there hasn't been a bit of a swap around with where he is in the rankings to come up to the main team.

Five seconds later, Nathan's barrelling towards us, blustering about us being late for the meeting. Best to just get this over with.

'Sorry we're late, but unfortunately Johannes won't be driving today. The doctor has recommended he doesn't drive because he has two fractured ribs that almost punctured his lungs.'

'How bad's the pain?' Nathan asks, turning away from me and practically glaring at Johannes.

We're all silent for a moment or two and I wait to see if

Johannes will downplay it and convince Nathan to go in there and fight the doctor for some strong painkillers, but his shoulders slump and he finally stops being stubborn. 'About a nine when I move. The doctor's right, I don't know how I'd drive right now.'

'Fucking brilliant. That's just fucking great. And three hours before qualifying. This is a joke.' Nathan storms off, but out of the corner of my eye I catch the documentary camera crew capturing every moment of this, so he's only fucked himself over here.

The crew chase after him to catch all the reactions – and the way he slams the meeting room door shut, cutting off their access to him.

'I'm going back to the hotel,' Johannes mutters to me. 'I don't think I can stick around to watch this, and I think I might be sick.'

'I'll get the doctor to draw up a prescription to ease your pain and then I'll find someone to drive you back to the hotel to get you settled.'

Then I really have to get to that meeting, because Lord knows I'm going to need all the car stats today to figure out how to guide Anton to any kind of success during qualifying today and the race tomorrow.

'This is the fucking worst day ever.' Johannes stomps off to who knows where, because he can't leave without his meds and a bit of assistance to get him back to the hotel, and he could probably do with being snuck out the back door before the media starts running wild with stories of why he's leaving. The PR team haven't even had a second to write up a press release yet.

Thankfully, the doctor releases the medication straight to

me, which I hand to two of the PR team who're going to get Johannes covertly back to the hotel and then write up the confirmation about him not driving this weekend for the press and our social media accounts.

Everywhere is a shit show, the engineers trying not only to sort the damage to both RBF cars, but also to refit the seat in Johannes's car – because Anton is four inches shorter than Johannes and we need it to suit him as well as possible to stand any chance of points this weekend.

When, three hours later, I finally settle at the pit wall for qualifying, I'm more than ready for this circus to be over. Especially when I have to give Anton an earful for blocking someone on a flying lap in Q1 – and even more so when he doesn't even make it into Q2. I still have to stick around for way too many hours to do my job, when all I really want to do is sneak away and make sure that Johannes isn't too mad at me for pushing him into not racing today.

Chapter Twenty-Five

Johannes

I can't believe two broken ribs are stopping me from racing this weekend. I'm furious to the point that I would love to trash my hotel room – but even shuffling along the floor hurts right now.

Not only that, but Nathan's pissed. I think even he knows that Anton isn't ready for today, especially without any practice, and even more so on a track like Brazil's Interlagos when the race tomorrow is destined for rain.

I'm trapped in the hotel room, my phone blowing up with notifications after the team put out the statement that I wouldn't be competing. My Instagram has never been so popular, and I've put out many a nearly-naked campaign shot in my lifetime. I can't bear to look at any of the comments – too much pity, and probably way too many fans of the other teams celebrating my demise because it gives their favourite drivers more of a chance at a podium today.

I have to turn my phone off an hour into being on bedrest. I've managed to give myself a stress headache worrying about what this means for my standings. I need the points. God knows I really need these points but there's just no way. It's difficult enough to get comfy on the plush bed without the pain reducing me to nausea, never mind squashing my body into the tight confines of the cockpit.

It's just one race. That's what I have to keep reminding myself. One race, and then by the time we get to Qatar I'll be on the mend and it won't hurt to fucking breathe. I eye the painkillers the team doctor prescribed. I don't want to take them, but there's also no point punishing myself anymore. Forcing myself to sit in agony just to suffer is not the kind of guy I want to be. So I open one of the many bottles of water within reach and pop two pills into my mouth before swallowing them down.

I don't even know what to do with myself. I don't think I could sleep if I tried. It would be far too uncomfortable right now. I don't want to watch qualifying. I can't bear to see everyone on track when I can't be. Plus, I'm not sure I even want to know how Anton gets on. Nice guy, but he's not ready for this. He looked green when he was told he'd be going into qualifying in just a couple hours' time.

I'm sure Caleb will look after him just fine, but more than anything and very selfishly, I wish he was here looking after me instead. It's not that I want him to play nurse, although him in that uniform, I could get on board with that. Mostly I just want him here with me because I love his company.

At some point, the first round of painkillers makes me drowsy and I actually fall asleep. When I wake up the room is much darker and as I try to get back into a comfy position I see the clock on the bedside table reads after 8 p.m.

Okay, so I slept for like five hours. That's something, at least. Plus, I don't even feel guilty about not watching qualifying now because the meds knocked me out.

I grab my phone from under my pillow, turning it back on and trying to ignore how the notifications roll in. Yet another reminder than I'm not racing tomorrow with all of the commiseration messages. Except, as I start to close them all down there's one that catches my eye. It's from a number I don't have saved.

> Just seen that you're not racing tomorrow. Harper said he's not been able to get a hold of you. Are you in hospital? Are you okay?

I double-check I haven't deleted Elijah or Kian's number by accident, but they're both still saved and then I make the mistake of saving this random number as a contact to check if they have a picture on WhatsApp. And there he is, dark-brown wavy hair tucked behind his ears, a Hendersohm logo in the bottom of the picture.

In what fucking world does Jackson Calder get to worry about me right now? Not this one. He can go fuck himself. I glare at the text, trying to think of a reply. Who does he think he is to text me out of the blue like he cares? I hate him. I hate him. I hate him! Like I'm not suffering enough right now.

I contemplate whether to delete the message and the contact when there's a quiet knock at the door. 'Come in,' I call out. I'm shirtless, but it's not like I can quickly hop out of bed and cover myself up for the hotel staff.

'Hey.' Caleb's head pokes round my door and I almost

forgot I'd slipped him a copy of my hotel card earlier in the week.

I'm not angry at him, per se – I'm angry at the fucking idiot who took out half the grid in FP3 and ruined my chances this weekend, sure – but not Caleb. But today I hate that there's an overlap between our relationship in real life and our relationship at work. I hate that today he couldn't understand why I wanted to compete so much. How I could have managed the pain.

'Come in.' I beckon, trying not to move too much. Even with the pain medication, I'm only just tolerating how swollen and tender my abdomen is right now.

'I wanted to check I was welcome before I barged in.' He laughs, but I can tell he's a little nervous. I probably didn't handle the situation well. I pat the spot next to me on the bed. 'Did you watch?' he asks as he slips off his shoes and carefully climbs onto the bed next to me.

I shake my head. 'Dare I ask how Anton got on?'

'P16. Nils was P5, though, so he's over the moon. But I think he's trying to be considerate of the fact that you can't race this weekend.'

'Nils knows how to be considerate?' I say with a chuckle before it turns to a wheeze. I must look like a right state. There's a champagne bucket full of ice and ice packs and my bedside table is covered with painkillers and there's a smattering of helpful things around my ring of pillows – the remote, my phone, fresh towels to put around the ice packs and some snacks.

'Yeah, he's trying, but he looked a bit lost without you today.'

When you spend so much time with someone, especially in

such an intense environment, you get used to that routine of the other person always being there. I can't imagine Nils not being around, either, and the sentimental part of me hopes he'll stick with RBF for a long while.

'He's probably been blowing up my phone, but I turned it off so I could sleep. I sometimes forget just how much I love this sport until I'm told I can't do it.' I want to be supportive of Nils, but right now I'm feeling a little bitter that he gets to be out on track tomorrow and I don't. It's incredibly childish of me, but my career's in detention for something it didn't do.

'I know I contributed to that today, but I only did it because I didn't want you to get hurt and, God, I'm sorry if—'

I raise a hand to stop his apologetic rambling. 'It's okay. It was –' I pause before continuing, reluctantly '– the right call. I've been in so much pain this afternoon that even with the ice and strong painkillers every little movement hurts. I don't think I could have even got in the car.'

I would have, though. I'd have forced myself into that car and endured the pain if it meant I didn't have to miss out on vital points. But I also would have hated myself even more if I'd ended up in hospital with a punctured lung or worse.

I try to push myself up a little, which leads to the blanket slipping down to my waist and exposing my bare, battered chest. Even with the rotating ice packs, the swelling has hardly gone down, and my ribs are already covered in midnight-blue bruises that look even angrier than they did earlier. His eyes are on them straight away, scanning the damage, and for a second I almost want to wrench the blanket up, but I can't move that fast and I don't think Caleb's about to turn his nose up in disgust.

'Can I do anything for you?'

How did I get so lucky with this man? He's just done a full, stressful day at work and here he is offering to do things for me.

'I'd love some dinner, but the phone is too far away on the desk.' I hate feeling like such an invalid, but the phone is corded so it's not like they could have brought it any closer.

'I'll order us some room service and then we could watch a movie or something?'

'You free for the rest of the evening?' I know he probably has work to do or some editing for his PhD thesis, but I'd love him to stay.

'You have my undivided attention. Anything you fancy?'

'Anything?' I waggle my eyebrows hopefully and he shakes his head.

'I don't think we should be doing anything too *physical* right now, but if you're a good boy and eat all your dinner and promise to rest afterwards, I could be convinced to blow you.'

'Oh, aren't I a lucky boy? You going to order me vegetables to help me grow up big and strong?'

'You're pushing your luck now, handsome.' He strokes a hand across my cheek and I lean into his touch. The painkillers are really doing their job and everything's a nice kind of relaxed haze.

'You think I'm handsome?' I ask, his thumb still swiping across my cheekbone as he takes me in. His stare is intense in the best possible way, and I'm convinced he's going to kiss me, but he just smiles like he knows what I'm thinking but it's not going to happen right now.

'You know I do. You know you are. You have the most beautiful smile. And these cheekbones are to die for. But it's more like … you have a glow. It's stunning. Like intoxicating levels of beauty.'

'It's the sweat. This room's a little warm.' Or maybe it's my face burning. Am I running a fever or is it the way he's speaking to me? Those words, him saying them, it's not like anything else I've experienced before.

'No, it's just you. The good person you are, how much you care about the sport, about your best friend, and about your little protégé.' I wasn't expecting this. My stomach flips at the praise. I am very used to hearing how good-looking I am – it's par for the course with modelling side gigs and posting thirst traps on Instagram. But that's not what he's doing. He's talking about what's on my inside and it's turning me to mush.

'Caleb…'

He presses soft lips to my forehead, cutting me off, and then slides carefully off the bed. Grabbing the room-service menu, he peruses it, before picking up the room phone.

'You don't know what I want,' I say from the bed as he clicks the number for the restaurant, but he just ignores me.

'Hi, could I order some room service for room eight three seven, please? Sure, the card is on file. Can I do the steak frites, medium rare with the salsa verde. A cheeseburger with fries. Then a sharer avocado and beetroot salad. A ginger ale, a Diet Coke and a bucket full of ice please. Yep, that's all, thank you.

'Did I do okay?' he asks as he hangs up, storing the menu back in its holder.

'As long as that steak's for me.'

'Of course it is.'

'How'd you know?'

'You always ask for it when catering are taking suggestions, and do you know how many times you put a steak on your

Insta stories when you're out for dinner? Plus, you've eaten several on the dinner dates we've been on.'

'You've been watching?'

'Of course. Am I okay to hop in the shower? I've been in these clothes for too many hours and they feel a bit gross right now.'

'Of course. You can borrow some sweats and a T-shirt if you want.' The thought of him in my clothes is intensely arousing, even more so than the fact he just ordered my perfect dinner.

'Give me ten.' He shuffles into the bathroom, whilst I glug down half a bottle of water, my mouth a little dry. I could also really do with a piss, but I'm a bit scared of standing up right now with the pain being as bad as it was earlier.

I also really don't want to have to ask the man I'm dating to help me to the bathroom. He's seen my dick plenty, but I feel and look a bit weak right now.

He showers quickly and my jaw drops when he leaves the bathroom with just a towel hanging from his hips. His hair's wet, water droplets dripping down his chest. What I wouldn't give to be able to chase them with my tongue. I want him so much, but he's right, I'm too injured to do much tonight.

'T-shirts are in the top drawer,' I say gesturing to the dresser. 'There's fresh sweatpants still in my suitcase.'

He grabs them both and then a pair of my boxers, which almost leaves me panting, and pulls them on. Everything's a little big on him, but it's a sight I want to remember forever. I unlock my phone to snap a picture and add it into the folder of us. 'You look fucking incredible in my clothes. Come here.'

I pat the spot next to me on the bed and he slides right in. 'How about I take care of that.' He grazes a hand over where

I'm erect under the duvet and I groan. 'But you have to lie still, okay?'

'I thought I had to be a good boy first and eat all my dinner?'

'We could wait, but that looks mighty uncomfortable to me.'

I'm not about to protest, so I just nod. He peels back the duvet and I'm glad that I stripped down to just my boxers when they got me comfortable in bed, because now he has easy access.

He doesn't even pull them down, just fishes my dick out and smears the pre-cum from my slit over my length. I have to force my hips to stay pinned to the bed because they are crying out to buck up right now and chase his hand. 'Fuck, Caleb, that feels so good, I can't even tell you. Love you touching me.'

His hand cups my balls and another filthy moan slips from between my lips as I watch him shuffle down the bed until he's got his knees either side of mine and is eyeing my dick like it's tonight's meal.

'You're so beautiful,' he says. His words are soft but in one swooping motion his mouth is taking my dick right to the back of his throat. This is something I never expected from polite, boy-next-door, Caleb Hughes. He sucks dick like a trooper and it's mind-blowingly incredible. I'm going to come way too quickly if he doesn't slow down.

He hums around my length, the vibrations causing my balls to twitch and draw up, and as he pulls away, he strokes his tongue along the underneath of my shaft. I'm fucked. I'm truly fucked. His hand disappears beneath my balls – and this time sweeps into my crack, massaging my hole. Fuck. Fuck. Fuck. I'm a goner.

His lips part again and the tip of my cock is poking down his throat and there's spit drooling out of either side of his mouth. He's not gagging, though, and I watch his throat as it relaxes, letting him take me even further down. It's frankly pornographic. No one should look this good choking on a dick. He makes it look effortless – and when his wet finger circles my hole and enters me I can't hold back anymore. I unload straight down his throat.

'Jesus Christ.' I'm pretty sure I entered another stratosphere for a moment. Everything goes fuzzy and there are stars flickering in my vision as my cock softens in his mouth. It's never been this good in my whole life.

He pulls his mouth off me, cum dribbling down his chin. 'It's Caleb Hughes, actually.'

We both laugh and he's an absolute sight. I can't stop looking at his swollen lips and the mess I've made of him. 'Kiss me.'

His kiss tastes like me and I'm greedy in the way I lap up the cum that's trickled down his jaw. All I can smell is me on him, my scent, my laundry detergent. It's intoxicating. I don't even hear the first knock at the door as he tries to climb off of me.

'Noooo,' I whine as his feet hit the floor. I just want to keep kissing him. It's the only good thing I have going for me tonight.

'The food's here.' He chucks me the remote from the end of the bed. 'Pick something to watch and I'll get everything sorted.'

It's not how I thought I'd be spending the evening. I was hoping we'd sneak in a round of celebratory sex after I pulled out the fastest lap in qualifying today. But as he sets up our dinners and I pick some comedy movie and we eat side by side chatting about everything and anything, I realise it could be so much worse. I'm lucky to have him, to be cared for by him and I can't take that for granted.

It's been such a nice evening that it makes it so easy to delete Jackson's message and his contact details once Caleb leaves to go and sleep in his own bed.

Chapter Twenty-Six

Caleb

A day at the racetrack without Johannes is not something I want to experience again.

Anton is way too green for this level of racing. He could do with some more time in the lower levels, and he struggles to take on board even the most straightforward command. I said box – box, and yet he managed to miss the fucking pit lane. I could have screamed. I did, when my mic was turned off, and Ian had to prevent me from throwing it out of reach so I didn't have to communicate with him.

Not a good day in the office, especially when Anton finished nineteenth and even that was only because another driver ended up not finishing due to an engine problem. It was almost embarrassing considering the incredible car he's in.

'How's Johannes doing?' Ian asks as we finish packing up. I'm not sticking around to assist with the garage pack-up tonight. I'm ready to run back to Jo and make sure he's doing okay.

'Two broken ribs and feeling absolutely distraught that he couldn't be out here today.'

'Yeah. And watching this shit show today probably hasn't helped. He going to be okay for the next one?' Ian asks, as he shoves his laptop into its case and throws his satchel over his shoulder.

'I don't think anyone will be able to stop him, even if he isn't.'

'He'll be back before we know it. Just one race, Nathan was saying.'

Yeah, well, Nathan would have liked it to be no races, so I'm not sure how much I value his opinion. 'Anyway, I'm off. Need to get back to, uh, work on my thesis this evening and sleep. Yeah, I'm tired.' I try to force out a yawn.

Ian eyes me suspiciously. Normally I'd be here all evening, but I'm out the door before he can even say goodnight.

'Honey, I'm home,' I call out as I slip my keycard into his hotel room door. He smiles, but frustration is etched in the way the room is an absolute mess of crumpled sheets of paper from the colouring book I thought might keep him occupied and several chocolate-stained room-service plates.

'Fucking finally,' he grumbles. It's much later than I predicted, but he knew I'd have no choice but to go to the grid today. It's not like the team has a backup race engineer.

I know Johannes is ready to climb the walls right now, but the doctor said for the first couple of days at least only light movement and exercise. Johannes is pulling threads out of the expensive bedspread right now, though, which tells me how bored he must be.

We've got each other off more in the last twenty-four hours than the whole time we've been dating, settling for messy hand jobs and blow jobs on my part, but it's been something to do. I'm pretty sure it was a blow job that convinced him to actually watch the race today. Even if he did say it would be on low volume and he couldn't promise he'd actually pay attention. I didn't believe him for a second. He'd want to catch Nils pulling up into fifth place on the grid, his highest starting position so far, and his pride wouldn't let him miss that success for his teammate.

I tug off the team jumper, folding it before draping it over the armchair and then slipping out of my trousers and boxers as he wolf-whistles. I'm in desperate need of a shower and to slip into something comfy before we spend the evening in bed together again.

'Let me wash quickly and then I'll take over keeping you occupied, okay?'

'Leave the door open so I can watch.' I almost do as well, just to give him a little bit of satisfaction, because this being unable to race thing is clearly making him cranky, but I know it'll only tempt him up out of bed and he'll be naked under the spray with me before I can blink an eye.

I grab a clean pair of his boxers and close the bathroom door behind me. 'How're the ribs feeling?' I ask, which is probably a stupid question.

'Urgh, not good. Feels like someone's trying to snap my body in half – and not in the good way like when I'm being bent over the back of a couch.' Well, at least he hasn't lost is sense of humour, or his libido. That's something.

'You're taking the painkillers, though, right?' I know some athletes can be too proud and stubborn to take them, not wanting to appear weak.

He grunts. 'I'm taking them exactly as the doctor said. They make me fucking sleepy though, so that's fun.'

I flick on the TV, trying to find something interesting to watch, but neither of us is interested in anything on offer.

It's 10 p.m. and I'm exhausted from the grind, but because he's hardly done anything today, Johannes is nowhere near ready to sleep. After the fourth groan and sigh in the last twenty minutes, I've had enough.

I remember the first time he brought me back to one of the villas in Europe and Nils had a Switch hooked up to their TV in the lounge. I'm sure I've seen it on the plane recently, too. Maybe Nils'd be willing to give it up for the night so I can keep Johannes from creating a damages bill for the team.

'I'll be back,' I say, sliding out of his bed. He mumbles something I don't catch on the way out, as I check the corridor before knocking on Nils's door.

He yells to come in, and I find the door unlocked. Not sure what's given me the nerve to knock on his room door, walk straight in and put my hand on the Switch console that seems to fly around the world with him. 'We're stealing this. Hope you don't mind.'

'Johannes has been a terrible influence on you. You used to be so polite,' Nils comments from where he's lying in his hotel bed, shirtless, watching some weird American reality show. I don't ask any more questions and I'm trying not to think about what I've interrupted as I notice both his arms are tucked under the covers.

'He's also got two broken ribs and is going absolutely mad having to lie in bed with nothing to do.' I think even I'd be going out of my mind, because though I'd have my PhD thesis to finally finish, I'd want to do everything I couldn't do in that moment.

'And he's got you playing nurse. Lucky him. I'm surprised he's not already got you in the uniform.' I hope Nils never repeats this to Johannes, because he'd be straight on Amazon ordering the skimpiest one with the fastest delivery.

'Should I be worried about you visualising that right now?'

'You're not my type, don't you worry, Hughes.' Johannes made it clear quite early on that Nils was straight, but I don't miss how his eyes scan my body in Johannes's T-shirt.

'I'm surprised you're not out tonight.'

'It's not the same without Johannes. We'll celebrate when his ribs are better. Even Harper and Elijah are having a quiet dinner with Cole and Ash. I didn't know Harper understood the word quiet.'

'Touché, team party animal.'

'I would be if your boyfriend wasn't being boring with his stupid broken ribs.'

I roll my eyes. There isn't a world in which Nils could have convinced me to let Johannes out this evening. Not that I own him, but I would have physically barricaded the door with my body before I let him be that stupid.

'Thanks again.' I wave the games console at him.

'Go, enjoy the rest of the evening with your man. Me and my hand will be in here feeling lonely.'

Not an image I ever want in my head. Gross. 'Ew. I did not need to know that. You need to get yourself a girlfriend, Nils!'

'You're telling me,' Nils mutters, but I'm half out the door, running the few steps between his and Johannes rooms before pushing open the door.

'Mission success,' I say, and his face lights up when he spots the Switch and HDMI cable in my hand and I make fast work getting it hooked up to our TV. 'I can't wait to beat your ass at Mario Kart.' He shoots me a glare now that says dream on, but he has no idea how much my siblings played this with me on the Wii when I was younger, and that I have been playing this game on Switch since the pandemic when I needed to unwind.

'Bring it on.' I chuck him a controller, before sliding back into bed next to him.

Turns out, you can be fantastic in an actual car and still be shit at a video game.

Johannes can't finish above fifth place after demanding we play it on the hardest settings because he can *manage*. I'm only familiar with first or second place, and it's all too satisfying to be beating a professional race driver's ass right now.

We only stop to order fuel – he insists that he's eaten way too much chocolate cake, but he still wants something sweet, so I ask if they'll make up a big fruit platter for the injured Johannes Müller and of course they are nothing short of happy to do so.

We eat it in between races, Johannes taking the most aggressive bite out of a slice of melon when he finishes last yet again.

He chucks the remote to the end of the bed when he loses for the fourth time in a row. He's lucky I can't currently put this on Instagram without revealing that there's something going on. What else would Caleb Hughes be doing in Johannes Müller's bed at close to midnight?

'I can't be both injured and humiliated, so I'm done for the night.' He yawns and for a second as he stretches, I think he's about to try and roll onto his bad side like an idiot, but he quickly catches himself.

'Hey,' I say, grabbing both remotes and placing them on the ottoman at the end of the bed, before turning the TV off and moving into his half of the bed. 'Come here.' I stretch open an arm so he can snuggle against me and get at least somewhat comfy before he tries to sleep tonight.

He reaches for his phone and for thirty minutes scrolls through the never-ending list of TikToks that Harper's sent him this evening. Half of them are fan edits of either one or both of them – which is only slightly concerning for their egos – but some of them are absolutely adorable clips of them as baby faced teens in go-karts.

It feels very domestic and all of a sudden, my mind is picturing many more nights like this. Cosy in bed together, him scrolling his phone, me typing away on my laptop. It feels so normal.

I can see us doing this for a long time. On the road, not hiding. Not saying we'll be doing PDA all over the grid, but I'd like us to be able to come into work together and have no one bat an eyelid. We could go away over winter break, maybe spend time at home together. Not that I have a home. I should probably start looking at a temporary rental for the winter or something, but for once I don't want temporary.

I want dinners with his – or as he keeps insisting – *our* friends. I want to make time for Cole and Ash like they keep texting me for. I want double dates with him and Harper and Kian. I want to spend every night with him and wake up in the morning to him clinging to me on one side of the bed.

I don't see why we can't have that.

'Soooo,' I linger over my words. It's not that I'm scared because I don't think he's going to decline, but it's never easy putting yourself out there. Plus, this will be the start of navigating a new era together.

'Soooo,' he teases, swiping up the last strawberry from the fruit platter.

'I was just thinking, we've been spending a lot of time together and doing these weird dates that we can manage between races and what not, and I guess what I'm trying to say is, would you wanna be my boyfriend?'

'Ooooh, boyfriend,' he says, mocking the way I rushed out that final word.

Rolling my eyes, I force out a sigh. 'Nope, I take it back. Rescind the offer. You remain just my little bitch driver.'

'Fuck you. I'm not shorter than you, asshole. I'm the tallest driver on the grid.'

'You might wanna put that on your Grindr profile.'

'Baby, I don't need a profile. I've already bagged myself the hottest boyfriend going. And, to be honest, I thought we already were…' He reaches for my hand, threading his fingers through mine and damn it if there isn't a little fizz in my nose as he squeezes.

We're doing this. I have a boyfriend. And yeah, it comes with risks to my job, but he's truly worth it.

He turns into my hold and kisses me softly, clutching the comforter to keep him in position without causing him too much pain. It's gentle and all kinds of soppy, until he winces and I force him off me to get him comfortable again.

'We should probably sleep,' I whisper into the darkness, kissing the back of his neck and then the top of his head as he slides back into a prone position.

'Caleb?' His voice is so low I almost miss the way he says my name as I'm trying to get comfy but also stay close to him without hurting him.

'Yeah?' His hand finds mine under the comforter and squeezes it gently.

'Thank you for looking after me.'

'If you'll let me, I always will.' It's a promise of a lifetime. I don't want it to come across as too much or too soon, but I'm falling for him whether I like it or not. Whether the racing world likes it or not.

Chapter Twenty-Seven

Johannes

Finishing P2 in Qatar is a fantastic feeling, but I'm absolutely desperate for that top of the podium finish again. It's been too long at this point after missing out on a whole race in Brazil, but I can feel it in my bones that it's incoming. It has to be.

Texas is where I'll finally make it happen. Where I start that final push to leapfrog Harper to the World Championship. I've made some good leeway in catching him up, but I need a win, and for him to have a really bad race and finish outside the points. I would never wish that for him – I love being his biggest competitor and our battle on the grid – but right now, I could do with his engineers fucking up a pit stop or two.

I've been trying to sleep for hours on the plane from Qatar to Austin, but I can't drift off. My usual podcast routine hasn't helped, nor has the fact that Caleb and I have sort of bedded down together, despite being in separate seats. Two separate blankets, but he's reached his hand across the lowered divide, clutching me close.

It's risky when we're surrounded by our colleagues, but the blankets cover us and Nils is the next closest person to us – and he's been conked out for longer than anyone. The plane is quiet as everyone tries to get some sleep, but what's going on in my head is stupidly loud right now.

I qualified first in Qatar, but it still wasn't enough. And, yeah, I was still recovering from two broken ribs and the pain had been a little bit bad in the actual race after taking my painkillers too early and the race being delayed.

But now, as we fly to Texas and the race isn't for a whole six days, I have plenty of time to be fully recovered and ready to make the last three races my absolute bitch. If I win all of them, it still won't be enough for me to beat Harper if he finishes second in all of them. I need Elijah to be on his absolute A game and push Harper down to third in a race – or three. I'll literally take anything at this point.

I am so fucking tired. I grab my phone from where it's on charge and, fuck, we are just an hour and a half from landing. How long have I actually been lying here? Why won't my brain just switch the fuck off? Why can't I just fucking win?

Texas. That's what I have to focus on. Visualisation. That's what my strategist is always talking about. It's not always been my go-to. I prefer the stimulator or to make the most of the free practices when it comes to getting a good feel for the track. But maybe it's what I need right now to get that win.

The Circuit of Americas is an easy one for this technique. That uphill climb at the first turn is significant and I know I need the speed to truly conquer it, so I need to be in Q1 to get up there right off the bat. Then it's all about making sure no bastard overtakes me on that sharp left turn. Not breaking too hard or risking a lock-up, but making sure I don't end up in the wall at the same time.

Then the esses – four, S-shaped corners that really test my precision. They demand a delicate balance of aggression and finesse, which is what Harper has in bucket-loads. And whilst I have the finesse, sometimes my aggression doesn't pay off.

I roll through the track in my brain, trying to picture where my weak points are and almost want to scream. This is the perfect track for Harper, damn it.

Caleb's arm slips from mine as the pilot announces our descent and people around us start to stir.

'Jesus, who's pinging off your phone?' Caleb asks as we finally land in Austin. Whoever put Qatar and Texas back-to-back needs their head checking. Worst flight of the season so far.

Peering down at my phone, I'm met with ten excited texts from Harper, letting me know that Kian's flown into Texas for the next five days to surprise him. Plus, three selfies of them together – one, very topless that I didn't need to see.

'That would be Harper. Kian's surprised him by flying in for a few days. He can't stay for the race, but I think they're both suffering withdrawal symptoms. Harper is of course very excited. He practically combusts any time Kian does something nice for him.'

'Hey, do you think they'd be up for a double date whilst we're out here? Maybe in the next couple of days before things get crazy.' Caleb's leaning across the middle of our seats and I'm so tempted to kiss him, but we aren't in private and the team would crucify us at this point in the season. We can't afford any distractions in these final weeks, and I'm sure a relationship between a driver and his race engineer would be nothing but.

'You serious? I think Harper would die if I even suggested it. He's been desperate to conduct a Spanish inquisition.'

'Well, on second thoughts…'

'Kidding, kidding. I'll make sure Kian keeps him on his leash.'

'Now I'm imaging your best friend in a harness and leash. Why would you even suggest that?'

'Stop imagining my best friend naked. That's gross.'

Nils finally stirs from the seat across the aisle, his fluffy blond hair sticking up in every direction. 'Did we land?' he mumbles.

'Yeah, we landed. You okay, bud? You look very dazed right now.' He's rubbing sleep from his eyes, blinking like he can't quite remember where he is. It's kind of cute, but then he yawns like he hasn't just slept for seven hours and I'm almost worried about him.

'I'm at the point in the season where I don't know which country or time zone I'm in. Plus, last night I was kept awake by two guys having very loud sex while I'm going through a dry period, so, you know.'

'Whoops?' Caleb offers up and I can't help but laugh. Maybe we're being way too obvious, but I don't actually care right now.

'I'm making sure our hotel rooms aren't sharing a wall tonight if it kills me. What excuse can I give the room coordinator to make sure of it?'

'Um…'

'Or we could just sleep in my room tonight?' Caleb suggests and I nod eagerly.

'Smart man. Knew there was a reason I liked you.' I brush the side of his arm with my hand almost about to rest it on his thigh when Nils clears his throat, bringing me back into the reality that we are currently on the team plane and he's the only one who knows about us.

Harper's so keen for a double date that we end up at dinner the next night. Caleb's chosen the perfect BBQ restaurant and the conversation comes easy, considering the thing we all share in common. It's nice as we enjoy a couple drinks and then the biggest platter of meat and sides anyone has ever seen.

'When I first met you two, nothing could have convinced me that a few years later you'd both be in committed relationships,' Kian says as he looks between his husband and me.

Nor me, to be honest. Even though I was more at the point where I wanted to step away from the constant sleeping around than Harper, I don't think I was close to being ready to settle down.

'Well, you are partly to thank for that. Considering you tied this one down and stopped him being such a slut.'

'I mean, tied down is one of my favourite—' Kian quickly shoves a fry into his husband's mouth, promptly shutting him up.

'Sorry, my husband possesses zero people skills, which is why he participates in such a solo sport.' We all laugh as Harper pouts. This is one of the many reasons I truly love Kian for him. He balances him out but doesn't completely restrain him from being the Harper James we all know and love.

'I'm surprised you didn't stick around in the sport,' Caleb comments as our desserts arrive. Half of us definitely shouldn't be eating them, but Caleb offered to split a piece of fudge cake and ice cream with me, and I'm weak when it comes to chocolate cake and this man sitting next to me.

I'm diving into the cake before Caleb can even finish his sentence because it looks so damn good. I'll happily pay for this with an early-morning run with Caleb tomorrow.

'Trust me, I had plenty of chances. Jackson's still trying to convince me to come back, but I can't leave the farm now. I don't even want to, which is still a shock to me considering how much I love this sport.' I'm surprised, too, because I thought Kian would die at Hendersohm. But nope, he's hardly even an affiliate at this point, except for his legacy.

'How much say does he have in the team?' Caleb asks as I steal another chunk of cake and glob of ice cream. Eating gives my hands something to do while they discuss my least favourite topic.

Nothing more uncomfortable than your current boyfriend discussing your secret ex-boyfriend with your ex-friends-with-benefits and his husband.

'Well...' Kian looks at his husband like he's not sure whether to say what he knows or not.

'What?' Caleb pushes. It's not like the whole of Hendersohm aren't aware at this point that Jackson will be taking over at the end of the season, but it hasn't been officially announced yet. There's been a ton of speculation, and no one will be surprised when it does finally get announced.

'If you were to ask me off the record, I think Jackson will be team principal by the end of the season.' Kian looks happy about that, smiling wide with pride for his friend. I know

Harper said they'd become close over the years, but this is torture.

'He's making his old man so proud,' Harper comments and my fingers grip the edge of the booth tightly. 'He's got a permanent supply of whisky in the bottom drawer, just like Anders. Can't tell you how many times I've found him a little drunk in there when he's been working late after work.'

'I've talked to him about this,' Kian replies. 'He can't keep doing that, but apparently, he's looking forward to being team principal, he's perpetually bummed about someone he lost to get there.'

'Yeah, he keeps saying the same thing to me – but he won't tell me who this guy is,' Harper says.

The last thing I need right now is Harper digging any more into that and putting two and two together. To be honest, I'm a little surprised he hasn't.

'We just need to keep being there for him, that's all we can do.'

'Hey, I'm trying. I put him to bed one night when he was too drunk to stand and I've taken him out for dinner in a lot of cities recently. Hang on, talking of that, you never did say where you went when you didn't show up for dinner with us in Zandvoort...' Harper's stare pins me to my seat as he waits an answer.

I'm about to remind him that he promised not to ask any questions, but the cogs are already turning in Caleb's head as he says, 'Hang on, didn't you say that night—' He turns to look at me and I'm frantically shaking my head.

'Oh, you bailed on us for your new boyfriend. That's low man. I told you he wasn't in a good place,' Harper quickly buts in.

I'm trapped in the corner of the booth, unable to escape this absolute torture. Caleb is staring at me and he looks confused, but also disappointed and a little angry.

I can't blame him. I kept my biggest secret from him, and that's not the basis any relationship should start on. I need to get out of here.

I feel trapped and panicky, like there's no way out. But then my rational mind kicks in, and I ask Caleb to move so I can get past. I'm up on my feet and heading towards an exit before I can stop myself.

I'm not even sure where I'm going until I'm at the back of the restaurant, pushing the emergency-exit door open, the chill of the late November air biting at my face.

For a couple of seconds, I lean my head against the brick wall, but in reality I want to slam my fists into it.

'What the fuck, Jo?' I'm trying to steady my breathing as my best friend steps out into the secluded alley behind the restaurant.

'This is all so fucked up,' I mutter, still facing the wall. I can't look at him right now and it's not even Harper's fault. I just feel like I've been transported back six months, trapped in a big secret as everything falls apart.

'What's fucked up? What are you talking about? I know I said I wouldn't ask any questions, but aren't we passed that?'

His hand touches my shoulder softly and I turn to my best friend, a single tear slipping down my cheek as he pulls me close, letting me rest my head on his shoulders.

'I fucking hate him,' I cry into his shoulder.

'Who, Jo? Who? Jackson? What did he do?' He's trying to be calm for me, but there's a nervous edge to his tone as he releases me from his grip to get a proper look at me. To try and understand what I'm saying.

He's right. We're passed that now.

'I'm sorry, Harp. I'm sorry. I couldn't tell you because he's going to be your new boss.'

'I don't understand.'

'Jackson strung me along for nearly three years and then ended it, just like that! He doesn't get to be sad about it when it was *him*. His choice. I *kept* trying, and he just pushed me away every single time for the team.'

'Ended … what? Jo, you aren't making any sense.' Confusion, then realisation is etched on Harper's face.

I've never actually said the words out loud before. It feels like a foreign language at this point.

'Our relationship. We were together.'

'I'm sorry, what?' Harper asks, his voice pitchy, arms splayed up in the air in complete and utter shock as he pulls away from me.

'You remember that night in Florida that you were pissed at me because I abandoned you and went home with someone. That was Jackson.'

'That was over three years ago! And you broke up when?'

'At your wedding.'

'Fucking hell, Jo. You're kidding me.'

'I wish I was.'

He shakes his head. 'It all makes sense now with what's happened and how you were performing earlier in the season—'

'It's why you were such a mess after Silverstone,' Caleb finishes from the doorway. I didn't even hear the door open, but he's looking silently between me and Harper trying to make sure he's pieced all of this together correctly.

He looks as broken as I feel, eyes shimmering under the luminous emergency light, hands shaking where they rest on the emergency-exit bar.

'Caleb, I'm sorry. I didn't want you to find out like this.' I go to step towards him, but he takes two back, arms wrapped around his chest, protectively.

'Find out what? This huge secret you've been keeping? Or that you're clearly still completely torn up over your ex? What has this been, huh? A rebound? Something to keep your mind off him? What the fuck, Johannes?'

'It's not like that at all.' I want to cry and scream and make him understand, but I can't because everything's a mess in my brain right now. A scramble of completely overwhelming thoughts and feelings that I can't get straight. More than two and a half years unravelling in front of my eyes that I can't even begin to process.

No matter how much my heart wants to save my current relationship, the rest of me is too much of a mess to even speak.

'I actually thought you were the good guy in this sport, Johannes. A little misunderstood after all of your antics, but if you can keep this a secret, what else are you hiding?'

Nothing. I want to say it but nothing comes out. I'm left looking at him wordlessly as he waits expectantly, before a surge of anger colours his face beetroot and he has to shake out his balled fists.

'Fantastic. And fuck you,' he grunts out, before turning back inside, the door slamming behind him again.

'FUUUUUCK!' I scream, and slam my fists into the wall, the ridges of the bricks grazing my skin.

'You need to calm down, Jojo. You don't want restaurant staff coming out here and selling some kind of anger-issues story to the press.' Since when did Harper care about the stories? He still did stupid shit even though he was happily married.

'Fucking hell, did you finally go to that PR training?' I ask, which causes us both to laugh. 'This isn't funny, he's probably going to break up with me now and never speak to me again.'

'I have to admit, even I'm confused. I'm not sure why you're this wound up. Do you still love Jackson?'

'No! I love Caleb, I just... Fuck! It was too much. Hearing all of that, hearing how hurt he is even though *he* did this. He chose the job over me. It hurt all over again, but not because I want him back or I'm still holding out hope, but because he put me through hell. He broke me and you don't just get over that in a couple of months, even if you've fallen in love with somebody else.'

'What do you mean?' His gaze narrows like he's trying to piece it together but doesn't want it to be true.

'He made me swear not to tell a soul. Ever. And then he gradually broke me down, piece by piece, day by day, and he knew I couldn't talk about it with anyone.'

'But you could have told me, Jo. I would have kept it a secret.'

'From Kian? I would never ask you to do that. And I would never ask you to choose between our friendship and your career. You know I would never do that.'

'But you're my fiercest rival and also my best friend and we make it work. I'd have found a way.'

I groan again. 'You don't think I told him that every time I pleaded the case on looping you in?'

'I don't get it.'

'Me either,' I reply, leaning against the wall to try and catch my breath after everything that's happened this evening.

'Maybe start from the beginning,' he suggests.

'We'll be here all day. The short of it is, everything was amazing at the beginning. I fell for him so quickly. Then we came back after that first winter break and things changed a bit, but not a lot. Like, he was around less, but not that it was super noticeable. Then, gradually, bit by bit, he pulled away – always leaving just enough breadcrumbs that kept me trailing after him but ultimately unsatisfied. He forgot my birthday – you remember? That night? When you all came to my room?'

Harper puts his head in his hands. 'Jojo...'

'At first it was exciting to be a dirty little secret, but then it was just dirty. Always sneaking around, like he was ashamed of me. It made me feel just so ... wrong. So bad about myself. So unlovable. I could see what you and Kian have, and I was fucking jealous, because I knew deep down he would never want that with me and that made me hate myself a little. You were right when you said in Monza that I stopped trusting myself. That I lost confidence in myself. This is why.'

'Oh, Jojo. I'm so sorry. I had no idea.' He quickly holds his hand up before he corrects himself. 'Actually, I did. I knew something was wrong. I definitely knew at the start you were seeing someone because it was written all over your face, but I had no idea it was him or that he was putting you through all of this.'

'What's going on?' Kian asks, joining us in the alley. 'I tried to stop Caleb bolting, but there was no stopping him. Did you guys have a fight?'

I shake my head, but I can't start the story again, so I look to Harper with pleading eyes. 'Johannes and Jackson were together for the last two-and-a-half years, Jackson made him keep it secret, treated him like shit and broke up with him at our wedding. I'll fill you in on the details later.'

To Kian's credit, he says nothing and accepts that he'll find out everything he needs to know later from his husband, but his face is anything but neutral.

'I'm sorry, Kian,' I say on a sob.

'I'm gonna fucking kill him!' Harper rages.

This is exactly what I didn't want. 'No, you're not, because he's about to become your team principal and he's one of your husband's closest friends. What happened between us is in the past.'

'I still wanna kill him. He's been hurting my best friend, right under my nose, for years.' Harper's practically foaming at the mouth until his husband lays a calming hand on his shoulder and Harper melts under it.

'There were good times, too... He was under a lot of stress...'

'Don't make excuses for him!' Harper protests, but I just shake my head.

'I need to go after Caleb and get him to hear me out.'

'I think that's a good idea,' Kian agrees. 'He's a great guy and I can tell how much he cares about you. I love Jackson, but ... he's like Anders in some of the worst ways and sacrifices everyone and everything at the altar of Hendersohm.'

'I don't care about any of that. I'm serious in what I'm

saying. You can't treat Jackson any differently. When he becomes your boss, Harper, he'll hold your whole future in his hands. Don't throw that away. Thanks to Caleb, I'm not broken anymore. I'm just not quite all put back together, either. But I will be. I will be.'

'Johannes Müller's words of wisdom.'

I'm not sure after all of this, that I actually have any wisdom, but I'm going to need some if I'm going to fix this between me and Caleb.

Chapter Twenty-Eight

Caleb

Stomping back to the hotel and not giving Johannes a chance to explain probably isn't the most mature decision I've ever made, but what else was there to say? It all makes so much sense now. He's been going through a break-up he had no chance of escaping. He's clearly still harbouring feelings for Jackson and how can I compete with him? The man is about to become a team principal!

He's also stupid handsome and has the racing insight of a freaking genius. I've read his blog and listened to his podcast for years. He knows his shit, even when he called Johannes an overhyped rookie four years ago.

I don't stand a chance against him. I've never been this self-conscious in my life, but I've also never fallen so hard for anyone before. Even Brad.

Yet I've given everything to Johannes – my heart, my head, my body. I couldn't have stopped it even if I tried. Johannes has his own gravitational pull. He's a star that shines so brightly, I cannot look away. But what kind of future can we have? The hotshot F1 champion and his nerdy, ginger earpiece. That's what we are, and I've been so stupid for letting myself think we could be more.

And then there's the fact that he lied to me. He could have told me in Zandvoort when I picked him up and coaxed him through his panic attack. He could have told me any one of a hundred times since then, but he chose not to.

A treacherous corner of my heart wonders if it's because he needed me to be his adoring doormat for the rest of the season because I helped him get back on top of the podium.

No, he's not like that.

I didn't think so, but I've always had so much more to lose than him. If we can't work together, Nathan will fire *me*, not Johannes. This is everything I feared when we began this relationship, and I ignored it because I wanted him so much. I used my stupid overworked brain to rationalise it away and took a risk – and now I have no choice but to guide him through the track like my heart isn't breaking because of him. I'll probably have to see Jackson, too, at least in passing, and try not to want to punch him and reveal his stupid big secret, too.

I get undressed and climb into bed, pulling the duvet over my head to try and quiet my mind and racing heart. But the second I close my eyes, my subconscious plays me an imaginary reel of Jackson and Johannes going at it, and now I need to bleach my mind. I'm restless all night, tossing and turning, phone on do not disturb so I don't feel tempted to reach out to him and tell him to come over. I just need a little bit of time to try and process.

I finally fall asleep and it feels like only seconds later that my alarm is going off and I'm dragging myself into the shower, dressing in RBF clothing and grabbing a Lyft with some of the other engineers in my apartment to the garage.

The next few days are bleak. They pass in a blur of misery and hard work as we gear up for the final three races of the season. I'm barely sleeping, and by the time Friday rolls around, I'm no use to anyone. I think I should fake being sick for the good of the team.

Of course, I have a day full of meetings, the first half just with Ian, reviewing footage, and then with some of the senior strategists. I could really do with a fully working brain today, except it's basically running on autopilot and as much caffeine I can fuel it with through energy drinks.

'Are you even listening?' Ian grunts out, banging his stack of notes against the table to straighten the pages.

'What?' I ask, not even sure what he was asking in the first place.

'Well, that answers my question. You look like shit.'

'Thanks, man. Kick a guy when he's down, why don't you.' I'm really not in the mood for Ian to be an asshole right now.

'What's going on?' he asks.

He's the last person I want to tell, but all my other friends are first and foremost Johannes's friends. I can't exactly call my parents when I never told them we were dating in the first place. So why not Ian?

'Johannes and I broke up.' There it is. Those five words that I really didn't want to say. I mean we haven't even officially broken up. I just told him to go fuck himself and then spent the next two days ignoring all his calls and messages, so it was as good as a break-up.

Ian hardly even bats an eyelid. 'Oh boy, I knew it had to be him, but I didn't think it would be this fast.'

'Yeah, well, rub it in why don't you. You were right. We got together and then it ended badly. Proved your point, didn't I.' Every word is a bitter mess. I hate that this is exactly what he warned me about. I hate more that I didn't listen and that I actually thought Ian was being a dick.

'This is exactly what I warned you about.' Ian sighs, pulling his glasses off to rub at the bridge of his nose. 'I could see it happening over the summer. You started looking at him differently and then you started hanging out with him, even flirting on the radio like idiots and now you're moping over him – and you still have to work with him. It's ridiculous.'

'Wow, thanks, man. Really appreciate it. I'm talking to you because I trust you and I've always admired the work you've done in this sport.' Or because I have no one else to talk to, and I at least don't think Ian will report me. Lecture me about being an idiot, sure, but I don't think he'll go running to Nathan telling him everything. He has nothing to gain from that, and the team needs Johannes and me to work together for the last few races for Johannes to have any chance of still bringing home the Driver's Championship.

'I'm just being honest with you. I'm not about to sugarcoat the fallout that could come from this. Plus, it'll be your job on the chopping block, not his. He could actually win this whole thing, so they'll never sacrifice him. You'll be wheeled quietly out the back door and for what?'

For him. It's idiotic to even still be thinking that it would be worth it when I've had to witness him breaking down and losing his damn mind over another guy. Someone he was with for *years*. Jackson Calder. Not in a million years did I see that coming.

I'd never have even guessed in my wildest dreams. But looking back now at how Johannes has been this season, especially in the second half, it's clear he was heartbroken. I hate that that's what Jackson did to him, and I hate that I feel sorry for him even now, when it's me that's heartbroken.

It's so easy to love Johannes Müller. He's fun, and playful but determined, and he has the kind of drive that any of the other racers would kill for. He's also caring and gentle, and when you're with him you can't help but feel cherished and safe. I already miss being wrapped up in his arms and it's only been two days. How pathetic is that?

'Well, it doesn't matter now, because it's over. And the season will be done in three races' time and I'm sure after winter break it'll all be forgotten about.' Maybe Johannes and Jackson will give it another shot. Maybe Jackson will poach him for Hendersohm. Elijah's getting on in age, and with two kids and one on the way, I'm sure he'll be wanting to spend more time at home.

That thought messes me up through every meeting of the day and then keeps me up most of the night.

When it's time for free practice one, I can't even look at Johannes. I feel his presence the second he comes into the garage. Every single hair on my body stands on end and my mouth goes dry, and that's before I turn around to get a look at him.

He looks like shit. Stubble on his chin, puffy eyes, no smile. He's courteous to the team and everyone around him, but his spark isn't there. It's like we're back on that beach in Zandvoort, or on the plane after Silverstone and he's a broken shell again. Then it was Jackson Calder's fault, but this time he bears his share of responsibility. He should have *told* me. And now it's up to me to coax a dazzling performance out of him or my head's on the chopping block. I can't help but be taken back to that alleyway, the thick and fast tears pouring from his eyes as he recalls to Harper how Johannes broke his heart. Their two-and-a-half-year relationship. All of that hurt, poured out into that alleyway.

'Morning,' he says as he approaches me and I grip my tablet to the point that it's causing indents in my hand. 'Can we, uh, talk before I have to go warm up?'

I shake my head, not trusting my words right now. If I speak, I'm either going to say something I regret or I'm going to tell him everything will be okay and haul him into my arms. And neither approach will solve any of my problems.

'Please,' he begs and at least he has the dignity and respect to do it quietly.

'I can't, Johannes. Not here, not right now. Can we just get the race weekend out of the way and then we'll talk?'

He deserves a chance to explain himself and I need to understand why this has all collapsed so spectacularly.

He sighs before resigning himself to the fact that I'm not going to give him any more than that. 'Okay, yeah. Thank you. Straight after the race, though, we'll talk in private. I have so much I need to say and I just, uh, I miss you, Caleb.'

My heart shatters on the spot, because I miss him way more than I'll ever admit.

'Me, too,' I whisper back, before pushing my chair away from him because I can't be so close to him right now. Not unless I want to do something stupid like blow off talking all together and just kiss him. That's what my heart really wants. 'After the race,' I confirm, and force my eyes back to my screen, hoping he'll take the hint that the conversation is over.

And then I'm disappointed when he walks away, as though that wasn't what I asked him to do. My heart longs for him to fight for us, for me, for him to tell me I've got it all wrong and he's over Jackson and I'm the one he wants, but I'm not stupid enough to believe that will happen. I watched him cry his heart out for Jackson Calder – no way would he ever do that for me.

This isn't some romcom, where the nerdy sidekick gets the super-hot megastar. This is real life. *My* real life. And in three weeks' time, when the season is over, I'll go back to Tennessee for a while and allow my mom to send me on some shitty first dates before returning to the factory to start the season all over again. On my own. Because that's how this story ends.

Chapter Twenty-Nine

Johannes

Free Practice 1 of Texas feels flat. I'm pushing hard on the track, maybe a little harder than I normally do, putting out great numbers, keeping myself in contention, but it all just feels like a giant ball of crap. Like I'm not enjoying being in the car. Like that fearless, reckless spark inside me isn't lit up today. I'm driving because I know I have to, not because I want to or because I have the desire to win.

'Looking good out there. Any feedback?' Caleb asks, and I miss him even more as I hear his voice in my ear. This is not the right time to plead with him, though it's all I want to do. This is our workplace, and I have to respect that he doesn't want to talk.

'All good,' I mumble. The car actually does feel good. The grip is great and everything feels smooth, but my brain is buzzing all over the place. I've managed to avoid seeing

Jackson until today, and then suddenly he's everywhere I look. It's like he's haunting me.

'Roger.' Caleb not pushing for more information than 'good' is a clear sign that he doesn't want to talk to me right now.

Even though he's promised me a chance to talk after the race on Sunday, I can't wait that long. I need to know we can fix this. I need to tell him that Jackson is nothing but the past. That he means nothing to me.

I pull into the pit as the hour ends and let the engineers get to work. When I get out of the car, I bump into Harper.

'You okay, man?' he asks and I just shrug. 'You and Caleb still not talking?'

I shake my head. 'I wish… Fuck, I've messed everything up. I want to prove to Caleb that I've closed the chapter on Jackson. How do I do that?'

Almost as if he's listening, my phone lights up and it's him. That number again.

'What does he want?'

'To talk, apparently,' I reply, my eyes skimming the message asking if I have any time before qualifying.

'Why don't you speak to him, clear the air and get all the closure you need and then you can go into the race and everything will be good.'

'I don't even know if I can bear to. I just want everything to work out with Caleb. I miss him so much right now.'

'Then face Jackson and tell him it's one hundred per cent over. Tell him to stop messaging you. I'll come with you, if you want. Kian and I both will. We'll be there to support you. Give us an hour and we'll meet you at his office.'

That's how I find myself being snuck in through the back

door of the Hendersohm garage after Free Practice 2 and deposited outside of Jackson's office. Harper knocks on the door before I get the chance to chicken out, and both he and Kian agree to wait outside for me.

'Johannes,' Jackson says softly as I close the door behind me and step into his office. 'How are you doing after Brazil?'

I groan, I hoped he'd get the message that I didn't want to speak when I didn't reply to his stupid text. He gestures for me to take a seat and it's only then that I see it. His tired eyes meet mine. His hair is a floppy mess and there's a stain on the front of his Hendersohm shirt. A tiny bit of my anger deflates.

'Better.' It's the only word I can force out, and I don't sit down. After all, I'm not staying. I just want to say my piece and get the fuck out of here.

'Good, I'm glad. It's no fun winning when my guys don't have any competition out there.' I'm almost offended on the behalf of the likes of Ogum and Kinsley and even Nils now, but I also don't care about his opinion.

'What do you want, Jackson? You asked for this meeting and I'm sure as fuck it wasn't to discuss my ribs.' I fold my arms over my chest.

'Is that Harper and Kian waiting outside my door?' he asks and I nod. 'They know?'

Of course that's the first thing he latches on to.

'Yeah, they know, and I'm not here to apologise for that. It should never have been this way, Jackson. You have to know that.'

He drops back into his plush chair and gestures for me to sit opposite him again, but I continue to stand. I'm not about to give him a single iota of control over me. I've fought too hard to claw my own power back.

'I know,' he agrees, and I am surprised at how easily and quickly his answer comes.

'You do?'

He nods. 'Yeah, fuck.' He looks around at the mess that seems to be taking over his whole workspace. 'I'm not sure any of this was meant to be like this, but it's where we are.'

'So, you're taking over the team?' He nods again.

'Don't you want to?' I ask, and he just laughs. 'I'm being serious. you threw me away like trash for all this, so I at least deserve to know whether it was worth it. Don't I?'

He sighs, closes his laptop and undoes the top couple of buttons of his shirt before leaning back in his seat. He looks rough, there's no denying it.

'Yeah, you do. Firstly, Jo, I am sorry about how everything went down. I was selfish and stupid, trying to have it all when this job was eating up every moment of my day. It's a lot. I don't know how Dad did it. But I want to find that balance like he did with Joyce, his new wife. I want that kind of peace … with you. I'm so sorry I hurt you. I wish I'd never broken up with you.' Every word depletes him, and I see the regret truly is there, but it doesn't hurt like I thought it would.

And in absolutely no way does it make me want to run back to him.

Jackson always spoke a lot about his dad. About how much Anders did for him, especially after his mum died. How his dad supported him, making sure Jackson wanted for nothing. It makes all the sense in the world that Jackson felt like he couldn't say no.

'So, that was your big plan? Get me in here and, what, convince me to give this another go?' I gesture between the two of us. 'After you strung me along for years, promised the world and only tossed me scraps of affection?'

'I loved you so much that I couldn't stop. Even when a month went by without us hardly seeing each other, to get to call you at the end of a tough week and know you were there made taking on this job so much easier.'

'For you, maybe. For me it was fucking hell, Jackson. You put me through hell.' I'm glad to hear anger in my voice rather than sadness. He doesn't deserve my tears.

'I am really truly sorry, Jo. I mean it. I see now how selfish I was. In the moment I didn't see that, and that's so fucked up. I wanted it all and I couldn't have it. The happier I saw my dad become, the more he brought up leaving the team, the more I knew I had to end things with you.'

Jackson's resigned himself to having nothing else but this job. I almost feel sorry for him.

'And you thought dumping me at my best-friend's wedding after a humiliating performance on the track was the right time to do that? You nearly cost me my season.'

'I know and there aren't enough times or ways I can say sorry—'

'You're right, there aren't,' I interrupt.

'You've pulled it back, though. It's clear from the way you're rising back up towards that top spot every weekend.'

'No fucking thanks to you! Everything I've achieved since then has been because I refused to let you break me. Because I have people around me who love me and support me and value me. When you stand at the top of Hendersohm, you'll realise you're completely alone and you'll always wonder whether it was worth it. But when I stand at the top of the podium, which I will at the end of this season, I know I'll never stand there alone, and that makes everything I achieve worth a thousand times more. Enjoy the view from the top, Jackson. I know I will.'

'Please, Jo, please will you give me another chance? I don't want to be at the top all on my own. I want you there with me.'

'Not a fucking chance. I've found something greater than you and I ever could have had. Someone who loves me in a way I don't think you're even capable of.'

His face falls, and I think this is when he knows there's no chance left at all.

'I'm glad for you, Jo, I really am. That's what you deserve.' He sounds earnest but I'm so over this. I truly don't care anymore.

'Good luck in the rest of the season. May the best man win,' I say.

I don't wait for his reply. I'm just glad my friends are waiting for me outside. Kian and Harper step away from the door as it opens. While Kian steps into the office, Harper slings an arm around me to guide me out of the backdoor they snuck me in.

'You okay?' He asks as we walk back through the paddock towards my own team.

'Yeah, I really am. Closure sure feels good.' The shaking hands that I walked into his office with are gone. My whole body feels the relief of the confrontation, and I hold my head high again.

'I don't like that glint in your eye at all. You're going to try and destroy me on track today, aren't you?'

I smirk at him.

'You have no idea, Harps.'

He grins and accepts the challenge.

'You might want to look into some therapy for your boss, though,' I say. 'I think he needs help.' The fact that I can be so objective about his situation is proof – if I needed it – that I'm free of his ghost forever.

'He'll have the support. Hendersohm is a family. We'll make sure of it.' Harper nods, and I'm glad that he's actually listened to me and not taken his personal feelings towards Jackson into the workplace. He's being pretty level-headed about it, but I do worry that when Kian goes back to the UK again that might change.

'All that's left now is to win back the heart of my super-hot race engineer,' I say.

'Maybe focus on one thing at a time, Jo.'

'I know, I just miss him.' Way more than I ever thought I would let myself miss anyone again. I never expected that I'd ever want to throw my heart into another relationship, yet here I am, having fallen hard again, and I'm determined not to hurt him with my past hurt.

'I'm sure you do, but this time tomorrow the race will be over and you can take some time out together before China.'

'Oh yeah, because back-to-back racing leaves lots of time for that.' I can't get on a plane with him to the other side of the world with all this animosity hanging between us. If I don't win, I don't want anyone to blame my performance on him. I won't risk him losing his job.

'You'll find time, or you'll make it, if it's important. Look, I need to get back to the team for the next practice. Speak later, okay?' Like the messy bastard that he is, Harper spots a camera watching us and leans up on his tippy toes to kiss my forehead. I push his face away with my palm, but we're both laughing, and damn, that feels good.

I wait for everything in my brain to click into place after the conversation, but things still aren't right because Caleb's not talking to me.

I need ten minutes on my own to focus my thoughts and get in the zone, so I glide through the garage with my head down praying no one stops me on the way to my room. The second I'm at the door, I step inside and lock it behind me.

Sitting right there, on the table next to my bed, is a piping-hot takeaway cup of coffee and my heart has never felt so full.

Chapter Thirty

Caleb

I'm on my third energy drink as I sit down at pit wall for the US Grand Prix. The concerning thing is I'm not even close to the vibrating, bouncing-off-the-wall mess I should be in after this much caffeine. One too many long days at work and one too many sleepless nights will do that to you.

It surprises no one that I've somehow thrown myself into my job even more to help Johannes bring the championship home over the next three races. Despite the fact that my brain and heart are at war, I was still working to the middle of the night last night with Alek, our lead strategy engineer, preparing for today.

Has it been easy coming to work the last couple days and having to see him, speak to him, be all up in his space, when we haven't had the chance to talk about him and Jackson? Absolutely not. But this is still my job, and I still care about him deeply. Even if we do end up calling it quits, it still matters to me whether he wins or not. It matters very much indeed.

I don't want to call it quits. I think now the shock's worn off, my emotions are less acute. And now I just miss him. So, he didn't tell me a really big secret – he never actually lied to me. He never betrayed me. Not my sweet, caring, country-music-loving Johannes. Not the guy who cooks for me every time he has the chance and who looks at me like he wants to give me the world. Not the Johannes who so clearly wants to be loved and made to feel worthwhile. My blood boils thinking of all that Jackson must have done to make him feel that way.

And nothing will stop me getting him his race day coffee. I have to courier it to the garage, but it's there waiting for him when he arrives for the day. It's tradition now. Superstition, or whatever. And the fact is I still want to do nice things for him, despite being mad at him, which says more about my stupidity than anything. Maybe I care too much.

I don't doubt that he cares about me, but the depth and breadth of my love is so vast that I could drown in it. Being cradled in his arms made me believe he felt the same way, but I was wrong once before, and now I worry that my inexperience in healthy adult relationships is really showing.

I shake off the emotions and put my headset on for the day so I can drown out all the thoughts with radio chatter. Nothing compares to a race day. There's no thrill like it. Sitting at the pit wall and seeing every decision Johannes makes on track is a privilege. Being a part of his process, assisting in every way I can, is a joy. Getting to be in the atmosphere that comes from ten teams battling to come out on top, the whizz of cars going by, the buzz of engineers working their asses off to change tyres in two seconds... I'm already dreading the post-season blues when my life becomes solely writing my thesis again.

Everywhere is already busy as we get ready for race day, and there's a sizzling tension up and down the paddock as the battle for the championship reaches its peak. I've seen Nils this morning looking more excitable than ever. He's going to finish in the top ten overall this season for the first time in his career and it'll probably be a mid-table spot, too, which is impressive. Next year I can see that being even higher. He must know what's going on right now, because he offers me a small smile with a hint of pity as he says hello to Ian and bounds into the garage.

Johannes was pulled straight into press briefings this morning, but the second I start thinking about him it's like the earth conjures him up for me and I watch out of the corner of my eye as he approaches the pit wall slowly.

'Hey,' he says, hands cradling the coffee cup I saw being delivered five minutes ago. 'Thank you for this.'

'Of course,' I reply, because I can't imagine having not gone out of my way to get it here for him. To keep that stupid superstitious luck going. When, really, I do it so he knows that he has someone who cares about him. Someone who's rooting for him.

'It's really good. Nothing will top Belgium's, but this is exactly what I need right now.' His eyes meet mine and he offers me a small smile and I'm instantly smiling back, hands itching to reach for him and pull him close, but I can't. We can't. Not right now, not here, not before the facts are straight and ironed out, and even then it's not appropriate to bring our relationship drama into the workplace.

'I'm glad.' Apparently, I'm unable to say more than two

words to him now. This is not what I want at all, especially as he takes a small step back away from the pit wall.

He's all suited up, waiting to be allowed to go do the formation lap and get situated on the grid. He might be sitting on the right-hand side of the front two spots, but I know he has it in him to knock Harper out of the way by that first corner. Johannes has won the last two US Grand Prix, and I see no reason for it not to be a third today.

'You done? I can toss that for you.' He hands me the empty cup and when our fingers brush, it's like a stupid romcom of electricity sparking between us, and I hate it. Except I don't. I love it.

He's still standing next to my screens, waiting, hand twitching where he's resting it on the table. 'Anything else?'

'No, just needed a second. Sorry.'

My heart physically hurts, like a pain twinges in my chest because this man seems to have experienced nothing but heartbreak and I can see it on every inch of his face. His eyes are a little glossy as he tugs his bottom lip between his teeth like he's contemplating the world.

'No, it's okay. It's going to be a busy day. Take all the time you need. I'm sure someone will be calling you soon.' He nods and I almost want to reach out and squeeze his hand, reassure him that it's all going to be fine.

I start my own race prep, and then in a blur the national anthem is finished and the race begins. The first forty-two laps are calm, although in the thirty-ninth lap, Nils overtakes Elijah for the first time ever and sits in P3 behind Johannes. It's a joy to be able to tell Jo that at least, but I can tell he's more focused on getting past Harper in front.

'Focus, Johannes, focus,' Nathan says from beside me and I

wish I could rip his headphones off and toss them onto the track to be annihilated. He must know how much Johannes hates hearing from him when he's driving. Part of me wishes Johannes would just tell him to fuck off – it's not like it would be the first time a driver's told someone in their ear to shut the hell up.

'I am fucking focusing,' Johannes grits out, and to prove it he closes the gap to just 0.5 seconds between him and Harper as they take turn ten together, heading straight into a DRS zone.

He's right up Harper's ass as they go into turn eleven and then on the last straight of sector two, he zips around him like a fucking ninja and steals the leading spot. I almost want to switch over to Harper's onboard right now. I bet he's swearing up an angry storm about his best friend.

'You're a P-One, man, P-One. This is exactly what you came to do.'

He whoops into the mic and then settles back into a focused silence, determined to bring this home.

The clean air between Johannes and the rest of the pack is beautiful. The distance he's put between him and Harper is even more so. He's cruising. There are still thirteen laps to go, but he has this sewn up. The tenths of a second begin to really rack up as he gets to the end of this lap.

'Oh, fuck,' Ian says from beside me and Nathan and me are both looking over his shoulder as we hear the loudest thump not too far from where we're sitting. On his screen, Nils is in the wall and there's another car in the side of him.

When I squint closer, I realise that not only is Nils in the wall, but his car's upside down and he's not moving. No! Christ. It looks bad on this screen. 'Who hit him?' I ask, pushing my mic up, even though I know it's not on right now so Johannes can't hear me, but I have to be sure.

The camera angle on my screen shows a Hendersohm car and Ian is quick to confirm. 'It's Harper. I don't think it was either of their faults. There's something on the track. The next screen over he zooms out and yeah, there's a fucking wing mirror on the track. How had no one seen that coming off? It's pure fucking negligence that it wasn't spotted and cleared up, even if they had to introduce a virtual safety car to do it.

Now there's two potentially injured drivers in the wall and the race is about to be slowed completely.

There's already double-waved yellow flags out on the track, and now I have to tell Johannes what's happened.

'Hey, Johannes, please make sure your speed is significantly reduced. Don't even overtake any cars that you might need to lap. Keep it slow for now, man.' It's inevitable that this race is now going to need a safety car, and seconds later, race control tells us one is about to be deployed.

'Tell me what's going on, Caleb.' The words come out tense, almost as if he's saying them through gritted teeth.

'There's been a crash. Both cars are in the wall. Safety car incoming, start to slow down, please.'

I'm watching as he grips the wheel, trying his absolute best to stay calm and focused. This is the worst part of this sport, how much risk and danger it can bring. The crash looked ugly, and my eyes keep flicking to Ian's screen as he waits for the emergency team to get to Nils or for Nils to respond.

The yellow flags are waving around the grid, while the safety car is leaving the pit lane to join the track and keep everyone under control until the situation is cleared.

'Any more information, man? Who is it?' Johannes asks as

he sits directly behind the safety car, zigzagging to keep some warmth in his tyres while obeying the speed limit.

I think about what to tell him.

'Nils!' Ian calls out into his mic next to me. He's done the gentle thing trying to get Nils to respond, and now he's desperate. We can see from the technology that Nils's heart's beating, but he looks knocked out and he's still not saying anything. 'Why is it taking so long to get to him, please?' Ian asks, and it's frustrating because he's in a part of the wall where getting access seems difficult.

It feels like it's been forever, but it's only been a minute or two of waiting. 'Nils!' he shouts once more and finally I watch Nils stir on the screen.

'The fuck happened?' he asks groggily and the whole pit wall breathes out a sigh of relief.

Ian confirms that he's crashed and to let the emergency-response team help him. When they get to him, they are quick to assess his safety to climb out of the car and even faster to confirm they think he's concussed.

'Jo, we're just waiting on updates that both parties are okay, but the crash was between Harper and Nils. Nils has been on the radio to Ian. He's all right, but a little bit spacey so they're thinking a concussion, but we're still waiting on an update on the radio from Harper.' I'm beyond aware I'm reeling off his worst-case scenario, but he handles it like the true professional he is. Probably aware that the TV cameras will be on him right now.

'As soon as you know, please, Caleb,' he begs, clearly not bothered that the whole world will hear him. This man. He has so much heart that not enough people get to see. How much he truly cares about the people around him.

'You know I will. Just keep your eyes on the road, keep it slow. They're definitely going to have to remove both cars from the track, so it's going to be like this for a few laps. No pit stop for us, but some guys behind you have got one in.'

I couldn't care less about what other teams are doing, I just need to keep Johannes focused and on track until the end of the race. I'm more than glad that Nils is talking. If he wasn't I'd be very concerned, it being his favourite pastime. A concussion isn't ideal, but the med team will take care of him.

I've got one of the guys next to me listening to Ash and Harper's radio stream so that I can update Johannes as soon as I know anything. If I were to look at the crash as an outsider, Harper came off much worse. He clipped the side of Nils's car as they were spinning out, and it flipped him multiple times until the wall caught him. It wasn't at incredibly high speed, but it was at a nasty angle that left the car upside down.

They are literally taking his car apart to get him out and it's not nice to watch, but when they free Harper gently and he walks to the medical car, the tempo of the world around me falls back into place.

'Jo, Harper's okay. Car's fucked but he's out and walking,' I confirm.

His voice is shaking as he replies, 'Thank you, Caleb. Tell Nils I'll win this one for him.'

'Yeah. He's not happy. Can't believe that he was in third and now he's out.'

'I bet he's pissed. Who's behind me now?'

'Elijah, and with Harper out, the second this safety car disappears he's going to be up your ass, so we're going to need to get some speed to pull away from him.'

'How many laps to go?'

'Eleven,' I reply. Eleven long laps for him to defend.

Plenty of time for him to find some pace again. Two more slow laps pass, and finally the green flag appears and the safety car slips back off the track and he's off again, picking up speed as quickly as he possibly can.

I know he'll do his absolute best to bring it home. No doubt every sports channel in the world aired his promise to Nils and Nils will one hundred per cent hold it against him if he doesn't keep to his word.

Chapter Thirty-One

Johannes

It would be the biggest lie in the world to say I feel level-headed as I race into the sixty-first lap at the Circuit of the Americas.

I've had to force my hands to stop shaking and I can feel sweat dripping down my forehead – and not just because it's a warm evening in Texas. Disturbing images that I can't seem to shake flash before my eyes of both my best friend and teammate in a tangled, bloody heap on the side of the track. I know it's not the case, I know they're both out of their cars and conscious, which is what's important, but it doesn't stop the way my thoughts race.

This sport. I mustn't think about it whilst I'm still behind the wheel. I need to focus on the road. Need to focus. The laps of the safety car fucked my tyres a little, but with Elijah behind me I know he's probably feeling a lot like me right now and he won't be one hundred per cent with it either. This should be an easy one-two to take it home for both of our teammates, but we both know the sport doesn't always work like that.

'Caleb?' I ask. 'Can you talk to me a little? I need something to drown my thoughts out.' I shouldn't be asking this on the radio, not when these channels can be broadcast live on sports networks all across the world, but I need him right now. I need a little soothing.

He might resent me a little. Might think I made him my rebound or second choice. Or that I was still in love with stupid Jackson, but he's still my race engineer and I know he takes that job seriously; and if this is what I need to get through the next eleven laps he'll do it.

'I have eleven nieces and nephews,' he starts, telling me again about his family, and I finally allow myself to get comfortable in the chair again, eyes solely on making sure I'm not fucking up. My brain relaxes again. 'Big family, the youngest of four brothers and I was a big surprise. There's nineteen years between my next brother, Gregg, and then twenty between me and Damon and twenty-two between me and Joshy. They'll love that they might get a mention on TV. I taught them to love this sport. They were all football stars growing up. American that is, not the other kind. Soccer.'

I pull a face at the word. *Soccer*. Nope. It will always be football and he knows that.

'There's only six years between me and my oldest niece, Laurie. I was an uncle at six, isn't that wild?'

I hum, because it is. Having no siblings, I won't ever get to experience that, but I can imagine Caleb is an incredible uncle. He's very doting, even on me, and I'm nothing but a pain in his ass – literally – sometimes. He must love being able to make eleven nieces and nephews feel special.

'They are also a wide range of ages with Laurie being the oldest and then Brent the youngest at just four. It makes for very loud Thanksgivings and Christmases, but I don't think my family would have them any other way. Ma loves hosting us all. They built an extension on the family house when my brothers started having babies. Their wives, I mean, not them. It meant there was always space for everyone to stay, for everyone to sit comfortably at dinner and TV time.'

I can picture it. Even though he's spoken about his parents and siblings before, I imagine him at home with them now.

'I bet it's cosy and full of love,' I say.

'It's very loud, but in the best possible way. All that joy in one building.'

'I bet you're looking forward to winter break so you can see them,' I say. We'll be apart. It'll be the longest we'll have been apart since getting to know each other. I can't think about that now. I can't imagine not seeing him all the time, hearing from him every day, being able to sneak into his room or him into mine and get completely wrapped up in him. I'll miss him in a way I don't think I've ever missed another person before.

His lanky frame in my bed, the way he likes to snuggle on my chest. His face in the morning when he squints to find his glasses because he insists he's basically blind without them.

'I really am.' His voice is so soft and the only thing I'm aware of now is the track and the way he's talking to me. Nothing else. He's so good at this. He should do audio books or something. 'Five laps to go, Jo. You've put an eight-second gap between you and Elijah. Beautiful pace. Because of the safety car you've got a lot of clean air out ahead. I don't think you'll lap anyone before the end at this rate.'

That's good to know. Ten minutes and the race will be over.

I'll be able to get out of the car and see for myself that the two of them are okay. Caleb continues to talk about his family and his childhood, and his words keep me going. The dulcet sounds of his voice lull me into a sense of safety and familiarity that strips away the panic I felt at hearing about Nils and Harper, and it drives me to finish the race.

It's hard to celebrate coming out on top with everything that happened during the race. I don't even need to be told by our PR team to downplay my excitement about the win, because I'm already there. It's a great and much-needed twenty-five points, but not at the expense of two other drivers. My team cheers for me, but I just want to find Caleb and get an update.

I push through a crowd of sweaty engineers in RBF suits until I find him.

'How are they?' I ask, the second I get to him. I wish I could steal a private moment with Caleb and get a hug from him – I really need it right now – but there are too many people around. Too many prying eyes already trying to catch my reaction to the race and the crash.

'Harper's right side was hurting so they've taken him in to be X-rayed and Nils went behind them. He's going to have a head scan and be kept in at least overnight for concussion check, but mostly they are okay.'

I know I have so much to do after the win today, but all I want is to get to the hospital and see them. The worst part is, I know they'll be showing the accident on repeat in the cool-down room, and I can't think of anything worse than having to watch that right now.

I can't even work myself up to fake excitement on the podium when Nils and Harper are in the hospital, but I know I don't have a choice. The fans who travel pay so much money to see this, to watch the podium celebrations from the track.

Yet I still can't shake the cold sweat that prickles my back, my mind still trapped in those silent, slow minutes in the car when nothing felt real and the world stilled around me.

'Hey,' Caleb says softly, reaching out to touch my arm. 'You okay?'

I shake my head, 'No, fuck. Can you convince Nathan to let me to sneak out the back door? I just want to see them both.'

'Not a chance in hell, but we'll rush you through as quickly as possible. Media will understand, and I'll talk to PR myself, if I have to. They can put some kind of statement out saying you headed straight from podium to go be with your teammate. Positive spin or whatever.'

I lean into his touch, wishing I could tumble into his arms right now and let him hold me. Maybe there the world wouldn't feel so fucking flat.

'I'm going to hug you, okay?' Caleb says. 'Just for a second, because you look like you need one. And no one in the world would dispute a hug between a driver and his race engineer, especially after the race you've just had.'

I fold into his arms and let him hold me, and I don't care what anyone says about us. About this. Make it what they want. All it actually is, is him giving me the comfort I need.

I make every second count as his arms wrap round me, engulfing my body. Breathing in his amber scent, I allow myself to relax for a moment, limbs softening as I let him hold me up. It's over all too soon, though, and he takes all the comfort with him when he goes.

Abi guides me to the cool-down room.

'Doing okay?' Elijah asks as I pull on my winner's cap and glug down half a bottle of water. I drop into the seat next to him and catch his hands gripping the underside of the chair. He's probably the only person who gets it right now.

'Ish,' I reply, wiping sweat off my head before pulling on the cap. 'What the fuck happened?'

'Missed debris on the track, from what I understand from Cole. Harper must have seen it or clipped it, and he swerved, but Nils couldn't slow down and they basically wiped each other out. Harper was going faster, and when they were spinning, he ended up hitting Nils and flipping the car. Don't fucking watch it, man. My heart was in my throat when I caught the replay. Trust me.'

It's definitely not something I will be seeking out anytime soon, not until I've seen in person that they are both alive and well with no permanent damage.

I know the cameras in here are streaming us across the world, so I limit what I say.

'I just hope they're both okay. Caleb says Nils has a concussion. He was chatting a lot of shit apparently and they need to do some scans.'

'Sounds like Nils.' Briefly, we both laugh, before the mood sours as they start to show the crash on the screen in the cool-down room.

'Jesus, fuck,' I groan as I bear full witness to the way Nils rolls three times before the barriers catch him from flying out of the circuit completely.

'He's lucky to have got away with just a concussion. That's a nasty crash. Ash said Harper was doing okay but he was in pain, so they obviously want to get him fully checked out in the hospital.'

Which makes sense, they don't want to miss anything and have him end up with a serious injury or an internal bleed or whatever. Fuck, I can't even think about it.

'Sometimes you forget how brutal it can be out there. I hope an official complaint is made about that debris. Even I could see it in that video. There's no reason it should have been missed.' I make a mental note to make sure Caleb pushes for the issue to be raised, given it could have been so much worse if there were more cars involved or if the cars had been going any faster.

Up on the podium, Ogum sprays us both with Champagne and I'm glad to keep a change of clothes in my cubby here because I don't want to go and sit in the hospital in a sticky, uncomfortable mess. I feel sorry for Ogum, because it's been a while since he's been up here and it must be exciting for him to score the big points, but I can't think about anything but my friends.

The second we're allowed down from the podium, I storm through the garage as far away from the press line as possible. I get changed and pull out my phone as I jog towards the cars.

'Hey, you ready?' Caleb calls after me. He's clearly been waiting for me.

'Ready?' I ask. I thought the team had agreed for me to skip the interviews? 'I can't talk to anyone right now, Caleb. I just want to make sure they're okay.'

'No, I meant to go to the hospital. Car's out front waiting for us.'

'Us?' I sound like a robot with all these single-word

questions, but I have no idea what's going on right now and I just want to get out of here.

'Of course. I wouldn't let you go to the hospital on your own. Come on.' He grips my elbow and guides me out the back door, where luckily the press haven't been allowed, and I get to slip into the car undisturbed.

'You don't have to do this, Caleb,' I say. 'I know we said we'd talk, and we will, but—'

'Jo, they are your priority right now and I'm here to support you. Nothing else matters other than getting you to the hospital.' He takes my hand and I'm thankful for the partition between us and the driver because I'm gripping his hand like it's my only lifeline. 'There's nowhere else I'd be other than here with you, Johannes. I hope you know that.'

It's the hope I need to see me through the journey to the hospital.

Chapter Thirty-Two

Caleb

'You look like shit,' Johannes says, his forced laugh getting caught in the back of his throat as we step into Harper's room. Harper's shirtless, and one side of his chest and arm is absolutely covered with angry-looking bruises.

He doesn't seem to be hooked up to any monitors, though, which is always a good sign, and there are no casts or slings on any part of his body. It's still not a sight you want to see in this sport. The thrill of it sometimes allows you to forget the danger until you witness the crashes.

I've loved this sport for a long time, but now that I'm close to so many of the drivers and engineers, accidents hit hard.

'You doing okay?' I ask Harper as Johannes perches on the end of the hospital bed.

'All good. No broken bones. Can you believe it? Just bruises.' He gestures to where he's turning black and blue. 'I'm just waiting to be cleared to go back to the hotel. But first I have to deal with this worrywart.'

He thumbs over towards where his phone is next to him on the pillow. Kian can be seen moving around frantically on the screen. 'My car is ten minutes away,' he says.

'I've told him he doesn't need to come.' Harper sighs, but I don't for a second believe he means it, and while we've only been friends for six months, I wouldn't be surprised if he's actually delighted that Kian's on the way. They seem to enjoy being joined at the hip.

'And I told him that there's nowhere else I'd rather be and that I started packing my bag as soon as I saw the crash.' Kian's tone, and the way he's throwing a duffel bag over his shoulder, tells me this isn't something anyone can stop him doing. I'd be the same if it was Johannes, and if I'm thinking that at this point, when I'm still not even sure what's going on between us, or between him and Jackson, then I can't imagine how Kian's feeling about seeing his husband all battered and bruised.

'No broken bones, no concussion or internal damage. Just cuts and bruises. I'm basically one hundred per cent,' Harper tries one more time, but Kian just shakes his head. There's a small smile on Harper's lips despite the amount of pain he must be in.

'Just let me come, okay? I want to be there for you. You're going to need someone to ice those bruises and help you out.'

I'm not sure we should be here for this conversation, but luckily Kian lets Harper know his car's outside and that he'll see him in around thirteen hours' time. They each hang up with 'I love you', and Harper tucks his phone back under the pillow.

'Your relationship makes me feel sick,' Johannes says as Harper stretches out to get as comfortable as possible on the hospital bed.

'Have you seen me? Of course my husband would get on a plane to check on this ass.'

Johannes rolls his eyes, before clapping his hands on his thighs and pushing up off the edge of the bed. 'And on that note, we're going to see what state Nils is in. I'll be back shortly.' He leans over and places a kiss on Harper's forehead and gestures for me to lead the way to Nils.

'So, it was worse than they thought it was,' Nils says as we step into his room and find that he's wearing a sling.

'Oh, fuck, man, I'm sorry. How bad?' Johannes is straight to his side, perching on the bed to try and get a better look at his injuries.

'Broken collarbone. Out for the rest of the season.'

Fuck. That's not what we want to hear right now, but it could have been so much worse and that's what I have to think about when it really comes down to it.

'At least there are only two races left, but that sucks. I'm sorry.'

'Next year we'll have it, though. I have a good feeling and there's nothing more I can do for the team this year anyway. Hendersohm basically has the Constructors all tied up, so you need to win the Drivers so we can have some silverware.'

'Absolutely.' Johannes pats his head in an adorable move and Nils preens. They're so cute, like brothers.

'Oh my God, you guys, have you seen this, though?' With his other hand, Nils scrolls on his phone until he finds what he's looking for and to my surprise he thrusts it towards me and not Johannes.

It's a Twitter hashtag. Of my name. With thousands of posts under it. What. The. Fuck. I'm not exactly anonymous because I'm the race engineer to someone who loves to win, so people post things about me every now and again, but these are all from today. This is next level.

'What am I looking at?' I ask Nils as Johannes peers over my shoulder.

'You went viral. I think Sky Sports or something aired your little story to Johannes, or at least parts of it, and everyone's lapping it up. They all think it was so cute and now they're basically worshipping you.' Nils is beaming and I can't help but notice he's liked a ton of these tweets.

I'm hoping that it's at least from a burner account, not his official one, because that would be really stupid of him. Especially the ones where people tweet that Johannes and I are #goals. Too many girls are saying they wish their men would speak to them like that and others are tweeting about being a part of a big family, too, which is kind of cute.

I'm sure when I turn my phone off do not disturb, I'll have a ton of messages from my brothers, but I made sure not to say anything embarrassing. I knew I was mic'd up, so I wasn't about to be stupid on the radio.

'When did you post this pic?' Johannes is on his phone now, too, looking at the same hashtag and someone's found a picture of me from like eight years ago. I'm shirtless, sitting by the pool with a book placed over my swim trunks so it looks like I'm naked – and possibly also pitching a tent. I probably shouldn't still have that up, but I'd clearly forgotten about it.

'Oh, fuck. Are people sharing that?'

He nods. 'This tweet alone already has over a thousand retweets. I suggest making your Instagram private, but it might be too late.' Sadly, he's right. 'They're all calling you hot, though, and of course I agree.'

'My ma's gonna have a field day with this.' I bet my brothers are screenshotting literally everything into the family group chat. She'll chastise me for the amount of skin I have on show, but she'll probably be tweeting back anyone she considers suitable for me. I wince at the thought of her getting carried away on Twitter, but it's a very real possibility.

'There are even news articles already. One of the sports channels in Europe has the full clip. They must be absolutely raking it in. This person who's tweeted it said they've already listened to it five times.' I don't even remember everything I said. I'm sure I was just chatting crap about being from a big family, something simple to soothe Johannes's nerves about his friends being hurt. That was all I wanted. For him to feel okay, for him to be able to get through the race, pull off the win and make it to the hospital quickly.

We have a lot to talk about, and we will, because it's not like I can just switch off my feelings. I care about him, no matter what. Plus, it's also my job. Maybe not to be that nice because I'm sure Ian would have just said 'You can do this' to Nils and kept feeding him the factual information he needed, but that's not me. It never has been and it never will be, especially with Johannes.

'Okay, well I might need a visit to the PR team, then.' That's something I never thought I'd find myself saying. At least they're easily accessible through the team, but I'm pretty sure they won't be expecting to have to deal with this. Maybe they already are, though. They probably started planning responses the minute I opened my big mouth and started reading Johannes the story of my life to keep him calm.

My phone rings loudly in my pocket. As my mom's is the only number that's set up to break through the workplace do-not-disturb settings I currently have on (because my dad refuses to get a mobile phone) I already know who's calling. And sure enough, when I slide my phone out of my pocket there's her name flashing up on the screen. 'I should get this,' I say, showing the screen to Nils and Johannes. Both of them grin as they nod, and I hate them. This is going to be awful.

'Hey, Ma,' I say as I slip into a quiet corner of the busy hospital corridor. 'I'm at the hospital right now visiting Nils so I have to be quick.' And mostly I don't want to have this conversation right now.

'We saw the race. Are the boys okay?' At least she cares enough to start with asking that, but I'm sure she's just getting the polite questioning out of the way before she begins to interrogate me.

'Yes, Ma. They'll both be fine eventually.'

'I'm glad it's not more serious because it looked really bad.'

'Thanks for calling to check up on them, though, Ma. I appreciate it, but I should probably go back in and spend some time with them before visiting hours are over.'

'My sweet Caleb, you think you're escaping your mom so quickly, but we have to talk about Johannes first.' My whole body twitches at the way she says his name. There's no way she can be implying what I think she's implying.

'My driver?' I ask. I'll play this coy until she admits to what she thinks she knows. I'm not about to hand it to her on a plate.

'Yes, your "driver". Don't pretend that's all he is to you,' she says. One thing I'll never do is lie to my ma. Obstruct the truth occasionally, sure. Fail to tell her vital goings-on in my life – has to be done sometimes. But straight up lie? Never.

'Ma…' I warn but she hears something in my voice that apparently confirms it for her.

'I knew it! I knew it! From the moment I heard how you were talking to him, I said straight away to all the family who're gathered here to watch the race that you're in love with him.'

All of the family? Great, just great.

'You do love him, don't you, sweetie?'.

'Ma, you can't go around telling people that. You know that, right? Tell me you know that.'

'Of course not, sweetheart, but *you* should have told me! I shouldn't have had to figure it out for myself.' She's right. Of course she's right, but I'm not sure I'd realised it myself until very recently.

'I know, Ma. I'm sorry. Things have just been so busy with work and, you know…'

'I need to hear all about him! My lord, Caleb, you're dating a celebrity!'

'Shhh!'

'Don't you shush me, Caleb Hughes!'

'Ma, please. I promise I'll call soon and tell you all about it, okay?'

'No need. Just bring him home to meet us! When the season's over, you get your butt back on a flight to Tennessee, ASAP.'

'Yes, Ma,' I say. Now is not the time to discuss the very complicated nature of our current status, so I just agree.

'One last thing, Caleb.'

'What, Ma?'

'I love you, son. You're a good boy and I hope he makes you very happy. It's been a pleasure being your mom and raising you.' I have to knead at my eyes with my fists to stop myself getting emotional.

'Love you too, Ma. I'll call you when I can.'

We end the call and I have to take a couple of breaths to steady myself. I wasn't expecting to have this conversation today. I wasn't planning on saying any of that stuff to Johannes, but he needed me and I'd do anything for him.

'Everyone okay at home?' Johannes asks when I step back into the room and take up the seat next to him.

'All good. They've heard the clip, of course, and my mom … well, we'll talk about it later, okay?' Johannes nods, before turning back to Nils who starts chatting our ears off about one of the hot nurses and how he's going to charm her number out of her. He's incorrigible.

Chapter Thirty-Three

Johannes

In the backseat of the car that Caleb's arranged to return us to the hotel, we're both quiet. There's hardly any space between us and I itch to reach for him.

He must be thinking the same thing, because he shuffles over a little and covers my hand with his, locking our fingers together. It's a small peace offering but it's precious.

The elevator ride is silent, neither of us even bothering to check for any of our colleagues in the corridor as I slide my key card into the door of my room and let him in.

The door is hardly shut when he pulls me into the tightest hug, my hands fisting in the back of his team jumper and clutching him like a lifeline. I couldn't be more grateful for this man right now, for the way he's given me everything I need today despite us being in a not-so-great place. He's stood by and supported me when he didn't have to, when I wouldn't have blamed him for abandoning me.

There are so many reasons that I love him, but his compassion and the way he supports me are some of the biggest.

'I know I owe you an explanation, but it's been quite a fucking day. When you said the crash was between Nils and Harper, I just about lost it. I didn't see it, but I heard it and it sounded so bad.' I finally pull away from where we've been clutching at each other and gesture to the bed for us to sit down. He discards his jumper and I take off my jacket before we shuffle up to the top of the bed to get comfy. I need to be if I have to tell this story again.

'Take your time, Jo, but don't leave anything out, because we can't move forward in this relationship with any secrets between us. You kept something huge from me.'

'I did and I'm sorry, but until that night at the restaurant, I'd never told a single soul.'

I launch into the story from the very beginning and spare no details. Caleb listens patiently and doesn't interrupt.

When I get to the end, he says, 'Christ, Johannes! I can't even imagine what that was like. I'm sorry you went through all that alone.'

He pulls me into his arms and I've never felt safer. He places soft kisses on my head, but I don't cry like I fear I might.

'He broke me but, Caleb, you put me back together. You and your beautiful cups of coffee and mind-clearing runs. You give so generously of yourself and ask for nothing in return, and that makes me want to give you everything. You are more than the voice in my ear. Little by little, you've come to mean everything to me. I hope you know that.'

Caleb nudges me gently.

'You put yourself back together, Jo. I just walked beside you while you did it.'

'You have no idea how much I love you, Caleb Huges,' I say, and it's such a relief to get it out there.

'You dick! I wanted to say it first,' he says, pinching my side, but then his lips meet mine and he's crawling into my lap like he belongs there. And he does. I can't imagine him being anywhere else now.

His arms ring around my neck and we slot together so perfectly that I don't ever want to let go. His tongue strokes over my bottom lip and I'm quick to let him in, the pacing soft and gentle like we have all the time in the world – and I really hope we do.

I hope I get to thread my fingers through his floppy curls for a very long time to come. I hope I get to watch him work away on his laptop, tongue poked out, hyper focused on whatever paper he's working on. I hope when we're fifty we're still going to watch our favourite country artists together. My heart truly hopes we'll be doing beachside runs until our knees can't take it anymore. There's so much hope, but at the same time I can see it. Like, truly imagine the grey strands in his hair as he listens to me complaining about my joints. I can't wait for all the memories we'll make together.

'Love you,' he whispers against my lips. 'Love you so much.'

The feeling is so deeply mutual I can't even cope. I don't want to get into comparing moments like this to moments in my relationship with Jackson – but that taught me enough to know that this is beautiful, special and so very real.

This love is unlike anything else.

We pull away from each other and I'm quick to open up the duvet to him so he can slide into bed with me. There's no way in the world I'm letting him go anywhere tonight. He's mine. We snuggle down, despite the hungry feeling in my stomach and the itch to be at the hospital with the guys. We can always order room service at some point tonight, and really, who's going to stop me if I want to sneak into the hospital in the middle of the night to keep my friends company while they heal.

'Two races to go, how are you feeling?'

I roll onto my side to face him and sigh. I'm still in second place, nine points behind Harper and it all feels like a lot of pressure. It's very overwhelming. Very much like I could throw it all away if I'm not careful and focused. Handing Harper a second world-championship win is not on the agenda. I've finished third the last two years. I don't want that again.

'Like we have a lot of work to do. I don't for a second want any of us to underestimate what a battered and bruised Harper James is capable of. I remember he broke his thumb when we were fifteen and he still competed that weekend. He won't be stopped. This will only make him more determined.'

'I know you have this in you. You've worked so hard to come back from everything after the summer break and to still be within touching distance even after having to sit out a whole race, you've done so well.'

It's awful to think that I've been lucky that my best friend had a big crash which left him gaining no points and that's helped me catch up. Sadly, that's just the way this sport works. It's kind of fucked up.

'So, what now?'

'We have to do this right,' Caleb says. 'No more sneaking around, no more secrets. We have to go to Nathan and declare our relationship.'

Does he not realise that's all I ever wanted?

'Absolutely. I agree. I have nothing to hide.'

'Good, me either. I'll get the meeting all set up and we'll just go in there and be honest. No lies. We'll tell him we're together and it's new but we're serious and want to give this a go.'

'Oooh, he's serious about me,' I tease and Caleb doesn't stand for it for a second, his fingers tickling the sides of my ribs so that I squirm against him.

'You're a brat sometimes, you know?' He uses his current advantageous position to pull me close and I'm not complaining at all, despite the tickle attack.

'I know, but you still want to be serious with me. So what does that say about you?'

'That I must be deranged, but here I am.' He presses a kiss to my forehead and just to disturb a perfectly nice moment, my stomach decides to grumble. We order room service – steaks, of course – and when we're full and happy we take a shower. Together.

We exchange wet, sloppy hand jobs, but it's the way he washes me down that truly makes me happy. The way his hands, covered in the most luxurious scented lather, move over me so softly, a million ounces of care in them. He's tender, even when he gives my hard nipples a cheeky flick. I wish I had hair for him to wash, because I can only imagine how loving that would feel.

He presses soft kisses to the back of my neck and I swoon against his touch, the steam and water cascading around us. This is all I want. He is all I want.

I don't deserve this man, but I hope I can hold on to him forever.

Chapter Thirty-Four

Caleb

We get through Shanghai – the team a mess, with Nils being out and trying to get Anton somewhat ready to drive in the final two races. Johannes finishes top of the podium, putting him just two points behind Harper.

I put in a call to our company's employee rep to ask if he can be available for a meeting with Nathan and some of the other higher-ups, as well as someone from HR. I'd like to get it sorted before we head to Abu Dhabi so Johannes can focus on his race and nothing else.

He can celebrate, hopefully as the new world champion, then we can get on a plane out of there where he'll post a picture of us together so the world can know we're together.

Nathan pencils us in for 6 a.m., which surely has to be a joke, but I know it's about to be stupid busy today as we go into the final race week. I'm lucky to get everyone I need in the room at one time, including my very sleepy boyfriend.

'What's this all about?' Nathan asks as he sits at the head of the conference table.

'Caleb and I wanted to make it official that we are together. Happy to sign any HR forms needed, as we want it to be all above board and in the open.'

I wasn't expecting him to take the lead on this, but it probably is best that it's coming from him. I've played all the potential scenarios they could take from this. My position of power, Johannes's position of power as star driver, the fact that I'm older than him, coercion etc... I don't want to give them any of that ammunition.

Nathan looks between me and Johannes, then to the CEO of the team. I can't quite read the CEO. It's almost like he doesn't believe us but at the same time is about to pop a lid at us for doing this to him now.

'Fantastic. Just what we need the week before the biggest race of this team's life.' Nathan drops his head into his hands like he's ready to thump the table and I'm left wishing we'd maybe left this till next week, after the race.

'We aren't planning to announce it till after the season is over. We obviously don't want to make it official while we're still in Abu Dhabi,' I throw in, hoping it'll stop him completely overreacting.

'I just... Are you serious?' We both nod at Nathan, and Johannes reaches for my hand where it's resting on the table. 'And I thought it was bad when we were sitting on the story about you and Jackson Calder.'

'You were what?' Johannes asks. 'You knew?' Jo's hand

tenses in mine and I'm glad this wasn't how I found out, because this would be shitty timing.

'The PR team informed me that someone had sent in an anonymous picture of you two about eighteen months ago. We squashed it but kept tabs on you both in case it blew up.'

'Jackson Calder and I have been over for a long time. There's no bad blood between us, not anymore, if that's what you're worried about.'

'Good to know,' Nathan says dourly.

'Caleb and I really want to give this a go. This isn't us asking for permission. This is more of a heads-up. We've got statements written that have been approved by PR, and we plan to post them in the days following the race.

I'm so proud of how he's stood his ground. He holds pretty much all the cards right now since it's possible he could win the World Championship in a matter of days, so it's about the only time he can afford to be cocky.

'You don't like to make this easy for us, do you, Johannes? First all the stuff with Harper, and then Jackson, and now your race engineer.'

I have a name.

I also feel annoyed on Johannes' behalf. I can't work out if maybe Nathan's slightly homophobic or just a dick at this point, because straight drivers often get caught doing much worse than having a couple of relationships. Plus, Johannes's thing with Jackson isn't and has never been public.

'Look, like Johannes said, we just wanted to let you know so you're prepared,' I add. 'Now, I'm sure we've all got a lot to do, given we fly out today.'

I'm about ready to cut this delight of a meeting short.

As we stand up, Nathan starts barking orders to HR and PR about how to handle this.

It doesn't matter either way to me. He can't fire us for this and it's done now. We have a flight to catch and the final race weekend to prepare for.

The week descends into chaos from that moment onwards. Someone in the meeting has clearly been breaking confidentiality because most of the team knows by the time we get to FP1. I'm subjected to a lot of whispering and second glances, but I can hardly bring myself to care. It makes it easier for me and Johannes to not have to hide. I don't go back to my accommodation with the other engineers and I'm not complaining, because every morning I get to wake up to Johannes and how could anyone complain about that?

In work we're completely professional like we've always been, and I'd challenge anyone to say otherwise. He's performing well. And with just two points in it between him and Harper for the championship, that's exactly what we need to see.

He qualifies in P2 – because Harper won't give up without a fight – but I tell Jo that it doesn't matter where he starts. He's going to take this. It's going to have to be the drive of his life, but he has it in him. I know it. I feel it.

Harper was just stupid fast in his single laps, but when it comes to today that's not important. Being good over one lap means nothing when there's fifty-eight to complete today.

Presenting Johannes with his last cup of coffee for the season is an emotional moment for both of us.

'This changed it all. I hope you know that, Caleb,' he says, coffee cup in one hand and my hand in his other as he squeezes it.

'Nah, you changed it. This was just fuel for the journey.' He's shaking his head, but he doesn't protest. He's got a race suit to put on and a national anthem to stand for and then it's go-time and I need to be at pit wall getting ready. 'You've got this, handsome. Go kick your best friend's ass.' I kiss his lips chastely before pulling away as he starts to laugh.

In the blink of an eye the race begins and all I can do is watch over him. He tries in the very first seconds to pull ahead of Harper, but he can't get through.

There were 123 overtakes on this track last year. Johannes just needs one to bring this home.

Except the laps begin to tick down and Harper's being, well, Harper, and making this impossible for us. He's determined, but I don't care. I want this for Johannes.

'Box, box,' I call out over the radio on lap thirty-two and he comes down the tunnel underneath the circuit into the pit lane. I watch the time it takes add up in the corner of my screen as I hope and pray for the quickest change over possible.

In a blink of an eye the wheels are on and '2.1' flashes in the corner of the screen. Someone around me lets out a 'Fuck, yeah,' and my brain screams it, too. That's exactly how it needed to be. You couldn't write this.

Lap thirty-three begins and I'm on the edge of my seat. The atmosphere around me grows tenser with every lap because the chances slip away with every one that goes by. But Johannes never stops pushing, and with his fresh tyres and knowing that Harper pitted earlier than him, he's playing it to his advantage. He's not overdoing it, but he's making them work so that he won't have to stop again.

Lap thirty-four hits us quicker than words and Johannes is now only 1.2 seconds behind Harper. If he can just knock that pesky point two off before turn four, he'll have DRS and a whole kilometre of straight to knock his best friend off the top position. Except he can't make it happen, not on this lap, because every time he gets closer, Harper pulls away. It's a frustrating game of push and pull and I'm ready to tear my hair out.

And then lap thirty-five begins, and my eyes light up when Johannes hits the 0.9 mark going into turn four and this could be it. This really could be it. 'You're in DRS range, Johannes,' I comment, trying to keep my voice steady. I don't want to put any pressure on him unless I really have to. He knows what he needs to do.

'Got it,' he confirms and he's not lying. He takes turn five like the absolute champion he is – and before I know it, he's pulling up to the very back of Harper, the gap between them hardly noticeable. Then the second he knows the time is right, Jo pulls out to the right and speeds past him.

The way the pit wall erupts! And then less than half a second later, the paddock behind us goes absolutely insane. I've never seen anything like this, and I've watched Johannes win a lot of races at this point.

Don't get me wrong, I'm out of my seat trying not to knock my headset off, keeping my eyes on the screen but celebrating, nonetheless. At the same time, I know it's not over.

It's wheel to wheel championship racing from then on. Lap forty Harper steals back, but lap forty-one comes just as fast and Johannes is right there taking it back and I'm sure the millions watching round the world are absolutely loving every second of this.

I've sweated through my RBF polo but I don't care. It's so fucking exciting.

'Hold on, just hold on,' I whisper to myself as they both brake going into turn six of lap forty-three and it could go either way as to who comes out on top after the turn. Luckily it's Johannes and I allow myself to breathe for a second, until they reach turn nine and Harper, the little bastard that he is, zips past Johannes into the lead again.

'Fuuuuuckk,' I growl and Ian lays a hand on my shoulder.

'He's got this,' he says over the noise of everyone panicking around us. He's at least given me a bit of a break after we made it official with the team – now that it's above board and signed off, it's like Ian actually approves. I didn't need it from him, but I have looked up to him since joining the team, so it is nice.

I have to wait till lap forty-eight to breathe again, when, as they go into turn twelve, Harper makes a small mistake as he blind-brakes and Johannes capitalises on it in the best possible way. He makes the last sector of that lap his bitch, putting a second and then two seconds between him and Harper – and finally he's free.

He laps two drivers and finally speeds into clean air, Harper stuck behind the pair as the clock hits a six-second gap going into lap fifty.

Five to go. It's my job to keep all eyes on the screen, but I couldn't look away even if I tried. It's not been easy, but it was never going to be, not against Harper. He's the current world champion for a reason. But right now, flying down the straight between turns five and six, I couldn't be prouder to be Johannes Müller's boyfriend.

It's beautiful to watch and this is why F1 is the best sport in the world. Nothing compares, nothing could possibly be as thrilling as this. Watching someone test the absolute limits of a car and a track and their mind and body. Don't get me wrong, there's a new layer of fear to the sport after falling for the man in the car, but I won't let that get to me. Not ever. It's my job to keep him safe and if I allowed that fear to creep to the surface, I'd have to quit.

Three laps to go and it's all coming together. I can hardly breathe, yet at the same time I'm beyond focused on being Johannes's eyes and ears, keeping him together on the track.

Nathan paces behind me, his headset discarded like he can't watch or listen. I can't imagine how much money he'll make if Johannes brings the team the biggest win of all. I hate that that's what it seems to be about for him, not that he truly cares about Johannes and this team.

I won't look away, though. Not with two laps to go, not with Johannes silent and focused. I don't want to miss a thing when the man I love becomes world champion.

'Last lap,' I say into the mic as he crosses the line again. I'm not sure why because he's definitely aware. Probably the most aware he's ever been of a lap in his whole life.

Chapter Thirty-Five

Johannes

'Last lap,' Caleb says quietly into my ear, and I can't find the words right now so I mutter confirmation that I've heard him. Anticipation and excitement and that tiny bit of stress crawls through my body as I go again for a final time this season.

This is it. The season has been so up and down and now I'm about to be world champion, as long as I don't hit a wall or do something stupid this lap. It's fucking insane. Through every high and low there's one person who's been beside me and that's Caleb. And, fuck, I might have dedicated my win in Monza to him, but this one is all his, too. I would not have got this far without him. I'd still be crying in the corner of the team jet as we cruised over Europe, clinging to the shattered pieces of my broken heart.

He mended it with every coffee, every run, every soft glance, every squeeze of my hand, every passionate kiss.

His love built me back up and I couldn't be more thankful to him.

As I whizz through the third sector of the final lap, I spot the mechanics in RBF colours shaking the cage up by the finish line, screaming for me. The chequered flag is mere seconds away. This is it.

'Johannes Müller, you're the new world champion.'

Nothing means more than hearing *Caleb* say those words over the radio as I cross the line. The screams of pure joy in the background mean so much, but they are drowned out as Caleb congratulates me. 'World champion!' he shouts again, so it sinks in that tiny bit more.

My eyes swim and I can hardly see as I slowly do my victory lap, before crawling into the winner's slot in the pit lane. I really, truly did it. I'm world champion. I did everything I set out to do in this race and I crushed it. I came back from the worst races of my life, and I took the top spot. I beat Harper, who's probably going to kick my ass – but who cares? I did it.

Today I proved myself as worthy. Worthy of this sport, worthy of this car, worthy of great love.

I climb out of the cockpit and I'm on top of the car within a matter of seconds, screaming, pumping both my fists in the air. On top of the world. Quite literally. The crowd around me is deafening and I'm almost glad to still have my helmet on, because right now it's just me in here. My moment to celebrate.

There may be cameras flashing all around me, tens of thousands in the stands looking on, millions of eyes at home watching this moment. But in here it's just me. I can catch my breath, the pure thrill of what this means crashing down on me. My team is in front of me celebrating me, us, and our hard work together to build and drive the perfect car. It's everything I've dreamed of since I was old enough to reach the pedals. It's everything I've worked my absolute ass off to be a part of.

And I can finally say that I deserve it.

And when the bliss of being world champion hits a second time it's a whole other host of emotions that have me sinking to my knees against the right front wheel of my car. Tears swim in my eyes as I bow my head, knowing there's at least ten to fifteen cameras around me capturing every angle. Except why should I hold back? I just won the biggest race of my life. So, with the visor still closed, I let the tears fall.

The tyres comfort me for a moment. They were so good today, getting me through the tough moments when I didn't think I was going to come out on top. They always had my back. I let my helmet rest against them to soak in the joy before I stand, push up the visor and run and fling myself into the crowd of engineers. I'm sure Caleb's among them somewhere, but it's hard to see or hear with all the chaos. I know we'll have our own celebratory moment alone together later.

Seconds later I'm being tossed into the air by my engineers, those guys who made the wonderful car that brought me here. The best thing I've ever driven. The whole team has been incredible this year, listening to me and Nils when things haven't been right and fixing them the best they can. I know next year is only going to be even better for RBF.

There's talk of podium and press, but I need a minute. I need to see Harper. And although I know we'll be absolutely fine, even though I've stolen this away from him, I still need to hear it from him. It was a fair fight today and all season, really, and I know there was a time when he thought he was going to romp home with the championship. But I was never going to let that happen, not in a million years.

I'm just trying to make my way back to the RBF garage, when, of course, I bump into Jackson Calder. Definitely not the first person I want to see after the win today. He was officially announced as team principal of Hendersohm this morning. Good for him, I guess.

'Hey,' I say smoothly, pulling at where my suit is tied around my waist. 'Congratulations.' I offer him my hand and he slips his into mine to shake.

I wait, a second, two, three, to feel anything, but there's nothing. It's one of the biggest reliefs of my life. I'm actually even a little bit proud of him. He might not have known that he wanted this, but he's been doing a great job with the team this year and in the other roles he's taken up over the last three.

'Thanks, Johannes. I really appreciate that.' He stinks of champagne and his face is a sticky kind of wet, but he looks at peace, which is good to see after how he's looked so conflicted for so long. 'Great win, by the way. Can't believe it came down to two points in the end.'

'And you, Constructors world champions again. Next year that'll be me and Nils.'

'You wish!'

He lets go of my hand and I go back to twisting the arms of my suit. It's weird to be congratulating the first man to break your heart.

'I, uh, I should go and rub my win in Harper's face. See you around, Jackson.' He nods, smiles and walks away. This time it doesn't hurt at all.

I should probably be heading to the cool-down room, but

the post-race schedule has already gone to shit and then I spot Harper, so at least we're both currently missing from it.

'You're such a dick. I can't believe you stole this from me,' he grumbles, punching me in the shoulder before pulling me into the biggest of hugs. 'And, I guess I'm proud of you. It was quite the comeback, Jojo.'

'You're telling me. There were a couple of moments there when I really thought I wasn't going to do it. You've had a great season, too, Harper. Don't be harsh on yourself just because you finished second. You guys still brought home the Constructors.'

'Yeah, I can see Jackson absolutely kicking our asses next year to make sure we actually get both.' He winces slightly. 'Sorry, I didn't mean to bring him up.'

'It's fine. He's old news.'

'You're a better man than I am, but still, I'm proud of you. It's been a tough year and look at you, taking home not only a world championship, but a great man. He's waiting for you, by the way.'

I look round in the direction that Harper is grinning and there he is, standing waiting patiently for me and Harper to finish having our moment.

'Yeah, I did good, huh?' I don't even mean just in the looks department. That smile, while beautiful, is full of pride and it's all aimed at me right now. To be subject to this level of support is absolutely wild to me, still.

'We both did.' I'd be lying if I didn't admit to the way tears prick the back of my eyes again, mirrored in the way that just for a second his eyes gloss over, too, as if we are almost sharing the same thought. Harper has his family with Kian and Elise and her kids and I'm about to be inducted into some crazy cult, if Caleb's stories of all his siblings and nieces and nephews is anything to go by. Yet we still have each other, despite everything. It's crazy to see how far we've come since we were fourteen and zooming around in go-karts.

'Go.' Harper gives a smack to my ass before letting go of me and shoving me in Caleb's direction.

'See you later, okay? We have big celebrations to partake in.' Although, I'm not sure what time I'll be able to get away from the team, I know our gang will all be out together this evening.

Before I can say anything, I practically sprint to reach Caleb. I can't believe he wasn't the first person I got to celebrate with.

'Oh, my God! You superstar, you did it! I can't believe how tight it was, but you did it.' I'm swept up and practically spun around by Caleb, shocked at his strength until he basically drops me, wheezing a little. 'Not sure that was a good idea, but so worth it. I'm so proud of you.'

'I can't believe we did it, like *we did it*.' I shake him a little too excitedly, but he still just grins at me despite my ridiculousness.

'Nathan actually looked happy for once in his life. You made his whole year.'

'Who gives a fuck about him? We did it, not him!' I probably shouldn't be saying that too loud when there are so many cameras around, but who cares what he feels when it's all about the money for him and I just bought him in a shit tonne.

'I can't believe my boyfriend is a world champion. How lucky am I?'

'You, lucky? It's me that's lucky, I couldn't have done

without that big analytical brain of yours and your velvet voice.'

'Velvet voice huh?' I want to lean into him and kiss him, but we're probably pushing our luck already. This is Abu Dhabi after all.

'I have to get to cool-down, but go get all wrapped up here so we can leave tonight.' We have a grand European break with our closest friends to attend. He shoots me a captain salute and because there's still press around I have to laugh him off before I make my way to find Harper and Elijah.

I don't even remember what I say when I'm interviewed. I'll watch it back on a sports channel at some point this week. I hope I'd stopped crying by that point. But standing on that podium, the German national anthem playing behind me as I receive the ultimate accolade in racing? That's not something I'll ever forget.

There's a thick, fresh batch of tears dripping down my face as I raise the trophy for the whole world to see. It's mine. I get to take it home. Maybe I'll actually go home, to Germany. Maybe it's time to make a place for myself there too.

I did it though, I made it to the top in the hardest season of my life. I never gave up, no matter how much I really wanted to at some points. On the days when I didn't think I'd get out of bed, on the track when I couldn't keep up with the car, at Harper's wedding when everything fell apart. This never felt possible on any of those days and yet I persevered and here I am.

Harper slams a bottle of champagne on the floor and the spray of it going everywhere pulls me from the top of the podium. They drench me, before I even open my own bottle and glug a hefty amount. It is my celebration after all. I spray my team, all the engineers, analysts, strategists, Nathan and of course, Caleb. Everyone cheers and whoops and screams my name. We get photos with our trophies and then it's time to go speak to the press and celebrate.

'Don't forget, we have to be at the airfield at 10 p.m., so keep the answers short and sweet, okay?'

A member of the team guides me from press station to press station, giving me a quick brief of who which interview is with so I can moderate my answers, but at this point they're all asking the same thing. 'How does it feel to be world champion?' I'm not even sure what answer I haven't used at this point. I try to find as many different words as possible for amazing and incredible, but without a thesaurus I'm slowly running out.

'There was a point in the season when you were struggling to stay in the points and it looked like Harper was going to race home with the championship, can you pinpoint what changed to bring you back into the game?' Beth from Sky Sports asks.

That was the easiest question ever, but simply saying 'Caleb Hughes' was not an acceptable answer. 'We spend nine months a year in this sport, and I think it's easy to forget that drivers do have a life outside of the car. We go through hard times and sometimes that reflects in our drive, but I just had to figure out what I wanted and where I was going. Once I had that down, I was nothing but determined to win this season.'

'Even at the expense of your best friend?'

'Yes, of course. He will always be my best friend, but on the track we're like any other competitors. That's how it's always been for us.'

'Your race engineer went viral in Texas. How much of a

part did he play in your win?' I feel the PR guide's hand on my shoulder tapping me to say move on, but I have to say something. It'll look weirder if I don't.

'Caleb Hughes is a genius. He's one of the smartest people I've met in this industry, but he also really cares about the sport and us as drivers. He went out of his way to keep me calm in Texas, when I'd just found out about the crash between Harper and Nils. This sport is lucky to have him. Thanks, Beth.'

'Congratulations, again,' she says with a nod, pulling back her microphone like she knows this interview is over. Thankfully, I'm at the end of the press line and I'm now free to leave. Everyone else already seems to have gone, so I'm finding someone to get me a car to the airstrip so we can get the celebrations started.

I'm not sure who booked the private plane, but it's the nicest one I've ever seen and there are more people on it than I ever imagined. Kian and his sister, who came all this way to support Harper, climb up the stairs, followed by Elijah and his wife, who've left the kids at home with Elijah's parents for a few days. Then Cole and Ash and my Caleb, and of course, Nils. This gang is my absolute favourite thing to come from this sport. We're a mix of teams and experiences, but we all come together because we love one thing: racing.

The drinks are flowing before we've even taken off and somehow there's a whole catered buffet set up for us. I guess that's what happens when you put five millionaires on a plane together.

'Where are we even going?' Nils asks, hugging a bottle of champagne to his chest with his good arm. I wasn't sure he was going to show today. I even told him it would be absolutely fine if he didn't. From my one missed race with those broken ribs, I know how shit it is to have to watch when you just want to be out there so desperately.

'Prague, maybe? I don't think we ever actually all agreed. I'm just going with the flow.' I shrug. I'm sure we're in for a hell of a celebration, and I can't wait.

I pick at the food, before being pulled into multiple conversations about the race today. I can't wait to watch it at some point when we're in our hotel room tomorrow.

'How are you feeling?' Caleb asks as I walk the aisle, half a spring roll hanging out of my mouth.

'Mmm, bit drunk. But, you know, I won.'

In our seats, Caleb pulls at my hand until I'm straddling him. I'm not sure this is what he intended but here we are. I swallow down the rest of the spring roll and he pries the bottle of champagne out of my other hand. 'You did, and I'm so proud of you.' He leans in to kiss me and yep, I can get on board with this. If we could just push everyone else out of the emergency exit, I'd ride him right here.

'Get a room!' Harper calls out from where he's using Kian's lap as a pillow. He can hardly talk. I shoot him the middle finger, before kissing Caleb one last time and turning myself round.

I sit in his lap, enjoying our little party in the sky, but all I really want is to be curled up in bed with the man I love, enjoying our own little celebration. That might have to be tomorrow night, though.

'The hotel room I've booked for the next few days is incredible. There's a jacuzzi in the bathroom. It can fit four.' I'm glad I left him to plan stuff, because outside of deciding to go somewhere in Europe with everyone after the race, I hadn't got much further.

'Ooooh, can't wait to soak in it. My muscles are fucking aching right now.' I groan, cracking my neck from side to side.

'Wow, for once I think we were thinking the opposite way around because I was thinking about riding you in it.'

'Caleb, you naughty, naughty boy!' We soar on towards Europe, the plane alive with the happiness of all my favourite people. I'm the new world champion and everything in life is falling into place. I've found my place in the world – and everything I'm worthy of.

Epilogue

Johannes

'I'm so stuffed. Just looking at that cheese is making me feel like I could be sick.' I push the plate away from our side of the table and open my arms so that Caleb can snuggle back up against me.

'I did tell Kian that it was just going to be the four of us, not the four thousand, but he and Grant have been working so hard on this stupid cheese, he was desperate to show it off.' I cannot believe that Kian Walker now has his own farm-shop cheese. Four-time world champion, Kian Walker has turned into a cheesemonger. What in the world?

'Well, it was so good, we'll have to take some home with us. Can we take food back into Germany?' Caleb asks, and the way my stomach squeezes when he says home, almost brings all the cheese back up.

'I'm sure it'll be fine,' I reply, pulling him closer so I can press a kiss into the side of his neck. We've spent the last two weeks post-season in Germany. I've been giving him a tour of the project house I've bought and talking about what we'd like to do with it. We haven't spoken about moving in together, and it's probably way too early to even contemplate, but we're both talking as if we're going to share the home, and I'm absolutely okay with that.

I think this is maybe one of the first winter breaks where I've not been out skiing or travelling the world. All I want right now is to spend time with him, cosy nights in on the sofa, watching cheesy films. I've even set up a desk in my spare room so he can work on finishing his PhD thesis.

Sometimes, I just linger in the doorway watching him deep in research on his laptop. I don't think I've ever been more in love in my life.

I get it now. I get everything Harper felt when he realised Kian was the one. I get why it basically drove him insane, because it's the weirdest feeling ever. It takes over your whole body, consumes your every thought.

I'm just grateful that it's Caleb. A man I trust, quite literally, with my whole life.

'Earth to Jojo.' Harper waves in front of my face from where he's sitting between Kian's legs on the opposing sofa. It's only the end of December and we're all aware that we'll be heading back to the grind of racing before we know it, but this, right here, right now just feels so nice. Even if we are trying to make a patio dinner work in the great British winter.

'Sorry, what did you say?'

'I asked you when you were heading out to Bahrain. I haven't managed to convince this grump to come with me for pre-season training. Apparently, he can't bear to be away from the sheep. So I'm going to need some entertainment.'

'I believe what I actually said, was that Grant and I have a production meeting and then we're working with the designers for the milk packaging. Sadly, I do not live to follow you around the world.' Kian punctuates that with a kiss to Harper's head.

I know Harper wants more time with him, and I also know that Harper wants to best Kian's four titles so he can come home and have children, but how they make it work in the meantime is just so nice to watch. It almost makes me feel guilty for taking away a championship from him this year and delaying his retirement. Almost.

'We're flying out start of February, waiting for Nils to confirm which day, but that boy is hard to get a hold of right now.'

'You don't need to tell me that. We were in Monaco at the same time and I was trying to get him to come play padel with me and Kinsley and Elijah. We had to ask Ogum in the end and I'm pretty sure that guy hates me.'

'Nils has had two different girlfriends in the last couple of weeks alone. I've asked if he's okay, but apparently he's just having fun.'

'Like that wasn't the two of you just four years ago, chasing after any man who'd give you attention.' Kian chuckles and the worst thing is, he's so right.

'And now look at us, both tied down.'

Kian quickly covers his husband's mouth with his palm to stop him making a tied-down joke, but Harper just licks his hand, which is equally disgusting.

'We're spending a late Christmas with Caleb's family and then we're doing a little bit of travelling around America. We'll meet up with you two idiots for the ski trip and then Caleb heads back to the factory and I'll be doing all my pre-season conditioning. We'll be at the penthouse while the kitchen and bathrooms in the German house are gutted and re-done.' I'm looking forward to all of it, but most of all I'm looking forward to that last month. A month of normal couples living, both of us going out to work for the day and then coming home to each other. I never realised until we were planning it how much I wanted a little bit of domesticity.

'What time do you guys need to leave tomorrow?' Kian asks.

'Our flight isn't till late evening, but it's from Heathrow so we'll call a car probably around 5 p.m.'

'Meeting the family, huh? How you feeling?' Harper knows exactly how I'm feeling – like I'll probably need to bring a change of pants with me.

'He's basically terrified of my mom. They've spoken on the phone a couple times, but she's like the biggest matchmaker ever and she's a bit disappointed she didn't pick Johannes out for me.'

And that only makes my stomach churn more. I can't imagine how I'll feel if she actually doesn't like me.

'I'm also just excited to go to Nashville. We've booked the most incredible hotel so we can explore for a few days and Caleb can show me the sights.' It's the first stop on our US tour and I'm already sure it'll be my favourite.

'And this is where I'm glad you exist, because Jojo's been talking about wanting to go there for years and I couldn't think of anything worse, so I've been making up excuses not to go.'

'On that note,' Kian says, clapping his hands on his thighs. 'We should probably start clearing away for the evening. I have the late feed to do, and Harper has an early-morning shoot.' They both start to collect the plates and cups, bidding us goodnight before they slip into the cottage, leaving us cosy on the patio.

'You fancy a walk? Go see the farm?' I ask Caleb.

'Mmm, I'm kind of comfy right now, but I guess I'd like to see the sheep Kian is clearly obsessed with.'

I give him the tour that Kian and Harper have given me plenty of times. I've suggested to Kian he do this for the public, but he's not interested in opening up their home to the crazy fans. The nearby farm shop in their village is the compromise, and Kian pops in every now and again as a surprise to people.

'Then up the top, that light in the distance, that's where his sister and family live. I think we're having lunch with them tomorrow. Elise is lovely, a great mum and sister, and her kids are brilliant, too. Crazy seeing Harper with them, but the first time I did, I knew he and Kian were going to be great dads one day.'

'Yeah, they are like stupid in love, huh? I was almost sick watching them, but they work so well together,' Caleb agrees.

'They really do. They make each other so happy. Harper won't want to be in this sport forever. He loves coming home to Kian, and there's no way that he'll start a family and travel for most of the year. He couldn't.'

'He's said he'll retire when he's won more championships than Kian, though, right?' I nod. 'So how will he ever retire when you're the best driver in the world?'

I can't stop the way I smile, the confidence and belief this man has in me. 'Honestly, I don't actually think it's that important to him. I think he just enjoys winding Kian up.'

Caleb

We're a little jetlagged, but after nine months and twenty-one different countries on the road, when aren't we jetlagged? Even so, Jo's still keen to make it to my mom's for dinner tonight. She promised him proper Tennessee BBQ – smoked chicken, wet and dry ribs and probably enough pulled pork to sink a ship. He's been salivating over it for weeks and I can't lie it'll be nice to have a home-cooked meal. Plus, she makes the best mac and cheese in the world.

'Gregg just messaged to say he's in the arrivals bay, so we should head that way.' Johannes is pulling two large cases behind him. I've never seen someone travel for a week's vacation with so much stuff, but I have a feeling half of them are full of late Christmas presents.

'And Gregg is the one with the three older kids, right? Sophia, Mikey and...' He pauses, his face pulling tight as he tries to recall the third name. I think it's adorable that he's even tried to learn my whole crazy family, but I know he wants to make a good impression. 'Sebastian!'

'Correct. Look at you go, you've got the whole Hughes family tree nailed already.'

I met his parents after the last race of the season. After Prague, we flew to Germany for a couple of days.

Johannes's parents were great, but it was a bit weird finding out they had no interest in racing and didn't really watch any of Jo's races. Still, I could see how much they cared about him in every other way.

He was in for a bit of a different experience here. My entire family adores sport, and they've all grown to love racing for the sake of it being the one sport I was interested in. Plus, they're all competitive as hell, and I wouldn't be surprised if they challenge Johannes to a race.

He stalls in the doorway of the exit to the pick-up area, wiping his palms on his trousers. 'It's going to be okay, right? She's not going to be mad that I'm not a doctor or a lawyer or something? Or that I'm not from your hometown so I won't force you to come back and live nearby.'

It's very rare to see Johannes nervous. He never is when he gets in the car, unless his head's been scrambled by some stupid ex-boyfriend, so the fact that he truly cares about what my mom might think, means a lot. 'She's going to love you, because I love you and you make me happy and that's all she's ever wanted for me.'

'Plus, I could learn to love Tennessee. I mean, Nashville has always been my dream holiday so that's a good start, right?'

I don't tell him that I don't need him to learn to love my hometown. I don't even know if *I* want to settle down here, so there's no reason for him to force himself to think about it.

'Let's just take it one trip at a time, okay? I'm not planning to give up my job on the road any time soon and I don't think you are, either. So we have years before we need to figure out where we want to settle down.'

'Years, huh?'

'Years,' I confirm before pecking a kiss to his lips. 'Now move your hot ass. Gregg will start honking the horn if we don't hurry up.

He's not wrong, I take another couple steps out the door to the short stay pick-up and a horn blares. We race to the car and travel the short journey to my childhood home.

Mom hardly hugs me for a second before she's scooting me out of the way to get a better look at Johannes. She eyes him way too appreciatively and then pulls him into the biggest hug she can manage. He's caught off-guard for a second, before quickly catching up and hugging her back.

'My boy, you did good. Look at this face, he's so handsome and strong. Great cheekbones.' She strokes a hand across the side of his face, and I swear Johannes is blushing. He never blushes when I do that!

'Mommm,' I groan and thankfully she retracts her hand.

'I'm just saying, he's very good-looking.'

'I mean, his side job is modelling, so I think everyone is well aware of how hot he is.'

'My son with a model. I raised you right.' She pats my head happily and moves out of the way to welcome us in.

Johannes doesn't get a second to adjust before he's led into the large sitting room full of kids and grandkids. He goes through twenty introductions before he's even been offered a drink or a place to sit. And then he's pulled into a conversation with Sebastian about cars and I've lost him.

I linger in the doorway, watching him converse with my nephew, who hangs off his every word like he's the coolest person he's ever met. The youngest pair, Erica being seven and Brent four, crowd him and pull him to sit down on the floor. Brent being the clinger he is quickly climbs into his lap as he talks about how fast he can go. It's the cutest thing I've ever seen and while I'm half sure I don't want children, it's nice to see that if we ever considered it that he'd be good with them. He doesn't even bat an eye when Erica starts to stroke his bald head as if trying to inspect for hair.

'He's a good one,' Mom comments from where she's standing behind me, also watching the scene unfold.

'He is,' I confirm. I haven't always been grateful for the home my parents continued to expand as the family grew, but it's nice to have this ridiculously large living room for occasions like this when we're all together. It's nice to bring Johannes into this when he's been an only child his whole life and for so long only really felt a true connection with his best friend.

Talking about expanding family, my eyes scan to where my oldest niece, who's only six years younger than me, has what looks like a growing belly. 'Is Laurie...?'

'Pregnant, yes sireee. Great-grandbaby number one is on its way. She and Euwin are getting married next summer, but the baby will be here first. Modern-day love huh?'

'Wow, I hope someone's prepared to tell Brent he's not going to be the baby of the family anymore. Kid ain't gonna like that.' He's sucking his thumb in Johannes's lap, the other hand playing with the ruffles on Johannes's shirt. He was a bit of a surprise when Damon and Jessie thought they were done after Erica, so everyone naturally showers him with love for the little miracle he is. He's way too used to it now and expects it from everyone. Even strangers he's never met before, like Johannes.

'I'm leaving that up to Jessie and Damon. Your momma's got plenty of love to give, though.'

'You really like him, though?'

'Yeah, I do. Look how happy you are! I couldn't not like him even if I tried, plus this is the earliest you've been home in the off-season, and while I know you're saying you won't be here for long, I love that he's already brought you home.'

I guess she's right. I'm normally not back until a day or two before Christmas and probably don't stick around long enough, which is on me. But it's not always been easy coming home as the single, childless brother.

'I mean it, baby, you picked a good one. Momma approves.'

She sweeps into the room and gets caught up immediately in a conversation with Laurie and Miley, Damon's oldest, but I'm happy to watch from the sidelines until dinner.

Dinner is chaos, so many people and way too much food, but Johannes slots in perfectly. Everyone loves him.

'I'm so stuffed,' Johannes complains as we lie in bed later on, the sheets rumpled around us from a make-out session, because under Mom's roof, that's as much as I can manage. It had been really hard to say no when the kissing turned to grinding and dry-humping, but we'd both been good little boys and called it quits.

He's massaging his belly, boxer shorts pushed down a little revealing the happy little trail of hair he seems to be growing. I want nothing more than to kiss down it till I'm mouthing at his bulge, but we have six more nights here and if we give in now that's six breakfasts I'm going to have to endure with the reddest face my parents will ever have seen.

'I told you not to have that last rib.'

'I don't think it was the rib, I think it was the banoffee pie. I love the off-season and being able to eat whatever I want for the first couple weeks, but you Americans take it too far.' Mom had gone way too hard refilling his plate and offering him all the extras in the world, and Johannes seemed incapable of saying no to her.

He snuggles into being the little spoon for the night, my

arms wrapped around him, our thighs slotted together like we're clinging to each other.

'I love you, you know?' I whisper into his neck. Even if today hadn't gone well and my mom hadn't fallen head over heels in love with him, I'd still have loved him.

'Love you, too, now let me sleep.'

I smile as the house is finally quiet, despite the ridiculous amount of people it's housing tonight, even though two of my brothers have houses on this street. Johannes dozes off, sleepy snores escaping his mouth, and for a few minutes longer I lie there in the darkness thinking about the fact that I've finally found someone to put down roots with and how I couldn't imagine it ever being anyone other than Johannes Müller anymore.

THANK YOU FOR READING
FIRST TO FINISH

IT WOULD MEAN SO MUCH IF YOU COULD LEAVE A REVIEW ON ALL YOUR PREFERRED PLATFORMS AND SOCIAL MEDIA TO HELP SPREAD THE WORD!

YOU CAN ALSO FOLLOW ME ON INSTAGRAM @RJCAFFERYAUTHOR FOR ALL THE UPDATES ON MY LATEST WORKS.

KEEP READING FOR AN EXTRACT FROM
POLE POSITION

DON'T MISS YOUR NEXT GREAT HIGH-OCTANE, HIGH-SPICE ROMANCE

Kian Walker has always been the golden boy of motorsport. The four-time Championship winner has racing in his DNA. His father was a legend on the track, but there's nothing Kian wants less than to be just like his reckless and unreliable dad.

Harper James is this year's rookie called up to compete with the big boys – and Kian's new teammate. Cocky, hot-headed and with a reputation for breaking as many hearts as he does new track records, Harper's the opposite of Kian in every way. But when the season starts, there's no getting away from him.

This might be one of the most dangerous sports in the world, so why then does Kian's heart feel safer flying around the track at 220mph than when he's anywhere near his teammate?

AVAILABLE IN PAPERBACK, EBOOK & AUDIO TODAY!

Chapter One

Kian

'What do you mean he's got a broken leg?'

I should be packing for Bahrain when my agent, Will, and the team principal, Anders, decide to drop an absolute shitstorm into my life.

'I'm not sure what more I can say, Kian, other than that it was a freak accident and Elijah slipped on the side of a pool. His leg's broken in three places, the muppet.'

Hearing the story a second time doesn't settle the riptide of stress my brain releases into my body.

It's a no-brainer at this point. My teammate's out for at least the first six months, maybe more, of the season and everything is truly about to go to shit.

I look down at my suitcase lying open on the bed. All the packing cubes in the world aren't going to make me feel better. And that's saying something, because I bloody love sorting my life into tiny, organised squares of neatness. Elijah Gutaga and I have been teammates for the last five seasons and we've developed a bond not only on the track, but off the track, too. I'm godfather to his three-year-old. He's my best mate in a world where it's hard to find people you can trust. In one of the most dangerous sports in the world, there has to be a level of trust within your immediate circle and within the wider team too. That bond, especially for the Constructors' Championship, is vital. Without this trust, everything falls apart.

It takes me way too many seconds to realise that I'm sitting in silence whilst the two people who hold my career in their hands wait for me to respond. I don't quite know what they expect me to say. Holding my nerve is one of the most important skills in this sport and it feels slightly shaken right now. Racing isn't exactly a team sport, but Elijah and I have been training together for years and we've always worked really well together.

With Elijah out, well, I don't know what that means for me.

Jeez I can't afford to think about it like that. There are already whispers about this being my retirement season – I'm thirty-three and I've been world champion four times, most recently last year. Even so, I need this to be a spectacular year in order to shut the press up.

'Okay.' I move away from the phone mic to take a calming breath. 'That's fine. It's not the end of the world. I'll give him a call. I did wonder why he hasn't returned my texts in the last twenty-four hours.'

Anders immediately pounces on my words. 'You'll be fine, Kian, and we'll make sure Elijah gets the best care. He'll definitely need surgery so we'll get Harley Street's finest surgeons on the case. We want him back and fighting fit as soon as possible.'

'So you think he might return before the end of the season?' I ask hopefully.

That would be something, at least.

'Best not to count on it at this point. We'll have to play it by ear. It depends first on how the injury heals and then his recovery. All you can do is focus on your own game plan and let us work with Elijah to support his recovery.'

'Okay, well, I'd best finish packing, then.' I survey the mess I've created whilst trying to organise myself. It's probably going to take all night. At least I can sleep on the jet.

And I can sleep well knowing we'll have London, the team's back-up driver, taking up Elijah's spot. He's come on leaps and bounds in the last year.

'Good man. That's what we wanted to hear. We'll see you and Harper on the runway first thing tomorrow.'

'Tomorr— Hang on, what?' *Did he just say* Harper? 'Did you just say Harper? As in, Harper James?'

'The one and only. We've called him up from the lower category to take Elijah's place whilst he's out. I dropped him a line before we called you.' Anders sounds completely calm about this, like it isn't the worst possible news he could be giving me right now.

Through gritted teeth I say, 'Of course. Makes sense. See you tomorrow.' The line drops and I have to resist the urge to lob my phone at the wall.

Harper bloody James.

I could write you a list of about twenty other drivers I'd rather share a podium with than Harper James.

Face like an angel but an absolute devil on the circuit. He's better known for his partying and seduction techniques than his skill on the track. Okay, maybe I'm exaggerating, because he did win the lower category last season, but his antics captured on social-media and in the press overshadow anything else he's achieved in his career. He makes the headlines every other day even in the off season and I've seen more of that guy's body than I could ever wish to. If there's a scandal in the sports pages, chances are his name is attached to it. I'm surprised that Anders is willing to put this aside and risk pissing off the sponsors – Harper James is good but he's not *that* good!

That's the only thing we've got in common, actually. Having been raised in the public eye from the second I was born, I've made enough headlines to last me a lifetime. The stories about you as a kid – and the awkward, unflattering helmet-hair pictures that accompany the lies – follow you around forever. He could do with learning that.

I shoot Elijah a text asking him to call me as soon as he has a moment. I'm sure he's devastated, and things at his end must be utter chaos right now. I can't even imagine how hard a season-ending injury has to be just days before we jet off again. I want to make sure he's okay and let him know I'll be by to visit as soon as I can.

As I hit send, my phone pings with a news blast, containing a press release I was sadly already privy to.

'Elijah Gutaga out for Hendersohm. Harper James in, with the new season just around the corner.'

Well. It's official.

The article quotes not only a tweeted statement from the

team, but also an Instagram post from Harper himself announcing his call-up. Of course he's tasteless enough to announce it shirtless in just a pair of Hendersohm shorts and baseball cap.

It's not enough that I've had to mingle with him at the occasional Hendersohm party in the past, now I'm going to be stuck with him every day for the best part of a year. All the excitement for the new season starts to drain from me. Normally, at this point I'm buzzing with energy for pre-season testing, but not anymore.

In the most insane way, I find peace from doing this sport, despite the intense pressure, and now Harper James is about to shake that all up with his bullshit attitude and recklessness on the track. I've had first-hand experience of his type and I don't need, or want, that kind of chaos in my life. He's a reminder of all that is wrong with this sport.

A few hours later, I park my packed case by the front door and pull on a jacket. It's time for my least favourite pre-season ritual – saying goodbye.

When I let myself into my mum's house, I'm instantly hit with a whiff of freshly baked apple pie. That smell used to soothe my soul as a child. Once she'd stopped touring, there was nothing Mum loved more than baking. Now, though, it's my sister who stress-bakes and it's always a sign that it's not been a good day.

A familiar niggle of guilt creeps into my stomach and I force myself to step over the threshold for the last time for the next nine months.

Cartoons are playing on the TV in the front room, which I quickly bypass, heading for what is now Mum's bedroom, downstairs. Peering in, I find her fast asleep, a contorted, distressed look pulling on her face. There's a fragility to the way her cheekbones protrude so sharply and I have to take a couple of seconds to watch the blanket on her chest rise and fall to reassure myself that she's breathing.

Not wanting to disturb her, I gently pull her bedroom door shut and find my sister amongst a mess of pots, pans, and plates in the kitchen.

'Hey, sis.' She jumps slightly, but nothing prepares me for the bloodshot eyes that meet mine as she turns to face me.

Wordlessly, I pull her into a hug, soft sobs ricocheting off my shoulders as I hold her close.

Four years ago, Elise was in the final year of her nursing degree when she found out in the same week that she was pregnant with my niece, Cassie, and that our mum had been diagnosed with Parkinson's disease. Both discoveries changed her, one for the better, the other not so much. She gave up her nursing degree and when Mum started to lose more of her faculties, Elise became her full-time carer.

Elise and her husband, Grant, rented out their house and moved into Mum's farmhouse set in several acres of land in Norfolk. Their first child, Cassie, and their second, Jesse, have been raised here for the last three-and-a-half years. I can't imagine them ever leaving now.

I admire everything about my sister, but the way she's taken care of our mum is truly something else. Especially as I haven't been here to pull my weight anywhere near as much as I wish I could. Elise would never say a bad word about that. She'll tell you she's grateful that I get to keep my career, that she more than appreciates the trust fund I've put aside for her kids to go to university or travel the world or whatever they want in the future. I wish it was enough. I wish I could do more than just pay for the best equipment and doctors and visiting support workers to make Mum's remaining time in this world comfortable.

I'm not sure how many minutes pass with us just standing there, me holding Elise up, but we never get too many undisturbed moments like this. And then Cassie is screaming her head off, causing the baby, Jesse, to cry, and we have to break apart before either of us are ready to let go.

Elise rushes off to sort them out and I make a start on the washing-up. It's the least I can do. Everything's on the draining board and the worktops are sparkling when Elise returns, peace restored in the living room, weariness carried heavily in every ounce of her body.

'I'll bathe and put the kids to bed. You go and grab yourself a glass of wine and chill in front of the TV,' I tell her. It's an order, not a suggestion.

'Lifesaver, thank you, Ki.'

I might have come over here to moan about Harper, but I can tell that now is not the time. I don't want to add to her burden when it's so clear she's already physically and emotionally worn out from the day. Even though I know she'd protest, saying she's always here, regardless, to listen.

'Who wants a story?' I call out as I enter the living room. Cassie cheers, racing into my arms so I can spin her around and Jesse springs up and down in his bouncer. I can't believe he's already fourteen months old.

Bathtime turns into a slip and slide, but it's worth it to listen to the sounds of my niece and nephew playing happily together. When they are dried and creamed, I lay Jesse down in his cot and thankfully he settles almost immediately, but Cassie is another story. Literally.

I finish one of her favourite books and she quickly requests a second, which turns into a third and it takes all my willpower to reject her pleas for a fourth. She's only three, but she's every bit as strong-willed as her mother and has the too-pretty-to-deny eyes to match.

'I've still got to go give your mum a story, so it's time for you to settle, missy. Come on, bedtime.' I tickle her sides and she screams, legs thrashing around under her duvet. I need to leave soon, and Elise won't thank me for riling Cassie up like this, but it's worth it to see the pure joy radiating off her face.

It's not the kind of bedtime I ever remember having as a kid. When we were on tour, Mum would be warming up or already on stage by the time Elise and I were put to bed, and Dad … well, the less said about that the better. I know it really matters to Elise that her kids have what we didn't, which is why I always find it so hard to resist their pleas for just one more story.

'Okay, Uncle Ki Ki, Mommy deserves a story.' She claps and then rolls on to her side to face the mountain of teddies she keeps with her. It's precious to say the least.

Pressing a kiss to Cassie's forehead, I pull the duvet up to her chin and wish her goodnight. She mumbles back but is more interested in how many of her bears she can cuddle at once. She's peaceful when I check on her after grabbing the baby monitor from Jesse's room, so I head back downstairs. One of the best things Elise and Grant ever did was make Mum's house feel like their own home so it feels like a wonderful multi-generational household.

Elise is curled up on the sofa in her pyjamas, hair scraped back, no remains of today's make-up left on her face. Her glass is full of a straw-coloured white wine and there's some crime drama on the TV. She appears calmer, but I can see in her eyes that her mind is still going a mile a minute. She'll only have one glass so she can hear Mum or the kids in the night, and yet again, I feel guilty that I'm about to disappear for the best part of nine months.

'You okay?' She asks, like it's been me taking care of the rug rats and Mum all day.

'I'm good, kid, are you?' My sister glares at me with the same stare she's been giving me since we were little – the one that reminds me that she is exactly thirteen minutes older than me.

'I'd be lying if I said I wasn't tired. Cassie's been full of beans all day and Jesse just wants to shove anything he can reach into his mouth.' I appreciate that she doesn't mention Mum and instantly feel bad about that.

'Mum okay?' It's a stupid question, because of course she isn't. She has a godawful disease which is slowly taking her from us.

The Parkinson's diagnosis came as a complete shock at first, and then within a few months we noticed every single symptom they warned us about. Elise was incredible and took it in her stride, and I just about coped with seeing it eat away at Mum for the three months a year I was around.

'Bad day. She thought I was Aunt Judith this morning.' I try to hide my wince, but a frown pulls at my sister's lips and I know she's concealing how bad it really is from me. 'Her memory is really deteriorating and it feels like the rate of decline is increasing every day.'

This is something else the doctors warned us about. Dementia. Another disease that often comes hand in hand with Parkinson's as the condition begins to worsen.

'I'm so sorry, Elise,' I apologise like she isn't my mum, too, but I know the burden is not shared equally between us. Mum will forget me first because I'm just not around enough. It will kill Elise to be forgotten, and she's the one who will have to face it every single day. It is truly the cruellest disease. I feel a stab in my heart every time Mum looks at me blankly, unable to place me as a part of her fading life, but at least I'm not confronted with it every hour of the day.

'Anyway,' Elise says as she waves the stress away, 'what's going on with you? I love you, bro, and I know you love us, but you didn't barge your way in here just to put the kids to bed.'

I groan, the lavender candle burning on the mantelpiece not doing a thing to soothe the anxiety that's been curling in my chest since the phone rang this morning. 'Elijah's broken his leg. Three places. It's bad.'

'Oh, shit.'

'Yeah.'

'Okay, so he's out for, what, three to six months? Half a season or thereabouts. Isn't that what the back-up guy is for? That's not what's got you in this funk.'

She knows me way too well. 'I think Anders has written him off for the whole season. Oh, and Harper James is his replacement.'

The room falls silent. Elise pauses the TV show to allow us to talk properly and the house suddenly feels unnervingly still.

'Look, baby bro,' she says, which only makes me want to groan louder. 'I know what's going on in that head of yours.

He's so much like the man you've desperately tried not to become, and I know you hate everything about his attitude and how he treats people, but it's temporary. *He's* temporary. Elijah's leg will heal, the team will go back to normal, and the rookie prick'll be shunted back down into the lower category faster than he's crawled up.'

And this is why she's the best sister in the world. She's the best mum, daughter, carer and, when she can finish her degree, she will be the best nurse, too. It's everything I need to hear. I know she's right. Deep down, in the rational part of me that's buried by the anxiety, I know this. My brain loves to catastrophise while hers is made of steel – or carbon fibre. I always joke that she stole all the sensible genes in the womb.

'I just…' I'm not even sure what's left to say. I just want everything to be okay. Easy. 'I thought this was going to be *the* season.' I can't find the words to say it, to say that I'm wondering if this will be my last season. I'm not sure I'm there yet. I'm not sure I'm ready to say it out loud. 'I thought this was going to be the one where everything would be—'

'You finished top of the podium last year and got your fourth world title,' she quickly interjects. 'You're already a legend. Way better than Dad ever was.'

'I know, but I still feel like I have everything to prove this year. I'd like to go for the points record, if I can.' She's heard the whispers about me retiring – and no one knows me better than Elise – so she knows exactly what I mean.

'Harper doesn't have to get in the way of that. *Elijah* doesn't stop you winning. As your second driver, he *supports* you and the team. You just have to put Harper into a little box in your head and focus on your own drive.'

If only it were that easy. We're going to be breathing each

other's air for months, sharing pits, simulators, private jets, locker rooms. The whole atmosphere is about to change and it's going to affect my performance, no matter how hard I try to prevent it. I've been around men like him before and I know what it will do to me. I don't know what Anders is thinking.

But my sister's right. I'm an elite sportsman and if I lose the mental game then I don't deserve to win. I mentally prepare a box and shove Harper James into it, padlocking it closed.

'Okay, smarty pants. You've got me there. I have every intention of bringing home the cup this season, don't worry. It's not like I don't already have four.' I shrug like it's nothing, but it means everything to me. The first one has pride of place in my home. The second lives in Mum's room, and the third was for Elise. The fourth is displayed in the premises of a local youth charity that I'm the ambassador for. I think it's finally time to bring one home for Cassie and Jesse.

'Good. Now can you let me get back to my show?' she admonishes with the most obnoxious eyeroll I've ever seen. I can't help but silently laugh.

She unpauses the TV, chucks a blanket at me, and I sink into the cosy L corner of the sofa. I fall asleep within minutes in the worst position for my back and neck, only to be woken by Jesse's screaming at 4am. It's perfect timing because a car is coming to get me in an hour to take me to the airport … to meet Harper James.

Elise comes downstairs carrying Jesse, face puffy and hair askew, grumbling about never getting a full night's sleep. I plant a kiss on her forehead and whisper my goodbyes.

'Good luck, bro. You can do this, regardless of who's in the other car. You've got this. And don't forget: we love you, whatever happens.'

I drive back home and wait for the car to pick me up. My sister's words stay with me until the second I climb the stairs to board the jet and find Harper James kicking back in a recliner, his trademark arrogant smirk curling the corners of his lips. My hope and excitement evaporate and I'm left with nothing but frustration and irritation.

'All right, Walker? How's it going, mate?'

His face is almost split in two by how wide his grin is, and I loathe him instantly. We've only met a couple of times, and we definitely aren't *mates*. Urgh.

It's going to be a long season.

Want to find out what happens next?
GET YOUR COPY TODAY!
AVAILABLE IN PAPERBACK, EBOOK & AUDIO

Acknowledgments

I would not have been able to write this book during the toughest period of my life without the support of my closest friends and family. I can't thank my little brother, Drew, enough for his endless support during those first few months after we lost our mom. I would not have got back into writing without it.

To my godmothers, Linda and Kath. Thank you for everything you've done for the both of us. My mom could not have picked two better best friends and godmothers for me and Drew. Thank you for your endless support on my writing journey.

And my friends. Han, Ella, Paige, Lou, Taylor, Kirst, Alice, Liv and Vi. Thank you for keeping me going. For showing up endlessly for me. For being my biggest cheerleaders as I tried to find enjoyment in writing again. I adore you all and would be nowhere without you. I love you guys.

To Charlotte at OMC. Thank you for being patient whilst I grieved and processed and put writing this book on hold. I love this book and I'm so glad it'll sit on shelves. Thank you for all your support on this journey.

Finally, to my mom. Thank you for making me the woman I am today. For the guidance and support and all your belief in me that I could be a successful author. The loss and grief I felt after losing you left me with nowhere for my love to go, so I put it into this book. I hope you would have loved it and have been proud of me for finding my passion and enjoyment for writing again.

ONE MORE CHAPTER

YOUR NUMBER ONE STOP FOR PAGETURNING BOOKS

One More Chapter is an award-winning global division of HarperCollins.

Subscribe to our newsletter to get our latest eBook deals and stay up to date with all our new releases!

signup.harpercollins.co.uk/join/signup-omc

Meet the team at www.onemorechapter.com

Follow us!

@onemorechapterhc

Do you write unputdownable fiction? We love to hear from new voices. Find out how to submit your novel at www.onemorechapter.com/submissions

The author and One More Chapter would like to thank everyone who contributed to the publication of this story…

Analytics
Imogen Wolstencroft

Audio
Fionnuala Barrett
Ciara Briggs

Design
Lucy Bennett
Fiona Greenway
Liane Payne
Dean Russell

Digital Sales
Laura Daley
Lydia Grainge
Hannah Lismore

eCommerce
Laura Carpenter
Madeline ODonovan
Charlotte Stevens
Christina Storey
Rachel Ward

Editorial
Rosie Best
Kara Daniel
Charlotte Ledger
Lydia Mason
Laura McCallen
Jennie Rothwell
Sofia Salazar Studer
Caroline Scott-Bowden
Emily Thomas
Helen Williams

Harper360
Emily Gerbner
Ariana Juarez
Jean Marie Kelly
emma sullivan
Sophia Wilhelm

International Sales
Ruth Burrow
Bethan Moore
Colleen Simpson

Inventory
Sarah Callaghan
Kirsty Norman

Marketing & Publicity
Chloe Cummings
Grace Edwards
Katie Sadler

Operations
Melissa Okusanya
Vanessa Coubrough

Production
Denis Manson
Simon Moore
Francesca Tuzzeo

Rights
Ashton Mucha
Alisah Saghir
Zoe Shine
Aisling Smyth

Trade Marketing
Ben Hurd
Eleanor Slater

The HarperCollins Contracts Team

The HarperCollins Distribution Team

The HarperCollins Finance & Royalties Team

The HarperCollins Legal Team

The HarperCollins Technology Team

UK Sales
Isabel Coburn
Jay Cochrane
Leah Woods

And every other essential link in the chain from delivery drivers to booksellers to librarians and beyond!